Christmas
Together

Enjoy!

Christmas
Together

Karen Rose Smith
Melissa McClone

*M&B™ and M&B™ with the Rose Device
are trademarks of the publisher.
Harlequin Mills & Boon Limited, Eton House,
18-24 Paradise Road, Richmond, Surrey TW9 1SR*

CHRISTMAS TOGETHER © by Harlequin Books S.A. 2008

Twelfth Night Proposal © Harlequin Books SA 2005
Special thanks and acknowledgement are given to Karen Rose Smith.

Rescued by the Magic of Christmas
© Melissa Martinez McClone 2008

ISBN: 978 0 263 86889 0

024-1108

*Printed and bound in Spain
by Litografía Rosés S.A., Barcelona*

Twelfth Night Proposal
Karen Rose Smith

Karen Rose Smith, award-winning author of over fifty published novels, is a former English teacher and home decorator. Now spinning stories and creating characters keeps her busy. But she also loves listening to music, shopping and sharing with friends as well as spending time with her son and her husband. Married for over thirty years, she and her husband have always called Pennsylvania home. Karen Rose likes to hear from readers. They can write to her at: PO Box 1545, Hanover, PA 17331, USA or visit her website at www.karenrosesmith.com.

Prologue

Montgomery Boat Company
Avon Lake, Texas

Glancing at the TV in his office, Leo Montgomery saw paradise. Well, a spot that was *supposed* to be paradise. There was a lake and grass and trees and a guy dressed in a tuxedo. But it wasn't the guy who captured Leo's attention.

There was a woman. The perfect fantasy woman.

Leo glimpsed her face for a moment—maybe half a moment—less time than it took to take a breath. He caught the sparkling, huge brown eyes. Then she was turning…away from him. When she turned, his palms tingled to touch her long, curly brown hair with its red highlights reflecting the sun. The dress she wore was some wispy material. It was short and bared most of her back, the fabric molding to her long legs as she walked away from the camera and away from him. She handed the guy in the tuxedo a can of soda. Large red letters proclaimed its name—ZING. Leo's gaze was still on the woman's back and those curls. When she lifted a parasol, tilted it over her shoulder and walked away, the letters on the parasol spelled ZING, The Fantasy Soda. As the jingle for ZING filled the airwaves, she disappeared into the trees.

To Leo's amazement, he found himself aroused… stirred in a way he hadn't been stirred for a very long time. Since well before Carolyn's death two years ago, for sure.

Giving himself a mental shake, willing his libido to calm down, Leo flicked off the TV with the remote. That fantasy woman on the screen was just that—a fantasy. He knew better than most men that fantasies don't become reality. On the other hand, however, maybe he should think about getting involved with someone from his country club. As his sister, Jolene, told him often, Heather needed a mother. His daughter needed more than the nanny-housekeeper Jolene had just hired.

Heather needed a mother, and *he* didn't want to sleep alone for the rest of his life.

Although the cursor on the computer screen blinked before him, Leo couldn't forget the fantasy woman's mass of reddish-brown curls, those long legs, that bare back.

He couldn't remember a feature on the model's face, but he supposed that was the whole idea—to charge a man's fantasy. Nevertheless, Leo wasn't the type of man to dwell on fantasies when reality was sitting right in front of him.

He checked the information on the computer with the boatyard orders on his desk. The dream woman forgotten, work filled his head. That's the way he wanted it for now. Jolene's advice might be sound, but he wasn't ready for it. He wasn't ready for involvement or commitment.

That's just the way it was.

Chapter One

"Montgomery here," Leo said as he flipped open his silver cell phone and stepped away from the boat trailer into the hot December sun.

"This is Verity. Heather's nanny."

The fact that he had to be reminded of her job position spoke of how little he'd paid attention to the new nanny. Maybe that was because he expected her to come and go as the rest had. Maybe it was because of her glasses, tied-back hair and oversize T-shirts. For almost a month she'd moved around like a ghost in his house, seemingly quite capable, as Jolene had predicted she would be, yet definitely always in the background.

Now he was on the alert because this call most probably concerned his daughter. "Verity, what is it?"

"It's Heather. I didn't want to bother you, but I

thought you should know that she fell against the coffee table in the great room and cut her forehead."

Leo's heart pounded and he felt panic grip him. "Is she all right? Did you take her to the emergency room?"

"I applied pressure and used a butterfly bandage, but you might want to have her checked. Just tell me what you'd like me to do."

Merely three, with her light-brown, wavy hair and her blue, blue eyes, all Heather had to do was look at him and his heart melted. The thought of her hurt—

"I'll be right there. Fifteen minutes tops. Is she crying? Is she upset?"

Verity's voice was helpfully patient. "She's sitting in my lap, sucking her thumb with her head on my shoulder."

"I'll be there as soon as I tell my foreman where I'm going. Keep her calm and call me if you see any change."

"Yes, Mr. Montgomery."

Leo headed for the production plant.

Fifteen minutes later he arrived at his house in a select section of Avon Lake, Texas, where the houses in his development were quietly luxurious. His ranch house sat back from the curb with a curved drive leading to it. He left the car in the driveway and hurried to the front door.

Usually when he came home, he was filled with the same sense of well-being he felt at the boatyard. Today dread clouded his thoughts as it had when he'd learned about Carolyn's brain tumor. What if Heather had seriously injured herself? What if she had a concussion?

His boots sounded on the ceramic tile floor in the entrance foyer as he headed straight ahead for the great room. The fireplace, cathedral ceiling and skylights made it his favorite room in the house. He barely noticed any of that now as he hurried to the denim sofa where Verity was seated with Heather. His daughter was dressed in red overalls with a little white sweater underneath. Her cheeks were pink and tear-stained, and her eyes were wide, as she kept her head on Verity's shoulder and stared up at him.

"Hello, baby," he said as he went to take her into his arms. To his surprise she hung on to Verity.

Verity whispered to her, "Go with Daddy."

But Heather shook her head, held on even tighter and mumbled around her thumb, "I wanna stay wif you."

Leo felt a stab to his heart.

With understanding eyes, Verity looked up at him, and Leo saw her, *really* saw her, for the first time since she'd been hired. There was a quiet equanimity about her that had calmed him from the first moment he'd met her. She was young—twenty-two. Her major in college had been early childhood education, and in the short time she'd been with him, she handled Heather as if she knew exactly what she was doing. He had a feeling that had more to do with natural ability than any schooling. Her blue wire-rim glasses had always distracted him from looking at her eyes before now. They were a beautiful brown, the color of teak. Her hair, tied back in a low ponytail, looked silky and soft. Her face was a classic oval, and her nose turned up just a bit at the tip. Although here on the Gulf most residents were suntanned, he noticed Verity's skin was creamy white.

"She's still upset," Verity said.

"Instead of the E.R., we'll take her to the pediatrician. I called him on the drive here. He said to bring her right in."

With utmost gentleness, Verity stroked Heather's hair. "Do you want me to go along?"

"I don't think I can pry her away from you," he responded wryly, realizing how that bothered him. Apparently, Heather had connected with this nanny. He was grateful for that, yet—

"Let's go," he directed gruffly, and would have turned to leave, but then he realized he'd been doing everything in a hurry lately. He'd also been working long hours. How many nights had he put Heather to bed since Verity had arrived and started caring for her?

Apparently not enough.

"Let's go with Daddy," Verity murmured to the little girl.

Leo looked at Verity again and found himself thinking how pretty she was, even though she was sloppily dressed. He found himself liking the sound of her voice. He found himself…getting stirred up in a way a man shouldn't around a nanny.

Their gazes connected and, in a flash, he saw the same man-woman awareness in her eyes that he was feeling. Then she glanced away, and he was glad. He certainly didn't want to delve further into that.

In his SUV, driving toward the doctor's office, an awkward silence surrounded them.

Leo headed north on Lonestar Way, Avon Lake's main thoroughfare, leading toward the college side of town. The college housed about 10,000 students, and the town itself had a growing population of more than 7,000 now. But Leo knew Avon Lake would always keep that small-town flavor. At least, he hoped it would.

Heather's pediatrician was located in one of the old houses near the college. Leo knew Verity took a course at the campus once a week, though he didn't know much else about her, except what she'd given on her résumé. She'd attended college at the University of Texas and had been born and bred in Galveston.

Maybe because of his reaction to her for those few moments, maybe because her silence made him wonder what she was thinking, he asked her, "What course are you taking this semester?"

As she shifted in her seat, he felt her gaze fall upon him. "I'm not taking a class officially. When I accepted the position with you in November, I was too late to register for the term. But I'm auditing a class on children's play techniques."

"You're working on your master's?"

"Yes, I hope to. I have an advisor now. I'll be meeting with him soon to choose courses for next term."

"It's hard to believe Christmas is less than a month away. Did you have an enjoyable Thanksgiving?"

They hadn't talked since then, and Leo didn't even know where she'd gone. She'd left early in the morning and come back late that evening after he and Heather had returned from dinner at Jolene's.

Quiet for a few moments, Verity finally answered, "It was fine."

Casting a sideways glance at her, his interest was

piqued, maybe because of everything she wasn't saying. "Did you spend it with family?"

"No. I went to Freeport for the day."

"And met friends?"

Again, that little silence, and then she shook her head. "No, I had dinner, then I drove to the beach for a while."

Now he was even more intrigued. Didn't she have family? Why would she spend the holiday alone? If he asked those questions, he'd become more involved than he wanted to be.

Heather suddenly called from the back in her super-fast baby voice. "Vewitee. Vewitee. I wanna feed duckee and go for ice cweam."

Verity gave her full attention to Heather as she turned. "Not today, honey. We have to go to the doctor's so he can look at your head."

"No doctor. I wanna feed duckees."

Peering into the rearview mirror to see his daughter, Leo caught sight of her lower lip pouting out. He hated to see her cry. "What if we go feed the ducks after the doctor looks at your head?"

After thinking about that for a few moments, she returned, "Ice cweam, too?"

"It's going to be close to supper. Maybe we could stop at the Wagon Wheel and get that chicken you like so much. They have ice cream for dessert."

"Chicken and ice cweam!" Heather said gleefully.

Verity laughed, a pure, free sound that entranced Leo, as she commented, "Ducks, chicken and ice cream all in one day. She's going to hold you to every one of those."

"Like an elephant never forgets?" he asked with a chuckle.

"Something like that. I can't believe how her vocabulary is growing, just in the few weeks I've been here. Each day she's becoming more coordinated, too. I've seen it before, of course, with the children I've worked with, but just caring for one child, and seeing her change almost daily, is absolutely amazing."

"I know Jolene probably mentioned it, but I don't remember how you heard about the position with me," he prompted.

"I have a friend in the career counseling office at UT. She knew I was looking for a change, called me and told me about it."

"A change from what you were doing or where you were living?"

"Both."

That concise word was the end of the conversation unless Leo wanted to pursue it. He didn't.

Sitting beside Verity, smelling the floral scent of her shampoo or lotion, very much liking the sound of her laughter, he felt as if he were awakening from a long sleep. It was disconcerting. He'd gotten used to his life, and although Jolene often told him he was in a rut, ruts were damned comfortable.

Activities in the town of Avon Lake often revolved around the small lake. After Leo unfastened Heather from her car seat and lifted her to the ground, she took Verity's hand and ran toward the black and gray ducks on the grassy shoreline.

In a few quick strides, Leo caught up to them, the bag of crackers he'd bought at a convenience store in his hand. "Wait a minute. You forgot something. You can't feed them if you don't have the food."

When Heather stopped short, let go of Verity's hand and ran back to him, he crouched down. "Do you want me to open the bag or do you want to try it?"

"*Me* try."

He handed it to her. But after jabs and pulls and a few squishes, she shook her head, curling tendrils along her cheek bobbing all over the place. "Can't do it. You open, please."

Leo knew his daughter's face was as close to an angel's as he'd ever see. Taking the bag between his two large hands, he pulled and a corner popped open. "There you go. Break up each one so they have lots of little pieces."

After Heather nodded vigorously, she took the bag and ran for the lake.

"Wait," he and Verity called at the same time and ran after her.

As he caught one of Heather's hands, Verity held her elbow. "Don't spill the crackers," she warned with a smile.

The sun's brilliance was fading into long shadows, though the air was warm and the day was still above 70. Standing by a tall pecan tree, Leo watched Verity as she and Heather sat on the grass and two ducks waddled closer. Heather crushed a cracker in her hand and opened her little fingers, waving her arm in the air. The crumbs blew this way and that. One of the ducks quacked and ran after a piece and she laughed like only a three-year-old could.

The doctor's exam had gone smoothly and quickly, mostly thanks to Verity. She seemed to be able to read his daughter's mind...seemed to know what to say to coax her into acquiescence. He didn't have that knack. He was learning negotiation was the highest skill a parent could master.

As he watched his daughter, he felt removed and didn't like it. After taking a few steps closer, he sat with Verity and Heather.

Heather offered him the bag. "You feed duckees, too."

How long had it been since he'd taken time to do just that? Taking one of the crackers from the bag, he broke it into a few pieces and tossed them so Heather could watch the ducks waddle after them.

"I should bring her here more often," he decided reflectively.

"You could use it as a treat so it doesn't become old hat."

Staring into Verity's brown eyes, feeling that stirring again, he said, "You're very good with her."

"Thank you. I've been waiting for some kind of sign from you—" She stopped and looked embarrassed.

"Sign?"

"Yes. To know if I'm doing a good job...to know if I'm doing what you want me to do with Heather. She's a wonderful little girl and I love being with her. But you're her parent, and I want to make sure she's learning what *you* want her to learn."

What *he* wanted her to learn.

He knew Verity wasn't talking about colors and numbers. "Jolene hired you and gave you a seal of approval, so I guess I thought that was enough. As she probably told you, I've tried nannies before. After two days, I know whether they're going to last or not…whether they fit with Heather or not. I fired one because she just wanted to watch TV and read all day and left Heather on her own. Another quit because she said she didn't have enough free time. You might decide that's true for you, too."

"I don't need much free time."

Curious, he asked, "Why not?"

"I'm new in town. I really don't know anyone. So when I'm free, I study for the course I'm auditing, read or knit. I'm not very exciting," she admitted, her cheeks pinkening a little.

The blush looked good on her. In fact, he was having trouble unlocking his gaze from hers. "You'll have friends once you start taking more courses. That is, if you stay."

"I'm exactly where I want to be right now," she murmured softly, and he felt himself almost leaning toward her. He imagined she had slightly leaned toward him. The urge to reach out and run his thumb along her cheek was so strong he balled his hand into a fist. He didn't know what was going on today, but he didn't like it.

After he picked up the bag of crackers, he motioned to Heather. "Come on, let's feed more ducks. Those over there didn't get any yet."

He was twelve years older than this young woman who'd begun to fascinate him. He'd never given a glance to younger women before. Not only was she younger, but he saw vulnerability and innocence in those eyes.

He could be wrong, but he doubted it. No matter what her life story, it was safest for him to keep his distance.

That was exactly what he was going to do.

Each stroke of Verity Sumpter's hairbrush through her hair was meant to be monotonous and soothing, but it wasn't. All too easily she could imagine Mr. Montgomery's hands stroking her hair. The thoughts were making her hot, bothered and agitated. From the moment she'd set eyes on Leo Montgomery her heart had tripped a little. If she had to admit it, her heart had tripped a lot. Today was the first he'd noticed her...*really* noticed her.

He'd probably have noticed her from day one if she'd applied makeup, highlighted her hair, spent the time on spiral curls and dolled herself up, as the casting agent had for that commercial she'd made.

That commercial.

Her twin brother, Sean, had encouraged her to do it and teased her saying, maybe if she did, she'd forget her tomboy days forever. Dear Sean.

When tears came to her eyes, she let them well up this time as she pulled her hair into a ponytail. He'd been gone for eleven months now, and the missing still overwhelmed her sometimes. She and Sean had been as close as any twins could have been. They'd shared secrets and jokes and sports and even attended the same college. He'd screened her dates and she'd always looked over the girls he'd brought home.

When a casting agent had approached her in the library on campus, he'd explained he was looking for college girls to make a series of commercials for a new soda—the company was targeting the college crowd. Verity hadn't given much thought to the idea until Sean had heard about it. He'd teased, cajoled and coaxed, insisting the experience would be good for her.

Her straight-as-a-ruler hair had become a mass of curls. She'd traded her glasses for contact lenses, and makeup had made her eyes look huge and her lips much fuller. No one knew if the commercial would ever make it to the TV screen, and she hadn't heard anything from the company other than receiving her payment for the hours she'd worked as a model.

After the shoot, Verity had decided curling her hair for an hour or more, applying makeup and dressing up was all simply too much trouble. The red highlights washed out of her hair, and eventually the curls straightened into looser waves and were caught up in a practical ponytail once more. When one of the soft contact lenses had torn, she'd gone back to using her glasses.

Then, last January, Sean had the skiing accident. When he'd died, her life had fallen apart. She'd gone through the motions to earn her diploma—

Noise in the hall startled Verity. Her bedroom, sitting area and bathroom were located at the opposite end of the house from the master suite and Heather's bedroom, along with another guest bedroom. Mr. Montgomery took over Heather's care on the rare nights he was home and, after he'd put Heather to bed, she usually didn't hear another sound.

Now, however, she heard little feet slapping on the hardwood floor, Leo's deep baritone calling, "Heather, you come back here," and the little girl's giggles as she came closer to Verity's door.

Verity had crossed into the sitting area when the door burst open and Heather ran through the room, naked, the ends of her hair wet, soapsuds still on her shoulders. The bump on her head hadn't slowed her down one iota.

Halfway across Verity's sitting room, Leo stopped. "I shouldn't have come in here without knocking."

Verity laughed. "I think Heather took care of announcing you."

Leo shook his head. "I'll collect her if she doesn't squiggle out of my arms again. She is so slippery when she's wet—"

"And she hates to stand still while you dry her off. I know."

Her gaze collided with his, and there was that shakingly, fascinating awareness again.

Breaking eye contact, he said, "Since I consider your room to be off-limits to me, do you want me to get her or do you want to do it?"

"I don't mind if you do," Verity murmured as she continued to stare at him. Leo was still wearing the black polo shirt and khakis he'd had on that afternoon. He was tanned, and his arm muscles were obvious under the shirtsleeves. His stomach was flat and she suspected hard. His hips were slim.

When he turned, she chastised herself for liking every bit of his backside, too. She couldn't be attracted to her employer. Besides the fact that she was tired of men letting her down, she was much younger than Leo Montgomery. She'd seen the picture of

Heather's mother in the little girl's room. Carolyn Montgomery had looked poised with her perfect makeup and blond pageboy. She was absolutely beautiful. Verity imagined any woman would have trouble living up to that. Jolene Connehy, Mr. Montgomery's sister, had told her honestly that he wasn't over his wife's death, even though it had been two years. Verity could understand that. She knew she'd never get over losing Sean.

Leo stepped into Verity's bedroom, and the very fact that he was so near her double bed disconcerted her. Maybe because ever since this afternoon pictures had been swimming in her head—pictures of Leo kissing her, pictures of her kissing him back.

His gaze had gone to the bed, too, with its white chenille spread, its maple bookcase headboard, where she'd lined up some of her favorite reads. But her mind wasn't on her books as she said in almost a whisper, "She likes to play hide-and-seek under the bed."

With a shake of his head, as if he couldn't believe he was doing this, he got down on his knees and lifted the edge of the spread. His voice was filled with affectionate frustration as he called, "Hey, you. You've got to get out from under there and put on some pajamas."

"I don't wanna go nighty-night. Wanna play with Vewitee."

Without hesitation Verity got down on the floor beside Leo. Her shoulder brushed his as she peered under the bed at her little charge. The touch of her shirt against his sent a jolt of adrenaline rushing through her. "If you come out and put on your pj's, I'll read you a story."

"That's bribery," Leo murmured very close to her ear, his breath warm on her cheek. Verity shivered.

"Would you rather kneel here and cajole for the next half hour?" she asked him, half joking, half serious.

"I'm too big to fit under the bed, and cajoling isn't my style."

"That leaves bribery," she decided, unable to suppress a grin.

His face was so very close to hers as they focused on Heather. When he turned his head to her, mere inches separated their lips. Leo's scent was pure male, and his light-brown hair fell over his brow in a rakish way. But it was the gleam of raw hunger in his eyes that kept her immobilized.

Suddenly he cleared his throat, bent lower, and extended his arm under the bed. "Come on, you little hooligan. Verity will read you a story. But don't think this is going to happen again. Next time I won't let you out of the bathroom until you have your pj's on."

Quickly recovering from whatever had overcome her when she'd been so close to Leo, Verity teased, "You really shouldn't tell her your strategy."

"Good advice," he admitted as Heather started wriggling toward them from under the bed.

"I'll go get her pajamas. Try to keep her from hiding anyplace else until I get back."

Verity laughed. "She likes me to brush her hair. I'll do that."

Less than five minutes later, Leo had returned with Heather's pajamas and Verity had helped him get her into them. She watched him as he fastened two small buttons at the three-year-old's neck, and his fingers fumbled with them. He was such a big man, but he was gentle with his daughter.

"Okay." He scooped her up into his arms. "To your room." In the middle of Verity's sitting area, he stopped. "I just realized you don't even have a TV in here. The last nanny who stayed here had her own."

"I don't need a television. I don't watch it very much."

He looked surprised. "You don't watch reality shows?"

She shook her head.

"Or the Discovery Channel?"

Again she shook her head and gave him a little smile. "I can always find so many things I'd rather do. Listening to music, especially." She pointed to the CD player on her night stand. "Now *that* I can't do without."

"You can use the stereo system in the great room anytime you want."

"I noticed you have an extensive collection of Beatles music."

"Sure do. Play it anytime."

"That's kind of you, Mr. Montgomery. I just might."

"It's Leo," he said gruffly.

They'd never really addressed that issue. Jolene had introduced her to her employer as Verity the first time they'd met, but she'd always thought of him as Mr. Montgomery…on purpose. Today, however, everything seemed to have changed.

"Leo," she repeated softly.

"Vewitee wead me a stowy now?" Heather asked, laying her head on her dad's shoulder.

"One story coming right up," Verity assured her.

* * *

A short time later Leo stood beside the rocking chair as Verity sat with Heather, rocked and read her a favorite Dr. Seuss book. Heather's eyes were almost closed as they finished, and Leo lifted her from Verity's lap and placed her in her crib.

Then he leaned down to her, kissed her forehead and said, "Good night, baby."

The huskiness in his voice tightened Verity's throat and she didn't know why. Maybe because Sean was gone. Maybe because her relationship with her father was strained. Maybe because she suddenly felt so alone.

Standing, she took a deep breath and said, "Nighty-night, Heather. I'll see you in the morning," and went to the door.

Leo joined her in the hall.

For a few moments they just stared at each other and a hum of attraction seemed to grow louder and stronger between them. They were standing very close, the toes of Leo's boots almost touching the toes of her sneakers. He towered a good six inches above her. When she looked up into his blue eyes, her tummy fluttered and her pulse raced. In fact, she almost felt as if she couldn't catch her breath. Leo didn't touch her, and she so wished he would. He looked as if he wanted to. He looked as if he wanted to kiss her.

With a shake of his head, he blew out a breath. "Do you feel safe here in this house with me?" he asked.

"Yes!"

"I didn't realize until tonight how this could look. Your staying here, I mean."

"I'm your nanny and housekeeper. Nannies often live in the residence where they take care of the children."

"That's true, but usually there's a wife. I don't want to compromise your reputation."

"I know who I am. I know why I'm here. What other people think really doesn't matter to me. Does it matter to you?"

"No, what other people think has never bothered me."

"Then we're fine," she said brightly. "There's nothing to be concerned about."

But the expression on his face as well as the wild beating of her heart told her that wasn't true. Besides that, if he knew how terrifically attracted she was to him, he might fire her. She liked this job, and she was beginning to like Avon Lake.

Tomorrow was Saturday, and to steer toward a safer subject, she asked, "Will you be going to the boatyard tomorrow?" He had worked the last three Saturdays she'd been here.

"For a few hours. I realized today I haven't been spending enough time with my daughter. That's going to have to change."

"I usually have breakfast for Heather around eight-thirty. Do you want to join us?"

After a pause he said, "Yes. I'll go to the boatyard afterward." There was an intensity in his gaze when he looked at her that excited her more than she wanted to admit. That excitement was as scary as the loneliness she'd felt as she'd watched Leo put his daughter to bed.

"I'll see you in the morning, then," she murmured.

When she turned to go, he finally touched her. His

hand clasped her arm, and the feel of his hot skin on hers sent tingles through her whole body.

"Thank you for taking care of Heather so well today."

"It's my job."

Releasing her, he nodded. "I'll see you in the morning."

Then she was walking down the hall into the great room, bypassing the kitchen and heading to her suite. Today Leo Montgomery had become more than her employer. She wasn't sure how their relationship had changed, but she knew she had to be careful or she'd get hurt all over again.

Chapter Two

Verity was selecting clothes from her closet when she heard Heather on the baby monitor chattering to her stuffed animals. Smiling, she pulled on indigo jeans and zipped them, then grabbed a T-shirt that had seen many washings. The soft, blue cotton fell practically to her thighs. Comfort had always come first with her, certainly before fashion or trends or what anyone thought a girl *should* wear. Climbing trees, riding bikes and playing baseball with Sean had always led her to choose practical clothes.

Heather's babblings were getting louder now, and Verity left her room and headed for the little girl's. In the past, Leo had gone to work before she was up. Last night she'd had a restless night, reliving those moments when they'd stood so close, when she'd thought she'd seen something in his eyes that had made her heart jump so fast. This morning, though, in the light of day, she just chalked it all up to her imagination.

Heather stood up in her crib when she saw Verity, grinning from ear to ear. She stuffed a pink elephant— her toy of choice this week—under one arm.

"Good morning, honey," Verity said, scooping the little girl up into her arms. "I'm hoping that big bed your daddy ordered soon arrives. I'm afraid you're going to crawl out of this one."

"I cwawl out," Heather parroted, swinging Nosy by his trunk.

"Let's brush your teeth. Then you can decide what you want for breakfast."

"Waffles wif bluebewies," she said as if she'd been thinking about it all night.

Laughing, Verity shook her head. "You've had those every day this week."

"Waffles wif bluebewies," Heather repeated.

"Okay. I'm sure you'll get tired of them eventually."

Cooking was a pastime Verity enjoyed. She and Sean and her father had always shared the chore. After she'd gotten her own apartment in college, she'd found experimenting could be fun. Now she was glad she had. Heather could be a picky eater, and coming up with fun and playful ways to serve food was always a challenge.

Fifteen minutes later, teeth brushed, dressed in pink overalls and a matching shirt, Heather ran ahead of Verity to the kitchen. The bandage on her forehead was still in place and she wasn't paying any attention to it.

Verity hadn't seen any sign of Leo, but he might be

working in his office in the pool house. She'd just started a pot of coffee brewing when a deep male voice made her jump. "Good morning."

Her hand over her heart, she swiveled toward the back door that led to the patio, pool and pool house. "Mr. Montgomery. I was going to call you when breakfast was ready."

He was carrying a folded sheet of paper in his hand. "It's Leo, remember?"

Oh, she remembered.

Without waiting for her response, he went on, "I thought I'd spend some time with Heather while you make breakfast. I realized yesterday I need to give her more attention."

Verity remembered how Heather had clung to her when Leo had arrived home to take her to the doctor. "I imagine it's difficult being a single parent."

"Funny," Leo said almost to himself, "I don't think of myself as single. But, yes, it is tough. After Heather's mother died, I guess I took refuge in work because Jolene was around to help me with Heather…or the nanny of the day. But yesterday when you called and said that Heather was hurt, I realized how very little I have to do with her day-to-day care."

"You're running a business."

"Yes, I am. Montgomery Boats will be her future, if she wants it. But in the meantime, I want to make sure I'm in her life."

Suddenly Heather ran to Verity with her coloring book. "Look what *me* did." She held up a page she had colored. Staying within the lines wasn't a concept she understood yet, but she knew her colors, and she'd used a lot of them on the page.

When Verity glanced at Leo, she saw the expression on his face and she realized he wished Heather had come to him.

"What a wonderful picture!" Verity exclaimed. "Show your daddy."

Looking puzzled for a moment, Heather tentatively held up the page to him. Verity could see Leo's uncertainty in exactly what to say or do. Then he crouched down, put his arm around his daughter, and offered, "That's a great blue dog. I bet he lives in the same place as pink elephants."

"Like Nosy," Heather decided.

"Just like Nosy."

"Heather insists she wants blueberry waffles for breakfast. Is that all right with you? I could scramble some eggs, too."

"It's been a long time since I had more than coffee for breakfast. Why don't I make the eggs?"

"Are you sure you want to help?"

He pulled one of the chairs over to the counter. "Sure. Heather can help, too. Heather, do you want to learn to crack an egg?"

"I wanna cwack *lots* of eggs," Heather said so fast, Verity could hardly catch it.

As Leo took the carton from the refrigerator, he replied, "I think we'll start with one."

Verity couldn't help but watch Leo as he made an effort to give Heather the attention he'd mentioned. He even let her stir the eggs with a fork. After a while, though, she tired of the process and told him, "I'm gonna color now." Leo lifted her down, and she went over to her miniature table and chairs to do just that.

When he frowned, Verity assured him, "Her attention span for most things is about ten minutes, unless it's something she's really into. Coloring is one of those things. Playing with blocks is another."

"Maybe she *will* grow up to want to design boats and build ships."

"Or houses or bridges or skyscrapers," Verity offered.

"I got it. I have to keep an open mind."

They smiled at each other and Verity felt all quivery inside. Leo's smile faded as he gazed at her, and the magnetic pull between them almost seemed to tug her toward him.

Then she remembered what he'd said earlier. *I don't think of myself as single.* That obviously meant he still thought of himself as married.

The timer beeped, signaling the first waffle was finished. Verity focused all of her attention into lifting the top of the iron, carefully removing the waffle and ladling in the next one.

The silence in the kitchen grew awkward until she finally asked, "When did you begin designing boats?"

"When I was ten."

She glanced at him. "What inspired you to do that?"

"My father. He didn't design boats, but he built them from someone else's plans. I spent every spare moment I could with him at the boatyard. I loved going out on the water with him, too. He had a real respect for the sea and taught me how to read it."

"Read it?" That idea fascinated her.

"Anyone can learn to pilot a boat. Instruments these days make the experience almost a no-brainer. But there are still times when the color of the sky, the direction of the clouds, the scent of the water can tell a pilot the story as well as instruments can."

After Leo took a frying pan from the cupboard, he poured the eggs into it. The scent of the sweet waffles with blueberries, the aroma of coffee brewing, the eggs cooking in the skillet filled the kitchen along with the sound of Heather humming as she colored. The scene was so domestic it took Verity aback for a second. It was almost like a dream she'd had a week ago—a dream in which she'd had a home and a place to belong. But she really *didn't* belong here with Leo.

Did she?

Whatever she was feeling toward Leo Montgomery was probably all one-sided, and she'd better put the brakes on it. As his nanny, she was convenient right now. When he no longer needed her, he wouldn't hesitate to say goodbye, just as Matthew had.

Snatching a topic, any topic, she asked Leo, "How about your mother? Did she like boats and the water, too?"

Leo cast her a sideways glance. "Not on your life. Mom's a high-heels, I-don't-want-to-get-my-hair-wet kind of person. She's never wanted anything to do with the boatyard or the business."

"Your sister told me she lives in Avon Lake, but she's away now."

"Lives in Avon Lake," Leo repeated. "Officially, I guess. She has an apartment, but rarely uses it for more than a few weeks at a time. She's become a world traveler."

"You come from such an interesting family."

He laughed. "That's one way of putting it. How about you?"

"Me?"

"Yes. Your parents. What do they do?"

Lifting the waffle iron before the timer went off, she saw the pastry was golden brown. Thankful she could stall for a little time to figure out what to say, she transferred it to a plate and decided to give an honest, short version. "My mother died when my brother and I were born. Sean and I were twins. Dad raised us. He's an accountant."

"A twin! That's great. What does your brother do?"

After Verity swallowed hard, she managed to say, "I lost Sean last January to a skiing accident." She went to pick up the ladle, but a blur of tears made her fumble it and drop it on the floor.

Leo stooped at the same time she did. His fingers brushed hers, and he took the ladle from her hand. When they both straightened, they were standing much too close, and he was looking down at her with so much compassion she couldn't blink away the tears fast enough.

"I'm sorry, Verity."

Embarrassed by the emotion she couldn't quell, she turned away from him toward the counter and took a few deep breaths. When she felt Leo's hand on her shoulder, she almost stopped breathing altogether.

"I'm okay," she murmured, feeling foolish.

Gently he nudged her around to face him. "No, you

aren't. And I understand why. I know what loss feels like. Losing a spouse, losing a twin… Those are bonds that aren't easily broken."

"I don't want the bond to be broken," she admitted. "Not ever." Suddenly she realized that's the way Leo probably felt about his wife. "The eggs are going to burn," she whispered.

"Can't let that happen," he said, and stepped away from her to tend to his part of the breakfast while she picked up a paper towel to wipe waffle batter from the floor.

Putting the breakfast on the table took little effort, but Verity busied herself with it as Leo helped Heather get settled on her booster seat.

Heather pointed to her waffle and looked up at Verity. "Please make a face."

The first day Verity had made the waffles for Heather, she wasn't sure if she was going to eat them. But after Verity had used syrup and a dab of butter to make a face on the waffle, Heather had eaten the whole thing. Now Verity fashioned a face again as Heather giggled and Leo looked on, making her feel self-conscious.

Suddenly there was a beep-beep-beep, and Verity realized it came from Leo's pocket.

After he answered his cell phone, he said, "Jolene. Hi. What's up? No, I'm not at the boatyard yet. I'm still at home having breakfast."

His sister must have made some comment about that because he explained, "I just needed some time with Heather. She hurt herself yesterday, and I realized I haven't been around very much." Then he explained what had happened.

After a long pause he responded, "I'm going to the boatyard as soon as I'm finished. I'm sure Heather would love it if you would pick her up and take her to the arts festival at the lake."

Today artists would have their work displayed all around Avon Lake. There would be vendors with various foods, activities for kids and wandering musicians. Verity had thought about taking Heather there herself.

Now she said to Leo, "I'd be glad to take Heather and meet Jolene there. I want to go, too."

After Leo relayed what Verity had said to his sister, he asked Verity, "Around ten at the Shakespeare statue?"

Verity nodded. "Sounds good."

Leo closed the phone, reattached it to his belt and asked, "Are you sure you don't mind driving Heather there?"

"I don't mind. Really. I was planning to go after you got home."

"Will you buy a painting?" he asked jokingly.

"Actually, I might, if I see something I like. If that's okay with you. I mean, hanging it."

"I'm not a landlord who's going to keep your security deposit if you put too many holes in the walls." His blue eyes were amused.

"I've just never been in this kind of position before," she said truthfully. "I don't know the rules."

"No rules, Verity. As long as you put Heather first, that's all that matters."

He was absolutely right on that score. She *would* put Heather first, of course, and try to block Leo Montgomery from her dreams.

* * *

Leo parked in a lot near the lake. As he'd sat in his office, studying each page of the new sales brochure, he hadn't been able to keep his mind on it. He hadn't been able to keep his mind off Verity. So he'd put in two hours, then driven to the festival.

His life had become a treadmill of work, putting Heather to bed now and then, sleep and more work. Even before Carolyn died, he'd started putting in longer hours. Had it been because of her remoteness? Had it been because he'd sensed she was keeping something from him?

She'd been keeping something from him all right... for three months—her brain tumor.

No point in thinking about that now. No point in thinking about how her lack of trust had seemed like a betrayal, how her independence might have cost her her life sooner than was necessary.

The day couldn't have been any sunnier, sometimes unusual in this part of Texas where cloudy skies and rain could prevail in December. The lake was blue and the scents on the breeze from food vendors were enticing.

His boots cut a path through the grass as he observed everything going on. Avon Lake was a Texas town through and through. Yet the college, and the influence of the bard who had written sonnets and plays, brought a uniqueness to the community that wasn't easy to describe. The statue of Shakespeare himself on the shores of the lake was a roost for birds, true. But it was also a reminder there was an aspect of life that had to do with poetry, artistry and creation that humans couldn't do without.

When had he even thought about that statue?

Around the lake, artists displayed their paintings on easels, pegboards and some on more elaborate contraptions. Some of the displays were adorned with Christmas wreaths or signs of the season. The past two years Jolene had bought Heather Christmas presents when she'd gone shopping for her boys. This year, Leo decided, he would find presents for Heather himself.

He'd gone a quarter of the way around the lake when he spotted Verity. She wore an oversize green sweater over her jeans. Although the outfit seemed to be an attempt to hide womanly attributes, he found it only enhanced them. The cable knit lay softly over her breasts, the breeze blowing it against her body, delineating her slim waist. With her hair tied back in a ponytail, her face tilted curiously to one side as she studied a painting, the sun glinting on her glasses, Leo found himself eager to talk to her again. There was something about Verity Sumpter that was strangely appealing.

Coming up to stand beside her, he nonchalantly slid his hands into his jeans pockets. "Interpretable?" he asked wryly, as he gazed with her at the swirls of color and motion.

After a quick glance at him, she laughed. "I'm not sure. I do think it would clash with everything else you'd put with it, though."

Leo chuckled, too, then looked at her. When their gazes met, Leo felt a tightening in his chest, and he didn't understand it at all. "Are you an art connoisseur?"

"Hardly. I like Victorian cottages, landscapes and paintings that take me away to someplace I want to be."

"Have you found any here today?" Blood was rushing through him faster now, and he chalked that up to his almost jog around the lake.

"A few. Have you seen Heather?"

"Not yet."

"The last time I spotted her she was at a stand making huge bubbles in the air. The wand was almost as big as she was."

"Did you eat lunch yet? We can grab a hot dog while we're looking." Then he stopped. "Unless you want to do this on your own."

She shrugged as if it didn't matter one way or the other. "I've made the rounds and I'm trying to decide between two paintings. A hot dog might help me make the decision."

For whatever reason, Verity Sumpter made him smile. She did more than that, he realized, as his gaze settled on her lips and he felt a pang of desire so strong he didn't think he'd ever felt anything quite like it before.

"Come on," he said evenly, nodding toward a concession truck that sold cold drinks, soft pretzels and hot dogs.

Strumming his guitar and dressed in purple velvet, a wandering minstrel serenaded them with a rendition of "Greensleeves" as they stood in line. Minutes later they each held hot dogs and sodas and went to stand under a pecan tree. When Verity took a one-handed bite of her hot dog, mustard caught on her upper lip. With her hands full and a napkin tucked under the bun, she couldn't wipe it away.

Not sure what possessed him, Leo set his soda between branches on the tree and caught the dab of mustard with his thumb. The touch of his skin on hers was electric, and her brown eyes widened with the jolt of it. What was it about Verity that stirred him up so?

She didn't look away, and he couldn't seem to, either. When he leaned toward her, she tipped up her chin.

All he had to do was bend his head—

"Verity. Hey, Verity," a male voice called.

A good-looking young man who appeared to be in his late twenties approached them. He had long, russet hair that curled over his collar and was brushed to one side. His green eyes targeted Verity and his smile was all for her.

As if she couldn't quite tear her gaze from Leo's, she blinked, breaking the spell. Her cheeks reddened slightly.

The man was approaching them then, and she was smiling at him. "Hi."

The guy's smile widened as he came up to them and stood very close to Verity. Much too close, Leo thought.

"Have you seen Charley's work? It's the style you said you liked—mountains and trees that make you feel as if you're right there."

Leo suddenly wondered if Verity had been dating this man. She could be, and he'd never know. He had no right to know.

"I've seen it," she offered with some excitement.

After another look at Leo and their half-eaten hot dogs, the young man gave Verity a slow smile. "I don't want to intrude." He rested his hand lightly on Verity's shoulder. "I'll see you Tuesday night. You can tell me then whether you bought the painting or not."

After the young man walked away, the silence that fell over Leo and Verity was louder than any of the noises around them. As they finished their hot dogs, Leo was very aware, again, that he was twelve years older than Verity and he had no business thinking about kissing her.

Yet questions rolled in his head, and he asked one of them. "Are you dating him?"

Her gaze flew to Leo's. "What made you think I was?"

Leo shrugged. "Maybe it was more his attitude than yours. If he hasn't asked you out, it won't be long until he does." He didn't like the idea of that—the idea of Verity and that guy in a dark movie theater, in a car or somewhere more intimate.

"I haven't dated much since…" She stopped and looked out over the lake. "Sean was protective of me. He screened my dates," she confided with a small smile.

Leo liked the idea of her having a protective brother who'd looked out for her. "Did you always go along with his advice?"

"I should have. Sean didn't like the man I was dating last fall, but I wouldn't listen. When you have a twin, a twin as close as Sean and I were, sometimes it's hard to distinguish your ideas from theirs, where you leave off and they begin. Being a twin is a constant battle to be yourself yet hold strong the bonds that bind you together. So I didn't listen to his advice about Matthew."

"What happened?"

"We'd been dating a few months when Sean was in the skiing accident. Afterward, I…I sort of withdrew. I just couldn't wrap my mind around the fact that Sean wasn't here anymore."

"That's not unusual," Leo offered, seeing her sadness, knowing what he had felt after he'd lost Carolyn.

"Matthew didn't understand that I just wasn't in the mood to go to parties or even the movies. Whenever I was with him, he didn't want to hear about Sean or how much I missed him. After a few weeks he told me that he needed to date somebody who was a lot more fun, and I realized my brother had been right about him all along."

Angry for her, Leo could have called this Matthew a few choice names, but he refrained because he could see how hurt Verity had been that someone she'd loved had deserted her at a low time in her life.

Verity had finished her hot dog and now took a sip of her soda. "How did you meet your wife?"

"I built a customized boat for her father. She came along to see the design, and that was that."

"So…you believe in love at first sight?" Verity asked curiously.

"I don't know if it was love at first sight. Carolyn was a beautiful, sophisticated, poised woman who could turn a man's head. She turned mine."

It wasn't until later that Leo had realized there was an aloofness about Carolyn that he could never really break through. Maybe that was the poise he had seen at first. That aloofness had never completely crumbled and had kept a barrier of sorts between them.

"Let's walk," Leo said gruffly.

When Verity glanced at him, there were questions in her eyes, but he didn't want her to ask them.

They hadn't gone very far when a little whirlwind

came barreling toward Verity. It was Heather, all smiles and giggles and excitement.

Wrapping her arms around Verity's legs, she looked up at her with the exuberance of a three-year-old. "Looky. Looky. I got painted."

Without hesitation, Verity sank down onto one knee before Heather who had a cluster of daisies painted on her cheek.

"You look beautiful," Verity exclaimed, and Leo's chest tightened at the sight of this nanny and his daughter bonding. It was evident Heather absolutely adored Verity.

Heather grabbed Verity's hand. "You get painted, too."

Rising to her feet, Verity began, "Oh, I don't know…"

"Let yourself go today," Leo advised her, guessing that wasn't something Verity did often.

Jolene and her two boys had come up behind Heather. Jolene's hair was blonder than his. At five-four, she was about twenty pounds overweight, but she was his sister, so Leo simply didn't care. Jolene liked to cook and bake. Everything she did, she did with gusto.

Now she told Verity, "They'll paint whatever you want—from flowers to kittens to parrots. And it washes off."

"Are you going to do it, too?" Verity asked with a twinkle in her eye.

"I could be talked into it. But my boys won't stand still long enough for me to have it done."

"I can take the boys and Heather over to the clown with the balloons if you really want to," Verity offered.

Jolene's two boys, Randy and Joe, seemed to like the

idea. Randy, the eight-year-old who was three years older than his brother, Joey, added, "And if Mom's not done until we get the balloons made we can play croquet. Kids are doing it over there." He pointed to an open area at the southern end of the lake.

"You're going to have your hands full," Leo warned her.

"They'll be fine as long as we keep busy."

Leo cupped Verity's elbow. Again, he felt a longing inside. But he realized it wasn't only desire.

Trying to ignore whatever it was, he decided, "First, you get your turn getting painted, then I'll help you look after the kids."

When Verity gazed up at him, everyone else around the lake seemed to disappear. The overwhelming desire to kiss her overtook him once more.

Releasing her elbow, he decided to keep his distance and concentrate on the kids.

Something had happened to him since Verity's call yesterday. He felt as if he was reacting and responding and living again.

All of it had something to do with this nanny. He just had to figure out where she fit into his life…if she fit in at all.

Chapter Three

Before Verity turned in for the night, she decided to make herself a cup of cocoa. Her mind was racing and she knew sleep wouldn't come quickly...not tonight. She'd enjoyed the afternoon with Leo and Heather so much she couldn't get it out of her mind.

She was stirring the mixture of chocolate and milk in the saucepan on the stove when she heard the sliding glass doors in the dining room open and close. Her heart rate sped up, and when Leo came into the kitchen, she told herself to calm down. This afternoon had meant the world to her. She'd had fun for the first time in a long time. However, she'd also realized her attraction to Leo wasn't something she could ignore easily.

Dressed in a denim shirt and black jeans, his tawny hair tousled, she wondered what had brought him back into the house. After he'd put Heather to bed, he'd told her he was going to work in the pool house for a while. The pool house was his office, and she knew he had a baby monitor in there like the one in her room so he could hear his daughter if she awakened or called for him.

"Is Heather awake?" She looked toward the little girl's room.

"Nope. Not after the afternoon she had. I wouldn't be surprised if she sleeps later than usual in the morning, too. I picked up my e-mail, and Jolene sent me these. I thought you might like to see them."

"What are they?"

"Pictures from this afternoon that Jolene took with her digital camera. I just printed them out."

Verity gestured toward the pot on the stove. "Would you like some hot chocolate?"

After a glance at the pot, he met her gaze. "Sure. That doesn't look like the powdered stuff I make in the microwave."

"It's not. It's the real thing. I found the chocolate in a candy store in town."

He was carefully studying her as if he was trying to figure something out. Unsettled by his intense focus on her, she reached for two mugs from the mug tree in the corner. Setting them on the counter, she poured the chocolate into them and carried them to the table.

Leo followed her, then lowered himself into a chair and spread out the pictures. There were four sheets of them with four pictures on each. Heather was the star of all the photos, whether she was gazing up at a strolling minstrel, learning how to play croquet with Verity, or licking her fingers from the cotton candy Leo held in one hand as he stooped down to her to give her another taste.

"These are great," Verity said, letting her chocolate cool a bit. "You ought to frame a few and put them in the great room."

"Maybe I will."

"Do you keep a photo album?"

"No, I haven't had the time. All of the pictures are in a box in the closet." Lifting his mug to his lips, he took a swallow.

Verity was mesmerized by the crow's feet at Leo's eyes...the shadow of beard on his jaw...his strong neck muscles as he drank the cocoa. A trill of attraction spun in her tummy.

Didn't she know better than to weave dreams? Didn't she know better than to think Leo Montgomery could be interested in her? He moved in the country club set. He'd had a wife who had been sophisticated and everything Verity wasn't.

With a smile, he set his mug on the table. "This is great!"

She felt inordinately pleased that he liked the concoction. "It's good with a little bit of coffee mixed in, too."

Again he was studying her. Yesterday, as well as today, he looked at her as if he hadn't really seen her before. That was odd since she'd been here almost a month.

"Did you hang the painting you bought?" he asked.

"Not yet. I need a hammer and a nail."

"I think I can come up with those. Do you want to hang it now?"

"*I* can do it, if you have something else you'd rather be doing."

Standing, he went to the kitchen closet, took a hammer and a box of nails from the top shelf. "It would be best to make sure the nail goes into a stud. I can do that for you."

A few minutes later, they were standing in Verity's sitting room, and she was showing Leo the wall where she'd like to hang the painting. It was an ocean scene at sunrise—pink, purple and gold spread across the morning sky as two horses grazed on tufts of sea grass along the beach.

After Leo made sure he knew where she wanted the painting, he rapped against the wall with his knuckles until the sound was slightly different. Then he hammered a nail right in. Taking the painting from her, he found the middle of the wire hanger and slipped it over the nail.

"What do you think?" he asked, stepping back, his arm brushing hers.

"I like it. It makes me want to go riding on the beach."

He was looking at *her* now, rather than at the painting. "Do you ride?"

"Just for fun. I never took lessons."

"There's a natural rhythm to riding. Some people catch on to it, some don't."

They were standing close together. So close Verity could see a scar on Leo's cheek, right above his beard line. So close that she could smell the maleness of him. So close that she could feel his heat.

When he reached out and traced the daisy that had been painted on her cheek, she trembled.

"Heather didn't want me to wash off her flower tonight." His voice was husky.

"This will fade away when I get my shower."

His thumb traced the petals of the flower. "So soft," he murmured, and her heart began galloping as it had never galloped before.

There was a look in Leo's eyes she'd never seen before. Although Matthew had kissed her many times, his kisses had been eager, enthusiastic, intended to convince her to want more. She hadn't wanted more with him. It was really the bottom-line reason they'd broken up. She hadn't been ready to have sex and he'd moved on. She'd grown up believing she wanted to save herself for the one, perfect relationship...the one man she'd love for the rest of her life.

Leo was a man. All man. The desire in his eyes spoke of a raw hunger that should have scared her because she was a virgin and he was experienced. Yet she wasn't afraid. She was curious.

The periphery of her life fell away. There was only that hunger in Leo's eyes and her desire to satisfy it. When he bent his head, he gave her time to back away. But she could no more back away than she could forget about the brother she'd lost. Leo's lips sealed to hers, and everything about her life turned and shifted. This man and his need awakened passion in her she'd never known she possessed. As her arms went around his neck, his mouth opened over hers.

Leo's kiss stunned her and swirled her into sensation that left her breathless and reaching for more. When her hands slipped into Leo's hair, she couldn't seem to get close enough to him. A groan sounded deep in his throat as his tongue stroked hers, as the kiss lasted for an eternity, as she responded to him in the way a woman responds to a man. Leo Montgomery stirred up excitement she'd never known.

Then suddenly his arms dropped, and his lips broke from hers. His hold on her shoulders loosened as he pushed her away.

"This is wrong," he muttered, his face taking on a stony expression.

Unable to find many words, she asked, "Why?"

"There are so many reasons I can't even count them all. First of all, I'm your employer. Second, I'm twelve years older than you are. Third…" He stopped.

"Third?" Unfortunately she guessed what was coming.

"Third, this isn't what I want. And you can't tell me it's what you want, either. Attraction is two parts chemistry, one part proximity and no parts common sense. I'm old enough to know common sense has to reign. Let's just forget that kiss ever happened."

For the first time in her life, Verity had had a taste of true desire. For the first time in her life, she felt something for a man that went beyond attraction and chemistry and reason. Nevertheless, from the look in Leo's eyes she could see that he was convinced they were wrong for each other. Words wouldn't convince him otherwise, and she didn't know if anything else would, either. Tears welled up and she quickly blinked them away.

Leo must have seen them. "If you want to leave, I'll understand."

"I don't want to leave. I like taking care of Heather."

To herself she added, *And I like being near you.* But she didn't dare say that aloud. He'd fire her for sure.

He went to the door. "I'll be taking Heather to a puppet show at the mall tomorrow. Do you have plans for your day off?"

No, she didn't. But she was going to pretend she did. That just seemed to be best. She'd make herself scarce, no matter what time he left or returned. "I'm going to Freeport to shop for Christmas. Do you decorate for the holidays? I can pick up some festive arrangements, maybe a door hanging for you."

He looked blank. "I haven't decorated since…" He stopped and cleared his throat. "A few decorations would probably be good for Heather. I'll get a tree closer to Christmas." Studying her closely, he added, "It's your day off. You don't have to be thinking about Heather or the house. I can always pick up a few decorations."

"I really don't mind. Christmas is a special time for children. I want it to be special for Heather this year."

Reaching into his back pocket, he extracted his wallet, took out a few bills and handed them to her. "If you want to pick out decorations for the house, go ahead."

As she took the bills, his hand closed over hers. His fingers were strong and firm. His gaze fell to her lips—

But then he released her and backed away. "Have a good day tomorrow," he said gruffly, then turned and left her room.

The magnetic pull between them had been so very strong since Friday. Had he left so abruptly because he wanted to kiss her again? Or did he simply regret everything that had happened between them?

Sinking into one of the chairs in her sitting room, she stared at the painting he'd helped her hang on the wall.

She'd better close and lock her heart if she wanted to stay employed here. She'd better remember Leo Montgomery was off-limits. What she remembered, however, was his kiss and the way it had made her feel.

Staring at the painting, she could imagine herself and Leo on those horses at the beach. When she closed her eyes, she blanked out the picture, knowing her imagination would only bring her heartache.

In the craft store on Sunday afternoon, Verity heard the rat-a-tat of rain on the roof. Selecting various items, she lowered them into her basket. She'd decided creating decorations might be more enjoyable than buying them. More economical, too. Not that Leo had to worry about that. But she and Heather could work on them together, and that would be fun.

She'd just arranged a pine-cone garland in the basket when a lilting musical tone emanated from her purse. It had to be the wrong number—not many people had her cell phone number. When she checked the small window, her chest tightened a little. It was her dad.

"Did I catch you at a bad time?" Gregory Sumpter asked.

She pulled her basket into an alcove at the end of the row. "No, this is fine. I was shopping."

"For you or your new job?"

"For my job."

"On a Sunday?"

She didn't want to tell him how her days off seemed

endless. She didn't want to tell him how she was feeling because she knew exactly how *he* was feeling. He missed Sean. Sean had been his golden child. Sean had been the male heir. Though Sean had taken engineering in college, her father had still held fast to the dream that he'd take over his three hardware stores someday, making them an even bigger father-and-son success.

"Did you have a reason for calling, Dad?" He didn't call her often. When he wasn't working, he closed himself in his study, staring at old photo albums, polishing Sean's trophies.

"I wondered if you were going to come home for Christmas."

Thanksgiving had come and gone without a phone call from her dad. She'd called him the week before a few times, not wanting to let the holiday pass without connecting, but he hadn't returned those calls.

"I don't know yet," she told him now. "I haven't thought much about Christmas." If she had dinner on the holiday with her father, they'd sit across the table from each other, not saying a word. She thought about being around Heather and watching the little girl's joy.

Being around Leo, too? a little voice inside her heart asked.

"Did you have anything special in mind?" In spite of her dad's remoteness, she still wanted to reach out to him. They didn't have relatives nearby. Her father had been an only child. Her mother had a sister, but she lived in Boston and they only saw her every few years. Verity wrote to her often and they called each other every couple of months, but actual visits were few and far between.

"No, nothing special. In fact, if you don't think you'll be coming home, I might drive to Corpus Christi. Ted Cranshaw—I knew him when I was in the Navy—just bought a big place there. He said if I wasn't doing anything on Christmas, I should come over."

So her father really hadn't called to say he missed her. He really hadn't called to say he wanted her to come home for Christmas. He'd called to see if she was tied up, because if she was, then he could do his own thing. She didn't him want to ask her to come home only because he felt that he should.

Keeping disappointment and a world of hurt from her voice, she said evenly, "You go visit your friend, Dad. That's fine."

"Are you sure?"

Of course she wasn't sure. Holidays were meant for family. But family had to involve more than duty, and that seemed to be all that was left with her father. "I'm sure."

An awkward silence fell between them—a familiar, awkward silence. He cleared his throat. "Oh, I almost forgot. What about your mail? Should I forward that to you? You got a letter that looks very businesslike from some production company."

Probably the company that shot the commercial. That seemed like eons ago now. Anything about it reminded her of Sean and his grin as he'd given her a wolf whistle and a thumb's-up sign right before the shoot. It also brought back memories of Matthew and his absolute fascination with her new look. She wondered if she'd met him with her hair straight, glasses on her nose, would he even have given her a second look. Probably not.

Leo had given her a second look. When she relived that kiss—

"Verity?"

She couldn't believe how thoughts of Leo could distract her. "I'm here, Dad. Don't worry about my mail. If you want to stick it all in an envelope and send it to me, that's fine."

"All right. That's what I'll do. Take care of yourself, Verity."

"I will. You take care, too."

When she closed her phone, tears came to her eyes that she couldn't will away.

On Monday morning Verity was folding laundry in the kitchen when Leo called around nine o'clock. He'd left for work before her alarm had gone off. She'd barely seen him yesterday after her trip to Freeport. Last night she'd worked on a paper for the class she was auditing, every once in a while hearing Heather's laughter, hearing Leo's deep baritone from the monitor, remembering their kiss.

Now she wondered why he was calling, since she rarely heard from him during working hours.

"How busy is your morning?" he asked.

"Just the usual chores and playtime with Heather. Why?"

"I have a favor to ask. I'd like to bring a client home for supper. I could take him to a restaurant, but Mr. Parelli is a family man. He has four kids of his own. I'll be piloting his cabin cruiser to Port Aransas in a week or so, and he's mentioned ordering another for his brother. Anyway, he talks about his kids all the time, and I thought he might like to meet Heather."

"What kind of dinner would you like me to prepare?" Leo was rarely home for supper. She usually left a plate for him in the refrigerator, and he ate when he got home.

"It doesn't have to be anything fancy," he added.

"I'll come up with something. But I will have to take Heather to the store. Is that all right with you?"

Leo had bought a second car seat for Verity's car, but she always let him know when she was taking his daughter someplace other than the preschool two mornings a week.

"That's not a problem. Just don't let her convince you to buy one of each kind of candy bar."

Verity laughed. "Don't worry. I have her almost convinced that granola bars are better."

After a brief silence, when neither knew exactly what to say, Leo broke it. "Thanks, Verity. Mr. Parelli is coming to Avon Lake this afternoon, so you can plan dinner for around six."

"I'll do that."

As Verity hung up, she thought about the menu. Glancing into the dining room, she realized she hadn't asked Leo if he wanted her to use the good china in the hutch, but she assumed she should.

There was something else she hadn't asked him. Did he want her to join them for dinner? If he and his client wanted to talk, she could distract Heather. She'd set a place for herself, and if he didn't want it there, she could take it away.

By 5:30 Verity thought she was ready. The table was set, the beef Stroganoff was simmering, the rice would be finished steaming in fifteen minutes. She'd dressed Heather in a pretty lilac flowered dress, and she'd taken more care with her outfit, choosing navy pants, a red knit top and a cotton camp shirt of navy and red. She'd even tied a jaunty red ribbon around her ponytail band. Whether she was serving or sitting down with Leo and Heather at dinner, she didn't want to embarrass him.

She'd just settled Heather on the floor of the great room with her coloring book and a plastic container full of crayons when the doorbell rang. Hurrying to the foyer, Verity answered it.

When she opened the front door, she found a balding man with a round face who looked to be in his fifties. He was wearing a white polo shirt and tan cargo slacks with deck shoes.

"Mr. Parelli?" she asked, wondering why he was at the door alone.

He smiled at her. "That's me. Leo got an unexpected phone call he had to take, and I told him I could find my way here. He said he wouldn't be long."

"Come on in," she invited with a wave of her hand toward the great room. "I'm just keeping an eye on supper and playing with Heather."

As Mr. Parelli stepped over the threshold, she closed the door. "Leo said you have four children of your own. How old are they?"

"Twelve, ten, six and two," he responded with a friendly smile. "Two boys and two girls. I've got a diverse bunch. Mary and I started later in life than most, I guess. But the kids make every day an adventure."

"Leo told me he'll be delivering your boat to Port Aransas. Do you live there?"

"Unfortunately, no. We just have a small getaway house there. I live in Lake Jackson. When Leo brings the boat to Port Aransas, will you be coming with him?"

She doubted that. But before she had a chance to say so, she heard a loud clatter in the great room, and Heather was running toward her, wailing, "My cwayons all spilled."

"If there's anything I can do to help, Mrs. Montgomery…" Mr. Parelli said.

Just as his words registered, the front door opened and Leo came in. "Hey, Tony. I see you found your way here."

"Sure did. Your wife and I are getting acquainted."

Heather was tugging on Verity's hand when Tony Parelli spoke, and she wasn't sure what to do. Stooping down, Verity picked up Heather and held her in her arms. "Just a minute, honey."

Leo looked from Verity to Mr. Parelli. "Tony, Verity isn't my wife. She's my nanny. Or rather, Heather's nanny."

An awkward silence seemed to reverberate from the foyer throughout the great room.

Finally, Tony Parelli gave a little shrug. "I see." His cheeks reddened slightly.

Totally embarrassed, Verity murmured, "Let me get Heather settled again, and then I'll put supper on the table."

"Will you be joining us?" Tony asked, obviously curious about their lifestyle. Verity saw Leo glance into the dining room and back at his daughter. "Yes, she will."

Why had Leo included her? Because she could tend to Heather? Or because he wanted Parelli to think they were a family, even if an unorthodox one?

Verity suddenly wished that was true.

Stepping closer to Verity, Leo took Heather from her arms. "Come on, kiddo. I'll keep her with us while you get supper out," he said to Verity with a cold look that she didn't understand.

For the most part, Verity kept quiet during dinner, simply taking care of Heather's needs. Tony addressed her specifically, once or twice. However, Leo's attitude was remote, and she wished she knew what he was thinking. Did this dinner with his client make him miss his wife even more?

When Verity offered to get Heather ready for bed, Leo politely thanked her. After she said goodnight to both men, she read Heather a story, then settled her in her crib for the night, Nosy tucked under her arm.

She'd just turned on her CD player in her sitting room and settled in an armchair with her knitting needles and yarn when there was a knock at her door.

Opening it, she saw Leo. "I think we should talk. Come into the great room, would you?"

His gaze cut to the painting that she'd bought at the arts festival, and she knew he was remembering their kiss. She had the feeling he might never enter her sitting room again, at least not while she was in it.

After she followed him to the great room, he didn't

sit and neither did she. Rather, he dug his hands deep into his pockets and asked, "Why did you lie to Parelli?"

The question was so far from anything she might have expected, all she could do was repeat, "Lie?"

"Yes. Obviously you told him something that gave him the impression you were my wife."

"Obviously I didn't do anything of the kind." Where she had been upset before, now she was angry. Why would Leo think she'd lied? "I'd never intentionally mislead *anyone.*"

Leo's narrowed gaze told her he didn't believe her.

"Mr. Parelli came to the door, I opened it and we started talking," she explained shortly. "I was trying to put him at ease. Then Heather spilled her crayons, he called me Mrs. Montgomery, and you walked in the door. I didn't have *time* to correct him."

"You could have said immediately that you weren't Mrs. Montgomery."

Had she hesitated? Had she liked the idea of the title? Or had she simply been so startled no correction had found its way to her tongue? "I'm sorry, Leo. I never meant to mislead your client. Believe me, I know my position here."

Before Leo could reproach her further, before she could wonder again about her own feelings on the subject, she turned her back on him and left the room.

Feeling more than attraction to Leo Montgomery wasn't acceptable, and she had to figure out what to do about it.

Chapter Four

As Verity walked down the tiled hall of the Arts and Sciences Building of Avon College the following evening, she thought about Leo and his reaction to what had happened with Mr. Parelli last night. Why had he ever thought she would lie? Where had that idea even come from?

She had never done anything that would give him the impression she wouldn't tell the truth.

Then again, they really didn't know each other very well.

Why did she want him to think only the best of her? Why did his opinion matter so much?

Arriving at Dr. Will Stratford's office door, she didn't answer the question. Tonight she was supposed to pick up forms to fill out for next semester.

The top portion of the door was plate glass and she

could see into the professor's office. Dr. Stratford was sitting at the desk, bent over some papers. His gray hair was mussed and sticking up all over. His bow tie was askew as usual. His suspenders today were bright red. The professor had the reputation for being highly intelligent but a bit kooky and absent-minded. Retired now from the English Department, he helped out where needed, sometimes even giving guest lectures. He'd taught everything from Shakespeare to William Blake and Lord Byron.

When she rapped on the door, he looked up and then motioned her inside.

Standing when she entered, he pushed his wire-rim spectacles up higher on his nose. "Hello, Verity. It's good to see you again."

From the moment she'd met the grandfatherly Dr. Stratford, she'd felt as if she'd known him all her life. "I was hoping to catch you. I couldn't remember if you had office hours this evening."

"Have a seat," he said, gesturing to a chair. "I'm here more than I'm not."

"But you're retired!"

After she sat, he lowered himself into the old wooden chair on rollers behind his desk and grinned. "Retirement is for folks who don't love their work. They think by quitting it, they'll find happiness. I knew better. I have my hobbies, and my cat meows that I'm not home enough, but keeping busy will keep me young."

"You have a cat?" she asked, amused.

"Yes, indeed. Sheets is a gray tabby who is overweight and entirely spoiled. He rules my house. I only reside there."

She laughed.

"That's better," Dr. Stratford remarked.

"What do you mean?"

"You were looking much too serious when you knocked on my door."

"I was thinking about something…someone."

"Are you having a problem I could help with?"

"Oh, Dr. Stratford. If only."

"Call me Will," he suggested.

There was a kindness that emanated from Dr. Stratford that helped her relax whenever she spoke with him. He seemed to truly care about what mattered to her, whether it came to classes or family matters. In her first meeting with him she'd found herself telling him about Sean. He'd understood everything she was feeling, and a bond had formed between them.

Leo understood, too, a little voice whispered.

Will Stratford leaned forward a bit, his arms crossed on his desk. "Whatever the problem, it's distracting you," he noticed with concern.

That was certainly true. "It's my job," she answered vaguely.

"You took a position as an au pair, right?"

"Yes, that's right. And my boss—" She stopped abruptly.

Will straightened, uncrossing his arms and gazing at her steadily. "Is he mistreating you in any way?"

Seeing the concern in Professor Stratford's gaze, she hurried to correct the conclusion he'd jumped to. "No.

Absolutely not. It's just…" She paused and then in a
rush added, "I'm attracted to him. He's a widower, and
I already love his little girl."

The teacher's expression relaxed, and he leaned back
in his chair, making it creak. "Ah, I see. Is this attraction one-sided?"

When she thought about Leo's kiss, her cheeks
caught fire. "I don't think so. It's just that I'm younger
than he is, and I think he's still tied to the past."

"You mean his deceased wife?" Will asked, catching
on quickly.

"Yes."

As soon as she'd uttered the word, she felt as if she'd
betrayed some kind of confidence.

Will must have seen that because he hurried to assure
her, "Verity, whatever we talk about in here, I will keep
confidential. I'm your advisor. If you don't trust me, I
can't advise you. In January you'll be starting your
work in earnest. If this situation you're in is going to in-
terfere with that, you should talk it through."

She knew he was right. "Nothing is going to inter-
fere. I don't think Leo's ready for any type of romantic
involvement."

After studying her carefully, Will's expression became sober. "Let me ask you something, Verity. You said
this man is tied to his past. Are you tied to yours?"

The question took her aback. *Was* she tied to her
past? Was she ready for a relationship? Or did she still
expect men to walk out on her? Her dad had always been
available for Sean, but she'd felt as if she were merely
part of the package. Matthew had left when the going

got rough. And Sean…he'd abandoned her, too, in a way. So even if she and Leo explored the attraction between them and found common ground, would *she* back away? Could she dare to dream that Leo would be different from her dad…from Matthew?

"I see that's a question you might have to think about."

"Yes, it is."

Taking a manila envelope from a stack on the side of his desk, Will opened it and took out a sheaf of papers. "Look over the catalog carefully, check out the classes listed here on early childhood education, and then fill out the paperwork." After he stuffed it all back in, he handed her the envelope. "Return them to me before Christmas, then we'll get your schedule moving for next semester."

Knowing she'd be late for class if she didn't leave, Verity stood and tucked the envelope under her arm. "Thank you for all your help."

"I don't help. I just listen and sort a bit." He stood, too. "In a little while I'll be sending you your official welcome letter for the new year. There will be another form for you to return to Student Affairs. Don't let it get lost in the Christmas shuffle."

"I won't."

With a wave, she left Will Stratford's office and hurried to her class. She didn't know how much auditing she'd be doing tonight. She'd be thinking about her ties to the past.

When Verity returned to Leo's house after her class, silence greeted her. She was both relieved and disappointed. After last night's fiasco, not seeing Leo lowered her stress level. On the other hand, she wished they could find an easy footing again.

If she checked on Heather, she might run into him.

Suddenly she didn't have to worry about running into him. He was standing there—in jeans, bare feet and an unbuttoned shirt.

"I was about to get a shower when I heard you come in. We need to talk."

His deep voice was sure and certain, and fear that he was going to fire her gripped her. After all, if he thought she'd lied—

"If you want to get your shower, I can wait." It wasn't in her nature to procrastinate or avoid the inevitable. But in this case...

"I don't want to wait."

As Leo approached her, trembling began deep inside of her and seeped through her body. She couldn't keep from responding to him even if she wanted to.

Taking a deep breath and squaring her shoulders, she stood up for herself. "I didn't lie last night, Leo. Mr. Parelli just jumped to the wrong conclusion."

"I know."

Those weren't the words she expected to hear. "You know? Did you talk with Mr. Parelli?"

Leo motioned toward the great room. "Let's go in and sit down. There's something I want to tell you. It might help you understand why *I* jumped to the wrong conclusion."

The intensity in Leo's eyes gave her pause for a moment, but then she took a deep breath and began to slip her backpack from her shoulders.

Before she could, he caught it, his large hand grazing her arm. Enticing tingles ran through her from the heat of his touch.

"This weighs a ton," he complained with a small smile, as he hefted it onto the table.

"Not quite that much," she responded lightly, feeling almost buoyant because she didn't think this discussion was going to be about firing her.

"You're much stronger than you look, aren't you?" Leo asked, his gaze immobilizing her.

"I've never thought about it. I work out every morning. I have weights in my closet."

"I wasn't just talking about physical strength."

Leo was looking at her as if he admired her. She didn't think any man had looked at her quite that way before.

After he motioned her into the great room, he followed her to the sofa.

When he sat beside her, she was much too cognizant of his unbuttoned shirt, his chest hair that was inviting her fingers to touch it. He seemed oblivious to his just-before-a-shower appearance and was totally focused on the conversation he wanted to have with her.

"Are you sure you don't want to get your shower?" Even his bare feet were sexy.

As if with a sudden flash of insight he was aware of the casualness of his attire, his fingers went to the buttons of his shirt and he quickly fastened them. "This won't take long," he said gruffly. "Then we can both call it a day."

Leo broke eye contact and then turned slightly to face

her. "I hate lies," he said. "Purposeful lies *or* lies of omission. One's as bad as the other."

"I'd never lie to you."

His gaze was steady and piercing. "I haven't known you long enough to figure that out. Even in the short time I *have* known you, I've realized there are areas of your life you don't want to discuss. You seem secretive about your family."

"Not secretive. Some things just hurt too much to talk about."

Leo digested that. "All right. I can accept that. I don't talk about Carolyn much for many reasons. Some of those reasons caused me to jump to a mistaken conclusion last night."

"I don't understand."

"Carolyn lived with a secret for three long months without telling me." He raked his hand through his hair. "She started having headaches and kept that information from me. I was working a lot, keeping the business going through tough economical times. Later she made the excuse that that's why she hadn't revealed she was having headaches. That's why she hadn't revealed the family doctor had sent her to a neurologist. That's why, for three long months, she didn't tell me she had a brain tumor."

Verity was absolutely stunned, unable to imagine a wife withholding that information from a husband. "Why did she keep it from you?"

"I've asked myself that question at least a million times, because I didn't accept her answer when I put it to her. She explained her brain tumor was inoperable.

She'd decided to accept the inevitable and live out whatever time she had with me and Heather in peace, adding as an afterthought that she was sure if she discussed her diagnosis with me, I'd want her to seek treatment—experimental treatment, any treatment—to keep her alive longer."

"She didn't want to live longer?"

"Carolyn was concerned with the quality of her life, not the quantity of it. You see, she didn't tell me about the diagnosis voluntarily. I came home and found her on the floor. She couldn't get up. That's how I knew something was terribly wrong, and her condition could no longer be her secret. A few months after that, she was gone."

"Leo, I'm so sorry."

He shook his head as if he didn't want her sympathy, and she realized he was a proud man. Because of that pride, the fact that his wife couldn't confide in him hurt even more deeply.

"I felt as if during those months she'd kept her condition hidden, we were living a lie."

"She was trying to protect you."

"No, I don't think she was. I think she was taking the time to decide what *she* wanted to do, and there was no room for my opinion. I don't think Carolyn even thought about what losing her mother would do to Heather."

He laid his hands on his thighs, stared straight ahead, then turned back to Verity. "Anyway, that's why I jumped to the wrong conclusion last night."

She had to make something very clear to him. "I won't lie to you, Leo. Ever. And if there's something you want to ask me, ask me and I'll answer it."

"I'll start making a list," he joked with a wry smile that was meant to lighten the mood.

However, as their gazes met, locked and held, the mood wasn't lightened. Her attraction for him was met by his attraction for her, and the resulting collision sent sparks flying.

"I've tried to forget about kissing you." His voice was gruff, low and deep, and her tummy did a somersault.

"It was unforgettable," she murmured honestly, not knowing what else to say.

When he reached out, when his hand caressed her cheek, she knew she was in trouble. No man's touch had ever affected her as Leo's did. "Maybe I should find another job."

"Maybe you should," he agreed.

"Do you want me to leave?" she asked, knowing that would make all the difference.

His turmoil was evident in the darkening of his blue eyes. "No, I don't. You're good with Heather, and you're good *for* her."

He dropped his hand to his side, and although he didn't move himself away physically, she felt him remove himself in every other way as he asked, "Do you want to stay?"

Although she was heading for deep water, although she didn't know if she could keep her boat afloat, she felt such a pull toward Leo she had to say, "Yes, I want to stay. I love taking care of Heather, and I feel safe here."

"Safe? How could you feel safe after I kissed you?"

"I knew what I was doing, Leo. If I had turned away, I have no doubt you would have left my room."

"You're so young," he growled with a shake of his head. "So naive."

That stirred up her temper. "I'm past the age of consent, and I can vote. I can also make my own decisions."

"But will they be wise ones, Verity? You and me…under the same roof—"

"I understand that I have the power to say yes as well as no. I understand the chemistry between us is powerful, but it doesn't change who we are."

Then, just as quickly as it had flared, the moment of temper vanished, and she had to accept the fact that she *was* younger than Leo and terribly less experienced.

On the other hand, he had to realize she was more mature than he thought. "Having a male twin taught me a lot about men."

Leo was silent for a few long moments, but then he grumbled, "Maybe not enough." Rising to his feet he said, "You did a great job with dinner last night."

"Thank you," she murmured, knowing he was relegating her to an employee once more. He wanted to keep her in a box because he thought that was safer for both of them.

As they said their good-nights and Leo left the great room, she didn't know how long she could stay in that box. She didn't know if she *wanted* to stay in that box. However, if she broke free, she had to make sure she was ready to face the consequences.

When the overnight package came for Leo the next day, Verity wasn't sure what to do. She could just let it sit until he came home, or she could call him and ask him if he needed it. As Heather pasted animal stickers onto a large piece of construction paper, Verity pulled the list of phone numbers from the refrigerator and dialed Leo's cell phone.

On the second ring, he clicked on. "Montgomery."

"Leo, it's Verity. An Express Mail package was delivered for you. It's from a company called Design Makers. Is it something you need?"

"Yes, it is. It's a computer program I've been waiting for. My secretary must have given them my home address." When he paused, she could hear the echo of voices, the sound of some type of machinery running.

"I'd like to have it as soon as possible, and I can't get away right now. I have a meeting in five minutes. How would you feel about dropping it off here?"

"I don't mind. But what about Heather?"

"I don't want Heather around the boatyard. I'll give Jolene a call and see if she can watch her for a little while. If she's not home, I'll call you back. I should be finished with the meeting by one."

"All right. If I don't hear from you, I'll be there then."

As Verity hung up, she had to admit she'd been curious about the boatyard. Now maybe she'd get a glimpse of it.

A little before one, Verity took the side road that led to Montgomery Boat Company. It was a large complex, about twenty minutes outside of Avon Lake, near Surfside Beach. There was more than one building, and rising up to the side of the main plant she saw huge cranes. The layout of the complex told her Leo did a lot more than design boats.

Heading for the front of the smallest building, she passed rows of employees' cars. Finally she slid into a visitor's spot.

The office was pleasant and inviting with framed photographs of boats hanging on the blue walls. A nameplate on the secretary's desk said Mrs. MacLaren, and the woman smiled at Verity. Mrs. MacLaren, with her salt-and-pepper, short-cut hair, looked to be in her fifties.

Now she saw the package in Verity's hand. "Verity Sumpter?" she asked.

Verity nodded.

"Mr. Montgomery said to send you right in. That door over there." She pointed across the sitting area where gray-and-blue armchairs sat.

Verity made her way to the door and knocked.

Leo's deep "Yes?" affected her in a way she couldn't quite explain.

When she opened the door, he was seated at his desk, surrounded by catalogs. Standing, he smiled. "Come on in."

"This complex is huge," she said as she stepped inside.

He laughed. "We build boats. They're big."

"I don't know what I expected."

"Maybe a little Mom and Pop shop and rowboats sitting around?"

She felt her cheeks redden.

"Sorry, I couldn't resist." He looked amused. "And it's not so far from the truth. That's how my grandfather started out—from birch hulls to fiberglass hulls."

She knew she looked blank.

"Would you like a tour?"

Laying the package on his desk, she asked, "You're not too busy?"

"I'm always busy." He motioned to the half sandwich on his blotter. "But since I didn't stop for lunch, I can take a break. Come on, I'll show you around."

Today Leo was dressed in jeans with a striped oxford shirt, the sleeves rolled up his forearms. As they left the office and went outside down a walk to the plant, he pointed and explained, warning her the smell of polyester resin would be strong. While he introduced her to his employees, she couldn't take her eyes off him, though she listened to his enthusiasm about the design of cabin cruisers and runabouts, the history of the business and the process of boatbuilding itself.

Often her attention went to his large hands as they glided over an unfinished hull. The timbre of his voice and the passion in it as he explained what he did, the breadth of his shoulders as he walked beside her glancing over at her, made her feel excited yet protected and safe.

"You have amazing responsibilities here," she noted as they returned to his office a half hour later.

"I guess it seems that way to an outsider, but I grew up here with all of this. Dad and I were partners, so running the business is second nature to me. I'll tell you, Verity, having sole care of Heather daunts me in a way this business never could."

"Why?"

"I guess it goes back to what you said the day we took her to the doctor's. You mentioned you want to teach her what I want her to learn. I knew then you didn't mean the alphabet or arithmetic. Teaching values is a lot more complicated than showing her how to do math. Sometimes I don't know exactly how to go about it," he admitted with a wry turn of his mouth.

"She'll learn values from *you*—from what you say and do and how you treat her."

"Now *that's* responsibility." His blue gaze caught Verity's. They seemed locked together in an intimate understanding when the phone on his desk rang.

Verity murmured, "I should go."

He picked up the receiver, then shook his head. "It's my mother," he explained, holding his hand over the mouthpiece and motioning Verity to the chair in front of his desk. "This won't take long."

Not eager to leave, Verity did as he suggested and perched on the hardwood captain's chair. She had no desire to eavesdrop, and so she cast her gaze around the office as Leo talked, studying a picture next to the TV on the credenza of Leo and an older man who must have been his father, as well as small framed snapshots of Heather. Models of clipper ships also decorated the office file cabinets.

"I know you don't like voice mail, Mom. Calling me here is fine, but if you leave a message on my cell, I *will* call you back."

Whatever his mother said made Leo frown. "You got into town last night?"

Another pause.

"Of course we all want to see you, but it isn't fair to expect Jolene to prepare dinner on such short notice. I'll call her. You can all come to my place and we'll order a pizza." Leo listened for a bit, then replied, "We can order more than one kind. The kids will love it. Come over around seven. Do you want to call Jolene, or should I?"

"All right, I'll take care of it. Are you going to bring your pictures of Hawaii?"

Again there seemed to be another long explanation.

"Jolene and Tim will love a cruise there as a Christmas present. I'll see you around seven."

When Leo hung up, he grinned ruefully. "I always feel as though I've been tossed around in a storm after I've talked to her. We didn't expect her back until a few days before Christmas."

"How long has she been away?"

"Two months. She's leaving again mid-January to visit a friend in England."

"You aren't really going to feed your mother pizza, are you?"

He looked puzzled. "When she jumps in and out of our lives on short notice, it seems the best thing to do."

"I can cook supper."

"You don't have to do that. Jolene and Tim and the kids will be coming over and—"

"I don't mind. Really."

As Leo's steady gaze asked her to give him a further explanation, she went on, "I often miss not having a mother. You shouldn't take yours for granted." That was a bold thing to say, yet she knew Leo always expected honesty from her.

Coming around his desk, he sat on the corner of it. "It's going to be a lot of work."

"It doesn't have to be," she objected. "I can buy tuna

steaks at the fresh market and broil them, make a relish for on top, toss a salad, bake a rice pilaf, buy a loaf of French bread. Voilà. Dinner."

"You never cease to amaze me." His low voice made her nerve endings tingle.

"That's because you underestimate me. You think that because I'm a few years younger—"

"Twelve."

"You think that because I'm a few years younger," she repeated, "I haven't had experience at anything. Well, I have, and *not* just with cooking."

As Leo's eyes seemed to linger on her face then drop to her mouth, he raked his hand through his hair. "Experience aside, you've probably never met anyone like my mother. She isn't always easy to take. She says what she thinks, sometimes without considering the consequences."

"I admire sincerity."

Leo gave a short laugh. "We'll see how long *that* lasts after you meet her." He studied her again. "You're sure you want to take on dinner?"

"Positive."

"All right. But I think it's a good idea if you let Heather stay with Jolene this afternoon. She can bring her along when they come to dinner tonight. That way you can shop and prepare without having to worry about Heather."

"Your daughter isn't a worry, Leo. She's a pleasure."

"Most of the time." He fished his wallet from his back pocket and took out several bills. "Buy whatever you need."

Taking the money, she tucked it into her leather purse. "This is going to be fun."

With a wry smile he stood and returned to his desk chair. "We'll see if you're still wearing rose-colored glasses when the evening is over."

After Verity left Leo's office, she was filled with the anticipation of meeting his mother. No matter what he said, she was going to like her.

Chapter Five

"I hope you're ready for this," Leo said, as he stopped in the kitchen when he got home from work. "Tim and Jolene pulled in behind me in the driveway. Mother's in back of them."

Preparations for the meal had gone well, and Verity felt that she was more than ready. "Dinner will be on the table in fifteen minutes."

After he took a bottle of wine from the refrigerator, Leo peered into the dining room at the vase and the set table. "Did you stop at the florist?"

"No, just at the grocery store. I bought two bunches of flowers and arranged them."

For a few moments he studied the red and white carnations with green filler, the red dinner napkins on the white tablecloth next to the good china that was white with a tiny gray pattern.

Then he remarked, "You should have been a party planner."

His words buoyed Verity because he apparently liked what she had done.

After his observation, he crossed to the counter where she was tossing a salad. She could feel his body heat and smell the scent of his aftershave.

"The corkscrew's in that drawer." He pointed to the area where she was standing, and the look in his eyes lit fires inside of her.

After she moved to the side, he opened the drawer, his hand brushing her hip. As always, she was shaken by the awareness straining between them.

His voice went husky. "I appreciate everything you're doing for tonight."

"Wait and see how it tastes before you tell me that," she joked.

For a second she thought he was going to say something else, but suddenly there was a noisy burst of conversation in the foyer. An instant later Heather ran into the kitchen and wrapped her arms around Verity's legs.

With a smile Verity stooped to give the little girl a hug. "Hi, there. Did you have fun today?"

Heather nodded. "We colowed and went to the playgwound. I swinged."

"That must have been fun."

"Now Randy and Joey came to *my* house to eat." In a sweet rush she added, "We're gonna play some more."

Heather was talking at superfast speed, and Verity could see she was in the souped-up mode that often happened when she was overtired.

"Did you have a nap this afternoon?"

Jolene and the other adults came into the kitchen.

Overhearing the question, Leo's sister answered, "No nap today. Sorry. I tried to put her down for a little while but she didn't want to sleep."

"That happens." Leo scooped up Heather into his arms and carried her over to his mother.

Verity could see at once that Leo didn't resemble his mother. He obviously took after the man she'd seen in the picture in his office at the boatyard. She was striking, though. She wore her white-blond hair in a short, sophisticated cut that angled against her cheeks. Tall—about five-ten—she was also slim. Tonight she'd dressed in beautiful green silk slacks and overshirt.

After Leo made introductions, Amelia Montgomery studied Verity curiously.

Unsure what to wear this evening, Verity had chosen a pair of beige slacks and a no-nonsense, cream oxford shirt. Her brown flat shoes seemed drab compared to Amelia Montgomery's green high-heeled pumps.

"Leo tells me you're the reason we're not having pizza tonight," his mother said.

"I like to cook," Verity responded easily. "I hope you like tuna."

"Salad?" Amelia asked with a twitch of her nose.

Verity almost laughed at Leo's mother's underestimation of her culinary talents. "No. Broiled tuna steak."

Eyebrows lifting, Amelia asked, "Sushi grade?"

"Of course," Verity answered, trying to keep a straight face.

Amelia's gaze went to the dessert custard sitting on

a rack on the counter. "I'm looking forward to a sit-down meal with my family. Thank you for making it possible."

There was more politeness in Amelia's tone than genuine warmth, but Verity didn't let that put her off. She was hoping to get to know Leo's mother. If she did, she might learn more about *him*.

"Let's go wash up," Leo said to Heather.

"I don' wanna wash," she said adamantly, her lower lip quivering.

With Heather pouty, Verity thought, *This might not be the sit-down meal Amelia Montgomery expected.*

Fifteen minutes later as Verity put the dinner on the table, everyone took their seats except for Heather and five-year-old Joey who were chasing each other around the chairs.

"Whoa!" Leo caught Heather around the waist. "Come on, let's get you settled in your seat."

"No, no, no, Daddy. I don' wanna sit."

On the other side of the table, Jolene was coaxing Joey into his seat.

"Joey's sitting down," Jolene cajoled. "We're going to eat. Aren't you hungry?"

Heather shook her head vigorously. "I'm not hungwy. Don' wanna eat."

Returning to the kitchen for the platter of tuna steak, Verity brought it in, set it in the middle of the table, then took the empty chair next to Jolene.

"You're going to join us?" Amelia asked, not looking as if she quite approved.

Leo, still trying to convince Heather to stay seated,

cut a short glance to his mother. "Of course she's going to eat with us. She's not a maid."

Verity knew she should have thought about this. She *didn't* belong here with the family.

When she began to gather her plate and silverware, Jolene caught her hand. "Uh-uh. You're staying here. Mother, Verity seems to have a quieting effect on the kids. Besides that, we've become friends. She's definitely more than a nanny."

Feeling embarrassed, Verity kept her gaze averted from Leo's because she knew if she didn't, he'd see too much there. She didn't even think of herself as a nanny anymore, and that was dangerous.

While the adults passed the serving dishes, Leo fixed a plate for Heather. But his daughter was definitely cranky, overtired and petulant. She batted at the dish, spilling the food on the floor.

Verity braced herself for what was coming.

Leo's expression was a study in patience. "If you don't settle down, Heather, you're going to your room. And you can eat when everyone else is finished."

At that, his daughter began to cry, loud wails that seemed to fill the whole house.

Amelia looked pained. Jolene just looked embarrassed. Her husband was enjoying his food as if nothing bothered him. And Jolene had told Verity nothing much did.

Although Leo was firm with Heather, when she cried, he was putty in her hands. He gave Verity one of those looks as if to say, Now what am I supposed to do?

Verity slipped off her chair but didn't go to Heather. Instead she took her own plate which was still empty

and quickly arranged some food on it in the shape of a
face. Then she took it over to the crying Heather, put her
arm around the little girl's shoulders and set the plate
before her on the table. "Hey, sweetie. Look what I
made for you. Bet you can't eat his nose."

The nose was a grouping of peas.

Suddenly the crying stopped. Heather looked up at
Verity, then back at the plate. "It's a *funny* face."

"Well, I guess you could say that. I didn't have a lot to
work with. Do you want to eat his nose or his hair?" His
hair was made of rice pilaf. Verity handed Heather a spoon.

"I wanna eat his mouf."

Verity had fashioned the mouth from half-cut cherry
tomatoes. Hopefully Heather would eventually eat the
tuna steak that dotted the face's cheeks. "Okay. You can
use your fingers for those."

A few moments later Heather was eating happily and
Leo was shaking his head. "I don't know how you do
it," he murmured.

"It takes imagination," Jolene offered with a smile.
"You use yours for designing boats. Maybe you should
take one of those classes Verity's auditing at the college."

Everyone laughed, including Amelia, but as Verity
took a clean plate from the hutch and sat beside Jolene
again, Leo's mother glanced at her often.

Verity knew Heather would finish her meal much
more quickly than everyone else. Since she didn't get
involved in the conversation around the table about people she didn't know and places she'd never been, she finished her food about the same time as Heather.

To avoid another scene, when there was a lull in the

conversation, Verity asked Leo, "Should I get Heather ready for bed?"

He saw that her plate was empty. "You don't have to do that. I will."

"If you want to spend time with your family, it's okay with me. As soon as she's bored…"

His smile was rueful as he nodded. "All right. But come back for dessert."

Not responding to that, Verity rose, gathered Heather into her arms, whispering to her that she could use bubble bath tonight, said good evening to everyone and started for the hall.

She wasn't two steps away from the living room when she heard Amelia's voice and stopped to listen. "She's certainly very capable, but what a plain Jane."

More than once, Verity had heard the old adage that eavesdroppers didn't overhear anything good about themselves, but she couldn't help the tears that sprang to her eyes. Not so much because of Amelia Montgomery's remarks but because she didn't hear the deep rumble of Leo's voice contradicting his mother. She didn't hear anything from him at all.

In the dining room Leo was fuming at what his mother had said about Verity. She *was* very capable, and she *did* dress plainly.

After he took a second helping of tuna and thought about his words carefully, he responded, "Verity is very easy to be around."

His mother looked surprised. "As compared to whom?" she asked promptly.

"As compared to anyone."

"Really? Or were you thinking about Carolyn?"

Maybe he was. Ready for a battle, he laid down his fork. His mother had adored Carolyn, constantly reminding him that his wife was perfect for him. "Maybe I *am* making a comparison. It's easier to be around a low-maintenance woman than a high-maintenance one."

Carolyn had definitely been high maintenance, just like his mother. Her hair had to always be perfectly in place, as did her makeup and her clothes. If she didn't have a manicure every week, she was embarrassed to go out.

"I'm not exactly sure what you mean by high maintenance," his mother replied haughtily, "but a little makeup never hurt anyone. Verity's basically a beautiful girl. She just doesn't know it. No one around her does, either. Contact lenses would make a world of difference."

"Mom, you can't change everyone you meet," Jolene admonished.

"Whom have I tried to change?"

"All of us," Jolene answered lightly. "You want Leo to dress in a suit and go to work every day as if he works on Wall Street. Even though he has an MBA, he works in a *boatyard*. And me. You think I should get out and go to book-discussion groups and join the bridge club when I enjoy spending time at home cooking and gardening more."

Amelia glanced over at Tim speculatively. "Do you have any complaints?"

"Not a one," he responded blandly, and Leo watched Jolene smile. That's what Jolene loved about her husband. He never got into an argument if he could help it.

"Look, Mom. Verity's doing a wonderful job with Heather. That's all that matters to me," Leo said.

"Is it?" his mother asked, as if she knew that every time he looked at Verity his blood pressure went up.

She couldn't know that. Could she?

When his gaze fell on Jolene, his sister shrugged her shoulders. "I can't wait to try that cream custard Verity made for dessert. Why don't I go put on a pot of coffee?"

Instead of sitting here having coffee and dessert with his family, Leo realized he'd rather be putting Heather to bed alongside Verity. That thought shook up his world, as did his mother's knowing glances as he finished dinner.

After his family left, Leo went to Heather's room. She was sleeping peacefully, Nosy tucked in by her side. She'd had an active day and with no nap, she'd probably sleep late in the morning. Not sure what prodded him, he went to the kitchen, spooned portions of the leftover custard Verity had made into two dishes and took them along with him to Verity's room. Her door was slightly ajar.

When he looked inside, he saw her lying on her sofa, a book on her lap. She was sleeping.

Studying her in sleep, he realized how very pretty she was. Her long ponytail lay over her shoulder, and he longed to unband it and run his fingers through her glossy hair. Not wanting to startle her, feeling like an intruder in her room, juggling the two dishes in one hand, he rapped on her door.

Instantly alert, she swung her legs to the floor and sat up. "Leo!"

Taking her exclamation as an invitation to come in, he crossed the room and sat on the sofa next to her, placing the custards on the coffee table. "Hi. I think the family exhausted you."

"I wasn't really sleeping. I just sort of dozed off."

He laughed. "You were sleeping. After caring for a three-year-old, making dinner for company and cleaning up, I can see why. I brought you dessert."

Glancing away from him, she focused on the custard. "Thanks."

"Why didn't you rejoin us in the great room after you put Heather to bed?"

"I didn't want to intrude."

Verity had brought something into his life that had been missing—peace, sunshine, energy that made him feel alive again.

"I told you my mother was hard to take sometimes."

A shadow crossed Verity's face. "She's just looking out for you. For all of you," she amended.

"She knows better than to think she has to look out for me."

"Heather, then. She wants to make sure any influence in her life is a good one."

"You're the best. She couldn't have anyone better looking after her." He wasn't just trying to reassure Verity. He meant it.

Apparently she could see that, and her eyes suddenly glistened. "Thank you, Leo. That's nice of you to say."

Sometimes he got the feeling that Verity didn't know her own worth. Cupping her cheek, he said gently, "That wasn't just an idle compliment. You're good for Heather." Honestly he added, "And you're good for me."

When her eyes widened, when her lips parted slightly, he couldn't help leaning into her. He couldn't help putting his arm around her. He couldn't help kissing her. Verity Sumpter brightened his world and drew him like a magnet. He still wasn't altogether sure why, but she aroused him in a way he'd never been aroused before. It definitely wasn't just physical, though that was a big part of it.

As Leo's lips angled over Verity's, he realized all the things he felt when he was with her. He felt taller, stronger, more of a man, as if he was capable of holding the world on his shoulders. He felt as if he could be a success at raising Heather. He felt his ties to Jolene more keenly, and even appreciated his mother a little more.

Why was all of that so?

Kissing Verity, he tried to find the answer. But as his tongue slipped into her mouth, as she caught her breath and then responded to him, he got lost in everything physical. When Verity wrapped her arms around his neck, when he felt her soft breasts against his chest, when he tasted her sweetness, and experienced arousal that was almost painful, nothing but the physical mattered. She seemed as lost to the chemistry between them as he was, as her hands slid into his hair.

After he broke their kiss to nuzzle her neck, he touched his tongue to the pulse at her throat, and she murmured his name. It was a sexy whisper that was as erotic as everything else they were doing. He brought one of his hands between them and pressed his palm to her breast. When she moaned, he did it again. Kissing her once more, he passed his thumb over her nipple. It was a hard bud, and he could feel it through her blouse…through her bra. Her tongue played with his and he teased the nipple, taunted it, made her want more. He could tell she did. As her tongue stroked his, as her hands slipped from his hair down his neck to his shoulders, as she curled her fingers into his muscles, he pictured her hands on his bare skin and thought about how he would feel. He hadn't been touched by a woman in so very long.

Without thinking about repercussions, only thinking about hunger and need, his fingers went to the buttons on her blouse. He started unfastening them rapidly, fumbling when one wouldn't come loose, all the while getting hotter because of Verity's willing responses, the soft sounds she made, her hand exploring what she could reach. Finally he slipped his hand inside her blouse. Her bra was silky, lace edging the cup. He dipped his thumb inside—

Verity froze. Absolutely froze. Her stillness was a sharp contrast to the playfulness of her tongue and the exploration of her fingers a moment before.

Breathing raggedly, he broke away and gazed down at her. "What's wrong?"

Her eyes were huge, velvety, and so vulnerable. She said, "I have to tell you something."

"Now?" he asked, lightly teasing.

When she nodded, her expression was completely serious. "I…I'm a virgin."

Leo wasn't sure whether to be shocked, amazed or

totally baffled. "A virgin? You've been to college. You've dated."

"Matthew was my first serious relationship. He wanted to, but I…" She scooted her gaze from his. "I wasn't ready. It's another reason he…moved on."

So many thoughts battled for dominance in Leo all at once. "If he couldn't wait until you were ready, then he didn't love you."

At that, her eyes came up to meet his. "That's what Sean said. I thought he was just being a brother."

"He was being a man, too. A man who knows how other guys should treat women." Leo raked his hand through his hair and moved away from her, as much from his own need to cool down as from what she'd told him.

"Leo, I…liked what we were doing. I just thought you should know."

"Now I know. Why have you waited?" he asked, needing to hear the answer.

"I was waiting for the right man…the man I wanted to spend my life with. I know that might seem silly. Maybe I should have been born a few decades earlier. But I just can't imagine being intimate with a man without knowing we have a commitment to each other and that being together is right."

"There's nothing silly at all about believing that," he said gruffly. "But I'm glad you told me because I'm not at all sure about the rightness of this. I don't think *you* are, either. We just got caught up in the moment."

"But…"

"No buts, Verity. I won't take advantage of you. You

were sleeping when I came in here. I shouldn't have let this attraction between us get out of hand."

"I was awake when you kissed me. I was awake when *I* kissed *you*. You seem to think because I'm younger than you I don't know up from down, left from right, or the consequences of what I do. Believe me, Leo, I understand consequences. I understand exactly what was happening between us."

He was going to see how really honest she was. "Were you ready for it?"

With a shaky smile, she answered, "I don't know. But I didn't want you to stop."

"On some level, you did. That's why you told me you were a virgin."

"No. I just thought you should know."

"You stopped me instinctively, and that was the right thing to do. The right thing for *me* to do now is leave."

After a moment she suggested, "We *could* eat dessert together."

"We could. But I think it's wiser for me to get a cold shower."

When she blushed, he felt every one of those twelve years that gave him so much more experience than she'd ever had. "I just wanted to apologize for my mother in case she made you feel uncomfortable tonight."

Still for a few seconds, Verity finally said, "Your mother put the situation in perspective for me. I'm not one of the family, Leo. You pay me to take care of Heather."

Yes, he did, and before he muddied the waters, he'd better make sure he was putting Heather's interests first.

Letting Verity's statement stand, he told her, "I have an early meeting in the morning. I'll be leaving the house before Heather gets up."

"But you'll be home for supper?"

"Yes. Even though you're excellent with Heather, I want to make sure she knows I'm always going to be around, that she comes first in my life, and that she matters to me."

After he crossed to the door, he stopped. "Thanks again for putting dinner together tonight. I won't forget it."

With Verity's soft "Goodnight" ringing in his ears he headed for his bedroom, knowing he wouldn't forget her response to his kisses or his response to her touch, either.

He didn't just need a cold shower. He needed a *long, cold* shower.

Rain drizzled down the following day when Leo came home from work and saw the letters shoved in the mailbox on the porch. Apparently Verity had been too busy with Heather to even come outside for the mail. Carrying it into the foyer, he sorted through it on the table and found a letter for Verity. In the upper left-hand corner was simply the name Will, instead of a return address.

Curious, yet knowing he had no right to question her about it, he strode into the kitchen where she was making dinner. Heather was standing on a chair next to Verity at the counter, watching her stir batter for biscuits.

After he kissed and hugged his daughter, he said nonchalantly to Verity, "You have a letter." He held it up to her so she could see the front of the envelope.

She smiled. It was a quirky little smile that made him wonder if it had come from the guy she'd spoken to at the arts festival. After all, she was young and pretty, and probably had lots of boys who wanted to date her. Boys. Leo was definitely a man. His thoughts about her were anything but pure, especially in his dreams.

Without giving any hints as to what the letter might contain, she simply asked, "Would you mind putting it on my desk in my sitting room? I don't want to lose it."

If she didn't want to lose it, that meant the letter was important.

Suddenly he found himself wanting to know where she went on her Sundays off. He wanted to know more about her, and there was only one way to do that—spend some time with her.

Still fingering the letter, an idea came to him, and he ran with it. "How would you like to do something a little different tomorrow?"

"Like what?"

"Every year, weather permitting, I have a party for my employees on the beach for Christmas. For years they've been telling me they enjoy that more than some dinner-dance in a hotel. It'll start about four and last into the evening. Would you like to go? The weather report for tomorrow sounds promising."

She looked a little puzzled, as if she wondered if he were asking her on a date. Damned if he knew!

"Heather, too?"

"Oh, no. This is strictly for adults. I'm going to take Jolene's boys Christmas shopping after school one day next week so I don't think she'll mind watching Heather.

My mom will have a chance to spend some time with her, too."

"Then I'd like to come to your beach party." Verity's eyes sparkled, as if a jaunt to the beach was exactly what she'd like to do.

He found himself looking forward to it, too. "Dress casually. Nothing fancy. Do you play beach volleyball?" he asked.

With a wide grin, she nodded. "Absolutely."

"Great. The employees have the afternoon off. I'll come home and pick you up and grab the volleyball gear."

The letter still feeling like a hot potato in his hand, he moved a little closer to Verity and peered over her shoulder at the batter. "I don't know if I've ever had homemade biscuits."

"Not even as a kid?"

"Mom wasn't very domestic." His lips were tantalizingly near her cheek. Her hair smelled fragrant…of spices and flowers. "What are we having with them?" he asked, his voice low.

She kept stirring. "Chili. If you like it hot I'll add more peppers."

"I like it hot."

She turned then, her skin grazing his, her gaze meeting his. "I'll remember that," she murmured.

"Daddy, Daddy. I'm gonna eat chili and biscuits, too."

Leo grinned. He realized that Heather heard a lot more than he'd thought she did. She was looking up at him as he stood so very close to Verity, and he almost felt as if they were a family.

That thought was a shock.

Moving away from Verity, he ruffled his daughter's hair. "I think we'll make some chili for you that isn't quite so hot."

Then he tickled his daughter and went to Verity's sitting room to deposit her letter on her desk. Already he was thinking about tomorrow and playing volleyball with Verity. He just wanted to spend more time with her…get to know her a little better.

In a flash of memory, he recalled Carolyn's first outing on the beach with his employees as well as her decision not to attend in the years after that. She simply hadn't been a sand-between-her-toes kind of person. He had a suspicion Verity was.

Realizing that, he knew he might have bitten off a lot more than he could chew.

Chapter Six

Waves sloshed on the beach as the sun dipped into the gold-and-pink horizon. Adjusting the elastic band she'd brought along to hold her glasses in place, Verity readied herself for the volleyball game.

She didn't feel as if she belonged here.

Although everyone was friendly, Leo was the one who was giving her that impression. Once they'd arrived, he'd become engaged in one conversation after another, leaving her on her own. Not that she minded that. She enjoyed going from group to group, getting to know people. But he was giving the impression he'd just brought her along for a game of volleyball. Maybe that's exactly what he'd done. Maybe she'd read more into this invitation than she should have.

So if he'd brought her along to play volleyball, that was what she was going to do. She was wearing purple running pants and a matching shirt she'd bought a while back and never worn. Volleyball was her game. She'd been on a team in high school, and she hadn't forgotten the moves.

She slipped into place on the side opposite of Leo. However, they had a shortage of players. The other side had an abundance, and Leo jogged over to stand behind her. She tried not to notice him in his cutoff shorts and a red T-shirt that stretched over his muscles like a second skin. She tried to ignore his hair blowing in the breeze and the strong cut of his jaw, as well as his powerful physique.

Staring straight ahead, she was determined to concentrate on the game.

Play began with a soaring high serve, and Verity was ready. The ball came straight to her, and she whacked it over the net. As the game grew fast and furious, she thought she'd forget about Leo behind her. But she didn't. She only knew she had to make every shot she could.

Verity was surprised that Leo was as expert at playing volleyball as she was and made it look effortless. When she swiveled to watch him take a shot, she marveled at everything about his tall, hard body.

As the sky turned purple with dusk, the ball became harder to see. They'd soon have to call it quits and were trying to get in as many shots as they could. When the ball sailed toward Verity again, she had to take a few back-up steps.

Suddenly there was a thwump as she and Leo collided, reaching for the same hit. The ball glanced off her shoulder and bounced away, but Leo's arms went around her to steady her. He was hot, male, sweaty, and she could feel the rise and fall of his chest at her shoulder. His arms were tight around her, and she knew she never wanted him to let her go. What a silly thought in the middle of a volleyball game!

He turned her around in his arms and steadied her. "Are you okay?"

She was fine, except she couldn't breathe very well. "Just had some air knocked out of me," she answered breathlessly, more from the contact with Leo and the hungry glimmers of desire in his eyes than from their collision.

"I thought it was too far back for you."

"I thought I could reach it," she murmured inanely, her pulse racing, every nerve in her body rioting.

As the waxing moon glowed down upon them, the shadows didn't seem so thick. Leo's face was so close to hers, she could almost brush her lips against his jaw.

Someone cleared his throat and a male voice asked, "Leo?"

Leo tore his gaze from hers and looked over his shoulder.

"It's getting pretty dark. Maybe we should quit." The man who said it was in his thirties, had short-cropped brown hair, and was trying to hide a smile.

His gaze went to Verity, and it was appreciative, as it passed over her clinging top and knit pants. "You did a perfect job. You can be on *my* team anytime. I don't think I caught your name."

"It's Verity. Verity Sumpter."

"And you're a friend of Leo's?" The man was waiting for some type of clarification.

"Verity came with me," Leo responded a bit posses-
sively.

"I see," the man commented with a frown. Then he
smiled again at Verity and extended his hand. "The
name's Jim Ross. It's good to meet you. Are you ready
for the bonfire?"

"Bonfire?" Verity asked.

"Yep. It's a tradition. I guess Leo didn't tell you. We
sit around it and cook hotdogs, eat marshmallows. There
are coolers over there filled with side dishes, too." He
winked at her. "The boss bought it all, so eat as much
as you want."

Leo hadn't told her much about what was happening
tonight. The bonfire sounded nice, yet she still felt uncomfortable and out of place.

The rest of the volleyball teams had broken up and
the players were scattering toward the fire that had been
started along the beach. Jim said to Leo, "I brought my
guitar and so did Dave."

Leo gave him a forced smile. "That's great. We'll
have entertainment after we eat."

"It takes everyone a while, but eventually they'll
warm up to a sing-along," Jim told her. "I'll expect you
to join in."

Verity nodded, and with a last look, Jim Ross
walked away.

She and Leo were left on the sand under the moon.
But only for a moment.

Someone called from the group gathering around the
fire. "Hey, Leo. We have everything all set up. Come and
get it."

"I have to stay for the bonfire," he told Verity. "But if you want to leave after we eat, we can."

"That's fine." She thought he just wanted to take her home because this was an awkward situation for him. Perhaps he was sorry he'd asked her along.

A short while later, Leo made sure everyone had enough food. As he headed toward the bonfire and took a seat in the circle around it next to Verity, he realized she fit in here better than Carolyn ever had. Verity had truly enjoyed that game of volleyball. She had a competitive edge and it showed. She also had a way with people.

He remembered the way Jim Ross had looked at Verity. A feeling so foreign had gripped Leo he hadn't recognized it right away. He'd felt a hint of it at the arts festival when Verity's classmate had approached her. Finally he labeled it—jealousy. Leo couldn't remember ever being jealous of Carolyn or feeling possessive. Although she'd been beautiful, a layer of reserve had kept other men from coming too close…had kept Leo from getting too close. Verity didn't have any of that reserve. She was genuine and friendly and approachable.

As Leo's shoulder brushed Verity's, he turned over the campfire appliance that roasted four hot dogs at once. The meat sizzled, smoked aroma filling the air along with the bonfire and the sea. When Leo glanced at Verity, she had her knees pulled up before her, her arms around them, and she was staring into the fire.

The tension between them was his fault, but it seemed safer than attraction. He'd been remiss in not introducing her properly to his employees. Truth be told, he hadn't known what to say. She wasn't his date, exactly. Yet he didn't want to simply introduce her as Heather's nanny. The lack of acknowledgment on his part had made her feel awkward, and he was sorry about that. With everyone sitting around, talking, listening to each other's conversations, this wasn't the place to tell her.

They'd eaten, and Jim and Dave were strumming a rendition of "Deck the Halls," when Dave's wife asked Leo, "What are you getting for Heather this Christmas?"

"I haven't gone shopping yet," Leo admitted.

"You mean she hasn't asked for everything she sees on TV?"

"We don't let her watch that much TV, so I think she'll be happy with almost anything Santa Claus brings."

"There's a new educational store for kids over on Yellow Rose Boulevard," one of the other wives mentioned. "I spent over an hour there. You might want to check it out."

Leo leaned close to Verity. "Maybe I could get home early some afternoon and we could stop in."

"Or maybe you and Jolene should check it out," Verity said quietly.

Leo had asked Verity along today because he thought she'd have fun. However, now he saw that he'd simply put her in an awkward situation. He hadn't meant to do that, and now he realized he had to take a stand where Verity was concerned. The silvery moon shone brightly on the water. They wouldn't need a flashlight if they went for a walk on the beach.

Leaning close to her he suggested, "Come for a walk with me."

She glanced at him, her eyes puzzled.

As he stood, he offered her his hand. When she took it, he tugged her up.

At the edge of the circle, he slipped off his deck shoes. Seeing what he had done, she slipped off her sneakers and socks, then rolled up her pants. Before Leo could even think about what came next, she was running across the sand to the packed part of the beach, letting the water catch her toes and slosh around her. He found himself doing the same thing, snatching her hand and running down the beach with her. He felt freer than he'd felt in years. Verity did that. She loosened something that had become coiled much too tightly inside of him.

When they stopped running and caught their breath, she stooped to pick up a shell and examined it in the moonlight.

Leo found himself clasping her shoulder and turning her to him. "I never meant for you to feel out of place tonight."

"I'm fine, Leo."

"Maybe. Or maybe you're just too polite to say what you're thinking."

She shook her head. "I'm not thinking anything. I'm just trying to live in the moment."

He wondered if she did that because of losing her twin…if now she realized how very precious every moment was. He was beginning to realize that, too. "Once we got here tonight I didn't know how to explain you. I haven't been out in public with a woman since I lost my wife."

She took that in. "You haven't dated?"

"Nope. So tonight, when I brought you along and we got a few stares, I decided to skip over introductions. That wasn't fair to you."

Turning away from him, she stared out into the ocean and then looked up at the sky, as if she expected to see something specific. Finally she said, "It's okay, Leo."

"No, it's not." Taking her hand, he tugged her a little closer. "I have to climb off the fence where you're concerned. It's just…you're *so* young."

"You've got a hangup about that," she remarked, so seriously he had to smile.

"I guess I do. But I can tell you why. You're unlike any other woman I've ever been attracted to. You make me see the world differently. Colors seem brighter. The days seem fuller. I appreciate everything Heather does in a way I didn't before. I was growing more distant from her, and you brought me back."

"You would have found your way back."

Leo traced her cheekbones with his thumbs and turned her face up to his. "I don't know what it is about you, Verity, but I can't seem to stay away from you. You've got your whole life ahead of you."

"So do you," she suggested gently.

After Carolyn died, his path had been clear—to work hard to make a future for his daughter. It had been a road without any turnoffs, a road without any forks to make it interesting. Verity had become a fork in the road, and he wasn't sure whether he should take it, for her sake as well as his.

Trembling all over, Verity felt as if she and Leo were

perched on a precipice. One false step and they'd fall. She wasn't too young for him, but she might be too inexperienced. As unsure as Leo was about them, she was that unsure, too. Could she trust what was happening between them? Could she trust that it was serious to him? Could she believe she was more than a distraction until he found the woman of his dreams? She was so afraid that once she offered him her heart he'd walk away. She was so afraid that the feelings she had for him were so much deeper than the ones he had for her.

She knew it was silly, but she wished, somehow, Sean could give her a sign. They'd always told each other when they were apart and they saw a shooting star, that star would be a message from one to the other. Because of their twin connection, they'd read the message and know what the star meant. She wished for a shooting star now. She wished Sean was here to give her advice. She wished so many things.

Her wishes took wings as Leo became her only focus. They lifted and scattered and flew as his arms went around her…as she breathed in his scent…as she tipped her chin up to accept his kiss. Tonight's kiss was different from the others. It was hungrier. It was demanding. It was possessive. The pressure of his lips, the sweep of his tongue, the tautness of his body told her he was letting go of more of his restraint. He was letting himself feel the chemistry between them, and he was going with it.

Far away, she heard the strains of a Christmas carol, voices blending with the guitars, a sea horn blaring out in the Gulf. The scents of saltwater and damp sand and

Leo's aftershave combined, until she knew she'd remember the mix forever. The sand was cold now between her toes, and it was a sharp contrast to the heat she was feeling in her body.

Leo's hand passed up and down her back, pressing her closer, until she could feel his arousal as keenly as she could feel her own.

Seconds later, however, he loosened his hold and stepped away. "We've got to slow this down."

She knew he was right, but not being in his arms didn't feel right, either.

"We both need time to think about what we want," he said, almost to himself.

"Sometimes thinking will get you into as much trouble as doing."

He blew out a breath, shook his head and smiled at her. "Where did those words of wisdom come from?"

Laughing, she admitted, "I don't remember. But they sounded good, don't you think?"

Still smiling, he wrapped an arm around her shoulders. "What I think is that we should get back before someone sends out a search party. Besides, we need to practice harmonizing on Christmas carols so we can do it with Heather. I'll stop for a tree tomorrow, and then we'll see if we can really usher in the holidays."

For the past month Verity had dreaded the idea of the holidays without Sean. Now she was looking forward to them. Leo and Heather were filling her life in a way she never expected.

Studying the sky, she hoped to see a shooting star. But only every-night stars twinkled back. However, as

Leo took her hand in his, she forgot about heavenly bodies and welcomed the warm, tingling feelings holding his hand gave her.

When Leo brought the tree in Saturday afternoon, Heather was napping.

"Good," he commented when Verity told him. "This tree will be a lot easier to put up without little hands and feet in the way. What's that great smell?"

"Heather and I made gingerbread men for the tree."

Leo straightened the evergreen in the stand. "Is this going to be an old-fashioned tree with popcorn strings, too?"

"I thought that might be fun. Heather might like to make a few ornaments to hang, too."

Their gazes connected and held, and Verity could see Leo liked her suggestion. After they'd come home last night, he hadn't kissed her again, but when they'd said good-night she'd seen the same hunger in his eyes that she'd seen on the beach. They were headed someplace exciting. She was scared and thrilled all at the same time.

Tearing his gaze from hers, Leo held the tree and tightened the bolts holding it in place on the stand. Then he angled a few feet away and studied it. "That's as straight as it's going to get. I have lights and ornaments in the attic. I'll go get them."

"Need help?" Verity asked.

"Not for this. I'll need your help when Heather wants to poke into every box and plug in every light." Then he went to the spare bedroom where there was a trap door and stairs that pulled down from the attic space.

Verity prepared and stuffed a chicken to roast in the oven for supper. By the time she'd done that, she realized Leo still hadn't returned with any boxes. Curious, suspecting the Christmas lights were tangled and he was trying to unravel them, she put one of the cooled gingerbread men on a napkin for Leo and carried it down the hall. Peeking into Heather's room, she saw the little girl was still sleeping.

The door to the guest bedroom was open and Verity went in. This room was pleasantly decorated in green and wine. The pine bedroom suite was substantial and the bed wore a geometrically designed coverlet. Stairs that had been pulled down from the attic hooked Verity's attention.

Crossing to them, she started up. When she reached the top step, she took in the area with a glance. There wasn't much stored there—a few boxes, a set of luggage, baby paraphernalia that Heather had outgrown already. Leo had found the lights. They were sitting in a neat coil at his feet. He was seated beside a cardboard ornament box and she could see he held a white-and-gold one in his hand.

"That's beautiful."

"Every ornament in this box is almost too delicate to touch."

Looking down at the opened box, she saw fragile, blown-glass ornaments as well as hand-painted ones.

"We had an artificial tree," Leo explained, pointing to a tall box in the corner.

Suddenly Verity understood that memories of Christmases past had grabbed Leo and that his ties to his wife might never be broken. She understood those emotions. Yet, seeing Leo like this with the ornaments hurt her because his reaction meant he wasn't ready for a new involvement.

Walking over to him, she crouched down beside him. "Do you want me to take the box downstairs? I'll be careful."

He looked at the gingerbread cookie in her hand and then back at the ornaments. "No, I don't think we can use them. I wouldn't want any of them to break. I'll keep them for when Heather's older. When she's not as likely to go over to the tree, pluck one off and toss it like a ball." His half smile was meant to tell her everything was fine, and she shouldn't be concerned about him or the ornaments.

She felt foolish standing there holding the cookie. "I brought this up in case you wanted to taste one."

Taking it from her he said, "Thanks. I'll be down in a minute."

It would take more than a minute for Leo to sort through his memories.

When Verity descended the attic steps, Heather was standing at the bottom, Nosy tucked under her arm. "*Me* want to see what's up there."

Heather's big bed was supposed to arrive on Monday. They'd ordered it so they wouldn't have to worry about her falling if she crawled out of her crib. Apparently she'd mastered the skill!

Crouching down to the little girl, Verity put her arm around her. "I'll bet there's something you'd rather see in the great room." She took her hand. "Daddy brought it in. Come on, I'll show you."

The idea of something exciting in the great room tantalized Heather. She only gave one more look over her shoulder before she let Verity lead her away.

True to his word, Leo joined them a few minutes later. Heather was still looking up at the tree with awe.

"We have to ice the gingerbread men," Verity explained to the three-year-old. "We can hang them on the branches. We can make other ornaments to hang with ribbon, too. Do you want to do that?"

Heather looked intrigued by the whole idea, nodded vigorously, then ran to the kitchen to get started.

"This is going to be messy," Verity said with a smile, trying to gauge Leo's mood.

"Anything concerning Heather and food is messy." He'd carried down a carton with coils of lights lying on top. "I'll work on the lights while you and Heather make ornaments."

She wasn't sure how to act with him, whether or not they should go into this Christmas full force for Heather's sake, or to tread lightly for his.

He must have read her concern. "I'll find CDs of Christmas carols. Heather will like them."

How about you? she wanted to ask...but didn't.

A half hour later, Heather had lost interest in icing the cookies, and Verity was just waiting for a few more to harden for the tree. The three-year-old had migrated to the small table and chairs where she'd arranged a doll and two teddy bears to watch her while she colored.

When Leo came into the kitchen, he took in the scene in a glance. "The tree has lights. Now we just need everything else."

"I'll be finished here in a minute. Then we can start stringing. This decorating process could take a few days."

Leo's somber mood seemed to have slid away. Or else he was hiding it well. "That will give Heather something to do."

Verity laughed and playfully dipped her finger into the bowl, then held it up for Leo. "Want a taste?"

There was no hesitation in him as he leaned forward and caught her finger between his lips. The sensation was so sensual she felt her knees wobble. She thought they would buckle altogether when his tongue laved her skin. The flare of desire in his eyes mesmerized her, and she couldn't look away.

Sensually, his lips slowly released her finger. She felt as if he'd touched her intimately. The smoldering heat in his eyes told her he was thinking of things other than cookies and icing and his daughter as he slipped his hand beneath her hair. "It's a shame Heather still isn't napping."

"Maybe it's not," she said quietly, realizing why Leo might be touching her now. "Maybe I want to be more than a distraction from your memories."

His expression changed. The smoldering desire became anger as his shoulders straightened and he crossed his arms over his chest. "Is that what you believe, Verity? Or are you just afraid to take the next step, and my history's a convenient excuse not to?"

Without waiting for an answer he strode across the kitchen, hunkered down beside Heather and asked, "Are you ready to decorate the tree?"

Verity knew she had probably just put another wedge

between them, but if he wanted her to be honest, she couldn't hide her thoughts. Sure, her inexperience and fear might be part of the mix. She'd overcome fear before. What she couldn't overcome were Leo's ties to his past.

Could she?

Chapter Seven

When Leo returned home from taking Jolene's boys Christmas shopping, he strode down the hall to Heather's room, wondering what Verity's mood would be. He had to admit he'd been angry with her Saturday night. Because she'd told him the truth?

His excursion into the attic had awakened sleeping memories. He was discovering that his marriage hadn't been all that he'd wanted it to be. So when he'd walked into the kitchen, seen Verity icing cookies, Heather playing so contentedly nearby, the tableau had created in him an unfamiliar yearning. Instead of dealing with that yearning and where it was coming from, he'd latched on to something easy—the desire Verity awakened without even trying.

Something about Verity got to him in such an elemental way, his usual ironclad restraint let loose. Yesterday had been her day off and all day he'd wondered how she was spending it…where she'd gone…if she was with another man. Her classmate, maybe? After she'd returned home in the evening, she'd looked in on Heather, then disappeared into her rooms.

Now as he came to the door of Heather's room, he stopped abruptly. Everything had changed inside of it. The furniture had been delivered, and it looked like a little girl's haven. He realized that didn't have as much to do with the furniture as what Verity had done with it.

"If you don't like it, I can take the spread and curtains back," Verity said from the bed where she was sitting next to Heather, a book across their laps.

The white wood bed with its turned spool design on the headboard, dresser and chest was elegantly feminine. He'd chosen this suite because Heather could grow into it, and the furniture would fit her even as an adult. However, beyond that, what someone had done to the room was charming. The quilted spread and matching curtains were printed with favorite nursery rhymes. On the wall hung a cloth tapestry of a cow jumping over the moon. There were pink scarves on the chest and dresser as well as a light with a pink-polka-dot lampshade.

"The room looked so barren," Verity explained. "I'd seen this set at the department store. But if you don't like it, I can pack it all up—"

Leo wasn't exactly sure what he felt about it. On one hand, he knew Carolyn would have hired a decorator to take care of the room. On the other, he felt as if Verity knew Heather better than he did. He wouldn't have known where to start. She had a mother's instincts where his daughter was concerned, and that seemed to bother him most of all because of the repercussions the fact carried with it.

"I think it's just right," he admitted. "How did you pay for it?"

"I had some money put aside for Christmas. I knew if you liked it you'd reimburse me. If you don't like it, I could return it for a refund. I probably should have called you and asked first, but things were kind of tense between us, and I didn't want to interrupt you at work."

Again, that truth that Verity seemed to have no trouble stating.

"You could have called. I'd put aside anything between us to consider Heather."

Apparently tired of waiting, Heather tugged on Verity's arm. "Can we wead the stowy now?"

Verity's gaze lifted to his, as if she were asking him if he wanted to read the book to his daughter. He did. "Hey, kiddo. How about if I read it to you?"

Heather looked from one of them to the other, then gave a little shrug. "Okay."

Verity gave Heather a hug and whispered, "Sweet dreams." Then, with a last look at Leo, she left the room.

He wished he knew what was going through her head. He wished he could control the attraction he felt for her. He wished he didn't feel in such turmoil about all of it.

After Leo tucked in his daughter, he went to the pool house. Losing himself in work had always helped him solve problems...or had insulated him from them. The night was cool so he lit a fire in the fireplace and settled himself at the drafting board. After he wrote a check for everything Verity had purchased and set it aside, he turned to his work. Nevertheless, the new design didn't call to him as it had yesterday. Still, he picked up his pencil and started making adjustments.

The fire licked at the logs as he became absorbed in his work. He wasn't sure how much time had passed when there was a knock at the pool house door. The baby monitor was quiet, so he knew Verity's visit didn't have anything to do with his daughter. He motioned her to come in.

After she opened the door and stepped inside, she smiled unsurely. "There's something I need to talk to you about."

Rising from his stool, he motioned to the sofa. It was tan leather and comfortable, as was everything else in here. He'd found a local artist to paint a lighthouse mural on one wall. Other than that, the space was simply furnished and the refuge he wanted it to be.

The thought suddenly hit him that he'd needed a refuge from Carolyn, the lifestyle she'd wanted, the pastimes she'd chosen. He'd have to dissect that later.

Perched on the edge of his couch, Verity looked as if she were going to fly away any moment. He suddenly realized how much he wanted her to stay. "What did you need to talk to me about?" He sat beside her with about six inches separating them, but he was angled toward her and could already feel the sparks.

"Heather's teacher called this morning. The school's having a Christmas program on Thursday."

"I know. I have it on my calendar. I can take her that day and give you a break."

"That's what her teacher wanted to talk to me about. Apparently, Heather assumes we'll both be there. Since her teacher's taking a head count, she wanted to make sure. If Heather wants me there, I'd love to go, but I didn't know how you'd feel about that."

He studied the nanny Heather had obviously become so attached to. As always, Verity had tied her hair back in a ponytail. Her skin was beautifully perfect with a healthy, peachy glow now that made his fingers itch to touch it. She wore jeans and a sweater that came practically to her knees.

But he knew what was underneath. He'd felt it when they'd pressed together. She was curvy and feminine, and the nondescript clothes were a tease in their own way. When he studied her serious expression, he realized she obviously didn't want to overstep any boundaries and found that aspect of her character totally endearing.

"Of course you should go to the Christmas program. Apparently, Heather will be disappointed if you're not there."

He still saw concern on Verity's face, then knew instinctively what was causing it. "You're thinking it will be moms and dads and you might feel out of place?"

"Not exactly that, but I don't want anyone to mistake me for someone I'm not."

She didn't have to say more than that. He was taken back to the night when Tony Parelli had arrived and jumped to conclusions. "It doesn't matter what anybody else thinks. If someone gets it wrong, we'll correct them. Jolene has been around, but Heather has never had a constant woman's presence before. I'm grateful for you, Verity. You've made a difference here. And you need to know that Saturday, in the kitchen, you were much more than a distraction."

After staring into the fire crackling in the hearth, she finally returned her gaze to his. "You accused me of being afraid. I am. I've never felt anything as strong as the chemistry between us."

He hadn't, either. Taking her face between his palms, he said huskily, "I don't want you to be afraid. But we need to take this slowly for both our sakes."

As he touched her, every cell in his body shouted at him to do a hell of a lot more. He actually ached to feel her under him…to join their bodies…to end this craving that was interfering with his life.

With their gazes locked together now, Verity's hands slid into the thickness of his hair.

"Verity," he breathed, leaning closer, tamping down primitive urges.

He kissed her forehead, the tip of her cute nose, and then his mouth was on hers, opening, eager to teach her everything she'd never learned. He'd kept his feelings in check, but now he couldn't deny his desire. As the kiss grew more incendiary, as their tongues played and mated, as he could feel her response down to his boots, he wanted more. Sliding his hands from her face to her shoulders, he stroked her arms. She strained toward him, and he was experiencing the same restless urgency. Still, he was aware that Verity was a virgin, and he didn't want to rush anything. He also knew he was going to have to stop.

But not now. Not yet.

Finally breaking the kiss minutes later, he murmured, "Have you ever been touched by a man?"

Her cheeks became red. "Matthew groped a little, but—"

He couldn't help but smile. "If at any time you feel I'm groping, you say so."

Her shy smile and her tiny nod filled him with the desire to take her in his arms once more. Kissing her again, he tugged her sweater up over her hips, but he didn't lift it over her head. He had a feeling Verity would be much too self-conscious naked. Instead, he slipped his hand beneath her sweater and let it rest on her midriff. He felt her shiver.

"Are you okay?" he asked.

She nodded. "Very okay. Can I touch *you?*" she asked.

"Be my guest," he answered gruffly, never more aroused.

"I want to touch your skin," she whispered into his neck.

He laughed and tugged his knit shirt from his jeans, then lifted it over his head. "There you go."

Reaching out tentatively, she let her palm rest in the middle of his chest. Just that soft touch made him feel as if he was going to explode...but he kept perfectly still.

"What do you want me to do?" she asked softly.

"Anything you want."

At that, she smiled and slid her fingers into his chest

hair, finding his nipple under the mat, running her thumb around it.

"You're awfully good at this," he growled, sucking in a breath.

"You like it?"

"Oh, I like it."

Then his hand was moving up her body and he was cupping her breasts. She was wearing a bra that seemed almost nonexistent. The material was like gossamer. As he cupped her breast in his palm, he heard her soft sigh. Her nipple was already taut, waiting for his touch. When he rubbed the heel of his hand around…against it, she moaned.

Laying her back on the sofa, he stretched out on top of her. "You make me crazy," he admitted, kissing her mouth, then her chin, then her neck, until the neckline of her sweater stopped him. She had her arms wrapped around him and was stroking his back. When her fingertips dipped beneath the waistband of his jeans, he shuddered.

Rising on his forearms, he peered down at her. "We've got to stop," he said hoarsely.

"Why?"

"Because I'm getting pretty riled, and I don't think you're ready for this. I don't know if *I'm* ready for this. Fantasizing about it is one thing. Doing it is another. If we finish what we've started here, everything will change between us. I'm not sure we've known each other long enough for that."

"You're afraid if everything changes, you'll want me to leave."

"I'm afraid if everything changes, you'll *want* to leave. You're twenty-two. You're a virgin. You have your future ahead of you."

"And you're thirty-four, with your future ahead of *you*. I don't see the conflict."

Verity knew how to turn his reason around on him and he had to admire that. Placing a gentle kiss on her forehead, he levered himself up and moved to the edge of the sofa.

She did the same, and then with a cautious glance she asked, "Where do we go from here?"

"We take one day at a time. We spend more time together. What are you doing for Christmas?" It was two weeks away, and Verity hadn't talked about any plans.

"I don't know."

"Well, I do. I want you to spend it with me and Heather. We're having dinner at Jolene's on Christmas Eve, and I want you to come along as my date."

She grinned at him. "You're going to make an announcement?"

"If need be. But in the meantime, I'm going to pilot Parelli's boat over to Port Aransas next week. Why don't you come along with me? We can stay overnight and fly back in the morning. I told Jolene I'll take the boys for a weekend in January so she and Tim can get away. So I don't think she'll mind taking Heather overnight."

"Heather would stay there?"

"She has before. Or sometimes Jolene brings the kids and stays here. It's like going camping for them. What do you think?"

She didn't hesitate. "I think I'd love to go with you."

He knew he was playing with fire taking her to Port Aransas and spending the night there. But he'd reserve separate rooms. He knew his boundaries, and he'd keep them...until he was sure they both knew exactly what they wanted.

As Leo drove Verity to the college Thursday evening to drop off her course selections for next semester, she sneaked a quick glance at him. After they'd watched Heather's program together this morning, he'd asked her if she wanted to go out for dinner to Heather's favorite restaurant where his daughter could eat her favorite meal—chicken and ice cream. When Verity told him she intended to run an errand at the college, he'd insisted he could drive her there on the way to dinner. Looking forward to tonight, she'd relived their evening in the pool house every spare moment. Although she understood he had called a halt to their lovemaking that night because he didn't want to rush her, she also knew he'd stopped because he wasn't sure they belonged together.

The difference in their ages didn't mean a thing to her, but she *was* concerned about his connection to Carolyn. She was even more concerned that the physical attraction he felt was all there was. He was obviously a virile man with strong needs, and she was there...handy...convenient. If he wasn't invested in more than a physical attraction, he'd walk away like Matthew had.

Since Monday night she'd felt close to Leo, as if they were on the verge of something important. They'd shared a few good-night kisses since then, but Leo had kept those kisses under strict control. Oh, how she wished she had someone to confide in. At times like these, she missed Sean the most.

In her car seat, Heather was babbling to Nosy who was propped beside her.

"She took a nap in her new bed without a fuss today," Verity told Leo, choosing a safe topic. "I think she likes it."

"She likes it because you made it special." His gaze as he glanced at her was filled with warmth, and Verity found herself looking forward to the future in a way she hadn't before.

In front of the Arts and Sciences Building there was a curb with spaces slotted for parking. Students were gone for the holidays so parking wasn't a problem.

"Are you sure your advisor will be here?" Leo asked her.

"If he's not, I can just slide the papers under his door." She unfastened her seat belt. "I'll try not to be too long. I don't want Heather to get restless."

"If she gets antsy, I'll take her for a walk. Don't worry about us."

One of the qualities Verity admired most about Leo was his patience. He made her feel as if she was worth waiting for. With a smile she left his SUV and shut the door.

Verity opened the heavy glass door and took the steps leading to the second floor of the Arts and Science Building. The halls were quiet and the tile smelled of fresh wax. She couldn't wait until next semester when she'd be involved in her new classes. She'd talked to Leo about it, wondering if being gone two nights a week would be a problem. But he'd been fine with what she'd planned. He'd told her he'd make sure he was home early on those evenings.

She didn't want to be naive about what was happening between them. She didn't want to wear rose-colored glasses only to have them smashed.

When she reached Will Stratford's door, she saw he was in the process of slipping into a jacket. She rapped softly and he opened the door.

"You caught me just in time," he said. He nodded to the envelope in her hand. "Is that everything I need for next semester?"

"I hope so. I scheduled two courses. I hope I'm not biting off more than I can chew."

"Are you worried about the time it'll take to do the work for them?"

"That's part of it. I really want to do this. I've always intended to get my master's. But Leo and I are becoming more involved and—" She stopped abruptly, not knowing whether she should go on or not.

"You want to have time for him, too."

Obviously, Will understood. "Yes."

"That's understandable. But you know, no matter what happens between the two of you, you have to make yourself happy. You have to be true to yourself before you can be true to anyone else."

"To thine own self be true," she murmured.

"'And it must follow, as the night the day, Thou canst not then be false to any man,'" Will finished.

"There's wisdom in Shakespeare's work. *Hamlet*, wasn't it?"

"Someone taught you well," he remarked with that kind smile of his.

"I loved his sonnets best," she confided.

"Don't use the past tense. You can read them anytime you want." He looked thoughtfully at his shelf with its volumes of Shakespearean works. "Are you familiar with *Twelfth Night*?"

"Not really."

"You might want to read it. The heroine, Viola, has a twin, Sebastian. She loses him for a while, then finds him again."

"What does the title mean?"

"The Twelfth Night is the last day of the Christmas season. Historians believe Shakespeare wrote the play for a Twelfth Night celebration. Like most of his comedies, it's about couples in love. You'd probably enjoy it."

Crossing to the door, he said, "Come on. I'll walk you downstairs. I have to stop in the language lab on the first floor. I'm picking up a set of Italian tapes."

"You're going to learn how to speak Italian?"

"I'm hoping to learn enough to get me by for a trip. I'm planning it for spring break."

They went down the staircase together. "How wonderful. I've heard there are so many treasures there to see—the architecture, the artwork, the history."

"You want to tour the world someday?" he asked, amused.

"I don't know. Sometimes I think people look all over the world when what they need is in their own backyard. I'm taking a trip with Leo to Port Aransas next week. I've never been there before."

After the last step, Will turned to her. "You're serious about this man, aren't you?"

"Oh, yes. I just don't know how serious he is about me, if he feels any of what I'm feeling."

Will laid a comforting hand on her shoulder. "Men aren't as quick to accept the whisperings of their heart as women are."

"Do you think men and women are really that different?"

"Oh, I think they're different, until somehow they find the same wave length." He dropped his hand from her shoulder. "Only nine days till Christmas. If I don't see you before, you have a good holiday."

"Thank you. I will. Will you be going out of town?"

"No. Believe it or not, I'll be cooking Christmas dinner. I have a few friends who are usually at loose ends on holidays, so we spend them together."

Verity thought of the envelope she'd received from her father yesterday with her mail in it. She'd dumped the pieces out looking for a note from her dad. She hadn't found one. Nothing else had looked important to her, not even the envelope from the production company. She certainly wasn't interested in making another commercial. She'd put everything aside because she was hurt her dad hadn't written a note. Maybe deep down, she'd hoped he'd change his mind about spending Christmas with a friend rather than her. She *wanted* to spend Christmas with Leo and Heather, but her heart ached because she wouldn't be seeing her dad this holiday when they'd both be missing Sean. Maybe that's why her father wanted to do something different...to run away from the pain. Maybe he wanted to run away from her.

After wishing Will a merry Christmas, Verity opened the door and went outside.

Leo had unfastened Heather from her car seat and carried her to the sidewalk. As dusk fell, he took her hand, and they walked around a row of loblolly pines to look at the Christmas decorations on the side of the Arts and Sciences Building. There was a replica of a long-horned steer pulling Santa's sleigh. The little old man was wearing a cowboy hat.

Suddenly the display was alight with red and green and white bulbs.

Heather pointed to it and giggled, and he scooped her up into his arms. "Santa's going to come and visit you."

"Vewitee said I haf to be good."

He chuckled. "You're always good."

"Not when I haf to sit in time-out."

"Does that happen with Verity or at preschool?"

"Bof."

His daughter hadn't even hesitated to tell him the truth, and that pleased him. "Do you want to walk by yourself or do you want me to carry you?"

"You cawwy me."

Leo's cell phone rang a short way from his car. Hefting Heather into one arm, he pulled his phone from his pocket and greeted the caller.

"It's me," Jolene said, "returning your call. What's up, brother dear?"

"I have to take a boat to Port Aransas next week, and

I've asked Verity to go with me. How does your schedule look? Can you watch Heather?"

There was silence at the other end. "You asked Verity to go along?"

"Yes," he answered, wanting to face this subject head-on if it was going to be a problem.

"I think that's a great idea. Are you staying overnight?"

Leo felt a bit stunned at Jolene's attitude. "Yes, we are."

"Great. I'll just bring the boys to your place and we'll camp out. I want to see Heather's new bed. Joey and Randy love your big-screen TV. They'll bring their DVDs and have a blast. Knowing Tim, he'll take a dip in the pool."

"This time of year?"

"You know Tim. He loves to swim."

"I hope you don't mind, but I also asked Verity to spend Christmas with us."

"Why would I mind? I like Verity. I hired her."

"That's the point. You *hired* her. But she's become more than a nanny."

"You know what I say to that? Bravo! Do you know how long I've been waiting for you to wake up and take notice of a woman again?"

When he didn't respond, she went on. "You've got a lot of wonderful years ahead of you, Leo."

"I know that. But I don't want to make a mistake. Verity's young."

"Verity's *younger*. She's not young. Don't use that as an excuse to act like a monk."

"Jolene…"

"All right. Talking sex with your sister is a little bit sticky. But I've seen you and Verity together. There's enough wattage there to light up all the Christmas trees in Avon Lake."

Leo had turned toward the building, and now he saw Verity coming down the stairs inside the door. There was someone with her—a man, though he couldn't see details because of the shadows—and they seemed quite involved in a conversation.

"I've got to go, Jolene. I'll give you a call when I decide all the details on the trip."

"You do that. I'll talk to you soon."

After Leo closed his phone, he stuffed it back in his pocket, all the while watching Verity. He saw the man beside her lay a hand on her shoulder, and she didn't move away.

What the hell was that all about?

He continued watching, noting how close they were standing. Then Verity moved toward the door.

After Leo opened the back door of the car and settled Heather in her car seat once more, he went around to the driver's side and climbed in.

A few moments later, Verity was sliding in, too.

"Everything all taken care of?" he asked her.

"Yep."

"Did you run into someone when you were coming out?"

"It was my advisor."

She looked a bit embarrassed when she said it, and her cheeks were rosy. If she'd been talking to her advisor, why would she be self-conscious about that? But he didn't ask any more questions. He simply wondered if she was telling him the truth.

* * *

"Did you see Leo's face when I came to the door with the kids and said *he* was going to be babysitting and *we* were going shopping?" Jolene asked Verity on Saturday as they strolled into a fashion store at the mall.

Verity laughed. "I don't think he really minded."

"No, I don't, either. He loves kids. He should have a whole mess of them."

Verity kept silent as Jolene found a rack of matching slacks and tops, then poked through it. She selected a red set in Verity's size and winked. "This should get him revved up."

"Jolene," Verity protested.

"Oh, honey. Aren't you absolutely excited about this trip?"

"I guess it shows."

"Sure, it does, and I'm glad. Leo actually looked happy today. I can't tell you the last time he really looked forward to something." Holding the outfit in front of Verity, she closed one eye and appeared to be imagining Verity in it. "Yep. This will work. Did you ever think of wearing contact lenses?"

"I tried them for a while."

"What happened?"

"They were soft contacts and one of them tore. I never had them replaced because I hadn't bought the insurance. I was saving money for a car and they just seemed frivolous."

"You should think about wearing them again... maybe having your hair styled."

As Jolene studied her even more closely, Verity asked, "What?"

"I can't put my finger on it, but something about you seems familiar."

"Maybe you're just seeing too much of me."

Jolene shook her head, obviously trying to remember. "Maybe you just look like someone else I know. Leo told me you're going to be sharing Christmas Eve with us."

"I hope that's okay."

"It's fine with me. But Mom's going to be there, too, so prepare yourself."

"I'm not exactly sure how to prepare myself for your mother."

At that, Jolene shook her head and laughed. "Isn't that the truth! At least this time *I'm* making dinner and you don't have to worry about preparing anything."

"But I want to. I want to help, anyway. I can make pies—chocolate cream, maybe?"

Jolene groaned. "You've found my weakness. All right. You go to it. And if you come over early, you can keep me from going crazy when my mom tries to tell me how to cook a meal I've made at least once a year for the past eleven years."

"Three women in the kitchen could be a nightmare," Verity warned.

"Yep. Close to it," Jolene agreed. "That's why I'll convince Leo and Tim to tell her all about their work and anything else they can think of until we get dinner on the table." Jolene wiggled the red sweater in front of Verity's nose. "But for right now, let's get you dressed to have a little fun."

There was no harm in buying a sweater and a pair of slacks, Verity told herself. She hadn't bought new clothes in months. If Leo liked her in the outfit, maybe she would find her tomboy days were definitely over. As the thought came and went, she almost believed she could hear her twin's voice whispering *"Atta girl."*

With alacrity, she took the slacks and sweater from Jolene and headed for the dressing room.

Chapter Eight

Aboard Mr. Parelli's cabin cruiser the following Tuesday, Verity looked around in admiration. The boat was fantastic. Leo had given her the statistics before they'd climbed onboard. It was a twenty-seven-footer with a large V-berth bed. All of its other fittings—the wraparound side seats, the built-in ice chest, the sink, icebox and head—had floated around her as Leo had described it so proudly. Although the boat was beautiful, she hadn't been able to take her eyes off *him* in his green T-shirt and gray stone-washed jeans. When he'd given her a tour and shown her the bed, her imagination had worked overtime.

Now sitting on one of the side seats, Verity watched Leo at the wheel. He'd explained the boat could practically navigate itself on autopilot. Still, he looked as if he belonged there—stoic, stalwart and strong.

The wind tugged strands of hair free from Verity's ponytail as she looked out to sea and wondered if she'd been approaching Leo all wrong. This time they were spending alone together could be important. Maybe she should confront the issues between them head-on instead of dancing around them. What did she have to lose?

They'd been on the water for most of the morning when she asked him, "How about some lunch? I can bring it up here."

Without looking at her, with his gaze still on the sea, he said, "Sounds good."

Ten minutes later Verity carried tall cups of iced tea to the control deck and set them in the holders by the seats. When she returned again, she juggled two paper plates that held thick roast beef sandwiches, macaroni salad, chips and carrot strips.

Leo swiveled around on one of the bucket seats while she sat on the side bench.

When his gaze met hers, it was like two firecrackers colliding and exploding. She practically shook from the power of their attraction, but forced herself to remain calm, to smile, as his hungry gaze passed over her red slacks and sweater.

"Do you get to do this often?" she asked, as if her insides weren't quaking.

"Pilot a customer's boat?" he asked.

"Yes. Deliver it this way."

"Maybe a quarter of the time. Usually the proud owner can't wait to get his hands on the boat, and he wants to navigate it himself."

"Do you own a boat?" she asked. It seemed only logical, after all, since he built them.

"Yes, I do. One much like this one. But it's in dry dock right now."

"Being repaired?"

"No. I realized I hadn't taken it out for about a year. I decided to have the controls updated."

She guessed dry dock had nothing to do with new controls. Not really. After his wife died, he'd withdrawn from life, too, just as she had.

"I guess you haven't had much time to go boating. Not with full responsibility for Heather and all. Did your wife enjoy boats as much as you do?"

With his sandwich halfway to his mouth, Leo stopped and laid it back on his plate. His sharp look almost made Verity lose her courage; nevertheless, she kept her gaze on his.

After a few very long moments, he admitted, "Carolyn didn't like to set foot on boats. She always got seasick."

"So you didn't take excursions together before Heather was born?" Verity thought about that V-berth bed, and how exciting and cozy making love on the water would be.

"No excursions. When we were engaged, I brought Carolyn out, just for a short jaunt. She got terribly seasick. After that, we tried it once more. Even though she took medication before we left, that didn't help, either. She decided boats just weren't in her karma."

"That must have been lonely for you, with you loving the water so much—being torn between wanting to go out on the sea or spend time with her."

A shadow passed over his face. "Verity, this isn't something I want to talk about."

"Why? Because it hurts?" She was pushing, and she knew it.

With a thump, Leo set his plate on the deck. "I don't want to talk about it because it's in the past."

"You can't forget the past, Leo. It's a shadow, always dogging you."

After a short silence he answered, "I suppose you're right. But just because I have a shadow, doesn't mean I want to dissect it."

"The past or your marriage?"

Now Leo stood and braced himself against the rocking of the boat. "My marriage isn't something I want to discuss with *you*."

His statement hurt, but she wasn't sorry she'd asked the questions. The subject of Carolyn was obviously a minefield. As long as it was, they wouldn't be able to move on, or move deeper into any kind of relationship.

"You say you don't want to talk about it with me, Leo. Why is that? Do you talk about it with anyone? Jolene?"

"My marriage is over. I can't fix what it was or wasn't by discussing it."

"Why would you want to fix it?" she asked quietly.

"Enough, Verity," he said curtly, turning away from her and checking the instruments.

He obviously thought he was shutting her down... shutting off the conversation. As she took a sip of her iced tea and watched his chiseled profile against the blue sky, she wondered if she'd done damage or good. Maybe she'd find out after they arrived in Port Aransas.

A few hours later, Verity watched Leo as they came into port, fascinated by the masterful way he handled the boat, how he easily and expertly backed it into a slip at the marina. A man on the dock helped him tie it down, and Verity suddenly wished she knew how to do all of the things that Leo needed help with. She'd like to be able to crew for him. Apparently he was used to doing this alone. He was used to doing a lot of things alone.

There was a car waiting for them in the marina's parking lot. Mr. Parelli had arranged for it to be there.

After putting their bags in the trunk, Leo held the door of the blue sedan as Verity climbed in. At her murmured thanks, he gave her a small smile, but it didn't reach his eyes. Their conversation about his wife had made the walls between them even higher and thicker. That wasn't at all what she'd planned.

The resort where they'd be staying wasn't far. When they turned into the drive, Verity saw the sprawling hotel, the rambling golf course, the lush vegetation encouraged even in December. Mexican fans and queen palms dotted the front lawn.

Leo parked and escorted her inside to a lobby. Soft music played, and their footsteps were muffled by velvety teal carpet. The reception counter was beautifully polished wood. Groupings of furniture in splashes of blue, peach and green looked comfortable and elegant. Checking in took only a few minutes, then Leo carried his duffel bag and her valise to the elevator.

When they rose to the third floor in silence, Verity wished she knew what he was thinking. She wished she knew why he'd asked her along.

In the intimacy of the elevator, silence grew long and tense until Leo asked, "Would you feel comfortable going riding on the beach?"

She remembered the painting in her sitting room and her dreams concerning it. "I'd love to go riding on the beach, as long as you don't challenge me to a race. I'm not sure I could stay in the saddle."

"No racing," he assured her, "just a leisurely walk, if that's all you want. Riding on the beach is much different from taking a trail ride. Especially at night. I checked and there's a full moon. If the fog rolls in, we might have to think about something else."

If the fog rolled in, she could think of a thousand things she and Leo could do, all of them making her blush.

Verity had watched the clerk at the desk give Leo two folders with keys. Now, as they came to one of the doors, he set down her valise and his duffel bag, reaching into his pocket for one of the small folders. "I'll go inside with you to see if everything's okay."

After he used the keycard, he let her precede him into the room. When he followed her, he laid her suitcase on the low chest next to the mirrored dresser.

The room had a nautical theme with a seascape mural wallpapered to one wall. The spreads were patterned with palm trees and surfboards, and drapes at the window were a pretty palm green over cream sheers.

Crossing to the window, Leo opened the blind to let sunlight pour in. Cerulean sky met green-blue water, and the view was absolutely breathtaking.

"Do you come here often?" she asked Leo, wondering if he'd ever brought his wife here.

"I stayed here once before when I came on business. There's a fine restaurant downstairs."

As she turned from the window, her gaze fell on the king-size bed. When she looked up, she found Leo studying her.

He motioned to a door across from the bathroom. "That connects your room and mine. But you can keep it locked if that makes you feel more comfortable."

"Did you request connecting rooms?" she asked, the idea giving her a thrill. Maybe Leo wanted tonight to be more than a minivacation.

"No, I didn't. But I did request sea-view rooms."

"Oh," she murmured.

Her soft exclamation must have held a note of disappointment, because Leo set his duffel on the bed and came to stand before her. Catching a strand of hair that had come loose from her ponytail, his fingers slid down it sensually, and he touched it as if he was enjoying the silky feel of it. "I asked you along on this trip so we could get to know each other better, not so I could take advantage of you. I don't want you to feel uncomfortable in any way."

"I only feel uncomfortable when you close down on me," she admitted.

He stopped fingering her hair and looked puzzled. "Close down on you?"

"You withdraw, Leo, when we broach a subject you don't want to talk about. If we get in the middle of something sticky, you turn off. You go somewhere where I can't reach you."

His silence was loud in the room until he asked, "You mean our conversation on the boat?"

"You shut down when we talk about Carolyn."

For a moment she thought he was going to do exactly what he had done on the boat and other times—close the door on the subject.

This time he didn't. "I wasn't aware I was doing that. I wasn't aware I was shutting you out." Encircling her with his arms, he tugged her close. "I guess I've gotten used to being alone. I've gotten used to keeping my distance from Jolene when she wants to give me advice, and walling Mother off when she tries to manipulate me into doing something she wants."

Feeling closer to Leo now, Verity asked, "Did you do it with Carolyn, too?"

When he tensed, she reached up and stroked his jaw.

Relaxing again, he turned his head and kissed her palm. The feel of his lips on her skin sent a thrill through her.

"Maybe I did," he admitted hoarsely. After a pause he added, "When I'm with you, Verity, I don't want walls between us." Tipping her chin up, he gave her a long, slow kiss.

After he released her, he asked, "Do you want to explore the grounds before dinner?"

His kisses always made her dizzy, made her dreams swirl around her like a cloud she couldn't grasp. She nodded.

"I have to put in a call to Parelli. Then we can go out."

Leo went to the connecting door, unlocked and opened it, then disappeared.

Verity thought about those connecting doors and what they could mean. One thing she knew—she wouldn't be locking hers.

* * *

Leo on horseback was even sexier than Leo on his boat, Verity thought, as they rode across the sand. The night was perfect, the sky an immense black canopy lit up by an almost-full moon and thousands of stars. They'd eaten a candlelit dinner at the restaurant, talked about Heather, places they'd traveled, funny stories from their childhoods. Memories of Sean had surfaced, and as Verity had shared them with Leo, she felt even closer to him. She'd told him about shooting stars and how she believed seeing one would be a message from Sean. Leo had told her about the night Heather was born, how watching her come into the world had been incomparable to anything else in his life.

As she'd sipped coffee, his gaze had lingered on her face. When they'd shared a fudgy, brownie dessert, their forks had touched, they'd both gone silent and she'd glimpsed the hungry desire in Leo's eyes.

Now, on the beach, she rode beside him, managing to keep up. As waves crashed on the shore, Leo led her just above them and came to a stop.

When she pulled up beside him, he asked, "Do you want to walk the beach?"

She remembered the night of his company party and thought about how much closer they were now. "Yes," she answered, hoping tonight would be the absolutely best night of her life.

Leo dismounted quickly, then held her horse while she slipped off. They hadn't gone very far when she saw lights appear on the horizon.

Stopping, they gazed out to sea together. "That looks big," she said, "but not as large as a cruise ship."

"It's probably a private yacht."

"Did you ever want a yacht of your own? You could build yourself one."

He laughed. "Yes, I could, I guess. But I never wanted a yacht. I did want to sail around the world, though, and I still might, after Heather's grown."

"Do you want to sail alone?"

Instead of looking out into the black night and the sea, he was suddenly looking at her. "I thought I did. I thought the solitude would be wonderful. But now I'm wondering if solitude is really what I want."

"Do you think you'd like to take someone along?"

"I'd like to take someone along who could enjoy the adventure as much as I would."

"I loved coming over here on your boat, if that means anything."

Closer now, he looked as if he might kiss her. But then his horse pulled on the reins, and he just draped an arm around her shoulders instead. "I think you'd be good company."

She wanted to be so much more than company, but Leo was still holding back, and maybe she was, too. Were their pasts tying them up again?

"You have a dream to sail around the world," she said softly. "Do you have other dreams?"

"I want to expand the boatyard. I want to fulfill dreams my father couldn't and make him proud."

"I'm sure your father is already very proud. Do you believe he's watching over you?"

"I believe he is, just as your twin's watching over you."

Their hips bumped as they walked, and Verity loved

the contact with Leo, the intimacy of touching, walking side by side and being comfortable with him. She'd worn a jacket and was glad of that now as the sea mist sprayed across the beach. Leo's arm around her kept her warm, and whenever their gazes met, her temperature went up another five degrees.

"Tell me about your dad," Leo suggested. "You don't talk about him much, and I have to wonder why you're not spending Christmas with him."

"He's spending Christmas with a friend." Then she added, "He seemed relieved I wasn't coming home."

"Why would he be relieved? If he raised you and your brother on his own, I'd imagine the three of you would be tight."

Memories flooded back. As the sea air brushed her face, she explained, "Sean and Dad always had a connection. It was as if I came along with the package. I guess that's why I was a tomboy as a kid. If I tagged along with Sean and played sports with him, my father seemed to know I was around."

After a pause Leo admitted, "At times I do think it would be easier to raise a boy. When I think ahead, I can't imagine talking to Heather about everything a mother would tell a daughter."

"You mean bras and boys?" Verity teased.

Leo grinned down at her wryly. "Exactly. So, I can understand how your dad probably felt. Yet I also know, as a single parent, I have the responsibility to talk to her about everything, whether I'm comfortable with it or not."

"Sean had always been the buffer between Dad and me. He smoothed conversations between us. After he was gone, it was as if Dad had nothing to say to me. Neither of us seemed to be able to talk about how much we missed Sean, and this silence grew between us until it was so big it pushed us farther and farther away from each other. I know how much he loved Sean, and when we're together, I feel I'm a reminder that my brother's not here."

As Leo's arm around her tightened, he stopped walking and pulled her to him for a hug. When he leaned away, he suggested, "Why don't you ask your dad to come to Avon Lake for Christmas?"

"He already has plans."

"Maybe he made those plans because it was the easier thing to do. But if you gave him an alternative, I can't imagine he'd want to be with a friend on Christmas rather than with his daughter."

If she gave her father the alternative and he didn't take it, then she'd know for sure he didn't want to be with her.

"I don't think you should let the holiday go by without making contact," Leo went on. "If you do, the chasm between you will become even wider. Don't you think?"

She knew Leo was probably right, yet she didn't know if she had the courage to face rejection again.

"Think about it," he suggested.

In the moonlight Leo's strong features seemed even more handsome. He wasn't wearing a jacket, and his polo shirt was open at the neck. The chest hair there tempted her to touch it. She wanted to touch *him*. Everywhere. The way he was looking at her, she guessed he wanted the same thing.

However, instead of kissing her, he said, "We'd better head back. It's getting late." After he released her, he took her horse's reins from her hands. "Come on. I'll give you a lift up."

After Leo helped her mount, they started back to the resort. Suddenly Verity saw it—a bright streak against the black sky—a shooting star.

Smiling, she now knew Sean was watching over her. He was sending her a message—he approved of her relationship with Leo.

She was ready for the next step.

An hour later Verity closed the volume of *Twelfth Night* she'd borrowed from the library, too distracted to read. She knew why. She'd missed her chance. She hadn't been bold enough.

After their ride Leo had walked her to her room, kissed her on the forehead and said he'd see her in the morning. She'd simply accepted all of that, when what she'd wanted was to be held in his arms. He thought he had to go slowly because she was a virgin. He thought he had to go slowly because she was younger than he was. He thought he had to go slowly because…because he might not be ready for a new involvement.

She already knew Leo was a man of integrity who wanted to be sure of every step he took. If he only knew how much she cared about him.

There was only one way he was going to know—she had to show him.

She'd brought along a pale-pink silk chemise for sleeping. She usually wore pajamas, but this had been a present from her aunt last Christmas, and bringing it along had seemed appropriate. It had come with a flowered, pink-and-green silk robe, and now she slipped from the bed and put on the robe, belting it at her waist. She thought about leaving her glasses in the room, but she wanted to see Leo's expression. He had a way of drawing his thick brows together as he pondered something. When he really smiled, the lines around his mouth deepened. Most of all, she wanted to watch his eyes, which were often as mysterious as the sea.

She knew if she thought too long about what she intended to do, she'd lose her courage, so instead of considering her actions another moment, she opened the connecting door and stepped into Leo's room.

A dim light glowed beside Leo's bed. He was stretched out on top of the covers, shirtless, wearing black shorts. There was so much tanned skin! His muscles looked powerful, and she was in awe of his male body which seemed perfect to her.

"Verity?" he asked, a multitude of questions in the sound of her name.

Frozen for an instant, she finally pulled herself together and stepped deeper into the room and closer to him. "Our good-night was so short, I thought maybe you'd like to do it over again." The last two words had wobbled a bit, but she'd gotten them out.

Leo's gaze absorbed everything about her, then lingered on the robe and the way the fabric molded to her. "This isn't a good idea." His voice was rough.

Taking a few more steps closer to the bed, she asked almost in a whisper, "Do you want me?"

His groan was deep and heartfelt and brought a half smile to his lips. "Oh, Verity, if only you knew."

"If only I knew what?"

"If only you knew how hard it was for me to keep my hands off you on the beach. If only you knew how hard it was just to give you a kiss on the forehead good-night. Now here you are, all soft and willing, and I'm trying to be a gentleman about the whole thing."

"Don't gentlemen make love?"

He laughed. "I suppose so. But they don't talk about it much."

"No kissing and telling?" she teased, her heart racing.

Taking her hand, Leo sat on the edge of the bed and drew her down beside him. "When a man's serious about a woman, he keeps his thoughts private."

"Are you serious about me?" She had to know if she was making a fool of herself.

"I'm attracted to you, Verity. But I don't know if I'm ready for serious. I can't make love to you until I'm pre-pared to make a commitment, and *I'm* not ready for that yet, either. I don't want you to tie yourself down to me and my baggage. It's as simple as that."

"But you brought me along so we could get to know each other better. And we have. Tonight on the beach, we were close."

"Yes, we were. I feel a bond with you I don't under-stand."

"Then stop fighting it."

"Is that what I'm doing?" His voice held a touch of humor.

"Yes, I think you are. I think you feel guilty because

you're beginning to have feelings for me, yet part of you still feels married. I think you've found something with me you didn't find with your wife, and you're wondering why that's so. You're thinking too much, Leo, instead of feeling."

Now he turned completely serious. "It's not that easy."

"It could be. It could be as easy as making the decision to go on with your life."

"When you're older and more experienced, Verity—"

Tears sprang to her eyes. "You're trying to find every excuse in the book."

Standing, she blinked, refusing to cry in front of him. "I shouldn't have come in here, Leo. Maybe that *is* inexperience. I thought we could come together as equals, but you don't see me as an equal. Until you do, we *don't* belong together."

She'd left the door between their rooms open when she'd walked in. Now, as she exited Leo's room, she closed it behind her. She didn't try to hold back tears. She was ready to take a voyage with Leo, no matter where it would lead. But at this point his baggage would sink them.

Taking off her robe and glasses, she laid them aside, then slipped between the sheets. After she turned off the light, she curled on her side and thought about all the preparations she'd make for Christmas. She had almost finished her present for Leo—a memory book that included photos of Heather over the past year. She'd taken pictures she'd found in the closet to an office supply store and had duplicates made. She'd finish the present in the next day or two.

Only four days till Christmas.

Her Christmas wish for Leo was an unfettered heart. Until he was free of his past, he wouldn't be able to return her love.

How long would she have to wait?

Chapter Nine

"Jingle bells, jingle bells, jingle all the way." Heather sang along with Verity as Verity slipped a stretchy bracelet surrounded by bells onto Heather's wrist. With a giggle Heather shook her hand and made them ring. She was dressed in a red velvet jumper with a satiny, puffy-sleeved white blouse, and looked absolutely adorable.

"You jingle, too," Heather directed, pointing to Verity's bracelet, which was just like hers.

With a grin, Verity shook her wrist. She'd bought the bracelets, knowing Heather would like the sound of the bells.

Leo poked his head into Heather's room. "Ready?" When his gaze landed on his daughter, he smiled. Then his attention shifted to Verity.

She'd dressed in green wool slacks and a cream, silky blouse, and now as Leo appraised her, the heat in his gaze warmed her all over. The past few days had been difficult because of the way she'd left Leo's room at Port Aransas. They hadn't said anything further on the subject, and it was like the proverbial elephant in the room. They walked around it, talked around it and pretended to ignore it. But there it was.

On their return from their overnight stay, she'd concentrated on making the holidays special for Heather— and Leo—from the wire wreath on the door, with its pine cones at the top of the circle and a cutout of the state of Texas at the bottom, to the red candles on the mantel and the pies she'd baked to take along to Jolene's tonight.

"I've loaded everything into the car," Leo said now.

When the doorbell rang, Verity glanced at him. "Are you expecting someone?"

"No. How about you?"

She shook her head.

"I'll get it," Leo offered. "You can make sure we didn't forget anything."

A few minutes later Verity was helping Heather slip on a jacket when Leo returned to the room with a man following him. Her father!

"Dad! What are you doing here?"

Her father looked ill at ease and uncertain. "You called and left that message."

That message.

After her talk with Leo on the beach at Port Aransas, she had decided to take one more step at communicating with her father. But when she'd called, he hadn't been home. She'd left a simple message: "Dad—If your plans fall through or you change your mind about how you'd like to spend Christmas, I'd be happy to spend it with you. You can come here or I can come home. Just let me know."

He hadn't returned her call. "When you didn't call back, I figured your original plans stood."

"I got to thinking. We haven't spent much time together lately."

"We never did spend much time together." A mixture of emotions washed over her as she said it. She wanted to spend Christmas Eve with Leo and Heather and Jolene and her family, yet her father was the only family she had left, and she wanted desperately to forge bonds with him, too. She just didn't know how. "Did you check in at a motel?"

"Not yet. I passed a nice one. But I wanted to see if you were even here."

"There's no need for you to stay at a motel," Leo interjected, scooping Heather up into his arms. "I have a spare room, and you're welcome to it."

"I don't want to impose," her father stated firmly.

"You're not imposing. In fact, you can come along to my sister's for Christmas Eve dinner."

"Leo, I don't know about that…" Verity began, thinking about Leo's mother who would also be there and her possible comments about a stranger joining in.

Heather reached her arms out to Verity. "Cawwy me?"

Verity looked from Heather and Leo to her father. What would her dad think about all of it? Would he be uncomfortable with Jolene and her family?

She wasn't sure what the best thing was to do, so she

decided to leave it in her dad's hands. "Dad, it's up to you. The two of us can go out, or you can come along."

Looking uncertain, Gregory Sumpter finally turned to Leo. "You're sure your sister won't mind?"

"I'm absolutely sure."

"Do *you* mind if I come along?" he asked Verity.

"No, I don't mind. The celebration might get a little rowdy."

"Rowdy's fine on Christmas Eve," he said with a smile. "In fact, I remember that Christmas Eve that Sean—" He stopped abruptly, and the old awkwardness and tension returned between them.

She finished for him. "The Christmas Eve Sean brought the whole basketball team home for supper. Yep, that was rowdy," she agreed lightly, then gathered Heather into her arms and hugged her close. The sweet-little-girl smell of her comforted Verity somehow. Maybe with enough people around, the awkwardness between her and her dad would dissipate some. She hoped so, or it was going to be a very long Christmas Eve.

At Jolene's house, Christmas Eve dinner became organized chaos, but Verity loved it. She couldn't remember ever being part of a holiday like this. Her father seemed a bit befuddled by all of it—the kids running around, the adults having conversations over their heads, the wonderful smells drifting into the living room from the kitchen. Verity soaked it all in, glanced at her father and Leo often, and felt as if her life were changing on all fronts.

Leo's mother was late, and Leo explained that that was a common occurrence, even on Christmas Eve.

Finally the doorbell to Jolene's ranch house rang. Tim hurried to answer it, and when he returned to the living room, Amelia Montgomery accompanied him... and so did another, younger woman.

"Hi, everyone." Amelia greeted them all with a wide smile. "Leo, look who I bumped into this week. She said she didn't have anyplace to go tonight, so I invited her along. I thought you two could catch up."

Jolene, who was sitting beside Verity on the sofa leaned over and out of the side of her mouth whispered, "Marjorie and Leo went to high school together. She's a stock broker."

The woman Amelia Montgomery had brought along was absolutely exquisite, with short black hair that looked to be styled by an expert, large green eyes and a model's walk. Verity knew that walk because a coach for the commercial she'd made had taught it to her.

"Everyone," Amelia said, "you remember Marjorie Canfield, don't you?"

Marjorie's gaze had targeted Leo as if she didn't care about anyone else in the room, and Verity felt a bit of panic. Had these two been sweethearts? Had they been involved? If so, did Leo still feel anything for her?

The gentleman that he was, Leo stood and approached Marjorie with a smile. "It's good to see you again. I didn't know you were back in Avon Lake."

"I returned more than a month ago. I bought a leather shop over on Bullhorn Road."

"Tired of big-city life?" Leo asked, as if he were genuinely interested.

"No. But with the financial markets being what they

are, I decided to plunge into a less stressful business. Selling leather products in Avon Lake should be a breeze."

Amelia laughed, and then turned her attention to Verity. "Verity Sumpter, meet Marjorie. Marjorie, Verity is Leo's nanny." Her gaze settled on Gregory Sumpter. "And, I don't know who this gentleman is. Jolene?"

After further introductions were made, Verity's father glanced at her often, as if he sensed some kind of triangle had suddenly come into existence.

As Leo sat next to Verity at dinner, his knee grazed hers more than once, their elbows brushed and their hands tangled when they reached for the salt shaker. However, Marjorie was seated on Leo's other side, and Verity caught tidbits of the conversation when Heather wasn't demanding her attention. Leo and Marjorie were obviously catching up. Verity didn't like the way the ex-stockbroker looked at him, as if she could eat him up along with the ham!

When Jolene served Verity's chocolate-cream pies and pumpkin-custard pies for dessert, everyone oohed and aahed over them, except for Amelia and Marjorie, who declined because they were watching their figures.

"I wish my crusts were as light as Verity's," Jolene admitted as she took her first enthusiastic bite of chocolate-cream pie.

"If you ever tire of being a nanny, you could open a bakery," Amelia suggested helpfully.

"I think the fun would go out of baking if I did that," Verity returned politely, realizing Leo's mother was trying to keep her in her place.

"How long do you intend to be a nanny? Do you have any future goals?"

In spite of her vow to herself to keep her equilibrium tonight, Verity felt herself bristling at Amelia's patronizing tone. "My goal is to enjoy any work I do. Taking care of Heather is teaching me more than any degree I could earn."

In explanation, Amelia turned to Marjorie. "Verity is taking courses at the college. Isn't that right, dear?"

Verity took a deep breath and answered, "Yes. For a master's degree. I'm not exactly sure what I'll do with it when I finish. I guess it depends on how long Leo needs me."

At her statement, silence settled over the table for a few moments. Finally conversation started up again, and Verity was relieved.

Tim announced, "As soon as we're finished here, we'll sing Christmas carols around the piano. Then I'll read the 'Christmas Story' before the kids fall asleep."

Little Joey piped up, "I'm not gonna sleep tonight. I'm gonna sit by the tree and wait for Santa."

Tim grinned at his son. "Maybe instead of sitting and waiting, you can go to bed and listen for the bells on his sleigh. I'm afraid he might not come in if he knows you're watching."

After thinking about that, Joey looked at Verity. "Can I leave him a piece of your pie? I think he'd like that better than cookies."

Everyone at the table smiled. "Sure you can leave him a piece of pie. And don't forget the milk to go with it."

"I want to give Santa pie, too," Heather decided, sliding off her chair and coming over to Verity's side. After a yawn, she laid her head on Verity's lap.

"I think this one's going to be asleep before we get home." Leo's gaze locked on Verity's.

As Leo sat at his sister's table, the woman his mother had handpicked for him on his left and Verity Sumpter on his right, he realized his need for Verity went far beyond any physical satisfaction he could find with her. Verity wanted to be his equal, and he suddenly realized that she was. There was a maturity, compassion and understanding about her that he found few women possessed. Where before doubts had plagued him, they were now replaced with a certainty that she belonged in his life...in Heather's life. As Verity stroked Heather's hair, Leo felt more right with the world than he'd felt in a very long time.

While everyone else gathered around the piano to sing Christmas carols, Leo cornered his mother in the hall outside the powder room. Leo could see she'd just made sure every hair was in place and her lipstick freshened.

"Why are you scowling, Leo?" she asked with a smile. "It's Christmas Eve."

"Yes, I know it's Christmas Eve. I'd like to know why you asked Marjorie to join us tonight."

His mother's face reflected complete innocence. "It's simple. She was going to spend the holiday alone. Just recently moving back to town, she hasn't reacquainted herself with her friends. She has no family here anymore. I didn't want her to be alone."

"I think your motive went deeper than that. What did you think would happen when Marjorie and I got together again?"

"You two dated in high school. You're both single. I thought you might find common ground once more. It's time you get on with your life."

His voice was calm but firm. "I *am* getting on with my life. You just don't like the direction it's headed. The type of woman you'd choose to be your daughter-in-law is *not* the type of woman I'd choose to be a wife and mother."

Amelia Montgomery looked stunned for a moment. Actually Leo had never seen her speechless before.

Hearing light footsteps, he looked up and saw Verity coming into the hall. She stopped as soon as she spotted them. "Oh, I'm sorry. I didn't mean to interrupt." In Verity's considerate way, she turned to leave.

But in two strides Leo was beside her, taking her hand and drawing her toward him. "Mom, I know you're worried about me because you think I should start dating again. Well, I have. I'm dating Verity. In fact, we're going to a concert at the college day after tomorrow."

Verity's eyes grew wide at his announcement, and she didn't seem to know what to say.

To her credit, his mother recovered swiftly. "I didn't know you two were serious." Her eyes were questioning. "I thought Verity just worked for you. After all, you're so much older—"

"I might be older, but Verity's mature. She's faced loss just as I have. Now that you know we're dating, maybe the two of you can get to know each other better."

Quick on the uptake, Verity offered, "You can come to dinner anytime. Just give me a call or drop in."

Amelia looked at her as if she were seeing her in a different light. "I'll do that." With a last glance at the two of them, she went down the hall to join the festivities once more.

"What did I miss?" Verity asked, looking a bit bemused.

"Would you like to go to a concert with me day after tomorrow?"

"Sure. I didn't know if you were just telling your mom that or if you really meant it."

"I meant it."

"Are you sure this isn't just an easy out so you don't have to date Marjorie?" she asked, half joking, half serious.

Taking Verity by the shoulders, Leo looked deep into her eyes. "This has nothing to do with Marjorie." Tipping her chin up, he softly kissed her lips, then added, "This has to do with *us*."

He could see there were still doubts in Verity's eyes, and his goal would be to eliminate them. Dropping his arm around her, he guided her back to the living room. This was going to be the best Christmas he'd ever had.

It was almost midnight when Verity and Leo positioned Heather's presents under Leo's tree.

On the sofa her father turned from the TV where a choir sang Handel's *Messiah*. "Don't forget to put out that pie for Santa," he reminded them. "I'm sure Heather will look for the empty dish in the morning."

Leo laughed. "I'm sure you're right about that."

"I can get it," Verity offered.

"Why don't we all have a midnight piece of pie before turning in? There's something I need to get in the pool house. I'll be right back."

After Leo had gone, Verity and her father were left in the great room. The lights on the tree twinkled on and off as the smell of pine filled the room.

After positioning the last present perfectly, Verity went to the kitchen doorway. "Would you like a piece of pie, Dad?"

"Sure." After he followed her into the kitchen, he pulled out a chair at the table. "You and Leo are involved, aren't you?"

"We're heading that way," she answered, hoping it was true. At first when she'd come upon Leo and his mother, she'd thought he'd told his mother they were dating simply to avoid her matchmaking. Afterward, however, when he'd looked into her eyes, she'd seen that maybe he *was* ready to move on with his life.

"His little girl seems attached to you," her father noticed.

"Heather and I connected right away."

"You haven't been here very long. Are you sure things aren't moving too fast?"

Words sailed out of her mouth before she could catch them. "You've never cared who I've dated before. Why now?"

Her father lowered himself into the chair. "Because this time it looks serious. Because…" He hesitated. "Because this time Sean isn't here to protect you."

"You relied on Sean to protect me?" she asked softly.

"I knew you'd listen to him."

"I would have listened to you, too. In fact, it would have meant everything to me to know you cared about me as much as you did about Sean."

Stunned, her father just stared at her. Eventually he responded almost sternly, "I have *always* cared about you, Verity."

"Not the same way you cared about Sean," she returned quietly.

After a few tense moments, her father ran his hand through his hair. "Sean and I were guys. I didn't know what to do with you. Especially when you started growing up."

"You didn't know what to *do* with me?"

"That didn't come out right," he sighed. "Verity, I was a single dad, and I did my best to give you and your brother guidelines. You were twins, and most of the time you didn't seem to need anyone else. When you were kids, you even had your own language. You did everything together. Remember when I tried to convince you to take dancing lessons and you said you'd only do it if Sean did, too? He wanted no part of it so you never got the lessons."

"I remember."

"That's the kind of thing I'm talking about. I didn't know how to go about helping you do girlie things."

"I didn't *want* to do girlie things. I liked sports. I liked climbing trees and hiking."

Her father shook his head. "I was never sure of that. I was never sure you were finding your own way, not just following in your brother's. But I never cared about you any less than Sean, and once you became a teenager…I was *really* out of my element. That's why I asked your aunt to have that talk with you."

That talk. The birds and the bees. Her aunt had come to visit one Easter and had sat her down and explained everything. At least everything she could fit into an hour. Verity had never realized her father had put her aunt up to it.

"I think Aunt April was as uncomfortable as you would have been."

"Maybe. But I would have turned red and stammered through it. I would have needed a script."

"Oh, Dad." Seeing fatherhood through her dad's eyes, considering parenting a boy compared to parenting a girl, Verity understood the difficulties…understood in a way she never had before.

"Why didn't you return my call before Thanksgiving? Did you want to spend it alone?"

"I was feeling absolutely raw," her dad admitted. "Ever since we lost Sean, all I wanted to do was crawl in a cave and lick my wounds. I know that was selfish. I know you were hurting as much as I was. But I didn't know how to make us both feel better, so it was just easier to retreat."

"I tried that for a while," Verity confessed. "But it didn't work. I missed Sean more. Since I've come here, though, all of it's been better. I don't know how to explain it, but when I'm playing with Heather, hugging her, it's almost as if Sean's looking over my shoulder. I know that sounds silly—"

"No, it doesn't. As connected as you and your brother were, I know he's looking out for you now. When you called and left that invitation for Christmas on my machine, I knew if we didn't make contact again, I'd lose you as surely as I'd lost Sean."

In the silence Verity knew he was right. Going to her father then, she hugged him. "You're not going to lose me. And we can keep memories of Sean alive by remembering him together."

When Verity leaned away from her dad, she saw his eyes were as moist as hers.

The sliding glass doors from the patio opened, and Leo came into the kitchen.

As if embarrassed by his emotion, Verity's father stepped away from her. "I think I'll turn in," he mumbled.

"Heather will probably be up at the crack of dawn," Leo warned. "Don't feel you have to get up that early."

"And miss the look in your daughter's eyes when she opens her presents?" Verity's father exclaimed. "I don't think so. It's been years since I witnessed a child's wonder. I think I'm ready for a good dose of it again." Then he capped Verity's shoulder and squeezed it. "I'll see you in the morning."

She covered his hand with hers. "Good night, Dad."

When her father had left the kitchen, Leo asked, "Did you two talk?"

"Is that why you left us alone?"

"Partly," he admitted with a smile.

"Yes, we talked. I don't know if we've ever talked exactly like that before. I guess I never realized how hard it was for him to raise me and Sean on his own. Seeing you with Heather has brought some of that home."

As Leo approached her now, she saw he had a small package in his hand.

"I also went out to the pool house to get this," he said.

"What is it?" She felt like a kid.

"Something for you I wanted to give you privately. Here. Open it."

"I have one for you, too."

"Mine can wait."

With trembling fingers, Verity took the present. The box was heavy and she couldn't imagine what was inside. Untying the ribbon, she laid it on the counter, then pulled off the paper and did the same with that.

Curiously she lifted the white lid. "Oh, Leo. It's beautiful!" She removed from the box a crystal paperweight in the shape of a shooting star. Tears came to her eyes as she ran her fingers over it. "It's beautiful," she said again, all of her heartfelt emotion in her voice. "I can't believe you remembered."

"I remember everything you tell me," Leo murmured, taking her into his arms.

She had to tell him something he didn't know. "I saw a shooting star the night we rode on the beach."

"When?"

"On our way back. It was as if Sean approved...of us."

Leo tipped her chin up and sealed his lips to hers. It was a hungry kiss that told her they hadn't kissed for far too long. It was a possessive kiss, and she loved the idea that Leo wanted to make her his. It was a masterful kiss, relaying to her that he wanted to teach her everything he knew about two people coming together, joining their hearts and souls and minds.

When he broke away, they were both breathless. "If your dad weren't a guest in my house tonight, I'd carry you to my bedroom."

"You can still do that," she teased.

"Tonight's too risky. Heather could come in and ask when Santa's coming."

They both laughed.

He ran his thumb over her lips. "We have time, Verity. Plenty of time. Besides, enjoying the anticipation is half the fun." After another quick kiss on her lips, he said, "Go on to bed. I'm going to catch the late news. I need something to distract myself from thinking about that kiss."

Still holding the box with the shooting star, she smiled at him. "Thank you for this. It means a lot."

"Good night, Verity. I hope you hear sleigh bells."

As she walked down the hall to her room, she knew she would. Tonight had been a perfect Christmas Eve. And tomorrow…if she and Leo had some time alone together, she'd tell him she loved him. Then maybe soon he could say those words, too.

She'd almost reached her room when she remembered the slice of pie they needed to leave out for Santa along with the glass of milk. She knew Heather would look for that empty glass and cleared plate. When she turned to go back into the great room, she heard music coming from a commercial on the TV. It sounded familiar.

ZING! It was the jingle for *ZING!*

She didn't intend to walk softly to the great room. She didn't really intend to spy on Leo as the commercial played on the big screen. But her gaze was riveted to him as she saw him stare at the images in fascination. He was watching her back as she walked away on the screen, the parasol over her shoulder.

Was that longing on his face?

Obviously, he hadn't recognized her. How could he? Only a glimpse of her face had shown for about half a second. And she looked so different in that commercial. She looked sophisticated and sexy and like everything a man could want in a woman.

With a flash of insight, she knew she could *be* that woman for Leo. If she could become that woman again, then maybe he could tell her he loved her.

When they went on their date, he was going to get the surprise of his life. She'd decided, after Matthew had bailed out of her life, she never wanted a man to be attracted to her again simply because of her physical appearance. She hadn't wanted a man who looked at the surface first, the inside later. But Leo had been attracted to her for what she was…for *who* she was. Now she wanted to show him she could be so much more. When they went on their date, he'd have a woman on his arm who would turn his head and keep it turned…toward her.

Chapter Ten

On the day of the concert, Verity stepped inside the doors of the exclusive dress shop with Jolene right behind her. "I pick up my contact lenses at three. Luckily the doctor had a cancellation and stocks the contacts I need. But he has a technician who explains how to wear them, how to clean them and all that, so that's why I'm going back this afternoon."

"When are you getting your hair done?"

"That's at four. Fortunately, the hairstylist could squeeze me in. So now, all I need is a dress. Are you sure women get dressed up for these concerts?"

"Absolutely," Jolene assured her with a wide grin. "They're an event in Avon Lake, especially around the holidays. You probably don't want anything sequined or beaded, but dressy is good. This store has great clothes as well as great sales after Christmas."

"Thanks for meeting me here. It's been so long since I bought a dress, I wanted another woman's perspective."

"I'll give you perspective. We'll find something that will wow Leo. What are you going to do with your hair? Have it cut?"

"Not much. Just trimmed a little. I'm going to get one of those spiral perms."

"Leo's not going to even know you."

He was going to know her, all right. She was going to turn into his fantasy woman, the woman who'd mesmerized him on the TV screen.

The store's racks still had a lot of selections. Jolene bypassed the sportswear and everyday clothes to head straight for the party dresses. Verity flipped through the dresses, dismissing any that were beaded or sequined and one that was silver lamé.

"Too gaudy," Jolene offered with a shake of her head.

Verity agreed. Finally they selected three—a black velvet halter dress with a short straight skirt, high neck in front and a low vee that would bare her back. The second was a red, silky fabric with long sleeves and low décolletage. It had a straight skirt and a slit up the side. Finally, there was a white, wool dress with a sweetheart neckline, long sleeves and full skirt. Verity knew before she tried it on that it was simply too virginal. That wasn't the look she was going for. But Jolene liked it, so she took it to the dressing room with them.

A half hour later, she left the store with Jolene, a wide grin on her face. "I knew I'd like that one best."

"I wish I could be there to see Leo's eyes pop out."

Verity laughed. "I didn't think I'd have an audience for the great 'reveal.'"

"I have a feeling it could be a night you'll never forget."

"I hope so," Verity decided fervently.

Jolene glanced at her watch. "We have time for lunch before you have to go to the ophthalmologist."

"Are you sure Tim won't mind watching the kids for another hour?"

"He won't mind. He takes days off over Christmas so he *can* spend time with them. There's a deli over on Bluebonnet. Why don't we stop in there? We could walk since the sun's shining today."

"I'm glad the rain stopped. My feet would get wet in those new shoes if I had to walk through puddles." The strappy, high-heeled sandals weren't like any shoes she'd ever bought before.

Suddenly Jolene grabbed her arm. "What about a coat? You can't wear a windbreaker with a dress like that." Jolene eyed Verity's jacket.

"Believe it or not, I have a cape I bought last year. It'll be perfect." She'd gotten it when she and Matthew had attended a dance at UT.

They stopped at Verity's car so she could put her packages inside.

"I got a call from Mom yesterday," Jolene disclosed.

"About anything important?"

"You could say that. She wanted to know why I thought Leo was interested in you."

Verity wasn't sure she wanted to hear this, but it

was better to know what she was up against. "What did you say?"

"I told her he was interested because you're perfect for him."

"I bet that went over like a lead balloon."

"Actually, it didn't. She was very quiet for a while, but then she revealed that on Christmas Eve she realized Leo hadn't been as happy in his marriage as she'd thought he had. She also realized that since you came into his life, he's smiling again, and that was important. By the way, I think she liked your dad."

"I think he was fascinated by her and all the places she's been."

"I think she admired the fact that he raised you and your brother on his own."

Verity and Jolene started walking down the street. "Dad and I had a talk on Christmas Eve," Verity confided. "We connected in a way we never have before. When he left last night, I felt as if I'd found something that had been lost for a long time."

Jolene glanced over at her. "So this has been a particularly special holiday for you?"

"I hope it has been for Leo, too," she said softly.

"I think it has," Jolene assured her.

"When Dad comes to visit again, if your mom's in town, I'll ask her to come to dinner, too."

"Matchmaking?" Jolene asked with a raised brow.

"I wouldn't call it that," Verity answered with a smile.

The two women exchanged a look, and they both laughed.

* * *

When Heather didn't want to take a nap, she was a bundle of energy that just wouldn't quit. Thankful for the sunny day, Leo had taken her to a playground, then fed her lunch, hoping she'd be ready to rest for a while. But resting wasn't on her agenda.

"Hide-and-seek, Daddy," she said with one of those smiles that made him feel like butter in her tiny hands.

"Okay, hide-and-seek. But only for a little while. Then you've got to rest. I don't want you cranky when you go see Joey and Randy tonight."

Jolene had offered to leave the boys with Tim, and she'd come babysit Heather. But he'd suggested Heather just stay overnight with her, instead. That way, he and Verity didn't have to worry about what time they got home. When they *did* get home, they wouldn't have to worry about being interrupted.

And just what might anyone interrupt? a little devil on Leo's shoulder asked.

Leo didn't have the answer to that. But he did know that tonight could be something special.

For the first round of hide-and-seek, Heather slipped behind the pink-and-white-striped chair in her bedroom, sure Leo wouldn't find her there. But he did, and she giggled when he tickled her.

Enthusiastically, she announced, "*Your* turn."

It didn't take Leo long to crouch down under the dining room table. After scurrying around the great room and calling "Daddy" a few times, she spotted him, ran toward him and gave him a giant hug.

"You're good at this," he told her with a laugh.

"I hide now," she said, and took off down the hall.

He knew where she was headed—to Verity's rooms.

Feeling like an intruder, he stepped inside Verity's sitting room and didn't see Heather at first glance. "Where are you?" he called.

After a quick look around, he pushed the bedroom door open wider, remembering how Heather had slipped under Verity's bed once before. He checked under there, but his daughter was nowhere to be found. Verity's closet didn't hold a little girl, either. Finally he knew what to do. Heather couldn't be quiet for more than a minute. He stood still and listened.

When he heard a rustling sound, he went into Verity's sitting room again. Then he saw the little feet peeking out under Verity's desk. When he went over there and pulled out the chair, Heather popped out, whirled around, and in her excitement brushed a few papers off of the desk.

As Heather ran out of the room and down the hall, Leo called after her, "I'm going to tickle you when I catch you."

He heard his daughter giggle.

Stooping, he picked up the papers that had fallen. One was a Christmas card that had opened, and in spite of himself, he read the writing inside. "You're a beautiful young woman who deserves love. Always, Will."

The Christmas card was a simple one with a Christmas tree on the front. There was no envelope with it.

Leo remembered the other letter Verity had received from Will. He remembered the man at the arts festival. He remembered Verity standing in the foyer of the Arts and Science Building in the shadows, a man close to her, his hand on her shoulder. Leo's gut turned, and all of it felt wrong.

Was Verity seeing this Will on her days off? Was she keeping secrets from him? Was she too young to understand monogamy and commitment?

That's what he'd been afraid of all along. Maybe she wasn't as inexperienced as he'd thought she was…or as she pretended to be. Was she really a virgin? Was *any* girl a virgin into her twenties these days?

Had he been an absolute fool?

The questions wouldn't stop swirling in his head. He had to confront Verity about it tonight before they went out. He had to know the truth.

He remembered Carolyn keeping a secret for three months, three months that had affected the rest of his life. If Verity was keeping secrets, he was going to find out what they were.

An hour later Leo had finally gotten Heather settled for her nap when the phone rang. Quickly snatching it up in the kitchen, he growled, "Montgomery here."

"You don't sound like a man who's going out on the town tonight," his sister jibed.

He didn't know if he was still going to be going out on the town tonight. He just knew that Verity had some explaining to do, and that was the first item on his agenda. "It took three stories to put Heather down for her nap. Somehow, I think her negotiation skills are better than mine. Did she learn them from you?"

Jolene laughed. "Could be." After a pause she said, "The reason I called is twofold. Verity said the two of you are grabbing leftovers to eat before you leave. You can give Heather a snack, but don't feed her supper. The boys want to order pizza after she arrives. And secondly, I'm going to come over and pick her up so you don't have to drop her off."

"I'm sure there's a reason you want to go out of your way."

"There is," Jolene admitted, with a lilt to her voice. "I want to see Verity before she leaves."

"Why?"

"Because I've been involved in the transformation process, and I want to see the result."

"Transformation?"

"You'll see. Anyway, the concert's at seven-thirty, right?"

"Right."

"I'll be there around six-thirty."

Since he wanted to confront Verity about what he'd seen in her sitting room, a talk would be easier after Jolene picked Heather up. "That sounds good. Thanks, Jolene."

After Jolene hung up, Leo went to the pool house for his briefcase. He would work at the kitchen table and stay occupied until he could have that talk with Verity.

When Verity came rushing into the house at 6:00, Leo heard her but didn't see her. Building a block tower with his daughter in the great room, he was aware of the front door opening.

Verity called, "Sorry I'm late. I've got to get dressed. Are you and Heather okay?"

"Fine," he called. "Jolene's coming to pick her up, so you have time."

Seconds later he heard Verity's sitting room door open and close. He'd already changed into his suit. All they had to do was grab something to eat and they'd be on their way—after he asked her about that card and letter.

A half hour later Jolene rang the front doorbell and came in. "Anybody home?" she called brightly.

Leo had packed everything Heather would need in a small pink suitcase he'd bought his daughter for just that purpose. Now he set it next to the little table where Heather was coloring contentedly.

When Jolene stepped into the kitchen, she smiled at him. "Don't you look handsome. Mother would be proud."

He straightened the knot of his tie. "Thank goodness I don't have to wear one of these every day."

When Jolene laughed, he gave her a wry grin.

"Leo," Verity's soft voice came from the great room.

When he walked in there, he stopped abruptly, caught up by the vision of Verity Sumpter, who looked entirely like someone else. The black velvet dress draped over her figure, flattering every curve. Her hair was a mass of curls. Her eyes were so big—

He swore. He'd seen her looking like this before. In the ZING commercial!

"You look like the woman—"

"I am that woman," she admitted with a smile that he took as seductive.

Confusion and then anger burgeoned inside Leo. She'd been playing a role with him...playing him for a fool. "Why were you pretending to be somebody you weren't?" he demanded.

Her surprise at his tone showed. "I made that commercial over a year ago."

"That's not an answer. That doesn't explain why you kept a secret from me or why you've been hiding behind drab clothes and glasses." Suddenly everything about Verity seemed like a mirage—a mirage he'd needed to pull him out of his past. Yet, if it was a mirage, it wasn't real. *She* might not be real. If she'd been deceptive about who she was, then she might be deceptive about other things.

"I don't know why you're playing at being a nanny or why you've hidden who you really are, but it makes me wonder what else you've been hiding. Are you seeing someone behind my back?"

Her brown eyes, which looked so impossibly large without her glasses, widened with surprise. "I have no idea what you're talking about. I haven't been seeing anyone."

He realized now that her innocent act could be just that…an act. He motioned angrily toward Verity's sitting room. "Heather and I were playing hide-and-seek this afternoon. She hid under your desk. When I found her, she accidently knocked down some papers. One of them was a Christmas card from Will. It sounded to me as if you two have something going on."

Verity had paled at Leo's accusations, but now spots of color again dotted her cheeks, making the blush she'd applied seem even rosier.

He heard his sister murmur, "Leo…" in a warning tone. But he didn't pay any attention to her until she gathered Heather into her arms and said to her, "We're going to play in your room for a few minutes," then carried her away.

Verity's gaze hadn't moved from Leo's. "Your question sounds more like an accusation," she said, her voice trembling. "Do you really believe I'd see someone behind your back?"

"If you would hide what you really look like all these weeks—"

"Hide what I look like?" She brushed her new curls behind one ear. "Let me tell you who I am, Leo, because you don't seem to know me. I grew up as a tomboy because I loved being with Sean and I wanted to earn my dad's approval. I never cared about dresses and designer jeans or having my ears pierced. Then I went to college, and still poured my attention into sports and studies, until one day a casting agent approached me. A new soda was going to hit the market, and the company wanted to use college-age girls and guys, to target that audience. I wasn't interested, but Sean thought it would be a blast. So, I agreed to do it. Professionals trained me how to walk and smile. A stylist curled my hair. A makeup artist applied makeup."

Suddenly she held out her arms and pirouetted. "This was born. Did I like the new image? I wasn't sure it fit. But I had the contact lenses, and the curls would take a while to grow out. Matthew was attracted to the new look, and we started dating. That should have taught me something, but I guess I'm not a fast learner."

Leo still wasn't ready to believe her and needed further explanations. "Why did you go back to wearing oversize sweatshirts? And glasses?"

"Because after Sean died, I just didn't care anymore.
I kept getting my hair trimmed and eventually the perm
relaxed, the red highlights washed out. Then I took this
job with you, and I began caring about everything again.
I came back to life. Heather filled my heart with joy. You
filled it with—" She paused, then went on. "I just
thought you'd like this version of me, that if I wowed
you, you might be able to admit your feelings."

"What about the card?" he asked hoarsely, still unable to let that go.

"That card is from my advisor, Dr. Will Stratford. By
the way, he's old enough to be my grandfather. He was
easy to confide in, and I told him I was…falling in love
with you. But my feelings don't seem to mean very much.
If you think I would see a man behind your back, then
you don't know me at all, no matter what I'm wearing."

With that declaration, Verity turned and practically
ran down the hall to her room.

Leo heard the slam of her door. Feeling shell-
shocked, he sank down onto the sofa. That's where Jolene found him a few minutes later. He looked up.
"Where's Heather?"

"She's changing the clothes on her doll. What happened here?"

"You tell me." He yanked on the knot of his tie and
opened it.

"In a nutshell, you blew it," Jolene concluded.

Finally he stared at his sister. "Did you know about
the commercial?"

With a shake of her head, Jolene sat on the sofa beside him. "No. Verity didn't tell me. It wasn't long

after she started working for you that I thought she looked familiar. That must have been when the ZING commercial started playing. But now that I think about it, you don't actually see her face on the screen for more than a split second. And all that hair. She looked so different."

"Why did she decide to make the transformation tonight?"

"Lots of reasons, I imagine. But I suspect the main one is because she wanted you to fall head over heels for her. She wanted to wow you and give you that sucker punch that would bring you to your knees and make you admit you loved her."

Verity had sucker punched him all right, but the blow had nothing to do with the way she looked. When she explained why she'd transformed herself again, he'd realized what a terrible mistake he'd made. He'd realized his doubts had ruined everything between them.

"She's probably packing," he muttered.

"Is there a good reason she *shouldn't* be packing?"

"Hell, yes! I need her in my life. Heather needs her. She's the best thing that's ever happened to us. And I—"

"Say it, Leo," Jolene prompted. "If you don't acknowledge it, and you don't say it, you're going to lose her."

Taking a deep breath, he admitted, "I love her."

The silence in the house was deafening.

Jolene glanced over her shoulder and down the hall to the bedrooms. "I'd better check on Heather."

Now that he'd admitted his feelings for Verity, he knew he had to do something about them…something concrete. "Can you stay here for a little while? I have to run an errand."

"Now?"

"Yes, now. Don't let Verity leave."

"What am I supposed to do, chain her to a chair?"

"I'm serious, Jolene. Don't let her leave. Make up some excuse. You have to keep her here until I get back."

"All right. I'll try. But if she wants to drive away, Leo, you know there's really nothing I can do to stop her."

He swore at the thought and the mess he'd made of everything. "I know. If she does leave, just make sure you find out where she's going...because I intend to go after her."

When Leo returned from his trip to the jewelry store, Jolene informed him Verity hadn't come out of her room. She hadn't tried to talk to her because she knew that was *his* job.

Gathering up Heather and her small suitcase, Jolene went to the door where Leo gave Heather a hug and a kiss. His daughter waved happily at him as Jolene carried her to her car.

Removing a tiny box from the jewelry store bag, Leo went to Verity's room and knocked. When she didn't answer, he knocked again. "Verity. Open the door."

After a few endless moments she did. He saw the tear tracks on her cheeks, and his chest felt tight. He'd never meant to hurt her. He'd never meant to doubt her.

She didn't say anything, just moved aside to let him enter. But he wasn't going to let her keep distance between them.

Taking her hand, he pulled her to the sofa and sat beside her. "I was afraid you'd pack your bags and go."

She stared straight ahead, rather than at him. "I thought about it, but I couldn't leave...." Then she looked at him, and he saw everything that she was feeling in her eyes.

"I hope that means what I think it means," he said huskily.

He'd been holding the small velvet box in his hands. Now he opened his fingers and showed it to her.

Verity's gaze went from the box to him.

"I've been an absolute fool. I *have* used every excuse in the book to keep from falling in love with you. But I *am* in love with you. Why else do you think I went so crazy when I saw that Christmas card?"

"You were jealous?" she asked a bit incredulously.

"Of course I was jealous! You are a beautiful, intelligent, talented woman, Verity." He brushed the curls from the side of her face. "Whether you have your hair curled, you're wearing glasses or you're dressed in jeans and playing with Heather, I fell in love with *you*, not a fantasy woman."

He opened the black velvet box. "Will you accept this ring? Will you marry me?"

Her mouth opened. Her voice was thready as she said in amazement, "I can't believe you're asking. I can't believe you want me to be your wife." She stared down at the princess cut diamond as if she couldn't believe her eyes.

Sliding the ring from the box, he held it out to her. "Will you let me put this on your finger?"

Trembling, she gave him her hand, and he slipped the diamond on her ring finger.

When she looked up at him, tears were brimming in her eyes. "Yes, I'll marry you, Leo. I love you."

Leo didn't realize he'd been holding his breath. Verity's answer meant the world to him. When his arms went around her, she lifted her face to his. When he kissed her, he let down all his walls, and his fervor told her exactly what he was feeling.

Breaking the kiss, but not leaning too far away, he asked, "When will you marry me?"

She was smiling now, and her eyes sparkled with her happiness. "Whenever you'd like."

"Soon," he breathed. "I don't know how long I can wait to make you mine."

"We don't have to wait," she assured him.

Holding her face between his palms, he kissed her again. Afterward he said, "Yes, we do. You told me once, you were saving yourself for the right man. I want to prove to you I *am* the right man. Our wedding night will be special for both of us."

Then he took his bride-to-be in his arms, grateful for all the love she'd brought into his life, grateful for the chance to share a future with her. He loved Verity Sumpter, and he would prove it to her for the rest of their lives.

Epilogue

On the evening of January fifth, the Twelfth Night—
the last day of the Christmas season, Verity walked
down the aisle of the college chapel, candlelight flickering on the white runner that showed her the path to
her groom. Her father's arm steadied her. Her satiny,
princess-style wedding gown billowed about her as her
veil flowed in front of her face. The chapel was still
beautifully decorated with poinsettias, but she hardly
noticed anything except for the man she was going to
marry. Jolene had walked down the aisle first in a green
velvet dress, followed by little Heather in matching
green velvet with a basket of yellow rose petals. Verity's
heart was so full she could hardly breathe. As she approached Leo, it beat even faster.

Once she and her father reached the altar, her dad
lifted her veil and kissed her cheek. "Be happy," he said

so fervently, she knew if she was happy, *he* would be, too. Then he placed her hand in Leo's, and she stood before the minister with her soon-to-be husband.

Always handsome, Leo was over the top tonight in his black tuxedo. He was looking at her as if he couldn't bear to turn away. She felt the same, and tears came to her eyes.

He squeezed her hand and said in a low, husky voice, "I love you."

"I love you, too."

The minister, a man with tortoiseshell glasses and gray hair, smiled benignly. "I think you two could do this without me. But just to make it official…"

The minister began the service.

As Verity promised to love, honor and cherish Leo, her heart overflowed with happiness. As Leo promised to love, honor and cherish Verity, she heard the deep sincerity in his vows, and knew they'd love each other for a lifetime…and more.

After the minister gave his blessing, Leo kissed her soundly with a yearning she was feeling, too…a yearning they would satisfy tonight.

They turned as husband and wife to greet their guests, and Verity spotted friends who had traveled from Galveston, spotted Jolene and Tim, Leo's mother and Dr. Will Stratford. The professor winked at her and she smiled. She barely noticed the photographer who'd captured every wonderful moment of the ceremony. Soon he would join them on a ship Leo had rented for the evening where they and their guests would enjoy the wedding reception.

Heather came running toward them then, and Leo scooped her up. The three of them walked to the back of the church together, a family at last.

The limo waited for them outside. They were stopping at the beach first where they could stargaze for a short while and breathe in the magnitude of the life they would share together.

Descending the church steps, Verity could see the night was filled with stars and promise. As Leo's arm held her close, Heather pointed up to the sky. "Look."

Verity and Leo saw it at the same moment—a shooting star, streaking across the heavens in an arc above them.

As moved as Verity, Leo said in a gravelly voice, "I think that's your twin's seal of approval."

Verity blew a kiss into the heavens and then raised her face to Leo's. His kiss was a mixture of gentle and sweet and possessive.

Together they climbed into the limo with Heather who Verity already loved as her own. Together they would make a life. Together they would form a family.

A car seat was waiting in the limo for Heather. Leo buckled her in and sat across from her with his arm around Verity.

"Are you ready for this new adventure, Mrs. Montgomery?" he asked with a wide grin.

"I'm ready for any adventure…as long as we live it together," Verity replied.

Leo held her close as the chauffeur drove them away…into their happily-ever-after.

* * * * *

Dear Reader,

In December 2006 three climbers went missing on Mount Hood in Oregon. The story captured media attention as rescuers struggled against weather conditions to find them.

Hoping to learn more about their fate, I stumbled across an online climbing forum where rescuers were posting about the search and rescue (SAR) operation. Sadly, the climbers perished, but the courage of the men and women on the mountain rescue units inspired and intrigued me. I knew I had to write this book.

One problem. I knew nothing about climbing. My husband climbed before we married, and he wanted to climb again, but I didn't want him anywhere near Mount Hood's summit. I decided not to ask him for help. Luckily for me, he wasn't offended. Through the internet I met climbers – some members of mountain rescue units – who not only helped me with my research, but became friends. The more I learned, the less I had to fear about climbing. I even gave my husband a guided trip up Mount Hood as a gift for our twelfth anniversary. He reached the summit during a climb in May 2007 and loved every minute of it.

My curiosity about climbing grew. Though I'm scared of heights, I took a class at a local rock gym for some hands-on research and discovered I loved climbing! I've been climbing ever since.

I've written several books, but not one has changed my life the way *Rescued by the Magic of Christmas* did. For those who helped me discover a new passion to pursue, all I can say is thank you and climb on!

Melissa

Rescued by the Magic of Christmas

Melissa McClone

Melissa McClone on *Rescued by the Magic of Christmas* :

"Christmastime is about love and affirming life. My youngest child was due in January, and I drew upon my own experiences for writing Hannah. Like her, I prepared endless lists, hoping to make the holiday the 'best ever' for my toddler and pre-schooler while preparing for the new arrival. Unlike me, Hannah didn't have things go quite as planned, but what better way to celebrate this special season than with the birth of a child?"

With a degree in mechanical engineering from Stanford University, the last thing **Melissa McClone** ever thought she would be doing was writing romance novels. But analysing engines for a major US airline just couldn't compete with her "happily-ever-afters". When she isn't writing, caring for her three young children or doing laundry, Melissa loves to curl up on the couch with a cup of tea, her cats and a good book. She enjoys watching home decorating shows to get ideas for her house – a 1939 cottage that is *slowly* being renovated. Melissa lives in Lake Oswego, Oregon, with her own real-life hero husband, two daughters, a son, two loveable but oh-so-spoiled indoor cats and a no-longer-stray outdoor kitty that decided to call the garage home. Melissa loves to hear from her readers. You can write to her at PO Box 63, Lake Oswego, OR 97034, USA, or contact her via her website: www.melissamcclone.com

For Portland Mountain Rescue (PMR), Central Washington Mountain Rescue (CWMR) and all the dedicated men and women who volunteer their time and talents to mountain rescue units.

Special thanks to Michael Leming, John Frieh, Mark Westman, Paul Soboleski, Lyneen Norton, Iain Morris, Steve Rollins, Keith Langenwalter, Hugh O'Reilly, Debra Ross, cascadeclimbers. com and Virginia Kantra. Any mistakes and/or discrepancies are entirely the author's fault.

PROLOGUE

JAKE PORTER double-checked the gear in his pack, his motions driven by habit and a sharp sense of purpose. Bivy sack. Avalanche transceiver. Probe. Shovel.

His friends were somewhere up on Mount Hood in the middle of one of the worst weather systems to ever hit the Cascades in December. And Jake was going after them.

Carabiners rattled as he closed the pack. Now came the hard part—waiting.

The other members of the mountain rescue unit sat at cafeteria tables inside the Wy'East day lodge, their faces tight and their voices low as they checked their own gear. Yawning reporters grabbed quick interviews between sips of coffee. Eager photographers snapped pictures of the early-morning mission preparations.

The overhead lights made everything look pale, stark and ominous, matching Jake's mood. The weather, too.

Outside, visibility sucked. The wind howled at forty miles per hour. The morning temperature hovered around thirteen degrees. The threat of frostbite and the very real avalanche danger made going to a higher elevation a fool's errand. But in his five years as a member of Oregon Mountain Search and Rescue, Jake had never been more eager to confront the elements for a mission.

He wasn't the only one. Every single OMSAR member had responded to the alert. More than a few had already heard the news and been waiting for the call. Others hadn't waited and had come here on their own. All they needed was the go-ahead to start moving out. Up.

Radios crackled as someone asked for additional gear from the rescue cache.

Jake tightened the strap around his shovel, ignoring the knot of concern in his stomach. The whiz of the rough nylon brushing through the buckle intensified his unease. His friends should have made it off the hill with no problem.

Where the hell were they?

Iain Garfield was one of the most talented climbers in the Pacific Northwest. Only twenty-three, he'd already made a name for himself, gaining sponsors and gracing climbing magazine covers with his numerous first ascents of peaks around the world. He could climb the Reid Headwall solo. Backwards. With his eyes closed.

And Nick Bishop. He knew the mountain better than almost anyone in the unit. When they were students together, Nick had once climbed the route overnight and made it to class the next morning for a midterm. After getting married and becoming a dad, he wasn't such a daredevil now. Nick knew challenging the mountain was always a stupid idea. The mountain never lost. That was why after seeing a nasty weather system moving in, he and Iain had changed their plans from a more challenging route to an easier climb.

Radios sprung to life once again as someone asked for the

ETA on a Sno-Cat. About time. Except what Jake really wanted was to see his friends walk through the doors with an epic tale to tell.

He stared at the door. No sign of Nick or Iain. Only two rescue leaders talking in hushed tones.

Damn. A heavy weight pressed down on Jake.

Nick had been his best friend since kindergarten class. They'd grown up together. Learned to climb together. Joined OMSAR together. Done everything together. Well, almost everything.

Jake swallowed around the lump of guilt in his throat. He should have been on the climb with them—a climb to celebrate Iain's upcoming marriage to Nick's younger sister, Carly—but Jake had said no. Attending the wedding was enough for him. A climb would have been salt to the wound. Okay, his heart. He thought he'd been following his gut, but maybe the decision not to climb had been selfish. If he'd said yes…

Sean Hughes, one of the rescue leaders who'd been talking by the door, motioned for Jake and two other experienced members, Bill Paulson and Tim Moreno, to come over. "Here's the plan. Avalanche hazard is high and the weather isn't the greatest. A Sno-Cat will take us to the top of Palmer. When we get there, SAR base is expecting us to call in a condition report to decide if we're staying put or if any searching is possible."

Every one of Jake's muscles tensed. At the top of the Palmer ski lift was a building where they could warm up, regroup and wait for the conditions to improve. Sitting around wasn't going to get the job done. They needed to head out in the field.

He zipped his parka. "Nick wouldn't hang around and wait if one of us was up there."

"We're not waiting, either." Sean lowered his voice so no

one could hear him. "We'll call in a report, then head up and bring them home."

Jake picked up his pack and swung it onto his shoulders. "Damn straight we will."

The two others grunted their agreement, even though rescuer safety came first in any mission. But when one of your own went missing, risk level changed.

"Let's hit it," Sean said, turning on his headlamp.

Jake followed Sean out of the lodge and into the frigid air. Tim and Bill brought up the rear. The media followed, taking pictures of them, the flashes like lightning, as they trudged their way through the heavy wind and darkness to the Sno-Cat. Freezing mist created a haze on Jake's goggles. Each breath stung. It had to be hell at the summit. What could have happened up there?

Maybe Nick or Iain had gotten injured. Hurt. Maybe they couldn't get cell coverage. Or the batteries had died. Maybe they were waiting out the weather in a snow cave. Maybe—

"Jacob."

The familiar feminine voice wrapped around him like an electric blanket set on high. Soft, warm, perfect. He reminded himself that Carly Bishop's heart belonged to Iain.

But that didn't mean Jake couldn't look and appreciate.

Even with her long, blond hair tucked inside a green ski cap, her cheeks flushed from the freezing temperatures and her eyes red and swollen from crying, she was the best thing he'd seen this morning.

"Carly." He noticed a photographer watching them. The press would sell their firstborn to get an exclusive interview with the fiancée and sister of the missing climbers. "Get inside. It's too cold out here."

She shoved her gloved hands in the pockets of her orange down jacket, which was actually one of Iain's. Her breath hung on the air. "Colder up on the mountain."

Where Iain and Nick were. His eyes met hers in unspoken understanding.

Jake blinked against the biting mist, against the sting in his eyes. "We're heading up to find them."

She inhaled sharply. "Th-they said the search was on hold until conditions improved."

"The conditions are good enough for us."

"Thank you so much." Her eyes glistened with tears. "You have no idea what this means to our family and me."

Jake knew. He was closer to the Bishops than his own parents. That was one reason he'd tried to never treat Carly as anything other than his best friend's kid sister. Well, that, and the age difference. She was twenty-two, four years younger than him. That difference in age meant nothing now, but the gap had been huge when they were teenagers.

Though right now she looked more like a kid than ever. Young and vulnerable. Jake wanted to say something to comfort her, but he hadn't a clue where to start.

"I know it's rough up there and what you're up against. But please, Jacob, do whatever…everything you can." Carly's voice cracked. "T-tomorrow is…"

December twenty-fourth. Christmas Eve. Her and Iain's wedding day.

Jake had the wedding invitation on his fridge and their gift under his Christmas tree. Tears streamed unchecked down her face. His already-aching heart constricted.

"I promise you, Carly." He wiped the tears off her cheeks with his gloved hand. He didn't dare allow himself to do more, and his caution had nothing to do with the photographer watching them. "I'll find Nick and Iain. Today."

Or Jake wasn't coming back down.

CHAPTER ONE

As SNOW FLURRIES fell from the gray sky, Carly Bishop stared at the charming log house surrounded by towering fir trees and decorated with strands of white icicle lights. A lopsided four-foot-tall snowman, complete with carrot nose, stood in the front yard. A single electric candle shone through a wood-paned window, the flickering flame-shaped bulb a welcoming light.

Carly walked along the snow-dusted path, dragging her wheeled suitcase behind her. A few feet from the porch she noticed a green wreath tied with a red velvet bow hanging from a brass holder on the front door. The scent of pine was sharp in the air. The same way it had been…

Her breath caught in her throat.

The house, the wreath, the candle, the snowman. It was as if time had stopped, as if the last six years had simply been a bad dream. Any second, Carly expected Nick to fling open the front door wearing a Santa hat, and greet her with a jolly ho-ho-ho. And Iain…

Iain.

She closed her eyes, fighting an onslaught of unwelcome memories.

I can't believe you're going climbing two days before our wedding. Why don't you just admit it, Iain? You love climbing more than you love me.

She'd wanted to forget. The argument and tears before and as he'd left to climb. The thoughts about his selfish behavior while he'd been climbing and dying. The grief and guilt after his body and Nick's had been found.

Carly thought she had forgotten. Put the past behind her. Moved on. She forced herself to breathe.

Coming back had been a mistake.

She should have stayed in Philadelphia, where she'd made a new life for herself, far away from the shadow of Mount Hood and all the mountain had stolen from her. If only staying away had been an option, but her brother's widow, Hannah, was expecting a new baby and needed help with her two children.

So here Carly was. Ready to be an aunt extraordinaire for her niece and nephew. For better or, most likely, worse.

Two weeks. All she had to do was survive the next two weeks, including December twenty-fourth, the twenty-fifth and New Year's Eve. How hard could that be? Given she hadn't celebrated the holidays in years, she didn't want to know the answer.

Carly tightened her grip on the suitcase handle and climbed the steps to the front porch. With a tentative hand, she reached for the doorknob then remembered this was no longer her brother's house. She pressed the doorbell and waited.

The doorknob jiggled.

Straightening, Carly forced a smile. Years of working with customers had taught her how to put on a happy face no matter how she felt inside.

The door cracked open.

"Welcome back, Carly," a male voice greeted her warmly.

She expected to see Hannah's husband of two years, Garrett Willingham, but the man standing in the doorway looked nothing like the clean-cut, non-risk-taking, business-suit-wearing certified public accountant. This guy was too rugged, too fit, too...familiar.

"Jacob Porter." Over six feet tall with brown hair that fell past his collar, he still had piercing blue eyes, a killer smile and a hot, hard body that had made the girls, herself included, swoon back in high school. But those things had only been made better with age. Her pulse kicked up a notch. "What are you doing here?"

"Waiting for you." His grin widened, the same way it had whenever he and Nick teased her about something. "Merry Christmas."

"Merry..." Simply thinking the word left a bitter taste in her mouth. She couldn't bring herself to say it. "Seasons greetings. Where's Hannah?"

"At a doctor's appointment," Jacob explained. "Garrett drove her. She didn't know if they'd be home before you arrived or the school bus dropped Kendall and Austin off so they asked me to come over."

Carly noticed Jacob's clothes—a light blue button-down oxford shirt, khaki pants and brown leather shoes. A bit more stylish than the T-shirts, jeans or shorts and sneakers she remembered him wearing. He must have been at work.

"Thank you." Though she wasn't surprised. Jacob had always gone out of his way for them, a surrogate everything to what remained of the Bishop family. He'd found her the job in Philadelphia. He'd taught Nick's two kids to ski and fish. He'd even introduced Hannah to Garrett.

"Hurry inside before you get too cold." Jacob reached for Carly's suitcase. His hand—big, calloused and warm—brushed hers. The accidental contact startled her, and she jerked her hand away. "You city girls aren't used to the temperatures up here."

Forget the cold. She wasn't used to her response to his touch. Carly couldn't remember the last time a man had had that effect on her. "It gets cold in Philadelphia, too."

As she stepped into the house, heat surrounded her, co-cooning her with the inviting comforts of home. She glanced around, noticing all the nice homey touches. Ones missing from her apartment.

"You look the same," he said.

He looked better. She glanced around. "So does this place."

And that somehow made everything…worse.

A fire blazed and crackled in the fireplace. The way it had that horrible, dark Christmas morning when a teary-eyed Hannah had told the kids to unwrap their gifts from Santa.

Carly wanted to close her eyes, to shut off the video of years gone by streaming through her mind, but the fresh evergreen scent, the twinkling multicolored lights and the ornament-laden branches wouldn't let her.

The popcorn-and-cranberry-strung garland, keepsake decorations marking special occasions, and silver bells and gold balls all reminded Carly of the rush to take the tree down before Nick's funeral. Hoping to protect the children, Hannah hadn't wanted the event to be associated with Christmas in any way. Her efforts seemed to have worked, but Carly couldn't think of one without the other.

The door closed. The sound made her glance back.

Jacob stared at her, an unrecognizable emotion in his eyes.

She remembered the time, during an argument with Iain, she'd turned to Jacob for advice. There'd been a moment when she thought he might kiss her. He'd been looking at her then the same way as now.

Her temperature rose—the combo of forced-air heating and fireplace, no doubt—and she shrugged off her jacket.

"I'll take that." He hung her coat on the rack by the door. "It's good to see you again."

"You, too." And she meant that. Funny, but seeing him hadn't brought back any bad memories. That surprised her. "How are things at the Wy'East Brewing Company?"

"Good."

Jacob's family owned and operated a microbrewery and pub in the alpine-inspired touristy Hood Hamlet, a small town set high on Mount Hood, fueled year-round by outdoor enthusiasts. Nick had worked there. Iain and Carly, too.

That seemed like another life. Who was she kidding? It had been another life.

"Hannah told me things are going well in Philadelphia," Jacob said.

"They are. Didn't you get my last e-mail?" Carly tried to keep in touch with him. Not daily, but an e-mail or two a month.

"I did. She mentioned you had a boyfriend."

"Wishful thinking on her part." It wasn't as if Carly hadn't had any boyfriends over the last six years—okay, two—but both relationships had petered out. "I date, but I'm too busy with work for a serious relationship right now."

"You've really moved your way up the ladder, Miss Brewpub Manager extraordinaire."

"I have, haven't I?" She loved managing the restaurant

portion of Conquest Brewery, but Carly had never wanted to be one of those focused career types working megahours. She'd wanted to be a wife. Iain's wife. Boy, had she been young, starry-eyed and idealistic back then. "But I still owe you for getting me that waitress job."

"You don't owe me anything—" Jacob winked "—but if I need an extra hand at the brewpub over the holidays, I'll give you a call."

"Deal." Jacob might be even better-looking than before, but he was still the same inside. She found that…comforting, as well as the memories now surfacing. A smile tugged on her lips. "Do you remember when we would brainstorm names for your seasonal brews?"

"I remember." He shook his head. "Especially the time you wanted to name everything after Macbeth."

Carly grinned. "Hamlet."

"Whatever."

She nudged his arm with her elbow. "Hey, some of the names were quite clever, and considering your brewery *is* located in a hamlet—"

"Yeah, like the guys buying the beer have a clue what a hamlet is."

"Maybe not the exact definition of a hamlet, I'll give you that. But the words 'brewed and bottled in Hood Hamlet' are printed on every single bottle."

Jacob raised a brow. "Nothing could justify naming a seasonal ale, and I quote, 'To Beer or Not to Beer.'"

"That was a great name." She searched her memory for the others. "Don't forget Lady Doth Protest Porter, Mind's Eye Amber, Less than Kind IPA, Soul of Wit Pale Ale. Instant classics. I'm telling you."

"You can tell me all you want, but that doesn't mean I'll ever use them."

She drew her brows together. "Maybe I should give those names to the master brewer where I work."

"Go for it, but that brewery isn't located in a hamlet so you might have a hard sell on your hands."

"Not if he recognizes genius at work."

"More like plagiarizing at work."

Carly laughed. Jacob's teasing filled an empty space inside her she'd forgotten existed. She had friends—good friends—in Philadelphia, but none who had watched her grow up. Who knew the people who'd mattered most in her life. Who knew what she had been like before being thrown the ultimate curveball.

"So what brilliant name did you come up with for this year's seasonal brew?" she asked.

Jacob's eyes met hers. Softened. "Nick's Winter Ale."

The name hung in the air as if a cartoon dialogue bubble surrounded the three words. Carly swallowed around the snowball lump of emotion lodged in her throat. "The beer he came up with right before…?"

Her life had been divided into two parts—before and after the accident. Things had gotten better with the passage of time. She no longer felt the familiar sting each time she thought about Nick. That dreaded prickling sensation hadn't brought a rush of unexpected tears in…years.

Jacob nodded once. "It's a good brew. He worked hard on it. Seemed time to use the recipe."

Nick had been so proud of the beer he'd created. He had been sure the brew would be the next year's seasonal ale. It probably would have been. "That's wonderful. Nick would be happy."

"That's what Hannah said. Your mom and dad, too."

Carly's parents had divorced after Nick's death. Her father now lived in Oregon. Her mother lived in Scottsdale, Arizona. Both had remarried. "You've spoken to them?"

"Yes, they sounded pleased," he answered. "Each asked for labels and a bottle."

She wasn't surprised. Nick had been the golden boy. No one, not Carly, their grandkids or each other, could fill the gap left in her parents' hearts with his death.

"So do I get any?" Carly asked.

"I have a whole case for you. Labels, too. I'll drop them off."

"Thanks."

"Come on—" Jacob motioned for her to follow "—the kids will be home soon. I need to fix them a snack."

"Wait a minute. You're going to fix them a snack?" The top of her head came to his chin. She looked up at him. "You guys always made me heat up the frozen pizzas and fix whatever else you wanted to eat."

"Good practice for when you're on your own," he said.

"I'll have you know, I've been on my own for—" Six years. She swallowed a sigh.

Jacob didn't appear to notice. "I meant with the kids. They'll expect you to fix their snack for them. And when Hannah goes into the hospital to have the baby—"

"I can handle it." Once upon a time, Carly had dreamed of having children of her own. But like her other dreams, that one seemed to have died on the mountain, too. So she made the most of whatever time she could get with her niece and nephew, meeting them wherever they spent their summer vacation. Anywhere except here in the Pacific Northwest.

She hadn't wanted to come back. "Spending time with Kendall and Austin will be great."

His smile crinkled the corners of his eyes, and her heart bumped. "We'll see how you feel in a few days."

Forget a few days. Carly didn't like how she felt right now. But that had nothing to do with her niece and nephew and everything to do with the man standing in front of her. Still, she was a survivor, and like everything else, she would get through this. She raised her chin. "It'll be no problem at all."

No problem. Yeah, right.

Jake had a big problem. Her name started with *C* and ended with *Y.* He grabbed a Granny Smith apple from the fruit bowl and placed it on the wood cutting board.

Maybe if he concentrated on fixing the kids' snack he could forget how Carly's turtleneck sweater hugged her breasts and the curve of her waist. How her well-worn jeans cupped her bottom like a second skin. How her blond hair, now shoulder length, would look spread out over a pillowcase or a man's chest.

His chest.

It was all Jake could do not to stare. Hell, drool. He reached for a knife.

Damn, she looked good. Better than he remembered.

The cold temperatures outside brought a natural color to her cheeks. Thick lashes, ones she'd had since she was little, framed expressive hazel eyes, eyes that no longer held the optimistic promise of tomorrow, but hinted at new depths he hadn't seen before. And those pink, full lips smiling up at him made him think about kisses. And the one time he should have kissed her, but had hesitated and lost her. Not that he needed kisses now. A taste of those glossed lips, simply a nibble, was all he really wanted, but that wouldn't be a smart move.

Hell, it would be downright stupid.

As he sliced the apple, the knife hit the cutting board with a thud.

"Be careful." Carly neatly placed cheese and crackers on a plate. "You don't want to lose a finger."

Right now, he was more worried about losing his heart. Dammit.

His heart was off-limits, especially to a woman who was the only person aside from his father to call him Jacob and had left town six years ago never to return until now. Okay, not exactly true. She hadn't been gone six years. Five years, seven months and twenty-eight days, if he wanted to be exact. Not that he'd been counting.

Granted she'd had her reasons. Good reasons.

But that hadn't made her leaving any easier. Which reminded him. She wasn't here to stay. Hannah had said two weeks. Long enough to turn everyone's life upside-down, including his. He wanted no part of it. No part of her.

Besides, she deserved better than him.

Jake cut another piece of apple.

"The cheese and crackers are ready." She placed an artfully designed plate on the table. "What next?"

"Hot chocolate." He handed her the kettle from the top of the stove.

She frowned. "Won't the water be too hot?"

"If it is, we add ice cubes."

"You've got this kid snack routine down."

Jake put the apple slices and a small container of caramel sauce on a plate. "I help out when needed."

She filled the kettle with water. "How often is that?"

Not nearly enough. He set the plate on the table. "Whenever Hannah or Garrett can't be here."

"They're lucky to have you."

Jake was the lucky one.

A door slammed shut. Thuds of varying volumes echoed through the house. Voices sounded, yelled, screeched.

He glanced at the clock on the microwave. "The bus was early today."

"So a herd of elk hasn't just walked into the house?"

"Elk would be quieter."

With a smile, Carly hurried out of the kitchen. Jake followed her, trying to ignore the sway of her hips. Maybe he needed to go out tonight. Between work and OMSAR activities, he hadn't been dating much. A woman—make that a woman other than Carly—would get his mind right where it needed to be.

"Aunt Carly!" Seven-year-old Austin ran into her arms before she took three steps into the living room. "You're here."

"I told you she was here." Kendall, nine years old, hugged Carly. "I saw a different car in the driveway."

Carly held both of the kids tight as if she didn't want to let go of them. "I can't believe how much you've grown since last summer."

Austin beamed. His blond hair stuck up all over the place. "We're big now."

Carly laughed. "So big."

"Mom asked us to stop growing," Austin said. "But I told her that was impossible."

Kendall rolled her eyes. "Mom was kidding."

"Kidding or not, I understand why she said that." Carly

kissed the tops of the kids' heads, staring at them with longing and love. "I wish you would stay little forever."

Watching the three together brought a bittersweet feeling to Jake's heart. The kids needed Carly. Not only when Hannah delivered the baby or when they went on vacations, but also on a regular basis, where they could share their lives and days with their father's sister. With their aunt.

Carly stared at Austin. "You look so much like your daddy."

A perplexed look crossed the young boy's face. "Which daddy? The dead one or the one who's alive?"

Kendall's long sigh could have propelled all the windmills in eastern Oregon. She tucked a blond curl behind her ear. "Our first daddy, right, Aunt Carly?"

"That's right." Her voice cracked slightly.

Jake fought the urge to reach out to Carly. He knew that kick to the gut the first time he'd heard the kids call Garrett "daddy" all too well. Jake still wasn't used to it. He didn't know if he would ever be, even though he liked the guy enough to introduce him to his best friend's widow.

"Every time I see you, Austin, you look more and more like him," Carly continued. "The two of you could be twins."

"Even if they look the same—" Kendall tilted her chin "—Uncle Jake says I'm the one who's more like him."

"It's true," Jake said. Austin might look like a mini version of Nick, but Kendall had identical mannerisms and her father's fearlessness. "You have the exact same personality."

Which made it harder for Hannah and Garrett.

But easier for Jake.

"I noticed that when we were vacationing in Gettysburg," Carly said.

Kendall grinned. "You have to see my room, Aunt Carly.

It's purple and blue and green. Uncle Jake bought me this cool, furry beanbag chair."

Carly glanced his way. "Sounds comfy."

"I have a space room." Austin held on to her hand and bounced. "Uncle Jake put glow-in-the-dark stars and planets on the ceiling. He also bought me a spaceship light. It's the coolest."

"Sounds like Uncle Jacob's been busy around here."

He shrugged.

"You mean Uncle Jake, don't you?" Kendall asked.

"Um, yes, your Uncle J-Jake," Carly said, as if testing the name for the first time.

That was the first time he remembered her calling him Jake. He liked how his name sounded coming from her lips.

"I can't wait to see both your rooms." She sounded every bit the enthusiastic aunt, much to the kids' delight. "But first you need to have your snack."

"Snack!" The kids stampeded into the kitchen.

Carly glanced at Jake. "Forget elk, those two could give buffalos a run for their money."

"You handled that well."

She shrugged. "Not much else I can do."

"No, there's not, but that doesn't mean it doesn't hurt."

Carly looked down at the hardwood floor. "They're just kids. And life goes on."

"Hannah does her best to keep Nick's memory alive. So do I."

"Thanks. I appreciate that. Nick would, too." Carly noticed a picture of Garrett, Hannah and the two kids sitting on the mantel. "Still, it's weird. I like Garrett. He's a great guy who adores Hannah and loves the kids as if they were his own, but he's so different from Nick."

"Hannah didn't want another Nick," Jake admitted.

Emotion clouded Carly's eyes. "I don't blame her for that."

"Come here." Jake placed an arm around Carly in a half hug. She leaned against him.

So nice.

Having her in his arms brought back a rush of memories. The time he'd found her shivering and whistling for help when she'd gotten lost snowshoeing at the age of fourteen. As he'd hugged her, trying to warm her up, he'd realized she wasn't a little girl anymore. Or the time she'd passed her driver's test and wanted to show off her license. Not to mention her short skirt and skimpy top. She'd given him a quick hug, letting him know she was a young woman, but still off-limits.

This time she was simply Carly Bishop, a beautiful woman. A single woman.

Against his better judgment, Jake brought his other arm around her, embracing her fully. He pulled her closer. Her body pressed against his. Warm, soft, perfect. The scent of grapefruit—her shampoo?—surrounded him.

Oh, man. Standing here with her in his arms was a dream come true. And even though he'd long since buried those dreams, Jake didn't want to let her go.

He brushed his lips across her forehead, offering what comfort he could.

Someone screeched.

Jake stepped back from Carly to see Austin staring wide-eyed and openmouthed.

Kendall bolted out of the kitchen. "What is going on?"

"Uncle Jake kissed Aunt Carly." Austin's grin lit up his face. "Now they have to get married."

CHAPTER TWO

MARRIED? TO JACOB? No way.

Carly stared at the kids, jumping and giving each other high fives. She needed to gain control fast or this could set the tone for the next two weeks.

She stuck two fingers in her mouth and blew, the way Nick had taught her. The loud, sharp whistle quieted Kendall and Austin.

Thanks, Nick. Once again her brother had saved her.

Too bad she hadn't been able to do the same for him.

The kids stared at her.

"Into the kitchen," she ordered in the same tone Hannah had used last summer in Colorado when a fight over whether to hike or swim erupted. "And sit at the table."

Even Jacob followed her instructions.

Carly hid a smile as he passed. Suddenly he stopped.

"This is all so sudden," Jacob murmured in her ear with an outrageous flutter of his eyelashes. Long, dark lashes, she couldn't help noticing. Ridiculously wasted on a guy. "Why didn't you tell me? I would have brought a ring."

Heat flooded her face. "Shut up. Sit down."

"Yes, ma'am." He took his place at the table with the kids. No one said anything.

"That's better." Carly followed them into the kitchen. She sat between Kendall and Austin, pushing the snacks toward them. "Why do you think we have to get married?"

"If you kiss someone, you have to marry them." Austin picked up an apple slice. "Sammy Ross told us at recess."

"You don't say." Jacob spoke with the utmost sincerity. "Sammy must be one of those guys who know everything."

Nodding, Austin dipped the apple into the caramel sauce. "He's got five older sisters. Three are in high school."

"That explains it." Jacob winked. "Better watch out who I kiss from now on."

Carly glared. Some help he was turning out to be.

Austin's eyebrows drew together. "You can only kiss the person you're going to marry, Uncle Jake. Aunt Carly."

Uh-oh. She straightened. Damage control was needed right away. "Austin—"

"I know you don't have to get married if you kiss someone, but wouldn't it be great if you got married anyway? You wouldn't have to go back to Philadelphia. And I could be your flower girl." Kendall's brown eyes implored her. "Please, oh, please. I've always wanted to be a flower girl."

Carly's chest tightened. She didn't want to hurt Kendall, but letting the nine-year-old think a wedding was in the works would be worse. The wedding march ranked right up there with Christmas carols when it came to music Carly didn't want to hear again. Besides, she didn't want Jacob to think she was interested in marrying him. It was bad enough Carly thought he was still hot after all these years. "No one is getting married, sweetie."

Kendall's face puckered.

Carly squeezed the girl's small hand. "I'm sorry."

The apology didn't keep the tears from welling in the young girl's eyes. Great, Carly had been with the kids for less than fifteen minutes and already made one of them cry. If this was any indication of how the next two weeks were going to go, she should drive back to Portland International Airport and fly home before she really messed things up.

"Come on, guys," Jacob said. "You're getting a new baby brother or sister next week. Your aunt is here for Christmas. That's plenty to celebrate."

With a frown, Austin stared at Jake. "But you kissed her. I saw you. You have to get married. Those are the rules."

"I only kissed your Aunt Carly on her forehead, buddy. That's what friends do." He flashed her another one of those teasing, tempting grins. "Good friends."

Carly caught her breath.

The gesture had been a little too friendly. As Jacob had comforted her in the living room, Carly had felt a security and a sense of belonging she hadn't felt in years. She'd forgotten everything and hadn't wanted the moment to end. Thank goodness for Austin's screech or she might have done something stupid like kiss Jacob herself. Not on the forehead, but on the lips.

What was going on?

She hadn't wanted to kiss anyone in a while. Nor did she want to feel compelled to kiss anyone, especially someone who lived on the other side of the country. Okay, she'd once been curious about his kiss, but she'd been a girl then. Not a grown-up. Best to keep her distance from him while she was here.

"So if you kiss a girl on the forehead you don't have to

marry them, but if you kiss them on the lips, you do?" Austin asked.

Carly bit back a sigh. "Sammy Ross might think you have to marry the person you kiss, but that's not how it really works."

"How does it work?" Kendall asked.

Feeling like a preschool teacher suddenly taking on a sex education class full of randy teenagers, Carly looked at Jacob for help. He tipped his chair back, clearly content to wait for her response. The devil.

"Well." She wasn't sure how to proceed, but catching a red-eye flight back East sure looked tempting. "First you meet someone you like, then you date, then you fall in love and then, once you know you'll get along for a long time, you marry."

Talk about an abbreviated lesson on dating. Maybe she should have told them to ask their mother instead. But Jacob flashed her the thumbs-up sign. She must have done okay to warrant that or he might have simply been trying to make her feel better.

"Where does the kissing come into it?" Kendall asked.

Carly didn't bother looking at Jacob this time. Hearing a nine-year-old ask about kissing would probably paralyze any single guy. "Kissing can happen at any of those steps, but that's something you do when you're older."

"Much older." Jacob told Kendall. Funny, he sounded more like a dad than a bachelor.

The girl's gaze darted between Carly and Jacob. "But you two could still get married. Then I could be a flower girl."

"We can't get married," Carly said. "We're…friends."

"Shouldn't you be friends with the person you marry?" Kendall asked.

The girl was too smart for her own good. Carly needed to be more careful with what she said. "Of course, you should be friends, but Uncle Jake and I are…more like brother and sister."

Though that wasn't really true. She'd never seen him as a brother. Growing up, she'd wanted him to be her boyfriend.

"He's not your brother though. My daddy was your brother." Two lines formed over Kendall's nose, the same way they used to on Nick, making Carly's chest tighten. "But if you married Jake, he'd really be our uncle, not just someone we call uncle, and I could be a flower girl, Aunt Carly. Jessica Henry has gotten to be a flower girl twice. And I've never even been asked to be one."

Carly knew what growing up and comparing yourself to someone else felt like. She needed to tell her niece something, even if it meant facing the part of her past she'd tried hard to forget. "Did you know a long time ago, when you were only three years old, you were going to be a flower girl?"

"I was?"

She nodded.

"Was I going to wear a pretty dress?" Kendall asked.

"Yes," Carly said. "A very pretty red dress made out of velvet and taffeta with layers of tulle to make the skirt poof out and a wreath of flowers in your hair."

"You looked like a princess wearing it," Jacob added.

Remembering, Carly smiled softly. "You sure did."

"But I never saw any pictures of me dressed like that," Kendall said.

Jacob started to speak, but Carly stopped him. "The wedding never happened."

Kendall tilted her chin. "Why?"

Why? That question still haunted Carly. "The boy…the

man I was going to marry, his name was Iain, had an accident when he was climbing with your daddy."

Kendall's mouth formed a small O. "He died with my daddy on the mountain so you couldn't get married."

"Yes." Carly felt Jacob's gaze on her, but she didn't—couldn't—look his way. She didn't want to see sympathy or pity in his eyes. She'd had enough of that those first few months to last a lifetime. That was one of the reasons she'd left Hood Hamlet and headed to Philadelphia. She'd wanted to go some-where—anywhere—where she could make a fresh start.

"Did I know him?" Kendall picked up a cracker. "Iain?"

Carly nodded. "He thought you and Austin were the two coolest kids around and loved you so much."

"Do you miss him?" Kendall asked.

Carly forced herself to breathe. This was fast turning into the trip home to hell. Not that she blamed anyone, but dredg-ing up the past this way wreaked havoc with her emotions. Ones she'd thought were long under control.

"Yes, sometimes I still miss him." She inhaled deeply. All she wanted was five more minutes with Iain. Thirty seconds would do. To say goodbye with love, not frustration and anger as had been the case. "But you know what? Iain is still with me. The same way your daddy will always be with you. In your heart."

"That's what mommy said," Austin said. He'd been so quiet Carly had almost forgotten he was there. "But I don't remember him at all. Not even when I look at his picture."

"That's okay, buddy." Jacob mussed the boy's blond hair. "You were only a year old."

"That's right. You were just a little guy back then." Carly put her arm around Austin's chair. "But I can tell you lots of stories about your dad if you want. You can remember him that way."

Austin smiled. "Uncle Jake and Mommy tell me stories, but I want to hear yours."

"And you will." Carly cleared her throat. "I know some really good ones."

"I remember him. Our daddy." Kendall got a faraway look in her eyes. "Well, his voice. He used to sing to me."

Carly felt a tug on her heart. She could almost hear Nick's voice drifting down from the nursery upstairs. "Your daddy sang to you all the time. You loved the song 'My Favorite Things' from *The Sound of Music*."

"If he stopped singing that song, you would cry," Jacob said.

Austin laughed. "Crybaby, crybaby."

"Be quiet." Kendall frowned. "You're the one who's a big crybaby."

Austin folded his arms over his chest and pouted.

"That's enough, guys," Jacob said.

Austin returned to his snacks, but not Kendall.

"You know, Uncle Jake," she said. "If you started dating Aunt Carly tonight, you could probably get married before she has to go back home, and I could be a flower girl before I went back to school after winter break."

"Uh-huh. Listen, kiddo—" Jacob stopped, obviously unsure how to proceed. He rubbed his chin.

"You go after what you want, don't you, Kendall?" Carly asked.

The girl nodded.

"Your dad did the same thing." Nick never used to give up when he set his mind on something. That's how he'd ended up with Hannah. Carly smiled at the similarity between her brother and his daughter. "Tell you what. If I get married, you can be the flower girl and Austin can be the ring bearer."

"Promise?" The girl's hopes and dreams filled the one-word question.

"Your aunt said *if,* not *when,*" Jacob clarified. *If* being the key point, and Carly was grateful for him pointing it out.

"But if you do, Aunt Carly…"

Even Austin leaned toward her in anticipation of her response.

She smiled. "I promise."

Married? To Carly? Too funny.

Jake could barely contain his laughter when the kids had brought that up, but the way she'd sent dagger-worthy glares his way kept him quiet.

Poor Carly. Those kids had pushed every one of her buttons. Some twice. With a shake of his head, he carried Carly's suitcase upstairs.

She followed behind him. "I'd forgotten all about the wall of infamy."

He glanced back and saw Carly staring at the photographs. "You mean wall of family."

She didn't take her eyes off the pictures. "I call it as I see it."

"Me, too."

Eight years ago, he had dreamed about being a real part of the Bishop family, of having his photo up on that wall. A wedding photo. He'd wanted to be Nick's brother-in-law, Carly's husband. And then, while Jake was taking his time waiting for her to grow up, Iain had taken his shot at happiness. The daring young climber had almost blown it though, and given Jake another chance, but when all was said and done, Carly stuck with Iain after he apologized for putting a climb before her birthday.

At the time, Jake told himself everything worked out for the best. But it hadn't.

Not for Iain, killed right before his wedding.

Not for Carly, widowed before she was a bride.

Not for Nick, dead before his time.

And not for Jake, either.

He continued up the stairs.

But what had happened or how he had felt about Carly was in the past. All that remained was for him to make sure she was happy and living life the way she should. Once he knew that, then he, too, could move on.

"Hannah will run out of wall space someday." He glanced back and saw Carly still staring at the pictures. "Or photos."

"Wall space perhaps," she said. "But thanks to digital photography, Hannah will never run out of pictures."

"True, she carries her camera everywhere." He listened to the kids in the kitchen doing homework. "Hope that wasn't too much for you downstairs."

"Well, it's not every day you get into a head-on collision with your past."

"Good thing you had an air bag to soften the blow."

"What air bag?" Carly asked.

"Me."

"Oh, yes, that thumbs-up was a huge help."

"You were doing great on your own." He respected the way she handled the situation. "I just provided a little cushion."

Her mouth twisted on one side. "How can Mr. Hard Body be a cushion?"

He grinned, remembering the teasing from years gone by. "I'll take that as a compliment."

"You would."

Jake laughed. "Still the pesky little sister shadowing her big brother, aren't you?"

"Being here brings it all back." The amusement had disappeared from her voice. "But that's not such a bad thing. Living so far away, it's easy to forget."

He entered the guest room and placed the suitcase on the bed. "Everyone's missed you."

"I've missed them."

Jake had missed her, too. But he saw a new maturity in her, a difference from the girl she'd once been. That hadn't come across in her e-mails. He liked the changes.

"The promise you made to the kids," he reminded. "They will hold you to it."

"I expect them to."

"So you plan to marry someday."

She shrugged. "I've learned you can't really plan on something like that. But if I met someone and fell in love...well, maybe I'd want to marry him."

Not the answer Jake was looking for. "You don't sound like the girl who started reading bridal magazines when she was sixteen."

"I haven't met anyone I've wanted to marry...."

Except Iain.

Though Jake wondered how marriage to an adventurous, full-time climber would have been for Carly. Still, the fact she hadn't seemed to have gotten over Iain's death made Jake feel guilty. Okay, guiltier.

"But you could." He wouldn't be happy until she moved

on with her life the way Hannah had. Carly deserved a happy ending, too. Jake would somehow make sure she found one. He owed her that much.

"I could." Carly didn't sound that confident as she opened her suitcase.

Jake didn't blame her. He hadn't known what to make of Iain the first time he'd met him. The kid's confidence bordered on cockiness, but Jake had soon learned the talented climber had a heart of gold. He couldn't help but like and respect Iain. Envy him, too. For his fearlessness. For his climbing talent. For being the recipient of Carly's love and adoration.

At least until finding Iain's bloody, bruised and broken body covered in snow. The image had given Jake nightmares for years. He blinked, hoping to erase the picture in his mind. "You really should."

Another shrug. "Do we need to check on the kids?"

He listened to the sound of voices drifting upward. "Nope. I hear them."

"I thought it was good when kids were quiet."

"Noise is good," Jake said. "Quiet means start worrying, but I can hear them. We'll help them with their homework later."

"What about you?" Carly asked.

"My homework days are long past."

"That's not what I'm talking about." She picked up a black camisole from her suitcase and threw it at him. The same way she'd tossed a dishrag or a sweatshirt at him years ago.

He caught it as he always had. "Nice throw."

But the action felt too intimate to Jake in a way it never felt before. This was the kind of top a man peeled off a woman.

Pink tinged her cheeks. "Sorry, habit."

"It's okay." Jake handed her the top rather than tossing it back to her. "What did you want to know?"

"Have you given marriage much thought?" she asked.

He was hoping she wouldn't go there, but maybe after coming home to face her demons—and the devil kids downstairs—she deserved the truth. It wasn't as if the information would change anything between them. "I was engaged, but other than that…"

Her gaze met his. "Nobody told me. You never told me."

He shrugged. "It was four…no, five years ago."

"So what happened?"

His jaw tensed. "I don't want to talk about it. I barely remember it."

He'd wanted to forget. While Hannah and Carly had been holding themselves together, he'd been falling apart.

"Come on. Tell me," she urged. "Did you kiss her and then have to get married?"

If only it had been that simple.

"Not exactly." Jake wasn't proud of what he'd become or done back then. "I was partying too much, met a woman who was nice but totally wrong for me and asked her to marry me. Luckily I realized getting married wasn't the thing to do at that time in my life so I broke it off."

And got his out-of-control life back together.

"Do you ever think about settling down now?" Carly asked.

"No. I see no good reason to change the status quo."

She grinned. "That's what I say, too."

Jake found her words hard to believe, even harder to take. Her joy and excitement over her upcoming wedding to Iain seemed a hundred and eighty degrees away from where she was coming from now, and that hurt. She was meant to be a bride.

Someone else's bride, Jake reminded himself.

He didn't deserve her.

If he'd been on the mountain six years ago with Iain and Nick, everything would have been…different. Better. Okay.

And it was up to Jake to make things right.

For Hannah, Kendall, Austin and…

Carly.

CHAPTER THREE

PATRONS PACKED the bar and dining area of the Wy'East Brewing Company. Carly hadn't seen so many familiar faces since…

She felt a pang in her heart.

Since Nick's and Iain's funerals.

With a sigh, Carly glanced around the lodge-style building. Jacob's place. She could see the care he'd taken with it, the improvements he'd made to the interior and the menu offerings since taking over after his father retired.

The aromas of beer and grease mingling and wafting in the air reminded her of the brewpub she managed back home. The conversations of customers drowned out the music being piped in through speakers. At least Christmas carols weren't playing.

Too bad everything else was decked out for the holiday.

A swag decorated with miniature lights, pine cones and holly berries hung around the bar. Wreaths dangled from the vaulted log-beamed ceiling. A twinkling Christmas tree sat in the corner next to a small stage with neatly wrapped packages underneath.

Talk about being dropped in the middle of a nightmare before Christmas…. She shifted in her seat. Since arriving in Portland earlier today, she'd been forced to confront the worst moments of her life over and over again.

"Your adoring crowd awaits," a glowing and very pregnant Hannah teased.

Carly forced a smile. She didn't want to leave the comfort of this table, but she couldn't hide behind her sister-in-law's family for the next two weeks. Hannah was obviously excited. And Carly wanted her sister-in-law to be happy.

Fortified by a serving of shepherd's pie and a salad topped with raspberry vinaigrette, she stood. Working her way through the jam-packed restaurant, she received hugs while having the same conversation over and over again.

Yes, she lived in Philadelphia now.

No, she wasn't married yet.

Yes, it had been a long time.

She missed Iain, too.

Carly could hardly breathe as she spoke. Facing her demons was one thing, but this… She plodded through the way she had six years ago at her brother's funeral and then at Iain's, gritting her teeth and smiling. This time, however, the answers got easier to say the fifth time around. They became automatic by the tenth. Progress? Carly hoped so.

She looked around the room once more. She'd expected to see Jacob at some point this evening. This was his brewing company. His pub. Where was he on such a crowded Wednesday night? She brushed aside a twinge of disappointment.

It wasn't easy to do. If Jacob were here, he would make this not such an ordeal. He would make her feel normal, the way he had at the house, and comfortable.

After what seemed like hours but was really only one, Carly reached the spot where she'd begun. The dinner plates had been cleared from the knotty pine table. A pitcher of beer had joined the kids' and Hannah's pitcher of root beer. A slice of half-eaten mud pie and five spoons sat between Hannah and Garrett.

They were sharing. Happy.

There was no reason for Carly to be here.

And no one for her to be with.

She swallowed the pint-size lump in her throat and sat opposite them. "Hey, you lovebirds. Where are the kids?"

"With Jake," Hannah said.

So he was here after all. "I didn't notice him."

"He's been here the entire time."

And he hadn't come over to say hello? At least, not until she left the table.

Ouch.

Carly rested her elbows on the table and supported her chin with her hands. Making the rounds down memory lane had drained her mentally and physically. The last thing she needed to worry about was Jacob Porter.

"Sorry that took so long," she said. "I can't believe all the people I know who are here tonight. Most of the local OMSAR members, too."

"Word's out you're back in town." Garrett looked at Hannah. "Though I can't imagine who would have told them already."

"I may have mentioned it to a few people," said a sheepish Hannah.

"That's a good one, my beautiful wife." Garrett laughed. "Since your definition of a few ranges from two to two hundred."

"I'm sorry," Hannah said.

Carly bit back a sigh. She didn't want Hannah to feel bad. Besides, if Carly got all the hard stuff over with her first day in town, she could breeze through the rest of the trip. "Don't apologize. Now I won't have to search people out since I saw them all here tonight."

Hannah tucked her shiny, long, auburn hair behind her ears. "That's the spirit."

"She's being a good sport, my dear." With a smile, Garrett poured a pint from the pitcher containing a deep, amber-colored beer. He slid the glass in front of Carly. "Here. You earned this."

"Thanks." She appreciated Garrett's thoughtfulness, as well as the way he honored Hannah's past, making sure Nick's memory stayed alive with the kids and accepting Carly as a part of their family. "I really need this."

"Yes, you do." Hannah's green eyes danced. "It's Nick's Winter Ale."

Carly should have known. A jumble of emotions ran through, but the biggest one—pride—made her raise her glass. "To Nick."

"Hear, hear." Garrett joined in the toast. "To the brewmaster extraordinaire."

"And Iain," Hannah added.

Carly took a sip. She wanted to remain impartial, to judge the beer on its own merits, to…

Delicious. Refreshing. Absolutely perfect.

The velvety smooth ale struck a perfect balance between the malt and hops. Full-bodied with a hint of cinnamon. She had never tasted something so yummy. Of course, Carly wouldn't have expected any less from her big brother.

"Extraordinaire is right." Her smile couldn't begin to match the joy in her heart at Nick's accomplishment. "An awarding-winning winter ale if I ever tasted one."

Two hands rested on her shoulders. Large hands. Male hands.

Jacob.

No need to turn around and see he was the one standing behind her. She'd recognize the warmth of his touch and his familiar scent anywhere, even in a crammed brewpub with all the noise, sights and smells competing for attention.

He gave a gentle squeeze, but didn't move his hands away.

The gesture, no doubt meant to be platonic, sent unexpected tingles shooting out from the point of contact. Carly gulped. She hadn't experienced tingles in…years.

No big deal.

"From your lips to the judges' scores," Jacob said.

She glanced up at him. "It's delicious."

His gaze met hers. "I'm happy you like it."

"My new favorite."

"Mine, too. Especially if it keeps that big smile on your face."

The way he stared at her, as if she were the only woman in the room, made Carly's insides clench. Her temperature shot up. She looked away.

"Thanks for putting the beer into production." She watched a bead of moisture run down her glass. "It means…a lot."

"I know."

Carly got the feeling he knew a little too much. She took another swig of her beer, but the liquid did nothing to cool her off or help her relax.

So what if he still had his hands on her shoulders?

No big deal.

He might still be a total hottie, but she wasn't a schoolgirl with a crush on her brother's best friend. No reason to freak out.

Jacob removed his hands. Thank goodness. Carly blew out a puff of air.

As he sat on the bench next to her, his thigh brushed hers. More tingles and a burst of heat erupted where he'd touched her. She scooted away. "Where are the kids?"

"In my office playing cards," he said. "They finished their ice cream sundaes and were still hungry so I gave them cookies."

Hannah tsked. "You spoil them, Jake."

"I indulge them," he countered. "A big difference."

His easy grin made him look younger and so carefree. Compared to him, Carly felt old and troubled.

Sure, she was home for the first time in years surrounded by family and old friends. Laughter and cheers filled the air, a good time being had by all the smiling faces. But something was missing.

Not something, Carly realized.

Nick and Iain.

She looked across the table at Hannah, resting her head on Garrett's shoulder. How did she handle this? Not just evenings like this, but every night, every day, raising Nick's kids in his house, in his hometown where memories lay waiting around every corner.

Somehow Hannah had found the hope and the courage to love again. And had made her peace with the past.

Not Carly.

She had barely made it through dinner tonight.

She stared at her bare hands. There hadn't been an engagement ring on her finger for years—never a wedding band like Hannah had worn. And yet…

Carly glanced sideways at Jacob, her cheeks warming. She almost felt guilty for being so aware of the man sitting next to her. It seemed strange to be feeling this way, for reacting to his nearness and his touch. This was where Iain had tended bar and she waited tables. Where they would have celebrated their rehearsal dinner had he made it down the mountain.

But he hadn't made it down. And she hadn't died up there with him even though it had felt like that at the time.

Losing him and Nick had hurt so bad.

She had wanted only to forget, but perhaps it was time to follow Hannah's example and remember.

Instead of avoiding the past, Carly could try to embrace it. Maybe then she could finally put the pieces of her heart back together and learn to love…again.

Chasing a woman was never a good idea.

It ranked right up there with "Don't talk back to your father" and "Don't glissade down a mountain wearing crampons."

The next day, Jake's feet crunched through the ice-crusted snow covering the sidewalk.

"Carly," he yelled.

No response.

He could see her bright purple jacket as she paused outside Wickett's Pharmacy.

That was what had caught his eye. The purple jacket.

Jake had been standing by his office window—talking back to his dad, actually—when she hurried by on the sidewalk and he saw her cell phone drop from her pocket.

Returning it seemed like a good idea. A good deed. It sure beat arguing with the formidable Van Porter over his desire to review the brewery's most recent financial statement.

Except now Jake was chasing after Carly Bishop.

Running, not chasing.

"Carly," he called again.

She stopped and turned. "Jacob?"

He caught up to her. "Why do you keep calling me that?"

"Because Nick once told me you didn't like it."

"And here I was being a nice guy and returning this to you." He waved the slim, red rectangular gadget in the air. "Maybe I'll keep it."

"My phone?" She reached for it, but he raised the phone over his head. "No fair."

"Who said anything about playing fair. Finders keepers—"

She made a jump for the phone, but missed.

"Nice try."

Carly pursed her lips. "In case you forgot, *Jacob,* you and Nick used to tease me unmercifully and order me around like I was your maid or something. Calling you by your full name was my small way of getting back at you."

"What did you do to Nick?" Jake asked.

"I turned all his underwear pink."

"That wasn't very nice."

"The two of you following me on my first date with Iain and sitting behind us at the movies heckling wasn't nice, either."

He laughed, remembering. Nick hadn't trusted any guy with Carly. "We may have been a little rough on you."

"A little?"

"Okay a lot." He placed the phone on the palm of her gloved hand. "I found this on the sidewalk outside the pizza parlor."

"Thanks. I had no idea I dropped it. Must be my lucky day."

His, too.

Carly looked great in her parka, jeans and boots, the way she had at the brewpub. When she had stared up at him with those warm, clear hazel eyes of hers and smiled, he felt as if he'd fallen into a deep crevasse. Climbing out hadn't even entered his mind.

"Thanks, too, for dropping off the beer and the labels." Carly tucked the phone into her pocket, but this time she zipped it closed. "The kids were sorry they missed you."

Kids, not her. Not that Jake expected her to miss him.

"Did you have fun sledding?" he asked.

"A lot of fun. Though Kendall and Austin like to go so fast. I was sure I'd have to break out the Band-Aids."

An SUV drove past and honked. Mr. Freeman, who owned the general store. Jake and Carly both waved.

"You used to go pretty fast yourself," Jake said.

Carly grinned. "I was faster than you and Nick."

"We let you think that."

Her mouth gaped as a group of snowboarders walked around them. "You did not."

"We didn't," he admitted. "But we told ourselves we did."

Her smile returned.

Good, he thought. She needed to smile more.

A comfortable silence settled between them, but the rhythm and sounds of the hamlet continued.

Down the sidewalk, Muffy Stevens knocked icicles off the awning in front of the coffeehouse. A truck driver delivered boxes of produce to the corner café. Laughing skiers entered a local inn.

"No matter how some things change," Carly said finally, "other things stay the same. Same locals. Even the tourists."

"And my dad."

Sympathy filled her eyes. "Still having trouble with him?"

"Like you said, some things don't change." Jake glanced across the street at the brewpub. "He's been retired for two years, but still wants to control things at the brewery. He doesn't think I have it in me to take the business to the next level."

Now why the hell had he told her that?

Jake rocked back on his heels.

"It's got to be hard for him to let go," she said. "To move on."

"Yeah, must be."

Blond hair stuck out from her wool ski hat. Jake fought the urge to push the strands back under. He stuck his hands in his pockets instead.

Was it time to move on?

Or time—finally—to make his move?

Carly glanced at the town hall's clock tower. "I'd better get back to Hannah and Garrett's."

"Okay."

But it wasn't. Not really. Jake didn't want to say goodbye.

"I'll let you go, then." For now, he thought. "But let's grab dinner sometime."

Her pretty mouth dropped open. "But—"

"Friday," he said, as if she hadn't spoken. "Hannah doesn't go into the hospital until next week. I'll pick you up."

"I—"

"Seven o'clock tomorrow night," he continued, before she could say no, and left without looking over his shoulder.

Move on.

She needed this. And so did he.

* * *

At two-thirty in the morning, Carly sat at the kitchen table with a steaming cup of herbal tea. Snow fell outside the window. The snowplows would be working overtime to keep the roads clear.

She took a sip of the chamomile tea. The box claimed the blend would make the drinker sleepy. She sure hoped so. She hadn't had a good night's sleep since arriving in Hood Hamlet.

Carly wanted to blame her sleeplessness on the three-hour time difference between the East and West coasts, but she knew that wasn't the reason behind her restless nights. Every time she turned around the past seemed to collide into the present, from being here with Hannah and her family to walking the streets of Hood Hamlet to reach the post office. Not to mention Jacob…make that Jake…

She hesitated to call their upcoming dinner a date. The word *date* made her nervous. Besides, he hadn't given her a chance to say yes or no. She didn't know what to make of that.

Or…him.

Footsteps sounded in the hallway. Hannah waddled into the kitchen, wearing a turquoise fleece robe that didn't cover her pregnant belly. "I thought I heard someone get up."

"Sorry if I woke you."

"Trust me—" Hannah patted her tummy "—I wasn't sleeping. This little jelly bean started kicking as soon as I lay down and hasn't stopped."

"Want a cup of tea?" Carly asked.

"No, thanks." Hannah lowered herself into a chair. "If I drink anything, I'll be going to the bathroom every five minutes instead of every fifteen. I keep reminding myself I wanted to get pregnant again."

"The end result will be worth it," Carly said.

"I know, but I have to admit, I'm happy they're taking this one early. I don't want to be birthing a ten-pound baby. Austin was hard enough at nine pounds six ounces."

She grimaced.

"Don't worry," Hannah said. "They make babies cute so you forget what you go through during labor and delivery."

Carly laughed. "So what's on today's agenda?"

"I want to finish up the last batch of Christmas cards, get them in the mail and do some shopping if the roads are clear. I wanted to be finished with all the holiday stuff by now, but it hasn't happened."

Carly did her holiday shopping in September before any of the red and green decorations hit the stores and carols played nonstop. She wasn't particularly organized, but Christmas had become so entwined with the accident she wanted no part of it. "I can take your cards to the post office."

If she dropped them into the box outside, she could avoid any more reminders of the holly-jolly season.

"That would be great. But I'm out of Christmas stamps. Would you mind—?"

She drew a deep breath. "No problem." So, she'd have to actually go into the post office. It wasn't as if Hannah had asked her to brave the mall with the kids or do any of those other things she avoided doing in December. All Carly had to do was buy stamps. "I'll take care of it."

"Thanks." The only light in the kitchen was from the stove, but Hannah's smile lit up her face. "That will be a big help. I don't have the energy to stand in line. Not to mention I'm as big as a mail truck."

"No, you're not." Carly wrapped her cold fingers around

her warm cup. "Just tell me what needs to be done. That's why I'm here."

"How is being back here going for you?" Hannah asked.

Carly took another sip of tea, the warm liquid coating her dry throat. "Fine."

"Fine as in everything's great or fine as in not really, but I don't want to bother you?"

"Something in the middle of those two."

Hannah rubbed her lower back. "Want to talk about it?"

"Not really."

"That bad, huh?"

"Not bad, it's just being back here has been a little… strange." Carly stared into her cup of herbal tea. "I look around and I can't help but wonder…"

"What?" Hannah asked.

This had been the elephant in the room Carly had avoided talking about. This probably wasn't the right time, either, but with the kids around she never had Hannah to herself. And Carly really needed to talk about this. Now more than ever.

"It's just…" She took a deep breath. "If I had convinced Iain not to climb instead of fighting with him, Nick wouldn't have died."

The only sound in the kitchen was an occasional ice cube dropping into the bucket in the freezer.

"Nick made his own decision to climb that day. He could have said no," Hannah said finally.

"I should have told Nick not to go." Carly stared at her fingernails. "Iain was upset when he left. If he was distracted… If his mind wasn't in the right space—"

"Accidents happen. It wasn't your fault. It wasn't anyone's fault."

Carly wanted to believe that. Desperately. "I still wish I would have talked Iain into staying home."

"And I wish I had told Nick to stay home," Hannah admitted. "But we can't change what happened. All we can do is live our lives the way Nick and Iain would have wanted us to live."

Carly reached across the table and squeezed Hannah's hand. "That's what you're doing. Nick would be so proud of you. I admire you so much."

Another ice cube clattered into the plastic bin.

"I climbed it," Hannah said, her voice a mere whisper in the dead of night.

It. The mountain. Carly shivered. "When?"

"Three years ago. In May. Jake and Sean Hughes took me up." Hannah stared out the window. "I wanted to stand on the summit the way Nick had done so many times and see what he saw. So I could try to understand."

"Understand?"

"Why he loved climbing so much." Hannah sighed. "I used to consider the mountain my nemesis. Mount Hood. The other woman in our marriage."

Carly understood completely. Iain had his eye on peaks around the world, including Antarctica. "I sometimes wondered who Iain loved more. Me or his mountains. Who he would have chosen if he could have picked only one of us."

"He loved you. Just like Nick loved me and the kids." Hannah tilted her chin. "But the mountains held an allure for them. Nick thrived on the mental and physical challenges of climbing, but he told me once the mountains were the place he found joy and felt most comfortable."

"Were you comfortable up there?" Carly asked.

"No, I was scared to death," Hannah admitted. "I didn't know if I could make it to the top. I remember standing in the parking lot at Timberline and looking up, thinking it was so far away. And it was. The slog up to Palmer took forever. The sulfur smell from the Devil's Kitchen made me so nauseous I thought I might throw up. I wanted to stop, but when I saw the triangular shadow of the mountain to the west Nick had told me about so many times…I had to keep going as much for myself as him. It wasn't easy. The ice on the Pearly Gates intimidated me, but I knew I was so close."

Carly listened, totally amazed by what Hannah, who had a paralyzing fear of heights and had never climbed anything in her life other than stairs, was telling her.

"Standing on the summit was…surreal." Hannah sighed. "All that snow and ice. I was so tired, completely wiped out by the climb, and I felt so small compared to everything around me, but there was such a sense of accomplishment. Of having made it to the top of something so big when I didn't think I could.

"The views were incredible and took my breath away. Jake had pointed out where Nick would have crossed the saddle of Illumination Rock to get to the Reid Headwall. It didn't matter that I couldn't see where the accident happened. I just thought about Nick and how he'd stood here and seen the same things. The morning sun glimmering on the Columbia River. The line of snow-capped volcanic peaks running to the north and south. All these other beautiful sights below me. I felt so…so close to him, as if he were right there with me, and everything was okay again. I could finally understand and not hate what he loved doing or this mountain where he'd died."

"Wow."

"It was definitely wow worthy, but I have no desire to climb again. I couldn't wait to get back down." The corners of Hannah's mouth turned up in a satisfied smile. "But I got the closure I wanted. Needed. And that's what you need to do yourself."

Carly's heart slammed against her chest. "Climb Mount Hood?"

"You've already done that."

Not since Iain had taken her up and proposed on the summit.

"You need to find whatever it is that will give you closure so you can move on," Hannah continued.

"I have moved on."

Hannah raised her eyebrows.

"Really," Carly insisted. "This trip has been good for that."

"And Jake?" Hannah asked. "Where does he fit into all this?"

A beat passed.

"We're friends."

Hannah drew her brows together. "Are you sure that's all you are?"

The concern in Hannah's voice and eyes sounded an alert in Carly's head. She straightened. "What do you mean?"

"Well, you liked him when you were younger."

Had her feelings been so transparent to everyone? Carly sighed. "Jake was my brother's best friend and always around. It was safe. A crush, nothing else."

"But he has asked you out to dinner."

"It's not a date. At least, I don't think it's a date."

"Uh-huh." Hannah used the table to help her stand. She rubbed her lower back again. "And what does Jake think?"

CHAPTER FOUR

MOVE ON? Or make his move?

Jake wasn't sure what he wanted as he sat across from Carly at Mama Amici's, a family-run Italian café. Things were not going well. The din of conversations from other customers only intensified the silence between them. He never expected tonight to be so damn uncomfortable.

Forget about what he might want. He needed to think about what Carly needed. Doing that, Jake knew exactly what he needed to do—reconnect with her as a friend. One who'd watched her grow up and cared about what happened to her. His job was to make her smile, laugh and relax so when she returned to Philadelphia she would be ready to move on. To love again.

Love someone else.

Jake shifted in the booth. Might as well jump on it. "It's just you and me here, Carly. No need to be nervous."

She placed the napkin she'd been toying with on her lap. "Do I seem nervous?"

So far, she had spilled her water, dumped the contents of her purse and dropped her knife onto the floor.

Jake shrugged. "Maybe a little tense."

"It's been a while since I've been…"

"Out to dinner," he offered.

She tilted her chin. "I had dinner at your brewpub the other night."

"That's right, and you didn't look as tense there." He swirled his glass of Chianti. "Or keep eying the door like you're ready to bolt."

"Sorry." Carly glanced around the restaurant until her gaze rested on the flickering votive candle on their table. "It's just…this feels sort of like a date and I'm not sure what it's supposed to be."

"It's not a date. Dinner with a friend."

He'd purposely picked this casual mom-and-pop café with its vinyl-covered booths and red-checked tablecloths so the evening wouldn't feel like a date. He hadn't wanted her to get the wrong idea. Hell, he hadn't wanted to get the wrong idea himself.

"If this was a date," Jake continued. "I would have taken you to a place where the smell of garlic doesn't smack you in the face when you walk in the door. You know, one of those fancy places where the waiter shakes out your napkin for you and they make you sniff the cork."

The corners of her mouth turned up. Her lips opened, giving him a clear view of her straight, white teeth. Those braces she'd complained about for three years had been worth it.

But he still wanted to see a full smile, one that reached all the way to her eyes. Time to send it.

"And I would have brought you flowers," he added.

A wide smile erupted on her face. Score.

"You bring flowers?" She stared up at him through thick

lashes, and Jake felt as if he'd been kicked in the gut. "Roses or daisies?"

"Different kinds of flowers," he said once he could breathe again. "Roses or daisies or whatever was your favorite."

"Sounds lovely."

She was lovely.

"I'd only bring those if this was a date." Which this wasn't, he reminded himself. "But I would never think of asking you out on a date."

Liar. Jake swirled the wine in his glass. He should have kept his mouth shut.

"Never? Once I thought… Well, it doesn't matter."

Damn, she was onto him. Suddenly bolting out of the restaurant didn't seem like such a bad idea after all. Instead, he met her gaze. "Okay, yeah. But I got over it."

Over you.

"Oh." Carly's mouth quirked. "That's good. Less awkward for everyone."

He smiled ruefully. "It would be hard to beat this for awkwardness."

"Oh, I can beat this."

"Please do, and take me out of my misery."

"That bad, huh?" she teased.

Jake shrugged.

"Okay." Amusement filled her eyes. "After Iain's funeral, someone came up to me to express his condolences. He also offered to be my friend with, um, benefits though his words were a little more blunt and left me speechless."

Jake's temper flared like lightning. "Who was it?"

"No one you knew," she said.

"Carly."

She sighed. "It was one of Iain's climbing friends from up north, a guy not worth the effort or a police record. Otherwise I would have asked you to beat him up."

"I still could have pushed him around a little."

She grinned. "Oh, one of your steely glares would have definitely intimidated him."

"What did you do?" Jake asked.

"Well, I didn't know whether to laugh it off or slap him. I couldn't stop thinking this was someone who Iain planned to climb with after we returned from our honeymoon. All of a sudden, the tears started flowing and wouldn't stop. The guy shoved his cocktail napkin into my hand and disappeared. I never saw him again."

"A good thing."

"No doubt, but that wasn't nearly as awkward as…"

She ran her fingertip along the stem of her wineglass.

"Tell me," Jake urged.

"Iain's parents." She took a sip of her wine and placed the glass on the table. "They showed up at the apartment the day after the funeral. I know they were in shock like me, but they acted like total strangers. They wanted any items Iain had left there and all the wedding gifts his family had sent. His mother kept picking up things and asking if they belonged to Iain. And then his father told me not to expect anything from Iain's estate since we weren't married. As if that's all I cared about, not the fact my hopes and dreams had died on the mountain with their son."

She didn't sound bitter, simply resigned.

"I had no idea." Jake reached across the table and touched her hand. "You should have told me."

"I didn't tell anyone, not even my parents."

Her skin felt soft beneath his fingers, the way he had imagined it would feel. "Thanks for telling me now."

As a comfortable silence descended, an invisible connection drew them closer. Wanting to reassure her, he squeezed her hand.

She smiled.

He smiled back.

"Out of your misery?" she asked.

"Completely. Thanks." Jake realized his hand still covered hers. He didn't want to move it, but did, lifting his fingers off her smooth skin and reaching for his wineglass. "But you might be the miserable one now."

"I've never been better."

He studied her face. No tightness around her mouth or creases on her forehead. "I believe you."

"You should."

Jake did. "Something's different about you."

She nodded. "I finally realized I can look back, but still move forward. It's been…good."

Those were the words Jake wanted to hear, but he wanted to make sure she didn't stop. "Keep at it. Those dreams of yours can still come true."

"I hope so."

"I know so."

"Thanks." Carly raised her glass. "To old friends."

"Hey, we're not over the hill yet."

"You're older than me."

"Only by four years."

"Well, you made it seem like a lot more when we were younger." She kept her glass raised. "Always taunting me about being older and wiser."

"I was older and wiser," Jake said. "And you could be a real pest."

"Oh, so me being a pest justified you comparing me to poison oak?"

She still made him itch.

He cleared his throat. "Admit it. You used to follow us everywhere. Spying. Annoying us."

"That's what little sisters do."

But she wasn't little any longer. And she sure wasn't his sister. "I wouldn't know. I'm an only child. But it looks like you've outgrown the pest stage."

"You sure about that?" she asked.

Her gaze, full of laughter and warmth, held his. Uh-oh. He felt as if he were treading where he shouldn't, traversing below a slab of snow ready to release and carry him off a cliff into the abyss below. He couldn't allow that to happen.

To old friends.

Jake tapped his glass against hers. The chime hung in the air. "Cheers, my friend."

As Jake drove his SUV along Highway 26, Carly pressed her head against the passenger seat's headrest. She couldn't believe how much fun she'd had with him. She wasn't looking forward to saying goodbye. "Thanks for dinner tonight."

"I hope we can do it again," Jake said.

"Me, too."

She meant the words. Being with him was so easy. Once they got through the initial silence and determined this evening wasn't a date, they could talk and joke. She couldn't remember the last time she'd felt so close to or so at ease with anyone.

And that worried her.

Carly liked keeping her distance, even with the few guys she'd dated, but surprisingly things had gotten downright cozy between her and Jake at the cute little Italian café. Oh, strictly platonic in spite of his holding her hand once. But another dinner for two, even a friendly meal, probably wasn't a good idea.

"Next time we should include Kendall and Austin," Carly added.

"The more the merrier," Jake replied easily.

His ready acceptance of the kids bothered Carly. She loved her niece and nephew, but a part of her wished he could have sounded a little disappointed at not being alone with her again.

Pathetic.

She glanced his way. The lights on the dashboard glowed, silhouetting his strong jaw and his straight nose. So handsome. Gorgeous really. If you liked that type. Which she did. Unfortunately.

Just friends.

She forced herself to look away.

The headlights illuminated a swath of snow-covered trees. The temperature outside had to be below freezing, but she felt a little toasty. Must be the hot air from the heater.

Yeah, right.

And maybe she'd wake up in a couple of days and discover Santa had left her the perfect present under the tree. She sneaked another peek Jake's way.

Too good-looking for her own good.

Better watch it.

He turned into the driveway, shifted the gear stick into Park and turned off the engine. He opened his door, hopped out and walked toward the front of the car.

Panic struck. She didn't mind the little man-woman gestures that added spark to a relationship. But she didn't want them from Jake. A two-week fling with an old friend who shared so much history with her wasn't a good idea.

Carly opened the door and slid out of the SUV. Her feet landed with a thud and sunk through the layer of new snow. She lurched toward the porch. Her foot slid on the layer of ice beneath the powder.

Oh, no. She slipped and tried to balance herself.

"Whoa." Two hands wrapped around her and held her upright. "It's icy out here. You need to go slow or you'll fall."

She felt as if she'd already fallen. No way could she get up without help.

His warmth and strength enveloped her. Her heart pounded. She struggled to breathe. She looked back at him. "Th-thanks."

A slow grin spread over his face. "At your service."

Heaven help her. She wanted his… No, she didn't.

Carly shivered and crossed her arms over her chest.

"It's cold out here." He removed his hands from her. "Let's get you inside."

Yes, because a list of words describing their dinner was running through her mind. Comfortable, cozy… If she weren't careful the next word on the list would be *couple*.

Not that Jake would want to be part of a couple with her. Or bring her flowers. Or kiss her good-night.

Kiss her? She really needed to say goodbye and get away from him.

Carly hurried toward the front steps, careful so she

wouldn't slip again. Jake followed. She stood at the front door, her hand gripping on the doorknob, feeling tongue-tied and all twisted up inside.

"Good night, Carly." He lightly tapped the end of her nose. A platonic, totally unromantic gesture.

She shouldn't complain. That was what she'd wanted from him. Not a date. No kisses required.

"'Night." She moistened her dry lips. "Thanks again. For everything. I had a great time. I really did."

She needed to stop talking. Now.

"You should come with us tomorrow," Jake said.

"Us?"

"I'm taking the kids to their ski lessons. Kendall and Austin love to show off what they're learning."

The kids. Not just Jake. Carly could do that. She appreciated the invitation. Besides, knowing Jake, he would be off skiing himself.

"Thanks, I'd love to go." She remembered her Saturday lessons when she'd been a kid. "I haven't been to Ski Bowl in years."

Jake hesitated. "The lessons aren't at Ski Bowl."

Her heart dropped. "Timberline?"

He nodded, his eyes serious.

"I can't go."

"I understand, Carly." Compassion filled his voice. "But remember what you said at dinner. About looking back, but still moving forward."

"This is different." She took a deep breath. "You're not asking me to look back. You want me to stand in the one place where my dreams began and ended."

"Maybe this is something you need to do."

Carly couldn't go back there. "Maybe it's not."

"There's only one way to find out."

She stared at her feet. "I don't know."

Jake raised her chin with his fingertip. "I do."

Carly couldn't believe she was standing at the edge of one of Timberline's freestyle terrains with an old pair of snowshoes strapped to her feet. Snow flurries fell from the gray sky, but the temperature didn't seem that cold. What gave her the shivers was the summit behind her. If not for the kids, she could have never done this. The kids and…well, Jake.

He stood next to her and gave a thumbs-up sign to Kendall.

Carly readied her camera to catch the next run. She concentrated on the kids and picture taking. Anything to keep her attention focused down the hill.

The top of Mount Hood held too many memories, both good and bad. Dealing with the bright Christmas decorations, the sparking lights on trees and the overflowing holiday cheer inside the Wy'East day lounge had been difficult enough when they'd dropped the kids off for their ski lesson. Carly couldn't handle seeing the summit this close up, too.

Jake adjusted his sunglasses. "We can grab skis and hit the slopes ourselves."

And get even closer to the top. No way. "Thanks, but I'll stick to snowshoes. You go ski."

"I'd rather stay here with you."

She was grateful for his understanding how hard being here was for her, but a part of her—the same one as last night—wished he would leave her alone. Of course, the other part wished he wanted to be with, well, her.

Face it. He'd been on her mind when she'd closed her eyes

last night and opened them this morning. She couldn't help herself. The guy was a total babe magnet, drawing second and third glances from females of all ages on the slopes, including herself.

Who could blame any woman for checking him out? In his red soft shell, black pants and a red patterned ski cap, he looked as if he'd taken a break from a photo shoot or stepped off the page of a ski magazine.

A good thing his sunglasses hid his eyes. Toss in those pretty baby blues and he'd be pretty darn irresistible.

To the other women, that was.

Not her.

Kendall, dressed in black bibs and a polka-dotted blue parka, waved at them. With a big smile on her face, she lowered her goggles from the top of her sticker-covered pink helmet.

"Is this how you spend every Saturday?" Carly snapped a picture. "Watching the kids in ski school?"

"Nope. Garrett usually brings them, but with the baby coming I thought he and Hannah could use some alone time."

Carly stared at Jake in amazement. "You're too good to be true."

A wry grin formed on his face. "I know a few women who would disagree with that statement."

"Only a few?"

He laughed. "The kids have really progressed with their skiing."

"Don't change the subject," Carly said, curious about the women in Jake's life. "We're friends. Friends share things, right?"

He shrugged.

"Come on."

"There's not much to say except most of the women I date are looking for more than a Saturday night date."

"What do they want?"

"A wedding date. A wedding date of their own," he clarified. "Since marriage isn't something I'm interested in, they aren't too happy when I won't get serious with them."

"Serious?"

"Make a commitment."

"So have you caught up to Sean Hughes with the number of hearts you've broken?" Carly teased.

"Nope, Sean still holds that record. I'm not even close to him."

"Not yet anyway."

"Though I may be able to catch up a little now that Sean's heart has been spoken for."

"Who's the lucky lady?" she asked. "A gorgeous snowboard model?"

"Close," Jake said. "A beautiful Siberian husky named Denali."

"I can't believe Mr. I-don't-let-anything-tie-me-down has a dog."

"Believe it." Jake pointed to the kids. "Kendall's turn."

As her niece sped toward a ramp, Carly held her breath and raised her digital camera. No wonder Hannah didn't like watching the kids ski. Whether they were skiing down a run or doing jumps, it was nerve-racking.

Kendall flew into the air, executed a twist and landed solidly as Carly took a picture.

Carly exhaled and clapped. "She is so much like Nick."

"Told ya," Jake said.

"You did, but Kendall reminds me of someone else, too."

"Who is that?"

"You," she said. "I know the kids have a stepfather now, but you have done an amazing job with them."

"Thanks. That means a lot to me."

"You mean a lot to Kendall and Austin. They talk about you all the time."

"Maybe now, but they're young. Soon they'll be teenagers and won't be so keen on spending time with their Uncle Jake."

"I doubt that."

"They are growing up so fast."

"I know." Carly watched Kendall talk to her instructor. "Remember when you and Nick took Kendall skiing for the first time?"

Jake smiled. "Hannah wanted to kill us."

"Kendall was only two."

"She did great," he said. "But Hannah wouldn't let me take her back out skiing. I had to wait until she started kindergarten. Austin, too."

Austin skied down another run with his class. The kid liked to go straight and fast. No fancy jumps or unnecessary turns for him. She aimed the camera at him. "Doesn't seem to have hurt her. Or Austin."

"Guess not." Jake's tone was far from indifferent.

"But you wanted them on skis," she said.

He focused on Austin, who had stopped to wait for the rest of the class. "It's what Nick would have wanted."

"And that's why you've gone above and beyond for Hannah and the kids all these years." It wasn't a question because Carly already knew the answer. "You've taught the kids about the outdoors. You introduced Hannah to Garrett. You've made sure what Nick would have wanted for them came true."

Jake shrugged. "I did what any best friend would do. Nick would have done the same for me."

Except Jake didn't have a wife and two kids. He didn't even have a pet. Just a father who never thought he was good enough.

"You're a good friend, Jake Porter."

"Sometimes." He pulled her hat down over her eyes. "Sometimes, not. I haven't been that good a friend to you over the years."

She pushed up her hat so she could see. "I'm the one who left and never came back."

"You had good reason," he said. "But your heart never really left Hood Hamlet. You can take the girl from the mountains, but you can't take the mountain out of the girl."

"I'm not exactly a girl anymore."

"Even eighty-year-old women still have a girl inside them. And before you ask, my grandmother told me that."

"Grandmas know everything."

"Mine thought so."

The two ski classes continued down their respective runs until the kids disappeared down the hill. Carly shivered, fighting a chill. She raised the collar of her jacket.

"The temperature dropped. Let's grab a hot chocolate in the lodge," Jake said. "The kids still have another hour of ski school."

"Sounds good."

In the bar on the second floor of Timberline Lodge, light streamed through the tall windows. Carly sat on a love seat opposite Jake, her huge mug of cocoa on the coffee table between them. They were the only two customers. "This really hits the spot."

As it always had in the past.

Some things never changed. Timberline Lodge was one of them. The historic building's timber and stone construction had a very northwest feel. The arts-and-crafts decor was comfortable and understated. But her favorite part had always been the view of the mountain from the Ram's Head Bar.

Carly tried not to look, but couldn't help herself. The large windows provided picturesque views of Mount Hood. The summit peeked through the clouds.

"Beautiful," Jake said.

The glimpse of the snow-covered peak where Iain had proposed and died was bittersweet.

She'd waited here for Iain and Nick to come down that fateful December day. She wasn't sure where things stood between her and Iain after the fight, and she'd needed to know. So she'd sat, watching the hours tick by until she realized something had to be wrong, terribly wrong, and she'd called the one person who would know what to do—Jake.

"I'm not sure what to think of the mountain even though it's been six years," she admitted.

"Sometimes it still feels as if everything happened yesterday."

"I know." Carly hadn't thought anyone else felt like that. "And the what-ifs…"

"Are still hell."

"They can drive you crazy."

He looked at the mountain. "If I could do it all over again, I would have climbed with them that day."

She shuddered. "You might have been killed, too."

"No, I *know* I would have made a difference and all three of us would have walked off the mountain together."

How many times had she dreamed that scenario? Too many to count.

"But I thought I was following my gut instinct by not climbing," Jake continued. "Instead I was being…"

"What?"

"Selfish."

The recriminatory tone of his voice clawed at her heart.

"It wasn't your fault." She found herself repeating the same words Hannah had said the other night. "I've never blamed you for not being with them. Hannah hasn't, either. I'm happy, relieved, you name it, that you weren't up there. I don't know how any of us would have made it through without you."

"Thanks for that." He sipped his drink. "What happened was an accident, but knowing that hasn't gotten rid of all the guilt."

Carly knew exactly how he felt. She wanted to help him. "Did you ever consider your gut instinct wasn't wrong? That your decision not to climb wasn't selfish, but self-preservation?"

He stared out the window at the mountain. "I never thought about it that way."

She reached across the table and touched his hand. "Maybe you should."

He nodded.

"Is there anything else that might help you?" she asked.

A beat passed. "You."

Her heart slammed against her chest. She pulled back her hand even though she wanted to still be touching him. "M-me?"

"Nick and Iain would want you to be happy."

"I'm…" Not exactly happy. She wasn't going to lie to Jake. He deserved better than that. "I'm doing okay."

Which was the truth. Not happy, not great, but okay. Nothing wrong with that.

"You've built a life for yourself in Philadelphia, but something seems to be holding you back. Someone. Iain, perhaps."

She stared into her mug.

"Think about what you said about moving forward," Jake said. "It's time for you to get on with your life, Carly. Fall in love, get married and have those kids you always talked about having. That's what Nick and Iain would have wanted you to do."

"It's not that easy."

"Especially if you won't let anyone get close to you."

"Have you been talking to Hannah?" Carly asked.

"She's worried about you. I am, too."

"I'm trying." She appreciated his concern. "You said you felt guilty about what happened. So do I."

"Why?" Jake asked.

"Because of that terrible fight Iain and I had over the climb. I should have tried harder to make him stay home, then Nick wouldn't have gone."

"Iain would have soloed the route."

"You're probably right." Carly took a breath. Iain lived to climb. Nothing would hold him back. Not even her love. She'd often wondered what marriage to someone like that would have been like over the long term. Probably not as wonderful as she'd thought at age twenty-two. "Okay, you're absolutely right, but Nick wouldn't have been with him. Hannah would still have her husband. Kendall and Austin, their father. You, your best friend. And me…"

"Your brother." Jake rose from the love seat opposite Carly and sat next to her. "Looks like both of us have been thinking along the same lines."

"We probably should have talked about this."

He placed his arm around her. "At least we're talking about it now."

With a nod, she leaned against his shoulder. He felt so warm. Strong. She wanted to soak up his strength. Him. "Hannah told me Nick and Iain made their own choices. No one's at fault."

"She's told me the same thing. Many times."

"Maybe it's time we listened to her."

He nodded.

"Seeing Hannah and Garrett together as a couple and so in love has made me realize there are second chances," Carly said. "Want to know what's helped the most?"

"What?" Jake asked.

"Actually a who. You."

He stared at her for what seemed like forever.

She didn't know if what she'd said was wrong, but it's how she felt. He was caring and understanding. Gorgeous and sexy. He had made a difference, and she wanted him to make even more of a difference in her life. Somehow. She moistened her lips. "I'm sorry, I shouldn't have—"

A wide smile broke across his face. "Yes, you should have."

She looked up at him with anticipation. She opened her mouth to speak, but he never gave her a chance to say a word.

His lips covered hers with such tenderness.

He kissed her as if this was the beginning and the end. As if he was afraid to ask for too much, but unable to keep himself from taking more.

She had never felt so special, so cherished, than in this moment.

His kisses heated her from the top of her head to the tip of her toes. Better than rich hot chocolate. Smoother than the dollop of whip cream floating in her mug.

His lips moved over hers gently.

Her heart felt as if it were finally waking up after a restless sleep. Her blood heated and surged through her veins. Desire, long forgotten, made her lean toward him.

Carly loved how his kisses made her feel. She didn't want the kiss to end.

But slowly he drew back from her. She stared up at him. The longing in his eyes brought tears to hers.

Jake brushed a strand of hair away from her face. "That was better than I imagined it would be."

Her heart skipped. "You imagined kissing me?"

He stared at her as if she was the last woman on earth. "Once or twice."

Her throat clogged with emotion. She remembered that one time. "When?"

"A while ago."

"Before…"

He nodded. "A long time ago."

Carly had been right. He had thought about kissing her. But she wasn't sure how knowing that made her feel. Flattered. Desired.

Unsettled.

She stared out the window, at the mountain as the backdrop to all the most memorable events of her life, and all she could see, all she could think about, was Jake. The past, the present, the future.

His kiss had totally rocked her world.

Carly couldn't remember Iain's kiss ever having such an affect on her. She must have forgotten.

Oh, no. How could she forget her fiancé's kiss?

Sure, she'd kissed other men in the past six years, but not one of them had made her forget Iain. She couldn't believe it would be Jacob Porter because that complicated…well, everything.

"Jake…"

"Shh." He placed his finger on her throbbing lips. "It's okay."

But Carly knew better. "No, it's not."

Jake had always been there. For Hannah. For the kids. For Carly.

She'd just gotten him back in her life. Did she want to risk that? For what? A few toe-curling kisses.

"We're friends," she said.

He grinned. "Good friends."

Her treacherous heart skipped another beat. Oh, no. "Hannah and the kids count on you."

"So?"

"With the holidays and the baby…" Her voice trailed off. She looked at him, willing him to understand. "I count on you."

"I'm glad."

He didn't get it at all. She tried again. "But what happened…"

"You mean my kissing you."

As her cheeks warmed, she nodded. "Kissing changes things. Complicates things. I like to keep things simple."

Simple equaled safe.

"What are you getting at?" Jake asked.

"I like you, Jake. A lot. But maybe it would be better if we stayed just friends. Friends who don't kiss," she added in case he still didn't get it.

From the look on his face, he did.

CHAPTER FIVE

LYING IN BED, Jake heard a ringing in his ears. Bells? He opened his tired eyes. The noise stopped.

Maybe he was imagining things. He felt completely wiped out. Carly's kiss had burned, branding itself on his lips, his brain and his heart. One kiss shouldn't have had such an effect on him. Yet thoughts about it and her had kept him awake past midnight.

Friends who don't kiss.

She'd given him a taste of heaven only to send him straight into "just friends" purgatory. He wanted to change her mind, but the worry in her eyes and the tightness around her lovely mouth had kept him from saying or doing anything. She'd been out of his life for so long. He didn't want to blow it by not listening to her. A temporary, strategic retreat was in order, but he wasn't about to roll over and play dead. He would think of a way to change her mind. More kisses were definitely in order.

The ringing sounded again.

Not bells. The telephone.

Adrenaline surged. Jake knew what a call at this hour meant. Someone was in trouble somewhere. OMSAR's alert system sent out pages, phone calls and e-mails when the sheriff called for assistance.

Sometimes the calls came during the day. Many times they came in the middle of the night. Each situation was different.

Reaching across the bed for the phone, Jake glanced at the digital clock on the nightstand.

3:23 a.m.

Next to the clock, his pager lay silent. That was odd. The alert system was automated. Usually he got paged for a mission, too.

He picked up the receiver and hit the talk button. "Porter."

"Hey, Jake. Hannah's water broke," Garrett said matter-of-factly. "The doctor wants her to go to the hospital now."

Jake jumped out of bed. He knew what "now" meant when it came to delivering babies. At least Hannah's babies. He headed to his closet. "She's not supposed to be induced until after Christmas."

"That was the plan, but it looks like we're going to need to hang another stocking on the fireplace." Garrett sounded calm, a little tired, but nothing to suggest something out of the ordinary was going on. Of course, the guy never lost his cool or got riled up. That was one reason he'd been the perfect addition to OMSAR's board of directors. Garrett Willingham could always be counted on to be the voice of reason. "Think you can pick one up for us?"

"No problem." Jake didn't understand the lack of urgency in Garrett's voice. "Did the doctor say go 'now'?"

"As soon as we can. Luckily, Hannah hasn't started contractions yet. Getting to Portland in this weather might take a while."

Jake glanced out the window. White flakes falling from the sky limited his vision. Uh-oh. Not good. He brushed his hand through his hair, a little concerned.

"I'll call everyone." One big, happy family sounded like a cliché, but the handful of OMSAR members who lived on Mount Hood year-round helped each other out. Even those who didn't live nearby were willing to lend a hand, too. Good times, bad times. At the beginning of a new life or at the end of another. "We'll get you there."

"That's what I told Hannah. She still needs to pack, but is doing laundry instead. Her way of keeping control of the situation."

"Forget control," Jake said. "Remind her how fast Austin came."

"She told me you almost had to deliver him."

"Yep, and I never want to have to go through anything like that again." Jake might be a wilderness first responder and have EMT training, but the last place he wanted to stick his head and hands was between his late best friend's wife's legs, even if it was to deliver her baby. "I doubt she does, either."

"That may get her moving faster," Garrett said. "Thanks."

"Get her packed no matter what she says or wants to do. I'll be there ASAP."

And that meant Jake would see Carly. Good. He hadn't liked the way she'd bolted out of his SUV like a downhill skier on a run for Olympic gold when he'd dropped her and the kids off. Usually women didn't want him to leave, not the other way around.

He made the calls as he dressed, then climbed in his SUV. The weather combined with the snow on the road made the driving tricky, even with four-wheel drive and studded tires. Headlights came toward him. He recognized the large pickup truck with a snowplow attached to the front and waved.

Sean Hughes leaned out his window and his Siberian

husky, Denali, stuck her head out, too. "What took you so long, Porter? Did you stop for an espresso first or did you need to put your date back in its pen before you took off?"

Jake ignored him. Sean always had something to say, anything from a smart-assed comment or a joke to diffuse the tension when they were out in the field. He also had no problem speaking his mind, which made him a favorite with the local media. But underneath that gruff exterior was a guy who would go out of his way for anyone, friend or stranger.

"How's the road looking?" Jake asked.

"Clear to the house. I'm heading to the highway now." With a nod, Sean rolled up his window and drove off.

Jake continued on to Hannah and Garrett's house. The plowed road made for easier driving. Jake parked and jumped out of his truck. The cold wind blasted him, and the snow pelted his face.

Floodlights illuminated the driveway where two OMSAR members—Tim and Bill, who Jake had also called—blew snow away. White icicle lights added a festive glow to the house. Granted, this wasn't the first time an OMSAR member made a middle-of-the-night hospital run to deliver a baby in a snowstorm, but if they didn't hit the road soon, this was going to turn into a damn birthday party.

Inside the house, the combination of the furnace, fireplace and bodies wrapped him with warmth, chasing away the early-morning chill. He hung his jacket and hat on the rack by the door. A bunch of familiar OMSAR faces, including paramedic Leanne Thomas, greeted him. Obviously, more calls had been made after his.

"The gang's all here," Jake said.

Leanne winked. "Gotta take care of the money man."

Garrett had been elected OMSAR's treasurer two years ago. He didn't ski or climb, but he knew finances and had become a valued behind-the-scenes unit member.

"Not to mention the money man's wife."

Nick's widow.

The words went unspoken.

The smell of freshly brewing coffee and the sound of all the conversations going on brought back images from six years ago. Almost to the day, in fact. But the mood was one hundred and eighty degrees different. This was a celebration of life. New life.

Jake glanced around. The twinkling tree lights, the Christmas cards hooked with clothespins on rope and interspersed with the kids' artwork made Jake think about family and home. Thanks to the Bishops, he'd always had those things.

"Garrett's trying to get things together for the hospital, but he could really use help," Leanne said. "Use some of that infamous Jake Porter charm and convince Hannah it's time to finish packing?"

"Where is she?"

"In the kitchen."

At least Garrett had gotten her out of the laundry room. "On my way."

Hannah sat at the table with a pen in her hand and a piece of paper in front of her. Carly, dressed in jeans and a bulky brown sweater, peered over her shoulder.

The sight of Carly took Jake's breath away. She looked like she needed a good-morning kiss. He could use one himself. Damn, she was sexy. Her tousled hair looked as if she'd crawled out of bed and not even brushed her fingers through it.

Voices drifted in from the living room. Sean Hughes must

have been on a cell phone with someone in there because he offered to lead the drive to the hospital. Leanne wanted to ride with Hannah in case she went into active labor and needed help. Other people chimed in to the discussion. Hannah, however, paid no attention to them or to anyone. She seemed to be in no rush to get to the hospital and kept writing.

"That's enough for me to get started, Hannah," Carly said, her tone concerned and her attention focused only on her sister-in-law. "You need to finish packing so you can get to the hospital."

"There's no rush. I'm not showing any signs of labor."

"Your water broke."

"My water broke prematurely." Hannah kept scribbling. "I'm not due for two more weeks. Remember, they were taking this one a week early. Contractions aren't going to start until they induce me so let me finish this list for you. You're going to need it."

The underlying worry of Hannah's words was clear to Jake.

Damn. He rubbed the back of his neck. For once he wanted something to go Hannah's way. She'd been through so much already. The last thing she needed to worry about was having the baby two weeks early and not being ready. But like it or not, she had to get moving.

"Good morning, ladies," he said. "I hear the jelly bean decided not to wait until next year to celebrate Christmas."

"Surprised us all, I must admit," Hannah joked. "Too bad I don't have a My First Christmas bib or outfit to take to the hospital with me."

She looked up at him. Jake expected to see a smile, not a hint of fear in her eyes. He wasn't used to seeing her like this, and he didn't want to say anything to upset her more.

Instead, he poured himself a cup of coffee. "Christmas is still two days away. We'll find a First Christmas outfit complete with Santa hat. Right, Carly?"

"Uh, sure," she said. "We'll find one."

"Come on, Hannah," Garrett said from the doorway. "It's time. I'm going to wake the kids so you can say goodbye."

"I need to finish my list."

"Honey, I know this caught you off guard, but we need to go. You can finish the list later."

Hannah clenched her jaw. "I'm not in labor."

"The doctor said—"

"The doctor is a man and, like you, has no clue about these things in spite of all his credentials and the initials behind his name." She glared at a taken-aback Garrett. "I will go to the hospital when I'm ready to go. Right now I'm busy, so leave me alone. Please."

Garrett started to say something, but Jake raised his hand to stop him. The guy might be Hannah's husband, but Garrett hadn't been through this before with her. Jake had. Twice. Tonight made it a hat trick. He motioned he would take care of it. With a nod, Garrett left to rouse the kids.

As Hannah continued writing, Jake took a sip of coffee. He watched the clock. A minute passed. "All packed and ready to go?"

"Almost. I need to finish this first," Hannah said.

Her stalling tactics bothered him. When she'd gone into labor with Kendall, Hannah had been in a rush to get to the hospital. She'd buzzed around the house like a hummingbird that couldn't find a flower while a pale Nick talked to the doctor, trying to figure out if they should go yet. Jake hadn't known what to do, so he'd helped Hannah get into the pickup truck and wished Nick good luck. Jake had shown up later that day at the hospital with a six-pack for the new dad, flowers for the new mom and a stuffed bear for Kendall.

Those had been the days. So young, so naive, so stupid back then.

With Austin, there hadn't been time to do much except to get in the car and drive with a lead foot. The labor hit hard and fast. Hannah couldn't reach Nick, who'd been climbing, so she'd called Jake. The baby's head was partway out by the time they made it to the hospital. Nick had arrived during the pushing, allowing Jake to get the hell out of there.

He took another sip of coffee and glanced at the clock once more. "Time's up, Hannah. You can finish the list later. Right now, you've got to go."

She dropped her pencil, staring at her list.

"You don't understand." Her voice cracked. "Having this baby early is going to ruin the kids' Christmas. I was hoping to finish everything up today, but now Carly's going to have to take care of it and she needs to know what to do. Otherwise—"

"Carly and I will make sure the kids have the best Christmas ever." He set his coffee on the counter and kneeled at Hannah's side. "Isn't that right, Carly?"

Her eyes met his in understanding. He saw the same worry on her face as he felt. The two of them had to get Hannah moving and on her way. "The most totally wonderful Christmas ever," Carly added.

Tears welled in Hannah's eyes. "But…I promised the kids I'd take them to see Santa today."

"We'll take them," Carly said.

Hannah glanced back at her. "Are you sure?"

Carly nodded. "It'll be fun."

Jake touched the top of Hannah's hand. "Just concentrate on delivering the newest addition to the family. Carly and I have everything else covered. No worries, okay?"

"There's really no rush," Hannah said, her gaze darting between the two of them.

"You know that," Jake said. "But for those of us who have never had a baby, would you please go to the hospital now?"

"I suppose."

"Thanks," he said quickly, not wanting her to change her mind.

"I should be the one thanking you." Hannah hugged him and squeezed Carly's hand. "I'm lucky to have both of you. So are the kids."

As Jake stood, Carly mouthed a thank-you to him. Seeing her lips move reminded him of kissing her. A spark of heat shot through him.

Hmmm. This could be the opportunity he needed, a chance to spend time with Carly, pint-size chaperones aside, and show her how they could be friends and still kiss. Jake grinned.

If things went the way he hoped, this might turn out be his best Christmas ever.

No matter where Carly went, she couldn't escape Christmas.

She stood in the mall surrounded by everything she'd avoided for years and never wanted to experience again. The over-the-top decorations, the teeth-grinding Christmas music and nonstop holiday cheer were driving her crazy.

Today, the sixth anniversary of Iain and Nick's fateful climb, was not the day she wanted to battle Christmas. Unfortunately, Carly had no choice.

Maybe this was the ghost of Christmas past's idea of a

joke? She closed her eyes, hoping it would all disappear, but when she opened them everything seemed brighter, louder, sparklier. She tried thinking about something other than the Christmas nightmare surrounding her, but her thoughts shot straight to one thing...make that person—Jake.

His kiss yesterday had opened the physical floodgates. She needed to close them. She didn't want to be led by emotion, by a physical need or desire of anybody.

Carly wasn't ready to go there yet. Especially with Jake, the subject of her childhood crush and teenage fantasies.

For someone who wanted life to be simple, hers had suddenly gotten very complicated. But she couldn't be concerned about herself right now.

She thought about Hannah in a hospital bed, worried and missing precious holiday traditions with her kids. More was at stake than Carly's comfort level. Kendall and Austin's Christmas rested in her hands. Okay, Jake's hands, too. They had promised Hannah the kids would have the best Christmas ever. They would have to work together to make sure it happened.

Together.

Talk about complications.

Carly rubbed one side of her forehead, trying to keep the headache threatening to erupt at bay. She wove her way through the throngs of shoppers, balancing bags and packages, while pushing strollers and holding young children's hands. Her packages were safely hidden in Jake's SUV so the kids wouldn't see them.

"Aunt Carly." Kendall waved. Her green sweater with a kitten wearing a Santa hat was hard to miss. "We're over here."

Here being the North Pole Village, home to the ambassador himself of this holiday horror, good old Kris Kringle. Kendall and Austin stood in a long line of children. Some in pretty party dresses, others wearing simple play clothes. All were accompanied by ragged and tired-looking parents, but where was…

"Where is Jake?" Carly asked, surprised she didn't see him nearby. He knew better than to leave the kids alone.

"He's at that store over there buying us smoothies," Austin said, pointing.

"Don't worry, Uncle Jake sees us or he never would have left us here by ourselves." Kendall sounded so much like Hannah. "He watches us like a hawk."

"That's because your Uncle Jake loves you so much," Carly said.

"Yep." Austin grinned. "He spoils us rotten."

"That's for sure." Carly wouldn't mind being spoiled a little. Not by Jake, but someone. Someday.

She looked around. The jolly fat guy wasn't sitting on the big red throne. No wonder the line hadn't moved. "Where is Santa?"

"He had to feed his reindeer," Austin said.

"And it's taking forever," Kendall complained.

"I'm sure he'll be back." Carly noticed the bag in Kendall's hand. "What did you buy?"

"A stocking and a First Christmas outfit for the baby." The girl bubbled with excitement. "There's a little red hat and matching bib, too."

"Sounds cute," Carly said, grateful Jake had thought to buy those. That would make Hannah feel better.

Austin moved closer to her. His wide brown eyes stared up at her. "Has Mommy had the baby yet?"

The concern in his voice squeezed Carly's heart. These poor kids. First they lost their dad and now their mom had to say goodbye to them in the middle of the night. At least they had Christmas to look forward to.

Carly placed her arm around his narrow shoulders. "Not yet, honey, but she will have the baby soon and then we can go to the hospital and meet your new baby brother or sister, okay?"

Austin nodded. "I hope it's a boy."

"I just want a healthy baby," Kendall said.

Austin's eyes narrowed. "Sammy Ross says all babies do is spit up and poop. Is that true?"

Carly bit back a laugh. Unlike the kissing and having to get married, this time Sammy was correct. "Well, newborns don't do a lot. They drink, cry, sleep, dirty their diapers and spit up."

"Yuck." Austin crinkled his nose. "Sammy said they smell. I hope our baby doesn't smell bad."

Carly bit back a smile. "You'll love your baby."

"Not if it smells."

She mussed Austin's hair. "Just you wait. The smell won't matter. You're going to be a great big brother."

Just like your daddy was to me, she thought with a pang.

Jake arrived with four smoothies in a drink tray. He handed a cup to each of them. Carly appreciated his thoughtfulness, but then again, as he'd proven buying those things for the baby, he was that kind of guy. Friend, she corrected.

"Thanks." She sipped her pink smoothie through a straw. The cold liquid tasted so good going down her throat. "Raspberry. My favorite."

"I know."

Carly was flattered he remembered after all these years. When she was around Kendall's age, maybe a little older, she'd memorized all of Jake's likes and dislikes. Not that bringing him a frozen Milky Way bar had endeared her to him in the slightest. He hadn't noticed she existed. At least not in the way she'd wanted him to notice her. They'd been like a Western Meadowlark falling in love with a Chinook salmon. Two different creatures. Two different ecosystems. The two weren't meant to be together. She stirred the smoothie with her straw.

"Look, it's Santa." Awe filled Austin's voice. "He must have finished feeding the reindeer."

The delight in the boy's eyes brought a smile to Carly's face. The way the children responded to the holiday was almost magical. She'd forgotten about that.

Santa hobbled past, using a cane as he walked. Not bad. Real beard, wire-rimmed glasses and rosy cheeks. He was better than some of the other Santas she saw when she was a kid.

"Sorry that took so long, children," Santa said. "But Vixen and Dancer wanted seconds."

The kids giggled.

"Do you think he brings his cane with him in his sled?" Austin whispered.

"I don't know," Carly answered honestly.

"You can ask him," Jake said.

Soon the line moved, and before she knew it, they were stepping through a white gate that had silver snowflakes painted on it. As Kendall watched the dancing penguins, mimicking their movements and singing along to their song, Carly videotaped her.

A singing snowman captured Austin's attention. He made Jake explain how everything worked, from the robotic movements to the sound coming from a tree. Jake's patience reminded Carly of her father. Her nephew's curiosity reminded her of Nick.

She pushed aside the bittersweet thought. This needed to be a happy day for the kids. The best Christmas ever was going to be a tall order for her and Jake to fill.

"Do you know what you're going to ask Santa to bring you?" Carly asked.

Both kids nodded.

"I want a snowboard," Austin said. "And a pirate ship."

"I want an iPod," Kendall said. "And makeup. But Santa already knows this because we sent him a list. We're here for the picture today."

Too smart for her own good. Hannah and Garrett had better watch out. "You can still tell him in person."

"Do you know what you're going to ask Santa for, Aunt Carly?" Kendall asked.

"I have everything I need right here." Carly glanced from Kendall to Austin, and then looked over at Jake. He looked so comfortable here, surrounded by this manufactured North Pole and the two kids. The way he casually rested his hand on Austin's shoulder made him seem more like a dad than a family friend who'd been made an honorary uncle. Carly had never imagined Jake Porter as a father before, but now she could see it so clearly. Her mouth went dry. "No need to ask for anything else."

Kendall pouted. "It's Christmas. You have to want something, Aunt Carly."

"Maybe she wants Santa to bring her a boyfriend." Jake emphasized *boy*.

Kendall drew her brows together. "That might be hard for Santa's elves to wrap, Uncle Jake."

Carly struggled not to laugh.

"If you tell Santa what you want," Austin said to her, "you'll get a candy cane."

"A candy cane, huh?" Carly asked. "Maybe I'll have to think of something. Got any ideas?"

"A video game system," Austin suggested. "Or a robot."

The line moved forward.

"Perfume might be nice," Kendall said. "Or a fiancé. If you had one of those I could be a flower girl finally."

Carly smiled. "Perfume might be an easier order for Santa to fill and it will fit into my stocking. Though I appreciate the other suggestions."

"Especially the fiancé," Kendall said.

Carly didn't want to get into that discussion. Boyfriends and fiancés meant more complications. She had enough right now. She caught Jake's eye, and her stomach tingled.

Darn him.

"Do you know what you want Santa to bring you, Uncle Jake?" Austin asked him.

"Not yet, but I still have a few minutes to figure it out."

"Better hurry," she said.

His lips curved into a slow, easy grin. "I don't like rushing."

A devilish gleam filled his eyes, hinting at things she could only fantasize about. Forget the snow outside, she suddenly felt hot.

"But I'll think of something. I don't want to miss out on a candy cane," he added.

Peppermint kisses, anyone?

She sipped her drink. "This smoothie really hits the spot."

One of Santa's elves, a young woman wearing a floppy hat, green costume, red-and-white-striped tights and pointy-toed shoes with bells on them, took their photo order. Kendall and Austin sat on Santa's lap. Another female elf told the kids to smile and snapped pictures. After the third flash, Carly lost track of the number of photos taken. Santa asked the kids what they wanted and gave each one a candy cane.

"It's my aunt's turn," Austin announced.

Santa motioned her over.

Carly gulped. This was the last thing she had expected or wanted, especially with the long line of children waiting behind her and Jake watching her.

Santa patted space next to him. "Come sit and tell me what you want for Christmas, Carly."

She sat on the arm of his chair, feeling self-conscious. "I just came for a candy cane."

"You have to believe," Santa said.

"I gave up believing a long time ago," Carly muttered, too low for the children or Jake to hear. Six long years ago, when her love and her hopes had died on the mountain.

"Still, there must be something you want," Santa said.

She caught her gaze lingering on Jake and looked away. "No, thanks. Too risky."

The mall Santa must have followed her glance. "Life is about taking risks…and love makes those risks worth it even if we end up disappointed or hurt."

Carly thought she would fall off the chair arm in embarrassment. "I'm not looking for love," she assured him.

Especially not with Jake.

"Ah, but love may come looking for you," Santa said. With a warm smile, he handed her a candy cane.

She ducked her head as she accepted it. "I don't think so."

As she stood, Carly noticed Jake watching her. Surely he hadn't heard her. His cell phone rang, and he answered it.

"One more thing before you go." Santa kept his voice low. "You used to enjoy the holidays so much. There's no reason you can't feel that way again. All you have to do is give Christmas another chance."

"How—?"

"It's Uncle Jake's turn," Kendall said.

"Merry Christmas," Santa said.

Carly walked to the cashier in a daze. She looked over the pictures of the kids with Santa, picked one and paid her money.

What was going on? When did mall Santas decide to dispense advice along with candy canes?

Not that she was going to listen to him. Carly knew better than to take risks. That was one reason she had wanted to keep her distance from Jake Porter. The guy had heartbreak written all over him.

And why would she want to give Christmas another chance? She was willing to do what it took for the kids' sake, but that was all. That was enough.

Besides, no seasonal mall hire could possibly understand what she'd been through. Who was that guy anyway? Take away the red suit and the glasses and…he still looked like a perfectly cast Santa.

Coincidence. That was all. He'd made a lucky guess. No reason to be baffled or bothered by what he'd said.

Carly followed the path out of the North Pole Village. The kids stood with Jake, who held a candy cane in one hand, his cell phone in the other.

"Garrett called," Jake said.

"Is my mommy okay?" Austin asked.

Carly drew the two kids close to her.

"Absolutely," Jake said. "She and the baby are fine."

"Baby?" Carly held her breath.

"By C-section."

Something must have gone wrong. No doubt there was a story behind Hannah's needing an operation to deliver the baby, but the kids didn't need to hear it.

"So do I have a brother?" Austin asked.

"Or a sister?" Kendall asked.

"A brother," Jake announced. "It's a boy."

CHAPTER SIX

AT THE HOSPITAL, Jake walked with Carly to the gift shop. The bounce in her step brought a smile to his face. She hadn't seemed this happy at the mall.

"Isn't he the cutest baby?" Carly gushed about her new nephew even though she'd seen him for all of five minutes before letting the family have alone time together. "He looks like Hannah. Well, around the mouth. I think he has Garrett's chin."

"And his hair," Jake joked, shortening the length of his stride so Carly wouldn't have to hurry to keep up with him. Garrett was starting to go bald.

She continued as if Jake hadn't spoken, still on some kind of weird baby high. "Tyler Michael Willingham is a great name."

"It's an okay name, but Tyler Jacob Willingham would have been better. They could have called the kid T.J."

Her mouth quirked. "You do know Michael is Garrett's grandfather's and father's name, don't you?"

Jake shrugged, happy he'd made her smile. "Guys don't talk about names much."

"Not unless they are female names. I remember how you and Nick used to talk about girls."

"We only said those things because we knew you were listening." He laughed at her shocked expression. "Come on. Did you really think we didn't know when you were spying on us?"

She pursued her lips, making them look even more kissable than ever. "And I thought I was so clever."

"You were, but we were more clever."

Mischief gleamed in her eyes. "At least you told yourselves that."

As he laughed, a warm feeling built up inside him. He hadn't seen her in years, but since her return they had picked up right where they'd left off. Jake didn't know too many people he could do that with. "I'm glad you're back. I've missed you, Carly Bishop."

"Me, too," she said. "You, I mean."

She stumbled over her words as if she were tongue-tied or embarrassed, the way she'd done when she was a young girl. Years ago, Jake hadn't known why, but he liked thinking he might be the reason today. He stood taller. Each thing she did, every word she said, made him want to learn more about the woman she'd become while living in Philadelphia.

An elderly man pushed a gray-haired woman in a wheelchair toward them. His bony fingers wrapped tightly around the handgrips, and he took short, careful steps.

Carly moved to the right side of the hallway. Jake followed her, noticing the way her jeans fit. The couple passed by.

She stared after them. "The way that woman placed her hand on his was so sweet."

He'd missed it.

"I used to want to be like that," she said wistfully.

"Old and gnarled?"

She gave him a look. "I meant in love."

Jake shrugged. Love came with too many strings. People wanting him to change or be something he wasn't. At least that had been his experience with his parents and with women, but he wasn't about to discourage Carly. "All you need is to find the right guy and in fifty years you could be like them."

"You make it sound so easy."

"It could be if you keep your eyes open. He might be closer than you think."

Especially if he was right here with you now.

Whoa. Where had that come from?

Carly drew her brows together as if confused.

That made two of them.

He liked her kisses. He liked her. But the next fifty years… Jake rubbed the back of his neck. He was used to thinking in days or weeks, not years.

"What I mean is don't close yourself off to the possibility of meeting the right guy or you could miss out," Jake clarified.

"I'll take that into consideration." She stepped around an empty gurney. "So are you as happy as Austin that Hannah had a boy?"

He was happy Carly had changed the subject. "Boy or girl, doesn't matter. I'll have this one on skis before he can walk."

"How can you ski if you can't walk?" she asked.

"I'm sure if he can stand, there's a way," he said. "And if not, I'll load Tyler into a pack and ski with him on my back."

Carly raised her eyebrows. "You think Hannah's going to allow this?"

"She might mellow with baby number three."

"She's always been overprotective."

"I'm embracing the glass-half-full approach to life."

"I haven't figured out what my approach to life is yet," Carly admitted. "One day at a time has been my motto."

"Nothing wrong with that."

"That's what I keep telling myself." She stopped in front of the gift shop. "So what do you think? A stuffed animal and flowers?"

"I bought the baby a polar bear, but another kind of animal might be nice."

"Let's see what they have." Carly walked into the store, stopped and turned. Her smile lit up her entire face. "You bought Kendall and Austin bears."

Her remembering pleased Jake. "Kids like bears."

Carly nodded. "It's a very special tradition you started. Both Austin and Kendall still sleep with those bears on their beds. I'm sure Tyler will be no different once he's old enough."

"Each kid is different."

"You sound so much like a dad."

"Nope," he said. "Just a guy who watches kids every now and then."

"Just a guy, huh?" She shook her head. "I think one stuffed animal is enough for a newborn."

"Yes, but flowers for the new mommy are a must."

"So Hannah gets flowers even though it's not a date," Carly teased.

The dinner conversation at the Italian café came back to

him. "Dates are only one time I bring flowers. Hospital visits are another," he explained. "But tomorrow I want to bring a small tree with lights and decorations. They can't spend Christmas in the hospital without a tree." He noticed the blank stare on Carly's face. "Hannah had a C-section like Tim Moreno's wife. That means she's going to be in the hospital for a few extra days. She won't be home for Christmas Eve or Christmas Day."

Carly's face paled. "I didn't even think of that. The kids—"

"Will be fine," he said. "Remember what we told Hannah."

"The best Christmas ever." Uncertainty filled Carly's voice.

"We will make this happen."

"We? I really appreciate all the help, but you have the brewery and your own family—"

"Stop." Jake stared into her eyes. "I've got the brewery under control no matter what my father thinks. And second, you guys are my family. Why would I want to spend Christmas in some fancy hotel eating overpriced food and being told I bought the wrong gift cards for my parents when I could be having fun with all of you?"

"Well, when you put it that way." Carly's tone was light, but she wasn't smiling. "Don't your parents miss you?"

"Not really. They liked the idea of having a child more than having a real child. Besides, I'll never live up to my father's expectations so not being around him much saves us from arguing more."

Compassion filled her eyes. "I'm sorry."

"No worries," he said, not wanting her pity. "It's the way things turned out. But at least now you know I'll be here to help. That's what friends are for."

"Thanks."

"Anytime." He wanted to reach out and touch her, but controlled the impulse. "You can always count on me, Carly. Don't ever forget that."

That night at the house, Carly laid out rolls of wrapping paper. The kids, exhausted from their busy day, were already sound asleep. She wondered how much sleep she'd manage tonight.

Jake carried a large black plastic bag full of items into the living room. She stared at the muscles beneath his shirt. Definite hard body. "This is the last of the presents."

"I don't know what I would do without you."

"Pretty indispensable, huh?" he asked.

"In some instances."

Carly didn't like that. She depended on one person only—herself. It was easier that way. Less complicated. And yet she couldn't have given the kids the Christmas they deserved on her own. She needed Jake. His help, that was.

He set the bag next to the others he'd brought down from the attic. "What next?"

A nervous breakdown.

Carly realized she was crunching a roll of blue-and-white snowflake wrapping paper. She loosened her grip and set the roll on the floor. She struggled to hold herself together, feeling as if she were about to unravel. She'd gone eight rounds with Christmas today, and felt emotionally raw. But it wasn't only the holidays she'd been battling. She'd been fighting her feelings for Jake, too.

She hadn't felt this vulnerable in years. The conflict inside her was talking its toll. If Jake knew how she was feeling, she'd be in big trouble.

"Nothing," she answered finally.

Best to send him on his way before he figured it out, or worse, she threw herself into his arms and couldn't let go.

Carly had a late, emotional night ahead of her. A box of tissues and chocolates were definitely in order along with the wrapping paper, ribbons and bows.

"Tomorrow's going to be a busy day." She placed the scissors and rolls of tape on the coffee table. "Go home and get some sleep."

He stood tall, his shoulders squared, as if he were ready to go to battle himself. "I'm not going anywhere."

She fought a rush of panic. "The brewery—"

"Manages without me when I go on a mission. It's no big deal if I don't stop in tonight. Don't forget, I'm a phone call away if they need me."

"You've done so much already. Talk about going above and beyond."

"You've done just as much. And look at all this." He motioned to the bags of presents. "You can't wrap all of this on your own."

"I can." She had to. Because however tired she was physically, emotionally, doing it on her own was better than continuing to rely on him for help.

"If I leave, you'll be up all night." He removed a box from one of the bags, his long fingers wrapping around a board game. "I'm not going to do that to you."

She needed him to leave her. Now. "I appreciate the offer, but I don't mind."

"I do."

The fire crackled. The wind blew outside. Carly could think of a million other places she'd rather be at the moment, but she was stuck here. She needed to be alone.

"Jake—"

"I know what's missing." He walked to the stereo and fiddled with the radio dial. "We can't do this without setting the mood."

Carly's heart slammed against her chest. Dread filled her. He wouldn't.

Except…she'd never told him about her discomfort with the whole Christmas season. She'd never told anyone except…Santa.

"Silent Night" played through the speakers.

She felt as if she might lose it any minute. Her shoulders sagged. "I'd rather we didn't have Christmas music playing."

He sorted the presents into stacks. One for Kendall. Another for Austin. "Why not?"

Carly took a deep breath, but didn't say anything. She couldn't say anything.

"Come on," he said. "Tell me."

"Christmas," she whispered as if it were some taboo word not supposed to be spoken. "I don't like it."

"Sure you do." He shot her a quizzical look as he placed a snowboard in Austin's pile. "You love Christmas. More than anyone I know."

She shook her head.

He froze. "You're serious?"

"Completely serious."

"But you used to bake all those cookies and spend hours decorating them with icing and candies. You'd make people gifts each year. And I'll never forget those Christmas carols you played all the time. Nick and I used to make up stupid lyrics to go with the music so you would turn them off."

Jake and Nick had irritated her so much with their words

and singing, but she had only turned up the volume when they did that.

"That was before," she admitted. "I—I don't celebrate Christmas anymore. I haven't since I moved to Philadelphia."

"The accident."

It wasn't a question. She nodded, grateful for his instant understanding. "I found it difficult, okay, impossible, to separate the accident from Christmas. Especially after the Christmas Eve wedding that wasn't. The feelings of guilt were so strong they threatened to suffocate me every time December rolled around. So I stopped celebrating Christmas. No one knew then. Or knows now."

His assessing gaze make her self-conscious. "You send gifts."

"I shop for presents all year-round, wrap them in September and package them so they're ready to mail after Thanksgiving. But now with Hannah in the hospital over Christmas I fear my secret is going to get out."

"Your secret is safe with me."

His words wrapped around her heart. She trusted he wouldn't say anything. "Thank you."

"Today must have been hard for you."

"I did what I had to do."

"You did a great job." He opened his arms. Carly went cautiously, but the moment he embraced her, she knew it was exactly what she needed. What she'd been wanting all night long. His hug offered comfort, strength and understanding. "Tell me what you need to get you through this and it's yours."

You.

What she needed was him. Uh-oh. She sure couldn't tell him that.

"Thanks," she said, not knowing what else to say.

"You know, maybe having to do Christmas for the kids will bring back your love of the holiday."

"That's not possible."

"Anything's possible," he said. "The Grinch figured out the meaning of Christmas in a night."

"And I thought you calling me a pest was bad." She crinkled her nose. "Now you're comparing me to the Grinch?"

"It's either him or Ebenezer Scrooge. Don't forget he learned what Christmas meant in a night, too."

This must be Jake's glass-half-full approach. She sighed. "I already know the meaning of Christmas. I just choose not to do anything about it."

"Be careful what you say."

"Why is that?" Carly asked.

He winked. "Because I'm always up for a challenge."

Forget about loving a challenge.

After four hours of wrapping, tagging and tying ribbons, Jake understood a little better why Carly felt the way she did about Christmas. But he wasn't about to give up. On the holiday or her.

She needed him. More than he'd realized. All he had to do was make her see it, too.

"That was harder than I thought it would be." Give him a length of rope, and he could tie one-handed bowlines with his eyes closed, but he couldn't tie a pretty bow around a present to save his life. "Good thing you were here to tie those ribbons."

"Well, I'm relieved you took the presents up to the attic. That was the last thing to check off my list for today." She sat on the couch, her legs curled underneath her and her eyes closed. "Do you think it would be bad if I slept here tonight?"

Not if he could join her. Oops. Wrong answer. He tried again. "It might get cold without a blanket."

"True, but I have the fire to keep me warm."

"Not unless you plan to keep stoking it so the fire burns all night."

"Stop." She yawned and covered her mouth. "It's too late for reality."

Jake was up for a little fantasy himself. He wanted to give Carly whatever she wanted.

"It's not too late for what I have in mind," he said.

"What is that?" she asked.

"Be right back."

"Take your time," she mumbled. "Please."

Jake returned a few minutes later. He set two glasses of eggnog on the coffee table. "This might make you feel better and give you enough strength to make it to your bed."

Carly's eyes sprang open. She saw the drinks and smiled. "Oh, this might give me the second wind I need. Is that nutmeg on top?"

"Freshly ground just for you."

Her warm, sleepy eyes brightened. "You are amazing."

He smiled at the compliment. "So are you."

Carly raised her glass to him. "To being amazing tonight."

"I'll drink to that." Jake sat next to her, picked up his glass and tapped it against hers. "Cheers."

She took a sip. "Delicious."

"Eggnog," he said. "A tasty Christmas tradition."

"This is one tradition I still enjoy." She took another sip. "See, I'm not the Grinch or a Scrooge."

"True." The carols playing in the background no longer seemed to bother her. "We could try another tradition to make sure."

"What do you have in mind?" she asked.

"Mistletoe?"

She laughed. "In your dreams."

Not quite the reaction he was hoping for, but at least she seemed more relaxed now. Jake wanted the joy back in her eyes. The way it had been at the hospital earlier.

He fought the urge to take her in his arms and hold her. To give her comfort, hugs, whatever she needed. But he couldn't. The line between friend and something more was already blurring. He needed Carly to give him a sign she was ready for more.

So he sat next to her, ignoring his need to touch her, to kiss her.

"You've been listening to Christmas music for the past four hours. It's time to sing along."

"I don't sing."

"That's true. I remember a couple of your Backstreet Boys renditions."

She swatted his arm. "Hey."

"Kidding." Jake laughed. He listened to the song playing on the radio. "I'm sure you remember the words to 'Jingle Bells.'"

"I could probably hum along…"

"That's the spirit."

"…if you got me a cookie."

"The ghost of Christmas present just rolled over in his grave."

She grinned. "Can I have his cookie, too?"

He tickled her side.

Carly erupted into laughter. She tried to tickle him back,

but he arched his body away from her. "No fair. You're bigger than me."

"Older and wiser, too."

"Older, yes." Amusement gleamed in her eyes. "But wiser?"

He tickled her more, until their bodies touched and their faces were mere inches apart. Her full lips drew his attention. He wanted to kiss her.

Instead he let go of her and moved back to his spot on the couch. A wise move? Time would tell, but it felt like the right move.

"I'm going home," he said. "I'll pick you guys up in the morning. We can get a tree and take it to the hospital."

"Sounds good."

"I have to be at work tomorrow afternoon," he said. "We're having a Christmas Eve buffet. Why don't you and the kids come?"

"That would be great. Hannah ordered a meal that only needs to be heated for Christmas dinner, but I hadn't figured out what to do for tomorrow night."

"I'll pick you up."

"You have to work."

"It won't take me that long to swing by."

"Okay," she said. "The kids will like that."

Jake was more interested in whether or not she was looking forward to seeing him again so soon, but he wasn't sure she was ready for the question—or that he was ready for the answer. He stood and walked to the front door. "See you tomorrow morning."

Carly nodded. "Jake."

He turned.

She stood, her eyes serious. "Thanks for everything. I appreciate all your help, but it was, um, really great having you here tonight. And not just to help me with stuff."

Her sincere words filled him with warmth. Jake smiled. He might not have gotten to kiss her tonight, but he would get his chance again.

Maybe sooner than he expected.

In thirty-six hours, Christmas would be behind her for another year. Carly couldn't wait. At least the day hadn't been too painful so far. Thanks to Jake.

She forced herself not to look at him. Not an easy thing in Hannah's cozy hospital room. But Carly had been staring and thinking about him too much. He'd become a part of her daily life, but she wasn't about to let him under her skin. Or into her heart.

Austin hung a silver bell on the small live tree they'd bought this morning. "This is so much fun."

The fresh fir scent and new baby smell masked the sterile hospital aroma Carly had smelled yesterday. And with all the noise—talking, laughter and Kendall's boot heels clicking against the tile floor—it seemed more like a party than hospital visit. "Christmas Eve should be fun."

"We've never decorated a tree on Christmas Eve before," Kendall said.

"That's because it's tradition to put up our tree on the first Sunday of December," Hannah said from her hospital bed. She hadn't stopped smiling or watching her kids since they arrived. She looked too rested to have given birth yesterday. "This one, however, is a very special tree. We'll plant it in the yard so it can grow with Tyler."

As Carly added hooks to the ornaments they'd purchased that morning, Austin removed a gold ball from the box.

"We can see who grows taller. Tyler or the tree," Jake said.

Carly glanced his way. He stood with the baby in his arms. Her breath caught in her throat. Her heart skipped at least two beats.

Talk about a natural. Okay, Jake had held Kendall and Austin as babies, but Carly remembered how he'd been back then. A little awkward trying to support the baby's head, but Jake's method couldn't be critiqued now.

An image of him holding his own child formed in Carly's mind. A beautiful child with the same piercing blue eyes and killer smile. A child that was hers, too.

The thought made her heart pound and her pulse race. Until she realized what she was daydreaming about.

Carly couldn't think of Jake as a father let alone the father of her baby. She'd given up on that dream. For now at least. And with Jake. A relationship with him could jeopardize the special place he held within this family. Not to mention the risk to her heart. She wet her dry lips.

"Babies can only see black, red and white," Garrett said.

"Not this baby." Jake's tone spoke of a deep affection for the child he held in his arms.

Austin nodded. "Our baby is the smartest baby. And he doesn't smell bad."

"At least not yet," Hannah muttered. "Come over here."

Carly sat on the chair next to the bed, noticing the photograph of the kids with Santa already set on her rolling bed tray.

"The kids are so happy being with you and Jake."

Hannah made them sound like a couple. Carly shifted in her seat. "It's been fun."

"I don't know how to thank you."

"No thanks are necessary. I'm having fun myself." Her gaze strayed to Jake. She forced her attention back to Hannah. "Don't worry about a thing. It's all being taken care of."

"What about you? Are doing okay?" Hannah asked, curiosity dripping from each word.

"I'm fine."

"You sure about that?" Hannah lowered her voice. "You and Jake seem sort of, well, chummy."

"We're friends," Carly whispered, ignoring the fact they'd kissed. She'd been trying hard to forget what had happened the other day. "That's all."

Hannah's eyes clouded with concern. "You're sure that's all?"

"Being friends is enough." After Carly had said the words, a part of her—the same part that liked when he pulled her into his arms and held her last night—wondered if that were true. She'd once liked the boy. She didn't have too many complaints about the man. Face it, men like Jacob Porter weren't easy to find.

But…the complications.

She had too much to lose if things went wrong. So did Hannah and the kids. Even Garrett. Carly wasn't willing to take the chance.

"Way more than enough," she added.

Hannah gave her a dubious look. The same one she'd given when Iain proposed and Carly had wanted a short engagement so they could marry on Christmas Eve.

"Just be careful," Hannah whispered. "I love Jake to death. I know he cares about you and has for a long time, but he doesn't exactly have the best track record when it comes to relationships. The last thing I want is for you to be hurt."

"I don't want that, either," Carly admitted. "I promise I'll be careful."

So careful she wouldn't have the opportunity to get hurt, let alone kiss Jake again.

CHAPTER SIX

CHAPTER SEVEN

THAT AFTERNOON after Jake had dropped them at home, Kendall and Austin decorated sugar cookies shaped like snowmen, stars, reindeer, candy canes, stockings and angels. The stove beeped. Carly turned off the timer. "The final batch is ready."

"They smell so good," Austin said.

The scent of freshly baked cookies filled her nostrils, bringing back memories of the Christmases that had come before. "They're almost better than gingerbread."

"We've never made gingerbread," Kendall said.

"You have." Six years ago. When Nick had still been alive. But that was the last time Carly had been with them at Christmastime. Her parents, too, since they'd moved after their divorce. "You were little, though."

And wouldn't have remembered.

That hurt. And yet, Garrett and Hannah, even Jake, couldn't be blamed for not honoring that particular Bishop tradition. It probably never even crossed their minds. But now all the things Nick loved growing up were unfamiliar to his children.

That wasn't fair to them. Or Nick.

Carly needed to fix that. "Your daddy and I always made a gingerbread house at Christmastime."

"I want to make one," Austin said.

"There isn't time tonight and we'll be at the hospital most of Christmas, but the next day I'll show you all you need to know about gingerbread, okay?"

Kendall beamed. "I can't wait."

"Me, either," Austin said.

Carly placed the cookies on a cooling rack. "That makes three of us."

"Four of us if you count Uncle Jake," Kendall added. "He'll want to help. Especially if food's involved."

Carly wouldn't mind Jake being there. She wiped her hands on the Mrs. Claus apron she wore. He'd been the one thing missing this afternoon. She kept thinking he should be here.

The song "I'll Be Home for Christmas" played on the radio. She listened to the lyrics, mentally composing a list like one Hannah had given her.

Snow, check.

Mistletoe, check.

Presents under the tree, check.

Not bad. Add in baking cookies and Carly was doing pretty good. Granted, this might not qualify as the best Christmas ever, but things were definitely better than she had expected.

Jake would be pleased.

Not that she wanted to please him. Carly placed the cookie sheet in the sink. Okay, maybe a little.

Uh-oh. She couldn't forget her promise to Hannah about being careful. Yet here Carly was, missing Jake. Wanting to please him. Becoming attached to him. Not smart. Carly washed the cookie sheet. The last thing she wanted to get was burned.

Austin popped a few candy sprinkles into his mouth. "Santa's going to love these cookies, Aunt Carly."

"Yes, he will." She pointed to the red candies on the snow-man's chest. "I like how you used cinnamon candies for his buttons."

Kendall tilted her chin. "It was my idea."

"Was not," Austin said.

"Was, too."

Carly whistled. Both kids stopped talking. "It's Christmas Eve. Santa still has time to take gifts off his sleigh."

The kids exchanged worried glances.

She looked at them both. "Let's concentrate on decorating the cookies and not arguing with each other, okay?"

Kendall and Austin placed new cookies in front of them and set to work.

"After we get home from dinner at the brewpub—" Carly placed candy sprinkles on the angel's wings she was deco-rating "—we can make a plate of cookies for Santa and one with carrots and celery for the reindeer."

Kendall's brow furrowed. "We've never left anything for the reindeer before."

Oh, Nick. I shouldn't have stayed away so long. Forgive me.

"Your daddy taught me to leave treats for the reindeer when I was a little girl," Carly explained. "Don't forget, Santa visits a lot of houses tonight, but it's the reindeer who do all the flying. They deserve something to snack on, too."

Austin flashed her a grin. "Will you come back next Christmas so we can do this all over again?"

Both kids stared expectantly at her. Carly took a deep breath. "I would love to come back, but we need to talk to your parents first."

"Oh, they won't mind." Kendall piped a red ball of icing on the end of a reindeer's nose. "Mommy always says she wishes you lived closer."

Carly stared at the angel cookie in front of her. "Sometimes I wish that, too."

"Then move," Austin said. "This is the best place to live in the entire world."

"Philadelphia's not too bad," she countered.

Austin looked at her as if she'd lost her mind. "But we're not there."

She thought about his words. The kids weren't there. Neither was Jake. But she hadn't been trying to escape them, only the mountain, a constant reminder of all she'd lost. "You're right about that."

They continued decorating cookies. Time seemed to fly. The sprinkles and colored sugars disappeared. Only a dab of icing remained.

"Do you hear that, Aunt Carly?" Kendall asked.

Carly realized she was humming along to the catchy Christmas carol spilling from the radio. Uh-oh. She wet her lips. "Hear what?"

Kendall pursed her lips. "Jingle bells."

"'Deck the Halls,'" Carly corrected.

"Not on the radio, silly! Listen."

She listened and heard a faint jingling in the distance. "You're right. It's not the radio."

"I hear it, too." Austin pushed his chair back from the table and stood. He looked up and down and all around.

"Maybe one of Santa's elves is checking to see if we're being good."

"You never know," Carly said. "Or one of the inns or resorts is offering sleigh rides tonight."

"I wish we could go on a sleigh ride," Kendall said with a wistful tone.

The longing in her niece's voice made Carly want to flag down the sleigh right then and there. She might not be in a position to make Kendall a flower girl, but this was something Carly could give her. "We could find out how much a sleigh ride costs and see if they are doing them after Christmas."

Kendall grinned. "That would be so cool."

"Very cool." Carly just hoped she could afford it. Seeing the look in the little girl's eyes, she almost didn't care.

"Did you ever go on a sleigh ride?" Kendall asked.

"No," Carly admitted.

Kendall's face fell.

"I went on a dog sled ride once, though," Carly offered. She had begged and begged for years, but her parents always said it was too expensive.

Austin stopped munching on a broken candy-cane-shaped cookie. "When?"

Carly remembered the wind in her face as the team drove around Frog Lake one chilly afternoon. She'd helped care for the dogs afterward. "When I was fifteen."

"Did your aunt take you?"

She laughed. "No, it was a special present from your daddy and…Uncle Jake."

Her brother had given her the gift, but Jake had played a role in the present. She suspected he might even have helped Nick pay for it.

"Uncle Jake gives the best presents," Kendall said.

"He does." The best kisses, too. Carly touched her lips with her fingertips. Careful. She knew more kisses were a really bad idea, but her lips seemed to disagree. Still she wasn't about to have a fling during her winter vacation and risk losing Jake's friendship forever.

And her heart again.

Austin cupped his ear with his hand. "Listen. The bells are getting closer."

Kendall ran to the living-room window. Austin followed at her heels. Carly took up the rear.

"It's on our street," Kendall said. "Coming to our house."

The kids pressed their noises against the glass and sighed.

"Look at the horse." Wonder filled Austin's voice.

Carly looked out the window. A large, black horse pulled a red sleigh hung with garlands. Two bright lanterns bobbed at the front. A driver, wearing an old-fashioned stovepipe hat on his head and a cape around his shoulders, held on to the reins. "Do you see anyone besides the driver?"

"Uncle Jake," the two said at the same time. They jumped and shrieked.

Who else but Uncle Jake? A warm and fuzzy feeling flowed through Carly. The only things missing were chestnuts roasting and carolers decked out in Victorian clothing. "He said he would pick us up, but I had no idea this was what he had in mind. Come on, guys, let's get ready."

As the kids washed and changed clothes, Carly threw away what little icing remained, snapped the lids back on the cookie decorations, washed her hands and removed her apron.

The doorbell rang. She smiled. Perfect timing.

"Merry Christmas," Jake said.

Her heart expanded. His cheeks were ruddy with cold, but his blue eyes were so warm.

"It's not Christmas yet," Kendall said.

"True, but it will be in a few hours," he said, looking stylish and handsome in his blue down jacket, olive-green pants and fleece hat. "That's why I thought a sleigh ride tonight might be a fun way to go to dinner."

Austin jumped up and down. "It'll be the funnest way ever."

"Thank you, Uncle Jake." Kendall hugged him. "I bet no one else gets to do this."

"Let's go, let's go," Austin sang.

Carly felt a tingle as she watched the scene in front of her. The kids' love and gratitude for Jake was just as strong as his for them. Lucky kids. But someone had to be practical. "Get on your coats, hats and mittens."

"What smells so good?" Jake asked.

"We baked cookies for Santa," Kendall said. "You can have one."

"I can't wait. Thanks." He looked at Carly and grinned. "Nothing like making Christmas cookies on Christmas Eve to put you in the holiday spirit."

Austin struggled with her zipper. "We're going to make gingerbread houses, too."

"Our daddy used to make it," Kendall added, jamming a hat over her blond curls.

"I didn't know that," Jake admitted.

"A Bishop family tradition," she replied.

"Maybe I could learn, too," he said.

"Sure." She shrugged into her jacket. "Thanks for arranging the sleigh ride. It's exactly what the kids need."

His gaze locked on hers. "I didn't do this only for the kids."

Her heart bumped. Had he done this for her? "Oh. Well…"

"We couldn't all fit into a dog sled. I figured a sleigh was the next best thing."

His thoughtfulness, his teasing, warmed her from the inside out. And so did the look in his eyes. "The best," she corrected. "Thanks."

"You're welcome." His smile widened. "Are you ready to go?"

At that moment, she would have followed him anywhere. Not trusting what she might say, Carly nodded.

"Hop on the sleigh, kids," he said.

Kendall and Austin ran outside, their footsteps crunching on the snow. Their laughter was a perfect complement to the jingle bells on the horse's harnesses.

Carly watched them. "The kids are so excited."

"What about you?" Jake asked.

A beat passed. She didn't dare look at him. "I'm pretty excited, too."

"The fun is only beginning."

Anticipation filled her. With the one-horse open sleigh in the driveway surrounded by all the snow-covered trees and delicate snowflakes falling from the sky, she felt as if she'd stepped into a greeting card.

Outside, the cold air tasted like…Christmas. She smelled snow, pine and smoke from fireplaces. By the time she crossed the driveway, Kendall and Austin were sitting on either side of the sleigh driver. Carly could see their breaths, but the low temperatures didn't seem to bother them one bit. Still, Jake covered the kids with thick blankets.

Carly sat on the padded seat in the back. He joined her, his thigh pressing against hers.

He spread a blanket over her. "Warm enough?"

Any warmer and her blood would boil. "Very cozy, thank you."

"Well, if you get cold, I know how to warm you up."

She wondered what he had in mind.

As the sleigh glided forward, the horse's bells jingled, almost drowning out the kids' conversation with the driver. Carly removed her camera from her purse and took a picture of them.

"They'll remember this forever," she confided with a smile.

Jake looked uncomfortable. "I don't know about forever. I just want them to enjoy tonight."

"They will. They are." She lowered the camera to her lap. "And if they ever forget tonight, they'll have a photo to help them remember. I still have a picture of me with those sled dogs. Did I ever thank you for that?"

"The sled ride was mostly Nick's present."

"But it was your idea," she guessed.

"Big deal." Jake took the camera from her and snapped her picture. The flash made her see spots. "Going on a dog sled ride for your birthday was all you talked about from the time you were ten. It didn't take much imagination to know it was time to make it happen."

"But—"

"Smile." He held the camera out in front of the two of them and leaned his head against hers. The flash blinded her again.

She blinked. "What nineteen-year-old guy would go to so much trouble?"

"A guy who realized his best friend's sister was growing up to be a beautiful young woman."

Carly's cheeks warmed.

Jake tucked a strand of hair back into her hat. The gesture was intimate, but felt so right.

"You're even more beautiful now, Carly."

Heaven help her. She forced herself to take a deep breath. "You're really determined to make this the best Christmas ever, aren't you?"

The festive atmosphere in the brewpub couldn't have been more perfect. The place was packed. Miniature lights around the bar flashed on and off. Small red foil-covered pots of poinsettias sat on each table. The fireplace crackled with a burning blaze. Conversations drowned out the Christmas carols playing on the sound system, but no one seemed to care. A few hardy souls at one table sang carols on their own. And the mouthwatering scent of the buffet had patrons thinking more about the tasty food than the beer on tap.

Jake couldn't be happier. No doubt his father would find something to complain about, but his father wasn't here to dampen his mood.

Satisfaction filled Jake as he stared from behind the bar at Carly and the kids eating dinner. All three were smiling and laughing. Fun times. Just as he'd hoped.

He would return to the table once things settled down, but he needed to help his bartender keep up with orders right now. He handed a server three glasses—two porters and an ale.

"Why don't you take a picture of her," a familiar male voice said. "It'll last longer."

Jake didn't look up. As he filled a pint-size glass with Nick's Winter Ale, he thought about what Carly had said on the sleigh ride.

And if they ever forget tonight, they'll have a photo to help them remember.

What was he going to have when this was over? A picture of Carly and a few memories? Or a whole lot of regrets?

Jake set the drink on the bar. "Merry Christmas, Sean."

"Same to you." Sean Hughes sat on the bar stool and raised his glass. "To Nick. Wherever you are, my friend, climb on."

Jake lifted his water glass into the air. "Hear, hear."

Sean glanced back at Carly and the kids. "You finally putting the moves on her?"

Jake clenched his jaw. "Thinking about it."

"You've been going to an awful lot of trouble for her."

"Not just for her. The kids, too." Jake placed his glass back under the bar. It hadn't felt like trouble to him. "I'm only doing what needs to be done."

Sean swirled the beer in his glass. "Is that what's best for Carly?"

"Since when do you offer dating advice?" Jake asked, filling another Nick's Winter Ale and two pale ales.

Sean shrugged. "Nick would be saying the same stuff to you if he were here."

"If Nick were here, he would have punched me out as soon as he found out I'd kissed Carly."

"True, that," Sean said. "I can punch you for him if it would make you feel better."

Jake handed a server two pints of amber. "Thanks, but no thanks."

Sean took another swig of his beer. "Just remember she's still Nick's little sister. Not some flavor of the month."

"I know that." But saying those words made the fact sink in.

"Thanks for the beer." Sean took a large swig. "Better get

back to the parents' house before Denali starts wondering where I've been."

"Denali is a dog."

"She's still a female." Sean downed the rest of his glass. "See you tomorrow."

"Looking forward to it." Jake filled another order, but his mind was on something else. Someone else. Nick.

Sean raised a good point.

What would Nick Bishop think about Jake wanting to be with Carly? He glanced at her and rubbed his jaw. Jake didn't think he wanted to know the answer.

Four hours later, Carly watched Jake. He sat in the middle of the living-room floor surrounded by pirate ship pieces. Frustration coupled with intense concentration creased his forehead. The look totally contradicted the carefree, almost messy style of his hair. Hair she wanted to brush her fingers through.

Oops. That wasn't being careful. Or smart.

Time to put the brakes on whatever attraction she was feeling. Physical attraction, she amended. When she returned to Philadelphia after New Year's, Jake would be out of sight. That would put him out of her mind and she'd be back to normal.

"You need a mechanical engineering degree to get the damn thing out of the box." He twisted the wire securing the hull to a piece of cardboard. "Forget about the packaging being kid-proof. This thing is fully adult-proof."

"I should have wrapped the box instead."

"And put this together on Christmas day with Austin standing over me asking every two minutes when it'll be ready to play with?" Jake succeeded in removing the last piece. "No way. I've done this enough times to know better."

"I feel like a total newbie," Carly admitted. "When the kids were younger, the presents were less complicated. A rocking horse, a toy box, a ride-on car."

"I remember those days." He held two ship parts in his hands. "But you seem to know what you're doing."

"Hannah's list." Carly arranged the presents under the tree. "Between that and you, I've had all I needed."

He gazed up at her. "Flattery will get you everywhere."

"I'll have to remember that."

"Just so you know. Being with you has been great." The way his eyes looked at her felt almost like a caress. "And I wouldn't have missed any of this. Christmas and kids go hand in hand. Wait until morning when Kendall and Austin run down the stairs, see the presents under the tree and scream at the top of their lungs."

"You must get here early to see all that."

He nodded. "Last year, Garrett and I took a long time putting together bikes for the kids so I ended up staying the night, but that made things easier in the morning. I didn't have to get up so early."

Easier in the morning, but what about bedtime?

The thought of saying good-night to Jake in the house alone filled her stomach with butterflies. Okay, they weren't totally alone, but their chaperones were fast asleep, dreaming about sugar plums, snowboards and the hottest new video game platform.

"I'm not fishing for an invitation if that's what you're worried about," he added.

"I didn't think you were. And I'm not worried." Darn. She sounded defensive. "I'm just not used to any of this."

"You mean, Christmas."

"Among other things." Like him.

"What other things?" he asked.

Carly blew out a breath. "I know we're just friends, but being with you these past couple of days has been like playing house."

His eyes gleamed. "You used to like playing house."

"I was eight, not twenty-eight," she said. "Everything has been so wonderful. Tonight was simply magical, but it's getting hard to tell what was pretend and what was real."

"It can be whatever you want it to be."

That's what she was afraid of. Part of her wanted it to be real, but that would mean taking chances again.

"You said it yourself, Carly. We're friends. We're having fun. It's Christmas Eve. Why don't we let whatever happens happen?"

The thought of doing what he suggested scared her. Carly didn't take chances, but she couldn't deny how wonderful being with Jake felt. It was as if a Christmas fairy had sprinkled magical snowflake dust on them. Maybe following his advice would be…okay.

Carly took a deep breath. "I—I can do that."

"Good." His smile reassured her. "Now want to help me put together this pirate ship so we can finish up everything?"

Relieved, disappointed, she nodded. "Where are the instructions?"

"I'm not big on instructions—" he reached under the box and pulled out a white booklet "—but you can use them."

She read the directions, found the necessary pieces and assembled the captain's quarter. "We might get the ship put together faster if we both followed the directions."

"I have a better idea." His eyes narrowed in on her. "Let's

divide the ship parts in half. Whoever finishes first wins. You use the instructions. I won't. What do you say?"

The challenging tone of his voice reminded her of the bets Jake and Nick had made over the years, decades really. "I thought you would have outgrown making stupid bets by now."

"Nope. And they're not stupid bets." Jake set the pieces of the ship on the carpet. "Sean ended up having to chop my firewood this fall after we bet on how much rockfall we'd see. He then wanted to go double or nothing by guessing when the bergschrund would be open. He, of course, lost."

"He shouldn't have bet to start with." She glanced over the directions. "I'm not much of a gambler."

"Even if it's a sure thing?" he asked.

"Nothing's ever a sure thing." Carly knew that better than anybody. She picked up two new parts of the ship and studied at the diagram in the instruction manual. "Though I must admit I'm partial to guarantees."

"I see nothing wrong with a friendly wager every now and then."

How friendly? She snapped a rail onto the ship's deck. "That's because you rarely lose."

"Losing is always a possibility, but that's what makes it exciting."

Exciting? Try terrifying. "I don't think so."

All Carly had done for the past six years was lose. Her fiancé. Her brother. Her parents being together. Pretty much everything and everyone she'd grown up loving had disappeared or changed. Every person she'd loved had disappointed her. She couldn't take anything else.

"We could make the prize something easy," he suggested. "Whatever you want."

She wanted Jake to hold her, to pull her against him and kiss her. Hard. The thought alone raised her temperature ten degrees. Not good.

His flashed her a charming lopsided grin. "I'll give you a head start."

"Don't try to egg me into accepting a bet. I've already put more pieces together than you."

"Then you can't lose."

She wished that were the case, but experience had painted a much different picture with wide brush strokes even she couldn't pretend not to see. "No, thanks."

"You said you would let whatever happens happen."

Carly stared at him. "Are you always so…?"

He raised a brow. "Charming?"

"Persistent?"

Jake laughed. "It depends on how much I want something."

"And you want it, I mean a bet, this much."

"Yes—" the intensity in his eyes took her breath away "—I want…it that much."

Oh, boy. Anticipation skittered down her spine.

"What do you say, Carly? Will you take a chance?"

His smile full of warmth and laughter hinted at a promise she couldn't even imagine. A simple bet with an easy prize. She was tempted—oh, so tempted, considering she'd already agreed to let whatever happen happen.

"Come on," he urged, those baby blues of his melting away her resolve. "What have you got to lose?"

Only one thing, she realized. Her heart.

"I can't believe I lost the bet." Jake ate another cookie. He'd already munched down carrots and taken bites out of celery sticks before tossing them outside so the kids would think the reindeer had eaten them. "But if you thought drinking milk and eating cookies left for Santa would be a chore, it's not."

"Somebody had to do it." Carly lay on the couch. "Better you than me. If I ate them, they'd go straight to my hips."

But they sure were nice hips. She had curves in all the right places.

"I'll do anything to help the cause." Jake bit into another cookie, a snowman with red candy buttons on his front.

"So you would have eaten the cookies even if you'd won the bet?" she asked.

"If you had wanted me to."

He wanted to help her. Not out of guilt, but because he cared. Not for the girl she'd been, but the woman she'd become.

Is that what's best for Carly?

Hell, yes. Jake only wanted what was best for her. Even if that might not be him.

A soft, sweet smile graced her lips, and Jake's heart did a flip-flop. "Thank you," she said.

"You're welcome, but are you sure you don't want something else from me?" He walked toward her. "You won fair and square, but I'm the one who got the treats."

"I'm good." She glanced at the clock. "I'm a little tired, but happy we got everything done before midnight."

"We're a good team."

She nodded.

Jake raised her sock-covered feet off the couch, sat and placed them on his lap. As he touched her left foot, she tensed. The moment he rubbed, the tension seeped from her body.

She sunk into the couch. "Oh, thank you."

"You deserve it," he said. "You've been on your feet all day."

"I'm on my feet at work."

"Yes, but you're not used to this kind of work."

"You're not kidding." Her eyelids closed. She sighed. "Is there anything Jake Porter can't do?"

"I suck at differential equations."

Her eyes remained closed. "When was the last time you did one of those?"

"On the final exam."

She smiled. "You're going to have to come up with something better than that."

He moved to the other foot.

"Oh, Jake." She practically purred. "This is wonderful."

He agreed. "Glad you're liking it."

"I'm loving it."

He wished he could give her more, but he didn't want to press his luck.

A cuckoo clock Nick had bought on a ski trip to Switzerland sounded twelve times. Midnight.

She opened her eyes and sat with her elbows supporting her weight on the sofa's armrest. "Merry Christmas."

"Merry Christmas, Carly."

A beat passed. And another.

Their eyes locked. Even their breathing seemed in sync.

What he wouldn't give for some mistletoe because if there ever was a perfect time for a kiss it was now.

Right now.

But Jake hesitated. He didn't want to make the wrong move. He'd known fear, on the mountain, not knowing if he'd make it down in one piece. The quiet. The waiting. The unknown.

Jake felt like that now.

Oh, the stakes weren't life or death, but they felt high nonetheless. What was the price of a kiss?

A brush of his lips on her forehead. A friendly peck on her cheek. A juicy one planted right on her lips. He wasn't about to be picky though if he had his choice he'd go for juicy. Especially if it was going to cost him. He rubbed her ankles.

If only he knew what she wanted him to do. Not that he had a clue himself beyond wanting a kiss. But the wanting alone pushed what he was feeling out of the friendship realm and into something else altogether. So he sat, his hands on her feet, holding his breath, waiting for inspiration to strike.

He'd told her to take a chance. Yet he was unable to do the same. Coward. He might as well plop down on a nest and warm a clutch of eggs.

Yawning, she stretched her arms above her head. "Sorry. It's been a long day."

"It's late, too," he said, breaking the mood like a glass dropped on a tile floor. "I should probably be going."

Carly moistened her lips. "Unless you want to stay the night."

CHAPTER EIGHT

UNLESS YOU WANT to stay the night.

Carly cringed. She couldn't believe she'd said those words out loud. Oh, she'd been thinking them. Boy, had she ever since his warm, strong hands had worked their magic on her sore, tired feet. Her entire body had responded to his foot massage.

But asking Jake to spend the night here?

He'd already spent the night before, she reminded herself. But not with her.

I promise I'll be careful.

So much for keeping that promise. She gulped.

"You want me to stay the night," he said, his steady tone the exact opposite of the way her insides trembled.

Carly noticed he hadn't asked a question. Was he that sure of himself? Or of her? She didn't like thinking she was so transparent. She was no longer the immature teenager who wore her heart on her sleeve. Maybe it was time to remind them both of that. She sat straighter.

"If you want to." Carly wanted a cue from him to tell her she wasn't making a big mistake. "Being here might make things easier in the morning."

"I'm all for easy."

She was afraid of that.

"I already put my presents under the tree," Jake said. "And I have a bag with extra clothes in the car."

As she thought about why he might keep extra clothes in his car, Hannah's words echoed through Carly's head.

He doesn't exactly have the best track record when it comes to relationships.

"I never know what's going to happen with OMSAR so keeping a dry set, something to wear after a mission, in the car makes sense," he continued. "Though sometimes I'm too tired to change and all I'll want is to get home."

OMSAR. Relief washed over her, but a little doubt remained. "It does. Make sense."

She sounded like an idiot. Or a thirteen-year-old with a huge crush. Maybe a combination of the two.

"There are clean sheets on Hannah and Garrett's bed if you want to sleep there," Carly said.

"I could take one of the bunks in Austin's room."

Not the words of a man burning with impatience to have sex.

Was she so out of practice she had completely misread his signals? Or was he letting her set the pace and parameters of their relationship? Not that she was even sure what they had could be called a relationship.

Why don't we let whatever happens happen?

She tried not to think of the queen bed in her room. A bed too big for one person. Especially on this cold winter's night. Right now Carly wasn't sure enough of her feelings or his to do anything.

"Whatever you want," she said finally.

Jake winked. "What I want isn't a possibility. Unless it's what you want, too."

The flash of desire in his eyes took her breath away. He made her feel as if she was exactly what he hoped to find under the Christmas tree tomorrow morning. She felt the same way about him. Tie a ribbon around him, attach a gift tag with her name on it and this would be the best Christmas ever.

What was happening to her?

When Jake was around, she forgot all about being careful and playing it safe. And yet...

He seemed to know it. Darn him.

His confidence undermined hers. She didn't know what she wanted anymore.

He put on his coat. "Be right back."

As the door closed behind him, Carly rose from the couch. She shuffled her way to the front door and stood by the window, waiting and watching.

Jake moved with the agility and grace of an athlete. The snow-covered driveway didn't slow him down. He disappeared behind the back of his SUV. A moment later, he reappeared with a dark-colored duffel bag in his hand.

So he was spending the night.

No. Big. Deal.

Too bad she saw right through the self-denial. Carly wanted to believe she'd asked him to stay for Kendall and Austin's sake, but she hadn't been thinking about the kids when she'd asked Jake to stay. She was the one who wanted him to be here. She was the one who hadn't wanted to have to say goodbye. She was the one who wasn't even ready to say goodnight.

As he walked up the step, she opened the front door for him. The cold night air felt good blowing against her.

Jake crossed the threshold, his presence filling the small foyer. He removed and hung his jacket on the rack. "Thanks."

Carly closed the door. As she clicked the lock in place, she felt as if she were sealing her fate, as well.

Stop overreacting, she told herself. Her reasons for asking him no longer mattered. Sure, she might have thought she was ready for something to happen, but she'd changed her mind.

"You're going to get cold feet," Jake said. "Standing in the doorway in your socks."

His warning was too late. Carly already had cold feet. She stepped back.

Jake stared at her with a wry grin on his face. "Better watch out."

Another warning? "Why?"

"You're standing under the mistletoe."

She glanced up to see the greenery hanging above. Flushed. "I forgot it was there."

Carly should move away, but his blue eyes mesmerized her, held her transfixed to the spot where she stood.

"I didn't," he said.

"But the kids aren't here to make us kiss."

His eyes darkened to a midnight blue. "This isn't about the kids, Carly."

A beat passed. She raised her chin. "What is it about, then?"

"Tradition."

Not the answer she had hoped for. And yet...

Why don't we let whatever happens happen?

Why not?

"I for one wouldn't want to stand in the way of a time-honored tradition."

Rising on tiptoes, she kissed him on the lips. Tentatively. Softly. Expecting him to back away at any second.

But he didn't.

Instead, Jake moved his mouth over hers with such tenderness she felt totally safe and in control. She parted her lips more and slightly increased the pressure of the kiss. He did the same. Carly liked being the one who decided what came next, as if they were dancing and he was following her lead.

A loud thud sounded. Not her heart. Maybe his bag? He wove his fingers through her hair. Yes, his bag.

Each step she took to deepen the kiss, he matched until she could no longer think straight to know what she was doing. Tingles flowed from her lips to every extremity. A toe-curling kiss, most definitely, but this one also had her heart doing cartwheels and her feet wanting to float off the ground.

This was far more than a Christmas tradition, far more than a kiss between friends, but Carly didn't care. She only wanted…more.

His arms wrapped around her. She arched closer, reaching up to embrace him. As she pressed against his body, she felt the rapid beat of his heart against her chest. The scent of him surrounded her. The taste of him filled her.

Her hands splayed over his back. She ran her fingers along the contours and ridges of his muscles. So strong and all hers.

For now. That was enough. It had to be.

Suddenly, Carly felt his arm come under her knees and she was no longer touching the ground. Jake carried her, as if she weighed nothing, his lips never leaving hers for an instant. He sat on the couch with her on his lap.

The mistletoe.

They were no longer standing beneath it, but that didn't seem to matter. Thank goodness.

Jake kissed the corner of her mouth. He trailed kisses along her jaw up and nibbled on her ear, shooting sparks through her.

She held on to him, her fingers digging into his back. If he let go she would slide right off his lap. But Carly knew, in her mind and in her heart, Jake would never let her fall.

He ran his tongue along her earlobe, the light touch making her quiver with delight. Desire burned like the blood rushing through her veins. "Jake."

Her voice sounded different. The word was more a plea than anything else.

"Hmmm?"

"Kiss me again."

Slowly, almost tortuously, he expertly trailed kisses along her neck until Carly thought she would burst with pleasure. Finally he reached her mouth and pressed his lips against hers.

"Like this?" he murmured.

"Uh-huh." She could barely talk, let alone think, as sensation washed over her.

She'd never felt so overcome by a kiss. Time no longer mattered. Nothing did. All she knew or could think about was Jake. How it felt to be in his arms and kissing him.

This was what had been missing in her life.

She hadn't thought she'd wanted it, but she needed it. Badly.

The cuckoo clock sounded once.

Jake kissed her hard on the lips again, and then pulled

away. His ragged breathing matched her own. He struggled to catch his breath, but never let go of her.

The way he held on to her made her feel precious and adored, a way she hadn't felt in years. A blissful euphoria surrounded her. She looked up at her friend Jake, at the man who had made her feel such passion.

The hunger in his eyes made her swallow. She'd put that look in his eyes. Her and their kiss. Make that kisses. Power and confidence blazed through her.

"I need to buy more mistletoe," he said. "And put it all over the house."

She wiggled her toes. "Sounds good to me."

"Over the bed," he teased.

Carly smiled, but her heart lurched. "That's quite a line. Have you used it before?"

Jake grinned. "Not that one. I made it up just for you."

Meaning there had been other lines, she deduced. Other women. Hannah's words came back to Carly.

He doesn't exactly have the best track record when it comes to relationships. The last thing I want is for you to be hurt.

Heat rose in her cheeks. She looked away.

"Hey—" he drew her chin back up "—don't do that."

"But I…" She glanced around the room, anything to keep from meeting his eyes. "We…"

"Let me give you the same words of wisdom someone told me once. 'Don't think about it too much.'"

"Your grandmother?" Carly asked

"Your brother." Jake's eyes softened. "When we bailed right below the Liberty Cap glacier on Rainier. I knew in my gut it was the right call, but I couldn't stop going on and on about it on our way down. Finally Nick said that to me."

"But how do you…."

"Not think about it too much?" Jake finished for her.

She nodded.

"He never told me that part."

Carly laughed. "Typical Nick."

"True." Jake ran his finger along the side of her face. Her skin felt soft beneath his calloused hands. "Though I wonder what he'd say about this."

"Does it matter?" she asked, reluctant to let the moment go even though she knew Hannah's concerns.

"I want you to be happy," he said.

Which was no answer at all, and all the answer Carly needed. She couldn't live completely in the moment as Jake did. And he wasn't offering her anything else. Not yet. Maybe not…ever?

She swallowed. "I am happy. I'm…I'm glad we're still friends."

"I will always be your friend no matter what," he said. "But I'm not going to lie and tell you I don't want to kiss you again. And more. But there's no rush."

Jake wasn't offering her any guarantees, but he did care for her. Enough not to pressure her.

Her heart overflowed with so much emotion her chest felt as if it might explode. Maybe the heart was capable of growing three sizes in a day.

"Just more mistletoe," she said lightly.

"I sure hope so."

"Thanks." She wrapped her arms around him. Jake hugged back, brushing his lips across the top of her head.

He let go and stood. "I'd rather not say good-night, but that's what I should do. And what Nick would want me to do. So I'm going to head up to Austin's room now."

She nodded, even though a part of her wanted to tell him to stay with her. "Merry Christmas, Jake."

"Merry Christmas, Carly."

Early Christmas morning, Jake stood in the kitchen. He added cloves, allspice and cinnamon sticks to the pot of apple cider and turned on the stove. The mixture needed to simmer.

He'd been simmering all night.

Sleep hadn't come easy. Not with only a wall separating him from Carly.

The kisses last night had been great. Amazing. A real turn-on. But what he felt went beyond the kisses they'd shared. The scars of the past faded away when he was with Carly. Somehow she made all the hurt, all the regret disappear.

As the oven preheated, Jake opened the refrigerator and pulled out the egg strata dish Carly had made last night using Hannah's recipe. The sun-dried tomatoes and spinach gave the dish a festive red-and-green look perfect for Christmas morning. Even the kids liked to eat it.

Kids.

Jake thought back to when he was younger. His teenage fantasy about Carly and being a part of the Bishop family had been nothing more than a pipe dream. He'd joked about it with Nick once, and if looks could kill Jake would have been six feet under. He hadn't a clue about love or relationships back then. But Jake wasn't the same, and neither was Carly.

The two of them were good together. Damn good.

"You're up early." Carly entered the kitchen wearing a purple robe and fuzzy pink socks. He wondered what she wore under it. "What smells so good?"

"Spiced apple cider." He picked up a wooden spoon and

stirred the liquid to keep from taking her in his arms and kissing. "It's tradition."

The echo of his words last night brought color to her cheeks. "Whose tradition?"

"Garrett's." Jake focused on the cider. That was better than trying to figure out what type of lingerie she did or didn't have on. "I'm going to take a Thermos of cider to the hospital."

"That's thoughtful of you."

He opened the oven door and stuck the strata inside.

Carly grinned. "Keep this up, and I may have to keep you."

That didn't sound so bad to Jake. He closed the oven door and set the timer. "Just make sure I get a little time off for good behavior."

He wasn't sure if he was joking or not. That bothered him. Jake had never felt this way about a woman before. He wasn't sure he liked it.

Carly sighed, reminding him of how she sounded last night. "This really is turning into the best Christmas ever."

That was what he was afraid of.

A half hour later, the kids ran down the stairs screaming. They stood in front of the tree in total awe and silence for about two seconds. The shrieking started up again as the kids dropped to their knees to search for their presents.

All their work the past two nights had paid off. Carly couldn't be happier. Nor could she stop laughing at the kids' antics. Thank goodness Jake had set up the video camera. Hannah and Garrett weren't going to want to miss this.

The day kept getting better. It wasn't a traditional Christmas by any means, but no one had any complaints. At the hospital, Hannah kept dabbing tears of joy from her eyes.

Garrett happily drank every drop of the spiced cider. Kendall and Austin loved opening more presents with their parents. Even baby Tyler seemed to enjoy himself. Being with Jake was the icing on top for Carly.

He looked so handsome and the way his smile crinkled the corners of his eyes kept her casting sideward glances his way.

As he drove them from the hospital to the house, she sat in the passenger seat singing songs with the kids. Pretending Christmas didn't exist might have made things easier, but celebrating the holiday this year made Carly realize how much she'd missed.

She didn't want to miss anything more.

"I wish today didn't have to end," Kendall said when a commercial came over the radio.

Austin sighed. "I wish there were more waiting for us at home."

Carly looked back. "We took all the presents with us to the hospital."

"Don't forget Christmas isn't about the presents," Jake said, glancing in his rearview mirror. "Remember what you heard in church this morning."

"We know, Uncle Jake." Kendall sounded years older than nine. "But it's still nice to get gifts."

"Very nice," Austin said.

"Hey, Uncle Jake," Kendall yelled. "You missed the turn to our street."

"We're taking a little detour," he said.

Carly looked at him. "Where are we going?"

Mischief sparkled in his eyes. "It's a surprise."

Excitement overflowed from the backseat as the kids guessed their destination. Even Carly joined in.

"The hot springs at Kah-nee-ta."

"Timberline Lodge."

"The brewery."

"Good guesses," Jake said. "But none are correct."

He made a right-hand turn off the highway, and Carly knew exactly what he had in mind. "Are you sure this is a good idea?"

"Yes. They're old enough." He parked at a Sno-park near other trucks and SUVs. "Remember, it's a tradition."

"What are Sean and Denali doing here?" Austin asked.

"There's Bill and Tim with little Wyatt in a backpack," Kendall said. "And Leanne's here, too."

"The whole gang," Carly mumbled, her chest tight.

Jake nodded. "It's what Nick would have wanted."

"Does Hannah know?"

Jake nodded. "Garrett convinced her it was time. Are you okay with this?"

Carly took a deep breath. "Yes."

"Then let's go," Jake said, exiting the car.

Denali, Sean's black-and-white Siberian husky with ice-blue eyes, barked a greeting and bounded in the snow.

As Kendall and Austin told everyone about their Christmas so far, Jake removed their snow boots and winter clothing from the back of his SUV. "Put these on."

"Are we going on a hike in the snow, Uncle Jake?" Kendall asked.

"You'll see."

Leanne gave Carly clothes and boots to wear.

Once they were dressed, Sean removed two gifts, awkwardly wrapped with bows stuck haphazardly on as if he'd let Denali help. "Look what was under my tree."

"Presents," Kendall and Austin yelled.

"That's right, presents," Sean said as Denali barked. "This one is for Kendall. And this one is for Austin."

"How come they were at your house?" Austin asked.

Sean shrugged. "Open them so we can figure it out."

The kids ripped off the wrapping while the dog ran between them, trying to snatch the paper away.

Austin's mouth formed a perfect O. "Snowshoes."

"Wow." Kendall hugged hers. "They're great, but Mom always says no when Uncle Jake asks to take us snowshoeing."

Jake kneeled so he was at her eye level. "Your mom gave her permission for this outing."

Kendall brightened. "Who are they from?"

"All of us," Leanne said.

Carly wiped the corners of her eyes.

"That's right." Jake helped Kendall into her snowshoes as Sean put Austin's on his feet. "You've been here a few times before, Kendall, with all of us."

Her small forehead crinkled. "When?"

"Christmas Day since you were born," Bill answered.

"Except you weren't big enough to snowshoe," Tim said. "So your dad carried you in a pack like I've got Wyatt."

Memories, long pushed aside, rushed back to Carly. Iain had offered to carry the baby pack so Nick could walk next to Hannah, but Nick wanted to do it himself. "Your daddy was sure you would fall asleep, but unlike little Wyatt, who's already napping, you stayed awake the entire time."

"Where was I?" Austin asked.

Carly put her arm around him. "One time you were at home in your mommy's tummy. Another time you were too little." There hadn't been a next time.

"We would meet here each Christmas afternoon," Jake explained. "Put on our snowshoes and hike around the lake. It was our Christmas gift to ourselves and each other."

"But we haven't done it in a long time," Bill said.

"How come?" Kendall asked.

Leanne placed her hand on Kendall's narrow shoulder. "Because three people couldn't be with us."

No. Carly looked at each one of them. That couldn't be.

This had been the best of the Christmas traditions, one Nick started when he was in high school. The first time only four of them had gone on the hike: Nick, Jake, Carly and Iain. Each year, more people had joined in. Until six years ago.

"Hey." Austin pointed to Carly, Kendall and himself. "We're three people."

"Yes, you are," Jake said.

Carly pinned him with her gaze. "You never came back?"

"It didn't seem right, but Sean thought it was time to start the tradition up again."

She hugged Sean. "Thank you."

"I did it for purely selfish reasons," the rescue leader said. "There's only a limited amount of time I can sit on my butt on my parents' couch without going stark raving mad or drinking way too much. Now I'll be able to go back to dinner and not want to kill one of my second cousins twice removed."

Carly laughed.

"By the way—" Sean handed her a present "—this was under my tree, too."

"You didn't!" She tore off the wrapping and found a brand-new pair of snowshoes and poles. "I love them. Thanks."

Leanne hugged her. "You're going to have to spend more time here so you can use them."

"Aunt Carly's coming back next Christmas," Austin announced.

Jake looked at her with a question in his eyes. Not knowing what to say, she simply shrugged.

Sean gave a quick lesson to Kendall and Austin in the basics of snowshoeing. "It might feel funny at first having these big things on your feet, but you'll get used to them. When you walk you might sink a little into the snow, and you have to lift your foot to take the next step. Try it."

The kids did, walking awkwardly.

"This is harder than it looks," Kendall said.

Carly remembered when she'd learned. "You'll get the hang of it soon enough."

Austin quacked. "It's like having big duck feet."

Jake laughed. "Sort of."

As the kids practiced, everyone strapped on their snowshoes. The way people joked and laughed the way they always had warmed Carly's heart.

"Where's Austin?" Tim asked.

"He's right…" She looked around, but didn't see him. "Austin."

No answer. Her heart dropped to her feet. As everyone called Austin's name, Bill studied the snowshoe tracks.

Austin popped out from behind a tree with a big grin on his face. "Gotcha."

Carly drew in a sharp breath of cold air. It was as if the ghost of Christmas past—okay, Nick—had just paid a visit.

"You got us all right," Tim said finally. "But when we're outdoors like this, it's never good to hide, buddy."

"Sorry." Austin walked over to them. "Uncle Jake taught me never to go off on my own, but I saw that tree and…"

"It's okay, dude." Sean tugged on the top of the boy's hat. "Your dad used to play jokes like that all the time."

"Really?" Austin asked.

Jake nodded. "He would always say 'gotcha' when he got us."

The boy beamed. "Like me."

Carly hugged him. "Exactly like you."

"Cool," he said. "Can I practice some more?"

"Go ahead," Sean said. "But stay close."

As Kendall and Austin practiced getting the hang of walking in snowshoes, Jake rubbed the back of his neck. "That was…"

"Eerie," Tim said.

"No kidding," Bill added. "The way he said 'gotcha' gave me chills."

Carly crossed her arms over her chest and rubbed them. "I got shivers."

"Me, too," Leanne said. "I don't think the goose bumps are going to go away anytime soon."

Jake nodded. "He sounded like Nick, an octave higher, but still…"

Sean agreed. "Total déjà vu."

"That was weird, and most likely a coincidence, but did anyone think we may have just gotten Nick's blessing for this little outing?" Leanne asked.

A breeze blew snow from the branches of a Douglas fir and onto the kids. They jumped up and down with gleeful delight. Denali barked.

Jake stared at them. "I think you're right."

The group stood. Silent. Watching. Carly couldn't help but think of Nick and Iain, but the memories weren't sad or even bittersweet. Peace surrounded her, both inside and out. She smiled. Coming here had been the right thing to do.

"We'd better hit the trail," Leanne said. "We don't have too much light left."

"And don't forget," Bill said. "We're supposed to be home for dinner."

"Please," Sean said. "Can't we forget?"

Carly called the kids over.

Jake laughed. "No, because your mother will call the sheriff, who will put out an alert and then we'll have all of OMSAR looking for us."

Tim laughed. "And the press will be out in full force since you brought along the pup."

As if on cue Denali barked.

"Don't forget the kids," Bill added. "They would be worth a few sound bites and scathing letters to the editor from city folk who wouldn't know a carabiner from a key chain."

"Is it time to go yet?" Kendall stood at the head of the trail. The same way Nick used to do.

"It's as if Nick's right here with us," Carly mumbled.

Jake smiled at her. "Who's to say he isn't?"

CHAPTER NINE

THIS WAS SO NOT what Carly had in mind.

Her legs burned. Each breath of cold air stung. Sweat ran down her back. She struggled to put one foot in front of the other as she snowshoed along the trail.

All Carly wanted was to be alone with Jake for a few minutes and pick up where they'd left things last night. So when someone had to go back to get the Thermos of hot chocolate they'd left after a snack break, she had volunteered, leaving Kendall and Austin with the group. Carly had imagined a romantic stroll for two in a winter wonderland, not wilderness adventure racing with an outdoor Adonis.

She blew out a puff of air.

"You're doing great," Jake encouraged. "We're almost there."

Easy for him to say, he wasn't huffing and puffing with each step. She wanted to plop down on a rock and rest for a minute. Okay, ten.

"When we get there, I want hot chocolate and cookies."

Jake grinned. "You can have whatever you want."

His suggestive tone brought a smile to her face. Maybe she'd get a kiss or two before they reached the gang.

"The kids aren't moving too fast," he added. "We'll catch up to them soon."

And maybe she wouldn't. Unless she did something about it.

She tried giving Jake a sultry look, the effect no doubt spoiled by her red face, runny nose and ducklike feet. "What if I don't want to catch up to them?"

"You can do it," he said encouragingly. "Remember the cookies."

His cluelessness knotted her spine with frustration, but she wasn't about to tell him she would prefer his kisses to cookies. Not when she'd been the one to kiss him last night. "Right."

Jake continued along the trail. Carly struggled onward.

She had been able to keep up with the guys when she'd been younger, but not anymore. Leaving the mountain meant leaving a life of outdoor recreation behind. But even though she was out of shape, out of practice and totally out of her league, she'd been willing to suffer a little indignity, a little inconvenience to be alone with Jake. She had feelings for him, deep feelings she wanted to explore. "What if my legs gave out and I couldn't walk another step? Hypothetically speaking."

"We'd stop until you could keep going."

Sultry had been a bust, so she batted her eyelashes. "You wouldn't carry me?"

He gave her a look. The look. The one her brother had used when she wanted to wimp out on a skiing run or hike. "Suck it up, Bishop."

Those were the same words Nick used to say to her. And that's when it hit her. All day, Jake had been treating her like

Nick's little sister. Not the woman he'd kissed last night. She wanted to know why. "I need to stop."

Jake turned toward her. "Have a drink of water. You'll feel better."

Carly drank. Physically, she felt better, but emotionally… She shivered.

"Cold?" he asked.

"What are we doing?" she asked.

His brow creased. "We're snowshoeing."

"That's not what I mean." She tried again. "What do you want out of this? Us, I mean."

"I want you to be happy."

She thought about his reply for a moment. "You want the kids to be happy, too."

"What's wrong with that?" he asked.

"Because I'm not a kid anymore," she said, irritated. "You alternate between wanting to devour me with kisses and treating me like Nick's little sister. I don't get this hot-and-cold treatment."

"Hot and cold?" Jake repeated.

She crossed her arms against her chest and glared at him. "How about just plain cold?"

He glared back. "You are Nick's little sister. I'm trying to be considerate here. Make you happy. What's wrong with that?"

She didn't want to argue, but Jake brought out the best and worst in her. "I know you've gone out of your way these past couple of days to make Christmas special for both the kids and me. I appreciate you and all you've done. It's been magical and wonderful. But instead of trying to give me what you think will make me happy, why don't you ask me what I really want?"

He flung his arms wide. "Okay. What do you really want?"

"I want what I thought I lost on this mountain six years ago. I want what I thought I could never have again. Love. A happily ever after. And I think I want it with you."

Jake stood silent. A beat passed. And another, while her hands and feet turned icy cold and apprehension froze her chest.

"I want you, Carly," he said finally.

A little warmth trickled through her. That was good. But it wasn't enough. "But do you want to have a relationship with me or just a fling? Which is it, Jake?"

Her question hung in the icy air.

"There you guys are!" The call came down the trail.

"Hot chocolate!" Kendall cried.

Jake's eyes met Carly's in unspoken apology as the group came down and surrounded them.

Or was that relief?

Do you want to have a relationship with me or just a fling?

Carly's question had been on Jake's mind ever since they got back from snowshoeing. And he still didn't have an answer for her or himself.

Outside, he placed the garbage bag into the can. His breath fogged in the cold night air, but he wasn't in a rush to go indoors. The kids were in bed. That would leave him and Carly alone.

Jake secured the top on the garbage can.

He'd always gone for what he wanted. The only time he hadn't was with Carly. First, she'd been too young. Then she'd fallen in love with Iain. And then there had always been Nick, who would have punched Jake out for thinking about his little sister that way. Even after Iain and Nick had died, Jake had hesitated to act on what he wanted because of Carly's grief and his own guilt. Those had all been good, valid reasons, but now... Now nothing stood in the way.

I want what I thought I could never have again. Love. A happily ever after. And I think I want it with you.

Nothing but him.

Jake wanted only the best for Carly, but he didn't know if he could give her what she wanted. He didn't know if he could be who she wanted.

He walked slowly to the back door, shoving his bare hands in his pockets. No matter what he decided, Jake had one thing left to do, one more thing to offer her. He entered the mudroom and made his way to the kitchen.

"Let It Snow" played on the radio. Carly dried her hands at the sink. She shot him a strained smile, her unanswered question still hanging between them. "The dishes are loaded. The only thing left is straightening the living room."

Jake's work was almost done here. Almost.

She walked into the living room, kneeled beside the Christmas tree and arranged the toys underneath. "It's hard to believe Christmas is over."

Jake leaned against the couch, watching her. "There's still a few hours left."

Carly got a wistful look in her eyes. "I guess."

He walked over to the tree. "Christmas can't be over because I haven't given you your present."

"You got me the snowshoes."

"Those were from all of us." Jake reached under the red-and-green velvet tree skirt and pulled out a gift he'd hidden two days ago. "This is from me."

Whatever else he could or couldn't give her, he could give her this.

She stared at the package, wrapped in bright red paper and tied with a white ribbon. "You didn't—"

"Open it," he urged.

Carly looked at him with hope and doubt before turning her attention to untying the lopsided bow and unwrapping the box. She removed the top of the box, unfolded the white tissue paper and stared at the front of the photo album made from wood. She ran her fingers along the stained and polished cover. "It's beautiful, Jake."

"You told me by looking back you could move forward," he explained. "I thought this might help."

She opened the first page and gasped. "This is from when we were kids."

"Hannah has all the pictures organized so that made them easy to find." Jake couldn't tell if she liked it or not. "The beginning of the album is filled with my favorite pictures of us. All of us. The rest of the book is blank so you can fill them as you make new memories."

Tears welled in her eyes. She blinked.

Carly thumbed through the pages, laughing and wiping her eyes at the all those times spent together, all those long-forgotten memories...

Jake got a funny feeling in his stomach that spread throughout his entire body and seemed to settle in his heart.

"Do you remember this one?" She pointed to a picture of her, Iain, Nick and Jake climbing at Smith Rock. "Or this one, when you and Nick took me backpacking?"

He laughed. "How could I forget the huckleberry ice cream incident or the run-in with Mr. Skunk?"

How could he forget any of this?

Jake had been dragging his feet, afraid to commit his life to Carly, but she was already part of his life. The proof was right in front of him. All those pictures of them. The good times and the bad. Sure, there was a six-year gap, but now that she was back, Jake knew exactly what he wanted. He wanted to be in the rest of the pictures. He wanted to fill all those blank pages with memories of the two of them. Together.

"This is incredible," Carly said.

No kidding.

"Thank you." She closed the album and looked up at him, her eyes shining. "It's the best gift ever. Well, next to the dog sled ride."

She laughed. So did he. Happy, relieved, nervous.

Jake hadn't felt so alive, so whole in six years. He felt as if he was starting all over again. As if his heart was brand-new, full of wonder and waiting for new discoveries. As if this woman sitting next to him was all that mattered, and would ever matter to him.

Carly parted her lips slightly. He took that as an invitation, pressing his lips against hers. Warm, soft, smooth.

Now this was the perfect Christmas present.

Moving his mouth over hers, he reveled in the taste—a mix of spices, chocolate, Carly. Exotic, sweet, unique.

And all his.

Finally.

Jake wrapped his arms around her and pulled her closer. He wanted to make the most of the moment.

No more "should have."

No more "what if."

No more regret.

He kissed her, holding nothing back. As his lips savored every sensation, heat sizzled through his veins.

She arched toward him, never removing his lips from hers. "Oh, Jake."

Her eagerness thrilled him. Turned him on. He combed through her hair with his hand, his fingers twisting in the silky strands.

He wanted…more. Okay, her. And for the first time, he had the chance he'd dreamed about all those years ago.

But this had nothing to do with then, and everything to do with now. He'd finally found home, where he belonged, and he wasn't ready to let go.

Jake didn't know if this was the best thing for Carly, but it was what he could give her. That had to count for something.

He kissed her as if she were the moon, earth and sun. And right now she was all three. The past, the present and, he hoped, the future.

His mouth moved against hers, wanting her to know how he felt. Words wouldn't do. He wouldn't know what to say or how to say it, but this kiss…

Yes, this kiss.

Hear me, Carly. Jake deepened the kiss yet again. *Please hear what my kisses are saying to you.*

Carly didn't want Jake to stop kissing her. Not now, possibly not ever. That fact alone should have sent off warning bells, but all she wanted was more kisses.

He had one arm around her back and his other hand in her hair. She scooted closer until she was on top of his lap.

For so long, she'd felt alone. But no longer. Carly wasn't alone. She didn't have to be alone ever again.

As he kissed her neck, she sighed.

Carly didn't want this to stop. She didn't want to let Jake go.

Don't think about it too much.

She focused on the now. On Jake's kiss. How his lips caressed her, showered her with love.

Don't stop.

"I'm not planning to."

Carly must have said the words aloud. She didn't know. She didn't care. No one had ever kissed her so thoroughly, so intensely. And…

Crying.

She stiffened, a nanosecond before he pulled away from her. "One of the kids."

Jake swore and then sighed. "Let's go."

Her swollen, bruised lips longed for more kisses, but she knew where her responsibilities lay. So did Jake. She crawled off his lap and stood. He laced his fingers with hers.

Carly smiled. She climbed the stairs with Jake at her side. The crying came from Austin's room. She pushed open the door.

"Austin," she said softly.

The boy sobbed from the lower bunk bed. "I miss my mommy."

"Aww." Carly pulled him into her arms. "It's hard when you miss your mommy and she's not here."

Austin hiccupped. Jake kneeled at the side of the bed. "Your mom will be home soon, buddy."

Austin sniffled. "I want her home now."

"I know you do." Carly combed her fingers through his short, tangled hair. "But she needs to be in the hospital right now to recover from having Tyler."

"What if she never comes back?" Austin asked.

Carly didn't know how to answer. He might not remember his biological father, but he knew his daddy had left one day and never come back. "Your mommy loves you very much. No matter where you are or where she is."

"Your mom wants nothing more than to come back and be with you," Jake added. "But she has to wait until the doctor says it's okay."

Austin wiped his eyes.

"Do you want to call her?" Carly asked. "Would that make you feel better?"

"What if the baby's asleep and Mommy, too?" Austin asked, sounding like a caring, considerate big brother. Nick would have been so proud. "That wouldn't be good to wake them up."

"She wouldn't mind," Carly explained. "She doesn't want you to be sad."

Austin looked at her. "I won't be sad if you sleep with me."

"That bed's a little small for two," Jake said.

Austin brightened. "I could sleep in Aunt Carly's room."

"Can I sleep there, too?" Kendall asked from the doorway.

Carly gave Jake a rueful look. The regret in his eyes matched her own.

He touched her shoulder. "It's okay."

His understanding touched her heart. This wasn't what either of them wanted, but they had no choice. She looked at the kids. "If you want to sleep in my bed, that's okay."

Austin jumped out of bed and grabbed his pillow.

"I'll go get my stuff," Kendall said before disappearing.

Carly glanced up at Jake. "I'm so sorry. I didn't think things tonight would end like this."

"Hey, no worries," he said. "We have plenty of time to be together."

Together.

The thought sent a burst of heat rushing through her veins. Anticipation built within her. "I can't wait."

He smoothed her hair with his hand. "You won't have to wait long."

She took a deep, satisfied breath.

"Go crawl in bed with them," Jake said. "I'll make sure everything's turned off and lock up before I go."

"You could stay—"

"I can't." He gave her a quick peck on the cheek. "But I'll be back tomorrow."

"Aunt Carly," a high-pitched voice called out.

"I better go," she said. "Thank you."

"For what?" he asked.

"For being you." Carly smiled. "And making this the best Christmas ever."

Jake grinned. "Just wait until next year."

CHAPTER TEN

THE NEXT MORNING, the doorbell rang. Kendall and Austin ran to the front door, their footsteps shaking the ornaments on the Christmas tree.

"Don't open the door until I get there," Carly said, padding her way from the kitchen.

"It's Uncle Jake," Austin shouted.

Her pulse quickened. "Go ahead then."

"Good morning." Jake stepped inside, for a moment his gaze met hers, then he closed the door behind him. He handed Austin a pink box. "Here you go."

Kendall peeked inside. "Donuts."

"Don't open the box until you're in the kitchen," Carly said as the kids skipped off, giggling the entire way. She felt like giggling herself.

Jake's hair looked damp and his face baby-smooth, as if he'd recently showered and shaved. Carly fought the urge to reach out and touch his face. There would be time for that.

"Thanks for the donuts," she said. "Much tastier than what I had in—"

He kissed her on the lips, hard and fast, taking her breath away and tripling her heart rate in seconds.

Jake pulled his left arm from behind him and handed her a beautiful bouquet of mixed flowers. "These are for you."

Her lips tingled from his kiss, her heart from his thoughtfulness.

"I didn't know what your favorite flower was," he admitted.

"These are." Carly took the bouquet and sniffed the colorful blossoms. A sweet floral aroma filled her nostrils.

"Which ones?"

Happiness swelled inside her. "All of them."

Jake winked. "Today's my lucky day."

"You might be right about that." She stared at the flowers. "But I thought you only brought flowers to dates and hospital visits."

"This could be considered a date."

Contentment settled over the center of her chest. "You think?"

He nodded. "Of course we have chaperones, but Hannah and Garrett should be home later today."

Excitement surged. Not that Carly didn't like being with the kids or didn't want to help out with Tyler, but she really wanted a little alone time with Jake. Okay, a lot of time, but she would take what she could get. "I know."

"I can't wait to steal you away."

"I'm yours for the taking."

"Promise?"

She laughed. "But don't forget, I'm still here to help Hannah."

"I've got you covered."

"How?"

"Leanne will come over to help Hannah with the kids so I can take you out."

Carly glanced at the cuckoo clock. "How did you manage to arrange help at eight o'clock in the morning?"

"My methods are top secret," he whispered, his breath hot against her neck. "I'd tell you, but then I'd have to kiss you."

"I wouldn't mind."

"Me, either." He peered around her shoulder. "But our audience might have something to say about it."

She glanced behind her. The kids stood in the doorway to the kitchen. Austin had chocolate icing smeared all over his face. "We'll be right there."

The kids didn't move.

Carly sighed. No rush, she reminded herself. Besides she needed to put the flowers in water. "Come on, let's eat breakfast so we can make gingerbread."

Standing in the kitchen, Carly inhaled deeply. "Okay, that's it! Everybody outside."

"Why?" Kendall demanded.

"The gingerbread needs time to cool," Carly said.

Jake's eyes met hers, still with that delicious warmth in his gaze. "I need to cool off, too," he murmured, too low for the kids to hear.

Enough of his accidental brushes and subtle on-purpose touches had Carly agreeing with him.

Everyone put on their coats, hats and gloves, headed to the front yard and made a snow family to welcome the baby.

As snowflakes drifted down from the sky, Carly wrapped a multicolored striped knit scarf around a snowwoman's neck. "What do you think?"

Kendall beamed. "It's perfect."

Things were perfect. Especially with Jake. Carly smiled, feeling warm inside even though snow fell from the sky. She couldn't wait until it was just the two of them.

Soon, she told herself. Very soon.

A pager beeped. A cell phone rang. Jake checked both. "Excuse me for a minute."

He took the call, but didn't speak. He didn't have to for Carly to know who was on the other end. She could see it in his eyes, had seen that similiar rush of adrenaline when a call came summoning Nick for a mission.

Jake would be heading up to Mount Hood for a rescue. She glanced in the direction of the summit, but couldn't see it. The weather must be bad up there.

She wrapped her arms around her stomach to fight the sudden chills and quell the knots forming in her belly.

He put his phone in his pocket. "That was a call-out for a mission. There's a briefing at Timberline."

"Cool," Austin said then returned to his snowman. Kendall didn't seem the least bit interested.

Jake nodded.

"You're excited about this." Carly had been through this enough times with Nick to know how pumped these guys got at the thought of heading up the mountain, but she had never worried that much about her brother. Sure, Carly might have felt an inkling of concern and told him to be careful, but she had never been afraid.

Not the way she was now.

"I'm not excited someone's in trouble, but I like getting out there," Jake admitted. "We all do."

"The weather has to be bad up there."

He shrugged. "Nothing we haven't faced before."

Maybe him. But not her. She hadn't faced anything like this before. Worry consumed her entire body. And she didn't like it.

A heaviness pressed down on her, threatening to over-whelm her. She felt as if a keg of beer had been laid on each of her shoulders, making it impossible for her to move or do anything. Was this how Hannah had felt each time Nick went out?

Carly didn't want Jake up on the mountain today. Not any day. Her chest constricted. "Do you have to go?"

He checked his pager again. "Yes."

The single word spoke volumes. She took a deep breath to calm her nerves. It didn't help. "When do you have to leave?"

"Soon."

Something flashed in his eyes. He meant...now.

Her heart pounded in her ears. A snowball-size lump lodged in her throat. She hadn't felt like this since...

Iain and Nick.

The kids hugged Jake goodbye. They laughed and smiled as if he were driving to the store to buy ice cream, not climb a mountain in whiteout conditions to find people who had lost their way or been injured. Or died.

The pit of dread deep down in her stomach made her nauseous. Carly thought she might be physically ill.

"Take care of your Aunt Carly while I'm away," Jake said to the kids.

"We will," Kendall said.

Austin nodded. "Promise."

"Thanks." Jake kissed each of their foreheads. "Now run inside and see if the gingerbread has cooled."

The kids ran up the porch stairs and into the house. The front door slammed close.

Tears stung Carly's eyes, but she wasn't about to cry in

front of him. She'd climbed enough with Iain to know Jake needed his full attention on what he was about to face. Nothing else could be on his mind. Especially not her.

Jake walked to her, his long strides putting him at her side in seconds. He cupped her face with his hand. "You've lost your smile."

She forced the corners of her mouth up. "It's still there."

He touched her lips with his fingertip. "Don't worry."

The tenderness in his eyes was nearly her undoing. She looked up at the gray sky.

"Worrying won't bring me back sooner, Carly. It'll just make you miserable."

"How can I not worry?" she asked. "And don't you dare tell me to try not to think about it too much."

He grinned. "I won't now."

Carly couldn't believe he was smiling and sounded so lighthearted. She pressed her lips together.

"Remember, we're trained for this. We know what we're doing." Jake held her hand and walked to his SUV. "But things usually take longer up there than you think they would."

Those were not the words she wanted to hear.

"As soon as I'm finished, I'll come back here."

"If you come back," she muttered.

"Oh, I'm coming back." He kissed her long and hard on the lips. She clung to him, afraid to let go, but he backed away. "You won't be able to get rid of me that easily."

"Promise?" she asked.

He brushed his lips across hers once more. "Promise."

She wanted to believe him. "Be careful. And safe."

Jake gave her a quick hug. "Always."

She wanted to reach out and touch him one more time, but he was opening his car door and sliding inside.

"See you later," he said.

Carly sure hoped so.

Excitement buzzed in the cafeteria at the Wy'East day lodge. The scent of coffee lingered in the air. Packs and poles rested against the walls. Duffel bags and jackets lay on the tables. The lousy acoustics made voices louder and echo through the large room.

As unit members talked about the past week, Christmas with their families, ice-climbing jaunts and skiing escapades, Jake sat at one of the tables and listened. For the first time, he had more in common with the first group, the family guys, than the other two.

Times were changing, he realized. For the better.

Sean sat next to him and handed him a coffee. "Just the way you like it, Porter, strong and hot."

"Thanks." Jake took a swig, needing both the jolt of caffeine and the warm liquid. The twenty-eight-degree temperature would make for a cold slog, but a break in the snowfall an hour ago and the resulting improvement in visibility would help. As one of the older, longtime unit members had told Jake during one of his first missions, it could be better, but it could be a helluva lot worse.

Sheriff's Deputy Will Townsend entered the cafeteria. He was the county sheriff's office's SAR coordinator. Jake had climbed with him several times and knew the deputy would shed his uniform and head out with the rescuers if he could.

Alan Marks, the incident commander, or the IC, followed. The IC was an OMSAR member who interfaced with the sheriff's office and kept everyone informed of what was going on out there. The IC cleared his throat. Unit members at the tables and those standing around quieted.

"Hope everyone had a nice holiday," the IC said. "The subject is a thirty-seven-year-old male, Samuel Sprague from Portland. He's an avid hiker who received new snowshoes for Christmas. He wanted to try out his present and see how high he could get on Mount Hood. The subject was last seen heading up climbers' right on the Palmer snowfield. He called his wife at ten o'clock this morning saying he was lost, and due to the conditions, couldn't tell where or how high up he was. We are working to pinpoint the position of his call. Attempts at further contact have been unsuccessful."

The guy had the sense to call for help, but that didn't mean he knew what he was doing out there or would stay put until someone came and got him. If he did move, Jake knew that during whiteout conditions people unfamiliar with the mountain usually followed the fall line down until they ended up in Zig Zag canyon. Not a fun place to be with the snow and cold temperatures if you weren't prepared and carrying the right equipment. But depending on which way the guy headed or how high he'd gotten, he could also be on the White River Glacier. Or anywhere else in between.

"The subject is carrying a pack, but he didn't fill out a permit so we don't know what supplies he's got with him," the IC continued. "We do know he doesn't have a GPS or MLU with him."

Sean looked at Jake with a raised brow. No doubt he was probably thinking the same thing. The use of Mountain Locator Units in winter had been a heated topic for a couple of years.

"The logical assumption would be he stayed put after calling his wife and is waiting to be extracted, but we all know logic doesn't always play out in these situations," the IC said. "The team leaders know their assignments. Good luck and be safe out there."

She hoped Jake was safe out there.

Carly tried to keep herself busy so she wouldn't think about him so much. She helped the kids make a gingerbread house and decorate gingerbread cookies. They played games until Hannah, Garrett and Tyler arrived home. The fuss over the baby kept Carly occupied. So did making dinner.

"Ready to call it a night?" Garrett asked after helping her with the dishes.

"I want a cup of coffee," Carly said.

"You won't sleep," Garrett warned as he went upstairs to help Hannah with the baby.

Forget being kept awake, Carly couldn't sleep. Not with Jake up the mountain.

Horrible what-if worst-case scenarios played out in her mind. A few real ones, too. She'd grown up on this mountain. She knew what could happen up there. She'd experienced it firsthand.

A car drove by on the street, the tires crunching on the snow and ice. Carly waited for the car to stop, prayed the car would pull into the driveway, but it kept going.

Not Jake.

Waiting for the coffee to brew, she remembered the last time the clock had moved this slowly. Carly prayed tonight wouldn't end up the same.

Hannah walked into the kitchen with the water bottle the

hospital had given her. A large plastic straw stuck out of the blue lid. "How are you holding up?"

"I would have brought you water. You're not supposed to climb the stairs too much."

"I know, but I went very slowly. I needed to walk, and I wanted to check on you." Hannah filled the bottle with cold water from the refrigerator. "So don't try and change the subject."

"I'm…" Scared to death. "Hanging in there."

"Then you're doing better than I did when I first started dating Nick." She refilled the water bottle. "I had heard the term SAR, but knew nothing about climbing let alone mountain rescue. I didn't know what to think or how to feel. I had both my radio and television on waiting to hear some word. I couldn't believe how relieved, how happy, I felt when he called to tell me he was finished and all right."

"You were Nick's girlfriend. You had every right to be worried about him."

"So do you." Hannah smiled. "Anyone can see there's something between you and Jake."

Carly blushed. "I did try to be careful."

"I'm sure you did." Hannah gingerly lowered herself into one of the kitchen chairs. "How's it going?"

Carly picked up the tin of cookies from the counter and placed them within Hannah's reach on the table. "Everything was so wonderful until…"

"Jake headed up the mountain."

Nodding, she sat. "Now I don't know if we…if I…"

"The waiting gets easier." Hannah reached for a ginger-bread man. "When I knew things were getting serious with Nick, I joined OMSAR. I did a few fund-raising events and helped out where I could, including the rescue base at Timber-line. Doing that showed me what really went on during a mission. How well trained everyone was, the work that's involved and why things take so long. It almost sounds like a cliché, but they really mean what they say about keeping rescuers safe. They don't take chances with their lives. The last thing anyone wants is to increase the number of injured patients during a rescue."

Carly remembered Nick telling their parents something similar when he joined OMSAR. "I guess being there would help."

Hannah nodded. "After Kendall was born, I couldn't be at the base. That was hard because I wanted to know what was going on. I would listen to the radio and check online. I still do that during missions. Friends are out there, and family, too."

Hannah yawned.

"Go to bed," Carly said. "You should sleep when the baby sleeps."

"I don't want to leave you alone."

She forced a smile. "I feel better after talking with you."

Hannah looked doubtful.

"Really," Carly reassured.

"Okay, but let me know if you need anything."

Alone again, Carly listened to the news on the radio and heard a brief report about a missing Portland man lost snow-shoeing, but no updates. She checked news Web sites and a Northwest climbing forum, but none had any new information.

She was just going to have to wait. Except…

Carly didn't want to wait. She didn't like this feeling of uncertainty, of being worried and afraid. She couldn't think straight or eat. It was exactly how she'd felt six years ago. She cringed.

What was she doing?

Carly had never wanted to experience those feelings again. Yet here she was. Her insides tied up in knots waiting to find out if Jake came back or not.

No matter how much Carly cared about him or wanted to be with him, she couldn't do this. She couldn't put herself through this over and over again, each time he went on a mission. Even if she were strong enough, which she wasn't, she didn't want to do this.

Not ever again.

Exhausted, Jake moved slowly from his SUV to the porch. Normally he couldn't wait to get home after a mission, but he hadn't even considered going there first. There was only one place he wanted to go tonight.

Scratch that.

Only one person he wanted to see.

As he climbed the front steps, the door opened. Carly stood with one hand on the doorknob. "You're back."

Damn, she was beautiful. A smile tugged on the tired corners of his mouth. "I'm back."

"How did things go up there?"

"Another team found him," Jake said. "Cold and hungry, but happy to be rescued."

"Are you hungry?" she asked.

"Starving." He kissed her on the lips. "Exactly what I needed."

She opened the door wider. "Come inside so you can warm up and get something to eat."

Jake looked down. He'd been in such a rush to get here he hadn't changed. "I'm dirty."

"You smell like the mountain."

True. All of his mountain gear and clothing had a particular scent, a mix of sweat and earth, of dirt and rock and mud—a smell that never went away. "I'll go around to the mudroom and change there."

"I'll heat up dinner for you."

Later at the kitchen table, he gobbled up the spaghetti with Italian sausage along with a salad and three slices of garlic bread.

She sat across from him. "You really were starving."

"It's not often I get a delicious home-cooked meal. Great dinner. Thanks so much."

Carly pushed the tin of cookies toward him. "You're welcome."

Jake took a one-eyed gingerbread man. He hadn't had one of these in years. "How's Tyler doing?"

"He's such a good baby." She stood and cleared his plate from the table. "Kendall and Austin aren't quite sure what to make of him since he doesn't do much right now."

"I'll wash the dishes," he offered.

"You've done enough."

He snatched another cookie. "I can handle a dirty plate."

"So can I." Carly rinsed his plate off in the sink. "And I wasn't the one out being a hero today."

"I'm not a hero."

"You saved a man's life."

"We were just doing our jobs," Jake explained. "We're not heroes."

"You volunteer. You don't have to do what you do."

"I have a skill and I'm trained to help people who need help. That's not a hero." Jake wiped his mouth with a napkin. "A hero is someone who finds themselves in an extraordinary situation and rises to the occasion like a guy driving by, stopping and pulling another person out of a burning car. That's a hero."

"I disagree." She tossed the dishrag into the sink. "What you do makes a difference. You help people. You save lives. That's a hero in my book."

"Why are we arguing about this when I could be holding and kissing you?"

Carly leaned with her backside against the counter. He didn't like seeing the wariness on her face, the tension bracketing the corners of her mouth. "I was worried about you today. Terrified something bad might happen to you up there."

"That's normal given what you've been through."

"Normal?" Her voice cracked. "There's nothing normal about what I went through today. I never went through anything resembling this when Nick went on a mission."

Jake didn't get it. He knew he was fine. She should trust his ability to take care of himself. "What's the difference?"

"You're not my brother," she admitted. "The feelings I have for you…"

Jake grinned. "I like hearing you say you have feelings for me."

"Well, I don't like saying it." She gripped the counter with her hands. "If I didn't have feelings for you, I wouldn't care what you did. It wouldn't bother me that you risk your life for yahoos who have no idea what the ten essentials are, but go up anyway ill-prepared and unskilled. I wouldn't care that you go after experienced, well-equipped climbers who run into really bad luck up there. I wouldn't care at all. But I do and it bothers me. A lot."

The tightness in her voice, the emotion in each word, made him realize how much she cared. He rose from the table.

"Rescuer safety is paramount in any mission. We don't put ourselves in harm's way."

"Not when you went after Nick and Iain?"

"That was different. And you know that." Jake lowered his voice so he wouldn't wake anyone upstairs. "OMSAR has said no to certain rescues when the risk level was deemed too high. We're out to assist people, not hurt ourselves."

"You're on an eleven-thousand-foot mountain, Jake. Anything could happen up there. Sure, rescuer safety is important, but you put yourself at risk for ice fall, rock fall and a whole bunch of other nasty stuff every time you go on a mission." She stared at the hardwood floor. "Don't tell me you don't."

"Look at me, Carly," he said, reaching out to her. She did, but didn't take his hand so he took hers instead. "You know me. I like a good rush as well as the next person, but I'm not some adrenaline-junkie, death-cheating thrill seeker looking for his next fix. I'm not going to take stupid chances with my life. You have to believe me."

"I want to believe you." Her words filled him with relief, and he squeezed her hand. "But today, tonight, I couldn't stop thinking about whether you were safe or not. Whether you would come back or not."

"I'm here." Jake embraced her. She felt so warm, so good in his arms. "I came back."

"This time." She sunk against him so he pulled her closer. "I want a family. I want what Hannah and Garrett have."

"You can have that, Carly." As Jake held her, he rested his

chin on the top of her head. "Nothing is standing in the way. Our way."

"But something is standing in the way."

His gut tightened. "What?"

"The mountain. Mountains," she admitted. "I can't live with the uncertainty I felt today. I don't want to."

He loosened his arms and looked down at her. "I don't understand."

"You can't guarantee nothing will happen to you, that every time you're going to come back."

"No one can guarantee that," he said.

"But the odds are higher with you."

Jake felt her slipping away. He didn't want to let her go. He touched her arm. "I could see why you'd think that after what happened six years ago. But it's not like I'm climbing a big mountain route in the Himalayas or Patagonia or even Alaska. You have to understand, there are always risks no matter what people do, whether it's climbing a mountain or driving to the store."

She said nothing.

"Carly."

"I need guarantees," she said softly, backing away from him. "I need to know you're safe. I need to know you will be coming off that mountain, alive and in one piece."

"There are no guarantees. You might want them or feel you need them, but they don't exist, Carly." He moved closer to her. "Even if I never climbed again, I could still be hit by a bus. That's how life works."

"Maybe that's true, but I can't go through it again."

His heart skipped a beat. She didn't mean... She couldn't...

Jake stared at her. He expected his father to tell him to change his ways because he wasn't good enough, but Jake never thought Carly would tell him what he ought to do. He'd given her everything he thought she needed. He was ready to give her everything she wanted. But if she wanted this... "Are you asking me to stop climbing?"

"No," she said without hesitation. "You love climbing. I would never ask you to give it up."

Relief washed over him. Climbing was a way of life for him, a life based in relationships with his partners and the mountains they climbed. "Good, because I don't want to give it up. I can't give it up. But I don't get where this leaves us."

"Where we've always been. Where we should have stayed. Friends. Just friends," she said, as if everything they'd shared had never existed, as if these past few days had been nothing more than boot tracks swept away by the wind.

Jake didn't buy it. He wouldn't let her dismiss what they had so easily. Sometimes a single boot print would be scoured into the snow and preserved when the others had disappeared. He wanted to hold on to the woman who had left her mark on his heart. He didn't see why anything had to change. "What if I don't want to be just friends? Then what?"

Carly's eyes glistened. "Then I guess there's nothing left to say except good-night."

CHAPTER ELEVEN

CARLY COUNTED the lunch receipts so she could close the register. She'd been back in Philadelphia more than a week, but still didn't feel settled. She missed Hannah and the kids, missed being in Hood Hamlet, missed…Jake.

Two weeks later, his words still reverberated in her memory.

What if I don't want us to be friends? Then what?

Then nothing.

Good-night had turned into goodbye.

She hadn't seen him again. In a town the size of Hood Hamlet, that took some effort on his part. But Jake had made it clear. He hadn't wanted to be friends. He hadn't wanted anything to change between them. But she couldn't allow things to stay the same, and she couldn't change the way she felt.

And that was that. Over. Finished. The end.

She'd been trying so hard to avoid heartache again these past six years, but it had found her anyway. The hurt still felt raw. She wanted it to go away.

Brian, one of the brewery's bartenders, motioned her over

to the bar. Two televisions hung from the ceiling on either side of the bar. A twenty-four-hour news channel played on one, a sports channel on the other. He handed on a tall glass of freshly brewed ice tea complete with lemon, a straw and a small purple paper umbrella. "Here you go, Carly."

"Thanks." She appreciated his efforts and took a sip, but her favorite drink didn't make her feel any better. Nothing had. She didn't think anything would. "The lunch rush takes its toll."

Brian wiped off the bar with a white towel. "So does spending nights in your office."

She stirred her drink with the straw. "Who said I'm sleeping in my office?"

"Rumor," he said. "You have to admit, you're always here."

"It's my job to be here." Better here at work than at her apartment. That place felt empty. Transitory. Lonely. After being in Hood Hamlet she'd gotten used to being around noise. People. Family. "But I may have been putting in a few extra hours this week."

Brian raised a brow. "A few?"

Ignoring him, she took another sip of her tea.

He tossed the towel under the bar.

Something on one of the television sets caught her eye. She glanced up. A picture of Mount Hood with the words *Missing Climbers* was displayed on the screen. A shiver inched down her spine. "Turn that off. No. Turn it up."

She was an idiot for watching this. The climber on the news wasn't Jake. It couldn't be. She was punishing herself needlessly because she couldn't be the woman Jake wanted her to be. The partner he deserved. But…

Brian adjusted the volume on the news channel.

"The two injured climbers spent last night on the mountain," the anchorman, who was dressed in a perfectly tailored suit with coordinating tie, said. "The deteriorating conditions have frustrated rescuers trying to reach the two men."

Jake? Fear slithered through her. No, not him. But someone she knew could be trapped on the mountain. No matter if it were a friend or a stranger, Jake would be looking for them.

Every single muscle of hers tensed. Her stomach roiled.

The news cut to a woman reporter standing outside Timberline Lodge. She looked like she was freezing to death even though she wore a blue down jacket, a matching hat and thick gloves. The swirling snow made it seem as if she were standing in the middle of a snow globe gone wild. More than once the reporter lost her balance when a gust of wind hit.

Carly's chest tightened.

If the weather was that bad at six thousand feet, it had to be a complete whiteout up top with high winds and—

"Weren't you just there?" Brian asked.

She nodded impatiently, her attention fixed on the screen. The camera panned the landscape. She recognized the lodge. The Sno-Cats. The men and women wearing OMSAR jackets with the white lettering on them. Where was Jake?

The picture returned to the studio. The news desk looked so safe, so boring compared to what had been shown on the screen before.

"But rescuers haven't given up and continue to battle the elements," the anchorman said with a polished tone and blinding white teeth. "The teams were pulled off the mountain due to high winds and whiteout conditions yesterday, but with the break in the weather this morning, they headed back up. As you can see from our live footage, the weather has begun to change again. Most rescuers are on their way down, but at least one team may bivouac, that is, spend the night on the mountain, to take advantage of another weather break."

Oh, Jake.

Rescuer safety is paramount in any mission. We don't put ourselves in harm's way.

Carly shook her head. That didn't mean he wouldn't be one of those spending the night on the mountain.

"Wow," Brian said. "I bet you're glad you're back here in civilization, huh?"

Of course she was. If Carly were there, she'd have to spend every minute glued to the news, shaking with anxiety, desperate to learn the fate of the climbers and the men and women searching for them on the mountain. Just like six years ago. Just like…

Now.

And that's when it hit her. No matter if Jake climbed or not, did mountain rescue or not, she wouldn't stop caring about him. She couldn't turn off her concern even if she lived across the country from him. Because no matter what he did or didn't, she would love him. She would always love him.

A new image appeared on the screen. The wives of the two injured climbers stood with Deputy Townsend. With amazing composure, one of them thanked the rescuers for battling the elements to search for her husband. She mentioned her husband was in the military and had just returned home after deployment in the Middle East. He'd been counting the days until he could climb Mount Hood with his best friend from childhood.

Hearing what the soldier survived during his tour of duty only to return home and be hurt on Mount Hood seemed ironic and wrong. But Carly realized Jake had right. Guarantees didn't exist. No one could avoid risk.

Unless they wanted to avoid love altogether.

Carly had. Once. But no longer.

The warmth flowing through her pushed the coldness away. She was ready to take chances even if it meant another broken heart.

Jake.

She loved him. Nothing else mattered.

It was that simple, that complicated.

Carly slid off her bar stool. She knew exactly where she needed to be.

And with who.

The mountain takes; the mountain gives back.

As Jake carved S turns with his skis in the powder, the cold wind stung his face. People had died on Mount Hood. Some who were lost had never been found and were part of the mountain now. It wasn't right or wrong. Just the way things worked. Which was why climbers, smart ones at least, treated the mountain with respect. No one wanted bad karma following them up there.

Today was one of the better endings. Adrenaline rushed through him. A happy ending.

Boo-ya.

The emotional high overcame his exhaustion. The team had found the two climbers, too late to bring them down safely with the weather conditions, so they'd built a snow cave and hunkered down for the night. Both men had suffered injuries from a fall, but they'd had the right gear and enough experience to survive that first night on their own. They'd been hurting, but relieved to learn they wouldn't be alone for a second one.

Fresh rescue teams had arrived early this morning to take the injured down. His team had handed off the two subjects and stuck around until the groups headed down the mountain.

Sean, who led the rescue team, swooshed down on his splitboard in front of Jake. Bill and Tim skied behind them. Just like old times. The four of them hadn't been on a team together in a while.

And like the old days, they turned down a Sno-Cat ride to the bottom. Nothing like the buzz of a successful mission to keep you going when everything else wanted to shut down. Even though they were cold and tired, not to mention hungry, no one wanted to pass up a run on new powder. Jake felt as good as a guy with a broken heart could feel.

Nearing the lodge, he saw the numerous satellite dishes sticking up. The media was out in full force on this multiday mission. No doubt the reporters would be waiting with microphones and questions.

Not that he minded.

Not when everything had turned out well. That was a welcome change from the way he'd been moping around. The last two weeks had been bad. A day hadn't gone by when he hadn't thought about Carly. Hadn't missed her. At least not until heading out on this mission, where he'd been able to push everything out of his mind, including her, and focus.

The team stopped and removed their skis and splitboard. As soon as the press noticed them, the mob with cameras, microphones and tape recorders surrounded them.

People shouted out questions. Jockeyed for position. Waited for a sound bite.

"What was it like spending the night on the mountain?"

"Did you ever think you wouldn't find them?"

"What led you to the climbers?"

"How do you feel right now?"

A knowing glance passed between Sean and Jake. Explaining to others how they felt right at the moment was nearly impossible beyond the clichéd "exhausted, excited, overwhelmed, running on adrenaline." At this moment, everything down here felt insignificant, almost trivial, to what they'd been doing up there.

"That's a good question for our rescue team leader to answer," Jake said.

Sean shook his head, but he was the one team leader who always had something colorful or incendiary to say. He hadn't become a media darling for nothing.

Jake would owe him a beer or three for sticking him with that though talking to the media was preferable to being left alone with thoughts of Carly hammering through his brain. Celebrating at the brewpub tonight might bring him out of his funk.

He wove his way through the crowd toward the day lodge where warm beverages and hot food awaited him. His boots crunched against the packed snow. His muscles ached. His stomach growled.

He looked at the double glass doors in front of him and nearly fell flat on his ass. It was all he could do to hold on to his skis so they didn't clatter to the ground.

"Carly?" The unexpected sight of her brought a rush of warmth. Forget about a cup of coffee, he had all he needed right here. She stood there in her bright purple jacket, black pants and snow boots, blond strands hanging out from beneath her hat, looking like a dream. Except for the worry etched on her face. "What are you doing here?"

"I saw the news." Her hazel eyes stared into his. All this time, he'd never noticed the gold flecks in them before. "I was worried, but most of all I just really missed you."

She'd dumped him.

But…she'd missed him.

Worried about him.

Jake got a grip. Yeah, and that's why she dumped him, because she didn't want to worry about him anymore.

"Let me get this straight, you dropped everything, hopped on a plane in Philadelphia and flew out here?"

She bit her lower lip. "Pretty much."

Who was he kidding? Jake rested his skis against the wall. He didn't care why Carly was here. The fact she was proved… Hell, he didn't know what it proved. He was just glad to see her.

Jake kissed her, a kiss full of need and pent-up frustration. She tasted warm and sweet. He wanted more.

Carly touched him, her hands shaking. Her arms wrapped around him, holding him, as if to assure herself he was all right.

"I stink," he said.

"I don't care."

She trembled.

"Honey, it's all right." He held on to her, holding her close to his body and his heart. "It's okay. I'm okay."

"I know." She ran her hands up his arms, cupped his face. "You're trained for this, you don't take unnecessary risks. I know. But I was still so scared."

And that's when he knew.

This wasn't okay. It wasn't worth it.

Jake followed his gut, knowing his instincts wouldn't lead him astray. He couldn't have her so worried about him all the time. He loved her too much to put her through this over and over again.

He looked down at her. The love reflected in her eyes nearly ripped his heart apart. She hadn't asked, but he knew this was what he had to do. "I'll quit mountain rescue."

Carly drew back. "What?"

"I'm not letting you go again." He ran his hand down her arm. "I won't climb again if that's what it takes to be with you."

She stared up at him, her expression full of wonder. "You'd do that? For me?"

"Whatever it takes." Jake squeezed her hand. "I love you."

"You don't have to stop climbing. The mountains are a part of who you are. I could never take that away from you." Her smile reached her eyes and touched his soul. "What you do with OMSAR is important. That doesn't mean I'll like it all the time or not worry, but I'll try not to think about it too much. As long as I'm with you, it'll be okay."

"Damn straight, it'll be okay." He picked her off the ground and kissed her. "You'll be with me."

"Yes, I will." Her eyes sparkled as he placed her on her feet. "I was afraid of taking risks, afraid of losing someone I loved again, but you taught me to take chances. I didn't know what would happen when I got on that plane yesterday. I don't know what will happen now. But I'm willing to let whatever happens happen. And I'm willing to do that with you. I love you, Jake Porter."

"Remember, I said it first."

She laughed. He kissed her again.

Two teenagers carrying snowboarders walked by and snickered. One muttered something about getting a room. Punks.

She stepped back. "As much as I'd like to continue this, you've got to be cold and hungry and wanting to get out of those boots. Let's get you inside."

"Not yet." Jake wasn't prepared, but it didn't matter. He knew this was the right time. Balancing with his pack on his back, he lowered himself to one knee and held her hand. "This hasn't been the most traditional relationship, and we haven't really had an official date yet, but I don't care. Carly Bishop, will you marry me?"

Tears slipped from her eyes as a smile lit up her pretty face. "Yes, of course I'll marry you. I want to be with you no matter where you go or what you do. Even if it means climbing the tallest peak in the world."

He stood. "Everest?"

"Whatever makes you happy."

"You make me happy, Carly." Jake pulled her against him and never wanted to let go. "It's always been you."

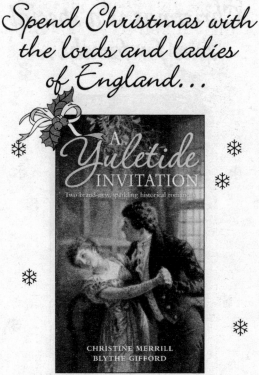

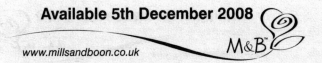

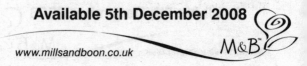

Celebrate 100 years of pure reading pleasure with Mills & Boon®

To mark our centenary, each month we're publishing a special 100th Birthday Edition. These celebratory editions are packed with extra features and include a FREE bonus story.

Plus, you have the chance to enter a fabulous monthly prize draw. See 100th Birthday Edition books for details.

Now that's worth celebrating!

September 2008

Crazy about her Spanish Boss by Rebecca Winters
Includes FREE bonus story
Rafael's Convenient Proposal

November 2008

**The Rancher's Christmas Baby
by Cathy Gillen Thacker**
Includes FREE bonus story *Baby's First Christmas*

December 2008

One Magical Christmas by Carol Marinelli
Includes FREE bonus story *Emergency at Bayside*

Look for Mills & Boon® 100th Birthday Editions at your favourite bookseller or visit
www.millsandboon.co.uk